TRAITOR ROCK

TRAITOR ROCK

JUSTIN D HILL

BLACK LIBRARY

A BLACK LIBRARY PUBLICATION

First published in 2021.
This edition published in Great Britain in 2022 by
Black Library, Games Workshop Ltd., Willow Road,
Nottingham, NG7 2WS, UK.

Represented by: Games Workshop Limited – Irish branch,
Unit 3, Lower Liffey Street, Dublin 1,
D01 K199, Ireland.

10 9 8 7 6 5 4 3 2 1

Produced by Games Workshop in Nottingham.
Cover illustration by Darren Tan.

See Black Library on the internet at

blacklibrary.com

Find out more about Games Workshop
and the world of Warhammer 40,000 at

games-workshop.com

Printed and bound by CPI Group (UK) Ltd, Croydon, CR0 4YY

For my favourite Snoots – the lock-down gamers.

For more than a hundred centuries the Emperor has sat immobile on the Golden Throne of Earth. He is the Master of Mankind. By the might of His inexhaustible armies a million worlds stand against the dark.

Yet, He is a rotting carcass, the Carrion Lord of the Imperium held in life by marvels from the Dark Age of Technology and the thousand souls sacrificed each day so that His may continue to burn.

To be a man in such times is to be one amongst untold billions. It is to live in the cruellest and most bloody regime imaginable. It is to suffer an eternity of carnage and slaughter. It is to have cries of anguish and sorrow drowned by the thirsting laughter of dark gods.

This is a dark and terrible era where you will find little comfort or hope. Forget the power of technology and science. Forget the promise of progress and advancement. Forget any notion of common humanity or compassion.

There is no peace amongst the stars, for in the grim darkness of the far future,
there is only war.

PROLOGUE

AFTERWARDS

I

Queues of warp-transports stretched out for hundreds of miles in the skies above Malouri, files of rusting steel freight ships chained nose to tail like the long mukaali caravans that trailed between underground hab-domes on desert worlds such as Goru-Prime.

Each shipmaster waited for their assigned turn to unload their cargo of war materiel, in fulfilment of hereditary treaties and planetary tithes. Failure could bring swift retribution upon their worlds. A purging crusade. A mob of frateris militia. A precision warhead taking out the upper mile of a hive, allowing a new, more compliant elite to be formed with Munitorum approval. But as the queues of warp-craft grew longer and the wait stretched out, the crews of each ship were faced with a terrible choice.

Some dumped their cargos and turned rogue, fleeing into the

black rather than face justice at home. Some abandoned ship. The dutiful starved to death, their ghost-ships hanging in space until gravity slowly tugged them down into a fiery death.

At the orbital unloading depots, penal serfs were worked to death. But the continent-wide subterranean warehouses on the planet's surface had long since surpassed capacity. There were towering silos of blood plasma, columns of Baneblades, mountains of munitions, millions of troopers stuffed into increasingly cramped and foetid conditions.

There was nowhere to unload and no way shipmasters could go back to their homeworlds with their tithes unfulfilled. And yet more freight-craft were arriving, their hangars packed full of war materiel for a battlefront that had already been lost.

Until a few years earlier, Malouri had been a critical hub in the web of supply routes that equipped the eternal warzone of the Cadian Gate. But Cadia had fallen. It was as if a drainage pipe deep in some hive had been blocked. Sewage was backing up by the hour while the arthritic wheels of the Imperium of Man ground on regardless, trapped in ruts worn ten thousand years deep.

There was no official news, of course. No word of the calamity that had befallen the worlds of the Cadian Gate. But there were always rumours. They spoke of the rout of whole sectors of Imperial control. An Imperium both rotten and decayed. The abject failure of their masters.

The truth of these rumours meant they had to be suppressed mercilessly. There were draconian punishments for even knowing someone who might have heard such dreadful whispers. Each morning, more offenders were strung up along the lines of barrack gibbets. But, as pus seeps from a wound, the truth was getting out.

The Cadian Gate had fallen. Malouri was a depot world without a war to supply.

Father Eris Bellona, a short, bearded priest attached to an Imperial Guard regiment of Elnaur Chasseurs, changed all that.

It should be clear: Father Bellona was no heretic seduced by whispers and lies. He was a veteran of many years and many battlefields. He had bled many times for the Emperor of Mankind. He knew enough of the Imperium to know that what he was being told was a lie.

The scale of the catastrophe froze his blood. The future of humanity hung by a fraying thread.

Sometimes, isolation from the madness brought clear thought. He withdrew to his cell, meditating on the perilous state of the Imperium of Man. A solution began to make itself clear to him. Nebulous ideas solidified. The logic of his reasoning led him to a cold understanding.

He spent a further fortnight in bouts of extreme fasting and devout prayer. On the last night, a glowing yellow light appeared in the air above his head. It was a golden skull, gleaming as if brightly polished, the inset diamond eyes radiant with an inner light. It spoke to him with words of sublime portent and meaning.

There was only one way that the Imperium could survive this calamity. Mankind would break free at last from the shackles that bound its mind and faith. The words he was to write would be the seed from which a new Imperium would grow.

The enormity of this endeavour chilled him. It made his hand tremble with fear and exhilaration. The responsibility was like a hab-block pressing down upon his shoulders. He was an unworthy vessel for the Emperor's love.

But he had been given the sign. The Emperor had come to him. From disaster, a new dawn might arise.

With tear-filled eyes, Father Bellona drew up a sheet of parchment and began to write.

He was inspired. He was honest. He was well-intentioned.

His ideas would cost the lives of billions.

II

The Astra Militarum headquarters on Malouri were located on the island fortress of Crannog Mons. That morning, black carrion birds squabbled over the rotting cadavers that hung in ranks of gibbets thousands strong. The stink of death hung in the air, and in the vast square before the towering Cathedral to Saint Helena Richstar, the Elnaur Chasseurs stood in their polished breastplates, plumed helmets and ceremonial cloaks, waiting for the morning's execution.

It was a matter of great pride to their commander, Lord-Marshal Holzhauer, that none of his Chasseurs had been gathered up in the purges of wrong-think. The Chasseurs were a proud regiment drawn from their home world's nobility. They lived by their own rigid code of honour and he had turned any heretic-catchers away from their camp. If there was any crime in their midst, they dealt with it themselves, as they were doing so this morning.

The convicted trooper had been found guilty of theft – a minor misdemeanour for other regiments, but to the Chasseurs it spoke of dishonour. The only way to deal with such a crime was execution. The condemned man no longer had a name. He had eschewed that when he committed his crime. But even now, as a non-person, he stood to attention, conscious that the manner of his death would affect the future of his brothers and nephews back on their home world of Elnaur.

As the executioner pulled the knotted thongs of the wire

scourge through his gloved hand to loosen them, the thief's silver-braided uniform was cut in strips from his body, to symbolise how the whip would flay the skin from his back.

'In the name of the Holy Emperor,' the executioner called out, looking to the commander, Lord-Marshal Holzhauer, for permission to begin the ritual flaying.

'Commence,' Holzhauer declared.

He stood apart from his officers to watch the man's slow and bloody execution. Holzhauer was a staunch veteran, and he looked down on the convicted trooper without pity or regret, only the hard stare of reproach. It was a matter of pride to him that the Chasseurs handled their own affairs. The Commissariat would not be needed to maintain order while he lived.

His Chasseurs were the bones upon which his reputation had grown. And iron discipline was the force that made them fear him more than any foe they had yet faced.

'And, unlike the Cadians,' Holzhauer liked to say, 'I have never lost a battle.'

When the punishment had finished, the Elnaur Chasseurs turned and marched under the gothic façade of the Cathedral of Saint Helena Richstar, back to their barracks halls.

The corpse was cut down from the whipping post and dragged away, leaving a pool of blood on the floor. Holzhauer turned his back on the mess, and as he did so his attendant aides-de-camp and officers did likewise, their smartly polished boots coming to a smart at-ease.

'A good death,' Adjutant Lehr remarked.

Holzhauer made no response. His thin lips remained sealed, his closely shaved cheeks as cold and blue as freshly whetted steel. The conversation died. The officers followed their commander's gaze.

Holzhauer was watching a black-robed figure march across the square towards them. The priest was not dressed in their usual barracks garb but in full battle dress – battered carapace breastplate and shoulder guards over his dark vestment and silk surplice embroidered with a golden skull.

As Father Bellona reached the doors of the cathedral, he pulled his pistol from its holster and used the butt to hammer a nail into the faded wooden doorway. It took only five sharp cracks before the deed was done. A scrap of parchment fluttered like a struggling prisoner beneath the nail.

An Ecclesiarchy adept had come running at the sound of the banging – a bald and hunched figure in his forties with the air of an over-officious clerk. 'Heresy!' he shouted. 'These words are heresy!'

Lord-Marshal Holzhauer lifted a finger and one of his aides stepped forward to hold the adept back.

The adept managed to get a few strangled shouts out. 'Stop this!' Holzhauer heard. The lord-marshal took no notice. He would decide what was or was not to happen here.

Holzhauer stepped forward to where the parchment still tugged against the nail, caught in the morning breeze.

The Imperium is a dying man. Filled with cancerous growths, the rot comes not from its body... but from the head itself. The Emperor's regents have failed him.

The words written upon it were...

'*Heresy!*' the adept hissed in strangled horror.

'Take the adept away!' Holzhauer snapped.

The sound of scuffles rose behind him. The adept managed to get his mouth free. 'Lord!' he gasped. 'These are the lies of the unclean!'

What Lord-Marshal Holzhauer read did not feel heretical. It seemed to express truths that he had never seen put into words before. 'Silence!' he ordered, and a backhanded blow from one of his aides enforced the command.

The words of Father Bellona outlined what had gone wrong with the Imperium of Mankind. They explained that with brutal surgery, a cleansing crusade and a return to the ways of the Saint Vandire, the Imperium of Man could be returned to vigorous health.

The thesis called for a military leader of great skill and purpose to lead the crusade. A warrior of faith and conviction and iron. The last chance to save the Imperium of Man.

Lord-Marshal Holzhauer considered all the skeins of fate that had come together in this moment. It seemed like divine providence that these words had been posted this day. That he should be here to read them.

He had never been defeated in battle. What greater proof did any have that he could be that warrior? With a moment's consideration, *could* changed to *should*.

Holzhauer beckoned the priest forward. Father Bellona stood before him, boots set squarely onto the rockcrete, resolute and defiant. He looked emaciated. His cheeks were pinched. His swollen eyes stared out from his face. But there was an inner light that seemed to glow from within him that spoke of great holiness and purity.

'There are many within the Imperium who would consider your thoughts heretical,' Holzhauer stated. 'Servants of the corrupt will try to destroy both you and your words. You will need a worthy protector.'

'Are you that man?' Bellona demanded.

'I am,' Holzhauer declared. With one swift motion he tore the parchment from the doorway. He turned to Adjutant Lehr. 'Make copies of this and distribute them to my commanding officers. And ensure Father Bellona has my personal protection.'

Lehr bathed in the lord-marshal's attention. 'It shall be done as you command, my lord!'

Lord-Marshal Holzhauer felt a new sense of purpose. *This was what he had been born for:* to be the cleansing flame that would start the Imperium anew.

From the towers of the Cathedral of Saint Helena Richstar, the bells struck the hour. After, when the true cost was being tallied, the Munitorum would fix this point as the moment the Malouri Uprising began.

PART ONE

ONE

Sergeant Minka Lesk shaded her eyes as the bombardment resumed. This was her thirtieth day upon Malouri. She was ten miles back from the front, sitting on her Gryphonne IV Chimera armoured transport, but even here she could feel the ground shudder as the building roll of Earthshaker batteries warming up became a rolling thunder.

The fyceline smoke grew thicker and darker as battery after battery added to the onslaught. The target for this fury was five miles off, across the steel-grey waters: the island fortress of Crannog Mons, known to them as Traitor Rock.

Beneath her, the five-inch thick ceramite armour of her Chimera, *The Saint*, rattled like a tin can. This was what the Imperium of Mankind did. It channelled blunt might from thousands of worlds and focused it into one square mile of utter destruction.

For the rank and file of the Astra Militarum the effect was

awe-inspiring. For the Cadians, who had seen war on a thousand planets, this was just the beginning.

It was five years since the whirlwind of the fall of Cadia had snatched Arminka Lesk up in its vortex. In that tumultuous time she had grown from a teenage Whiteshield to trooper to sergeant. She'd learnt many things with the Cadian Shock Troops. To kill in the name of the Emperor. To drink. To sleep anywhere. To own every room she walked into. To always twist the bayonet.

Now she was a young woman of twenty-one years with scars and bad memories and nightmares as twisted as the roiling swirls of the Eye of Terror. But she was still alive, and there was still fight within her yet.

That morning Minka was dressed in seasoned Cadian drab, her flak armour scuffed from action, her bull-pup Accatran-pattern lascarbine slung over her shoulder, a pair of grenades hanging from her webbing. Her tri-dome helmet lay next to her. Her sleeves were pushed up above her elbows.

An ornate tattoo had been worked into the skin of her forearm, with the symbol of her home fortress of Kasr Myrak surrounded by the motto *Cadia Stands* in High Gothic script.

Jaromir came up behind her. 'Traitors?' he said simply.

She nodded. Jaromir was a well-built giant with a mop of sandy hair. He'd been a handsome man once, but he'd taken a bolt shell to the head long before he was assigned to Minka's squad. His injury had left him unable to express himself with ease. Sometimes his mouth stopped working, and he could not connect his thoughts together well. In the old days he'd have been retired to the reserves.

But despite his injuries, Jaromir could still strip a carbine, could still hit a bullseye at a hundred yards, and when given an order he responded with the sharpness of a new recruit. His training ran deep.

Orugi had been lying on the open rear access ramp, his helmet beside him. He sat up from the shade of the Chimera. 'Nothing like a bombardment to wake you up,' he said as he stood and stretched.

A klaxon rang. Minka slapped the Chimera's front slabs of armour. 'Come on! We're moving out!'

Breve had been fretting over the machine-spirit ever since they'd landed. He made the sign of the aquila before engaging the engine-stud. 'Here goes!' he called out as he coaxed the Chimera's machine-spirit to life. The first gritty puffs of promethium fumes began to splutter through the armoured slats that screened the twin exhaust pipes.

'So far so good...' Breve said, keeping the engine turning over. All across the camp, every trooper, every squad, every company of the Cadian 101st, 'Hell's Last', was already moving with prompt efficiency.

Minka clambered back over the hull, dropping into one of the roof hatches and pulling the top closed to keep the dust out. The air-filters were already kicking in, blowing warmed air about their feet. It smelt of burning unguents.

'Breve!' Allun shouted. 'Can we turn this thing off?'

Breve shouted something that Bergen, the front gunner, relayed into the cabin. 'They're overheating. If you need ventilation then open the hatches.'

Allun kicked the vents closed. 'Last thing we need is cooking alive.'

They'd been on Malouri for four weeks, drilling incessantly and preparing themselves for the battle. There was a serious air to them now, underlined by the crackling static of orders that came through on the vox-unit.

It was routine traffic. Orders of the Day. Crude jokes. Mundane banter between the signal officers of the various companies. It went on and on until Colonel Sparker's ident code cut through it all. All other voices fell silent.

'General Bendikt commands.' The attack on Traitor Rock was about to begin.

The interior of *The Saint* had been their home for years – mass produced, unadorned, utilitarian in every way, but home nevertheless. Every inch held some memory for Minka: the Black Five tally marks scratched over Baine's head, old sentry rotas from their time on Potence, a few fading sketches of exercises on Crone B9 that she had engraved with her knife-blade, the scorch marks from when Dreno had accidentally discharged a las-bolt within the tight confines and miraculously no one had been more than alarmed and singed.

She took this all in. This was her squad and she was their leader, and they could not wait to get to grips with the enemy. It was not just her who felt it. A thrill went through the tight confines of *The Saint*. The months of travel and practice and training were over.

Even Baine sobered up. 'So, this is it,' he said.

Minka adjusted her helmet and slid the chin strap down. She nodded. 'We're going in.'

TWO

Minka's regiment, the Cadian 101st, 'Hell's Last', had travelled to the planet of Malouri aboard the Endeavour-class cruiser *Right of Will* – a tough little scrapper that originally hailed from the shipyards orbiting Morten's Quay, in the Agripinaa System.

The regiment had spent six months on the ice world of Crone B9. After successive campaigns on Potence, Leymas and Eastea, a spell of arctic training had raised their spirits. The air on Crone B9 was so still and quiet that they could hear the snow squeak under their boots.

Not only had it been cathartic, but it had allowed troopers from other Cadian regiments that had been decimated by action or considered 'lesser', to be easily merged into the 101st. Nothing but amasec and ice, they had joked as they swapped their stories and memories and melded their many pasts into a new whole.

Minka's squad had been two short of the requisite ten. 'I'll fix that for you,' Colour Sergeant Tyson promised as he stood with a clipboard and scribe. Minka was still wary of him. He was a short, bullish man with an overlarge chin that was always shaved so close it looked pale blue.

'Here are your two,' he said, and waved the men forward. The first was Thuja Baine, a square man with a boxer's face. Baine was a rough, bare-knuckle fighter with 'Cadia Stands' and the Imperial aquila tattooed in a band about his arm. What remained of his nose had long since been smeared across the left side of his face and reset in a crooked V. Minka herself had broken it a few months back, sparring.

He was shorter than she remembered. From the colour in his cheeks it was clear that he remembered her as well. She was used to this.

'Baine, is it?' she smiled, not giving him a chance to speak. 'Welcome to Seventh Company.'

If Baine held a grudge, he did not show it. He smiled and shook her hand. 'Greetings, sarge.'

The other man was Elias Orugi, a poseur with a bald head and neatly trimmed black goatee. A solid looking trooper, he had a burn scar on his right cheek that had left the skin stretched. His right eye had been replaced with a cheap field-augmetic of bare steel and simple red targeting orb.

'Plasma overheat,' he said when he caught the look in her eyes, 'on Potence. But I've retained my marksmanship. Marksman, First Class.'

'Welcome to Seventh Company,' Minka repeated. 'Don't know if you've heard, but we're heading back to El'Phanor.'

El'Phanor was an ancient warrior world that was being brought back to life. It was also the headquarters of this section of Imperial Command.

'Can't wait!' Baine said. But it turned out that Minka had

spoken too soon. Their orders had been altered and they were diverted.

'It's an emergency, apparently,' Colour Sergeant Tyson told the collected officers of the 101st. He had to try to buoy up their spirits. 'Local commanders have made an Imperial mess of things. We'll go in and bang some heads together.'

The *Right of Will* had a smooth passage through the warp.

When it transferred into realspace in the outer circuits of the Malouri System, it relayed its arrival to the local Imperial commander. Coded ciphers gave it priority over all other craft. All previously plotted courses and docking times had to be refigured. Logic circuits whirred as banks of slaved servitors recalculated the many ship-approach routes as its course was meticulously plotted.

Imperial Navy wrecks still hung in low-orbit, those further out hanging in pale nebulas of frozen gas, those nearest to the planet ever falling in slow death-spirals that would end in a fiery doom. The *Right of Will*'s plasma-engines roared past them, the blue-green glow of the afterburners trailing like comets as they left queues of Munitorum transports behind.

While they travelled in system, General Bendikt was transferred straight to the planet aboard the colonel's personal lighter. 'He's keen to get this battle wrapped up,' Sparker told them. 'It won't be long till you're down there as well. And there'll be plenty of action for you all.'

In the days before disembarkment, the Cadians were briefed on the war they were going to end. The progress of the Malouri Uprising had followed a predictable pattern. A local potentate had seized power and declared independence from the Imperium of Man. Waves of conquest and brutal suppression followed until the whole planet was in the grip of heretical forces and calling out to neighbouring planets for all-out revolt.

At the company briefing, Sparker went on, in a long monotone, to tell them things they already knew. Crannog Mons was an island fortress. The siege had lasted for nearly five years. Munitorum calculators had predicted the fall of the planet within – and here he fudged the numbers he knew – at least seven years.

Sparker referred to the papers in his hand. 'Usual rank and file units. Mainly local, though with some solid fighters. Notably the Lethe Rifles and a number of Elnaur regiments. They're the system elite.' Sparker paused as he consulted his notes. Evrind pointed to the relevant part. He did not think to thank her. 'At time of siege starting there were millions of defenders. No doubt they've slaughtered many of their own. They fought well, according to all accounts, in the land war. Expect battle-hardened veterans, more dangerous because of their heretic philosophy.'

He ended by looking up and scanning the room. 'This world was part of the supply network for the Cadian Gate.'

They all knew it, of course. But the link between this world and Cadia was worth repeating. This battle was personal now. There was only one option left to them, and that was utter victory.

Unfortunately for the traitors, the Imperium had not been slow to respond. An armada carrying local regiments, led by Mordian General von Horne, had arrived in the Malouri System largely unchallenged.

As the traitors lacked a sizeable naval strength, von Horne's armada had bludgeoned their way in-system and landed on the planet in force.

Furious battles had taken place across the planet before the traitors had shortened their lines and pulled back to the island fortress of Crannog Mons, blowing the land-bridge as they did so, determining to sit out the siege for decades, if necessary.

'The siege is already four years old, and it seems that the Mordians are not moving fast enough for Lord Militant Warmund. So he's sending us.'

Sparker pulled up a map of the island. 'The whole place is filled with magazines and barracks. The traitors could hold out for decades.' At the landward end was the great gatehouse of Tor Tartarus. The image was greeted with studied silence.

'What are those markings?' Dido asked, pointing.

'A suspension bridge connected the island to the mainland. Those are the supports.'

'Anything of the bridge left?'

Sparker checked with Evrind and then shook his head. 'I don't think so. It's just the isolated columns.'

He went around the island. In the centre was the cathedral. Halfway along the island, perched on the northern and southern cliffs were the fortresses of Margrat and Baniyas. 'Baniyas is now in ruins. The traitors have stationed a few batteries here but there is nothing of any particular consequence.'

'What about Margrat?'

Sparker brought up the data-slide that showed the plans of the fortress. It was built on the same plan as the bastion that lay at the centre of Kasr Myrak. The sight of it stung Minka.

At the opposite end of the island was the tower of Ophio. It was the smallest of the bastions, star-shaped, with a narrow tower rising from its centre. Guarding the approaches to this far end was the small island bastion of Tor Kharybdis. Sparker tapped it with the end of his stick. 'Volcanic atoll. Fortified with a single main bastion, nicknamed the Lone Redoubt.'

Sparker next brought up picts of the traitor generals and their forces. First was General Kirkin, a vain looking officer with his hair pulled back into a small bun.

'An excellent duellist,' Sparker reported. 'Personally brave. He leads the Ongoth Jackals. They earned battle honours on Scarus and Lethe Eleven. Poor quality troops according to Militarum sources.'

The Jackals were a shabby looking bunch in ill-fitting great-coats and scavenged uniforms. 'There were nearly two million Jackals at the time of the rebellion. They didn't all turn traitor, but they've long since purged their ranks. How many are active defenders now we cannot say. Expect solid if uninspired leadership.'

The next commander of note was General Conoe of the Swabian Fusiliers. He had an augmetic eye, an aquila tattooed under the other and a goatee that hung in a heavy grey plait down to his chest. 'He leads a number of units – the Lethe Rifles, the Scarus Light, and the Swabian Fusiliers.' The data-picts showed troops in smart uniforms of black worsted with enclosed helmets and rebreathers. 'A solid unit poorly led. Personally, I hold him responsible for the fall of Lethe Eleven to the greenskins. Another heretic.'

Dido called out. 'Sir, what heretical belief do the traitors hold?'

Sparker lowered his voice. 'They are followers of the apostate Goge Vandire.'

The hush that greeted his words said it all. Vandire was one of the worst heretics of Imperial history. He had brought corruption to the very throne room of the God-Emperor. Minka had never paid much attention to the annals of Imperial history but even she knew enough to know that. It wouldn't have mattered either way. They were traitors.

Sparker was holding the best – or worst – until last. 'Commander of the heresy is self-styled Arch-Duke, Lord-Marshal Holzhauer. He leads five regiments of the elite Elnaur Chasseurs.'

The data pict showed a line of troopers smartly turned out in ornamental black carapace with plumed helmets and ceremonial cloaks over one shoulder.

'This is the only data pict I could find of Holzhauer.' Sparker brought up a cold-faced man with brightly polished breastplate and heavily starched velvet jacket. 'He claims to have never lost a battle,' Sparker said. There was a long pause before he added, 'He has clearly never met the Cadians.'

While the others laughed, Minka looked into Holzhauer's blue eyes and saw cold arrogance and an inexhaustible self-regard. A man willing for others to die on his behalf.

In her heart, she felt that the defence of Cadia had been crippled by traitors like Holzhauer. It had only taken a moment, but as she looked at their enemy, she felt hatred.

THREE

They disembarked the next day. Troopers marched with packs, armour and webbing, loading up by company alongside their Chimeras, while the heavier armour and supplies were all safely stowed and tied down to grav-pallets. Seventh Company was loaded half an hour ahead of schedule. Minka's squad was on the third level, at the back, near the engines of the second craft.

Each squad found their transport and dropped in through the top hatches. Minka counted her troopers in before following them. There was only one seat left, next to Baine. She ignored him as she slid into the chair and sat back, resting her head against the metalwork behind her.

'That's thirty-two days aboard ship,' Viktor said, and scratched the tally up on the interior panel above his head. Minka paid no notice. Viktor liked to count things. It was how he was.

She closed her eyes when she heard the rattle of the fuel pipes disengaging from the lighter. The engine whine rose in volume, the sub-sonic vibrations making her teeth ache. She started to sweat and began to feel sick. The stuffy air was unbearable.

Dreno pulled out his pack of well-thumbed cards. 'Who's up for it?' No one took him up.

Minka sat with her back to the metal struts. Out of boredom she took her combat knife from the sheath she kept strapped to her thigh. It was kasrkin issue and had once belonged to a soldier named Rath Sturm who'd kept her alive in Kasr Myrak. The pressed emblem read '94th' with a crossed rifle and knife beneath it. Sturm was the kind of man held together with scars and skull-plate and titanium pins. By sheer force of will he had kept them fighting, street by street, ruin by ruin, room by room, long after they should have been mopped up by the Black Legion kill squads.

Among his many honours he was also an Armageddon veteran. 'Any warrior who's fought greenskins and survived is hard to scare,' he'd liked to say.

He still came to her in her dreams. When she was cut off behind Statue Square, or picking through the ruins of her former scholam. Then she would hear the inhuman keening of the enemy forces, her heart beginning to race and her body sweating.

She struggled to wake in those moments, as if the enemies would not let her surface from sleep. But then Colonel Rath Sturm would appear, leaping over a broken wall, or kicking a door down and shooting her foes.

She held that image in her head now, and it calmed her as their lander began to fall towards the planet.

Minka had seen enough landing craft get hit on their descent. She'd seen them fall like fireworks from the sky, the hailstorm of blackened bodies landing a few minutes later. It was an image that always tormented her at moments like these. She hated planetary landings. She clenched her jaw and thought of Rath Sturm.

But this time she could smell Baine's closeness. The nausea kept rising.

Minka pushed herself up at last. 'Dreno! Deal me a hand.'

She had lost a month's wages by the time the klaxons sounded for imminent landing.

Baine had been watching her the entire time. 'Got a problem?' she snapped at last.

'I wouldn't have played that,' Baine said.

'No?'

'No,' he said.

She gave him her coldest smile. 'And why should I take any notice of a man I beat in the sparring pits?'

'You got lucky.'

'I didn't *get* lucky, I carry it around with me.'

Baine clapped his hands and laughed out loud. 'Good. That's the kind of sergeant we need.'

The lighters' bulky forms settled like large, lumbering birds on the vast rockcrete plain of Starport. It would take days for the regiment's full cargo and support staff to unload, but the fighting strength of the 101st was sent straight up to the camp to acclimatise and start training.

Once they were under way, Minka ran through the basics. Gravity. Daylight hours. Hostile life forms. Diseases. Having covered the pertinent details, she said, 'It's pretty normal. And of course, there's an intractable siege that we're here to sort out.'

They had not yet seen Crannog Mons, so it was all theoretical to them. But they were weary of confinement aboard ship and were just glad to be planetside. They opened up the top hatch, climbed onto the Chimera and stretched out.

It wasn't long before the stench of smoke and old decay surrounded them. Their humour quickly faded as they left the radar masts, control towers and flat rockcrete slabs of Starport and got their first true sight of the planet of Malouri.

The land was white. Baine picked up the auspex and checked it out. 'Bone fields,' he said. He passed the auspex around. It was a bleak sight. War had crossed over the planet like wildfire, with hundreds of thousands dying in the opening skirmishes. There were mountains of bones and excavation teams were busy bulldozing them into mass graves.

An hour or so later, they saw jagged mountains rising from the ravaged landscape.

'They seem familiar,' Baine said.

They looked, not quite able to determine what was strange about the terrain before them.

At last, Orugi said, 'They're battleships!'

Minka suddenly understood. The land about was strewn with fragments of warp-craft that had fallen to the planet, their towering metal wrecks forming ranges of burnt and blistered armaplas and steel.

The exoskeleton of an Imperial battleship lay across the road close by, its vast bulk stretching away for miles in either direction. Its spine had fractured upon its fall, forming a road that cut through the ship's centre. The interior of the craft rose up on either side, a rusting canyon, hung with tendons of pipe and ducting. The darkness was occasionally lit by the flash of arc-lights as Adeptus Mechanicus recovery crews slowly cleared the most salvageable parts of the wrecks.

It took ten minutes to pass through the void-ship's innards. The mountains of fuselage soon began to diminish, and before them lay a vast flat plain, acne-pitted with craters, each one silvered with putrid floodwater. As far as the eye could see, reflected light silhouetted barricades of knotted razor wire and tank traps, and the hulks of destroyed tanks, transports and carriers. There was no life, except for swirling flocks of black carrion birds. Nothing to offer variety except for the sight of a crashed Marauder or the rusting hull of a burnt-out Leman Russ.

The gunner, Bergen, was sitting half in the open hatchway, one boot up on the roof plating, his chin resting on his bent knee. He puffed out his cheeks. 'Well. This is bleak,' he said.

'It's better than being aboard ship,' Orugi replied. He lay stretched out on the front decking, helmet drawn over his face.

The others were sitting with their legs dangling into the open rear cabin. Viktor passed a bottle of grog around.

'So where is the island?' Baine said.

Bergen pointed. 'Due west.'

After a few swigs, he started up a sing-along.

Hours rolled by. The lights of Starport dwindled behind them. Far off in the distance the rolling thunder of a bombardment rose to a roar. Mile by mile, the flat grey was gradually replaced with cities of reserve emplacements. Temporary tent and prefab townships began to take on an air of permanence. There were broad medicae tents, latrine huts and dimly lit black-market camps, where the weary trooper could trade their pay for something resembling comfort on this benighted world.

They were onto their third rendition of *Flowers of Cadia* when Baine clambered forward to where Minka was sitting propped up against the turret, the spooled rolls of autocannon shells cushioned with her old kit bag.

'Still not there yet?' he said.

She shook her head. 'Looks like we'll be going through the night,' she said.

'Why didn't we land closer to this place?'

'Brass says they've still got formidable and functional defence laser silos. We're too precious to risk.'

Baine nodded. There was a long pause as he sat silently, rubbing his hands. At last he started, 'Well, this is better than ice-world training.'

'Yeah,' she said.

He paused again. Minka could feel him thinking of something to say. She didn't give him the chance. 'Listen. About your nose. Sorry about that.'

'Better you broke my nose than I yours,' he said at last, and winked.

FOUR

It was nearing dusk on that first day when they passed close to the first penal labour camp. Razor wire and watchtowers ringed its perimeter. The penal work-gangs were heading back, their armed guards walking behind them, lasrifles slung over their shoulders.

Dirty conscript faces stared up as the Cadians went by. Somewhere far ahead there was the lightning flicker of another bombardment, followed by the low thunder of ordnance. Lumens began to glow from the outer limits of the siege camp. Searchlights scissored the sky, lighting columns of smoke from within. Distant sirens rang out.

The Cadians looked on impassively. They passed long convoys of Munitorum cargo-20s, yellow hazard lights flashing. The semi-trailers creaked under their loads of replacement artillery barrels, crates of ordnance, giant rolls of razor wire, stacks of duck boards, medical boxes, powercells and kilolitre vats of sloshing blood plasma – all feeding the warfront with materiel on an industrial scale.

Hour after hour and still the front lines seemed no nearer than before.

Minka fell asleep, woke briefly to note that they were moving again, and then fell back asleep. She half-listened to the conversation of her squad.

'Welcome to Malouri,' she heard Baine say.

Dreno nodded. 'Yeah. Another shitty war.'

At dusk they passed an isolated prayer chapel standing among high walls. Pseudo-flames guttered from grates set into the high stone buttresses. The gothic windows were lit from within with warm light. Over the roar of tanks and tracks Minka thought she could hear the sound of singing.

It woke an old memory within her. Each morning, as a child, hurrying towards Statue Square for morning drill as the night glare of the Eye of Terror slowly receded with the dawn. Veteran choirs had sung all night, dispelling the dread for the unholy rift that swirled above their heads.

The sound of their singing faded behind her. She paused and turned, pushing the hair from her face as she looked back, but the chapel was soon lost behind the military silhouettes of the Chimeras of Seventh Company.

The chapel in her memory had been dedicated to the Cadian Saint Gerstahl the Martyr. Squeezed into a gap between a dome-topped defence silo and a marshalling yard, the chapel had a small, narrow interior with high gothic windows that looked out onto the stacked habs. Along both walls were side chapels, each one hung with the mouldering banners of Kasr Myrak regiments, the oldest having rotted down to the bare skeleton of threads, the symbol of the Cadian Gate little more than an impression.

Each wall had been patchworked with brass plaques memorialising troopers who had died on far-off battlefields, too distant for their bones to ever be returned. She had stood there as a child and tried to pronounce the names of places. They spoke to her imagination of heroic deaths across the Imperium of Man.

There was one statue that she had loved more than any other. It was of cast bronze, depicting a colonel with a stern and tragic look in her one remaining eye. The statue was so old that the bronze had a deep, dark patina and only the aquila on her breastplate shone. Many hands had rubbed that mark for good luck; the two eagle heads, one blind, one sighted, and the raised ridges of the eagle's wings gleamed.

The name of that warrior was Colonel...

Minka frowned.

She closed her eyes and summoned those details back, making the memories parade before her. There was a time, not long ago, when the name would have come to her in an instant. She strained for it, but the cherished object had been snatched up by the past, and however much she stretched and scrabbled for it, it was lost now, beyond all reach.

The sadness of Cadia did not come from the terrible months of battle as she had fought for her home city. The loss came from little separations like this.

Fragment by fragment, she was losing her past.

She closed her eyes. She was a child again walking along Euphrates Street. It was a safe place to be. Her mother and Tarli would be home when she returned. But then, in a moment, her mind rebelled. The setting about her scrambled. It was now a city of smoke and ruins. Empty windows stared blankly out. Dead bodies lay hidden under the rubble. She could smell their rotting cadavers. She saw herself as she crept forward, lasrifle in hand, her skin white with rock-dust. She was ready for any danger as the keening of the Broken rose up as they hunted through the ruins.

And then Colonel Rath Sturm appeared, his face broken in a lopsided grin. 'Ready, Lesk?' he said.

Minka blinked her eyes open. It was still night. In the shelter of the squad cabin, Viktor had brewed up recaff with a promethium stove. He passed mugs round.

'Sarge,' he said, and shook her shoulder.

In a moment she was sitting up.

'Cheers,' she said, taking the mug and holding it tight. The recaff was thin and watery, but it was warm enough.

She passed the empty mug backwards as the artillery bombardment spread across the horizon, battery after battery of Earthshaker cannons adding to the fury, each one a flaming yellow tongue licking against the sky.

Each member of the squad got sleep as well as they could, lying in the cabin, packs for bedding. Minka slept head to toe with Lyrga – one of their new reinforcements – in net hammocks used for stowing baggage.

Breve and Wulfe took it in turns driving through the night. Baine and Dreno were passing a bottle of grog about. The songs stopped and started and faded away to low conversation.

At some point in the night they had to stop for a convoy of cargo-12s carrying a squadron of three Baneblades. The Cadians pulled over to let them pass. The engines of their Chimeras and tanks idled as they waited. Minka was barely awake as she watched the great beasts pass by.

Behind came a tail of Adeptus Mechanicus support vehicles and shrine-walkers, skitarii centaurs and cherubs carrying heavy brass censors. At the head of the convoy strode three banner bearers, each carrying the colours of the ancient engines. The engines of war were a wondrous sight, the colours of the Cadian 101st emblazoned upon their flanks.

In the wake of the procession, a pair of drab coloured cargo-8s were nosing forward, the vehicles rusting and ill-maintained. They did not look as if they had anything to do with the previous convoy. They were clearly not Cadian.

Anger came quickly. Minka grabbed a lumen and jumped down, waving the lead cargo-8 to a halt. It tried to go round her, but she stood in front and lifted her hand for it to stop.

The driver was dressed in some tribal weave. He was unaugmented. There was nothing of the Adeptus Mechanicus about him. He was free-riding, she realised, keeping close to the Baneblades to cut through the convoy.

'What's your unit?'

'Drookian Fenguard,' the driver said.

'This is a Cadian convoy. Pull over. You're going to have to wait,' she told him.

The driver nodded, but instead of pulling over he surged forward. She had to jump out of the way. Minka cursed.

It took only three single las-bolts before the rear pneumatic tyre burst with a blast of compressed air. Debris shredded off, and then there was the screech of steel rim on the rockcrete road surface.

Minka reholstered her pistol as the Drookians dismounted. There was a captain among them, his Imperial insignia incongruous among his tribal garb.

'You!' he shouted. 'You shot out our wheel?'

She squared off before him. 'Yes, sir.'

His hand felt for his blade.

Her chainsword was on the Chimera, but she was not afraid. She shifted her weight onto the balls of her toes, ready as he closed the last steps through the gloom.

'Is there a problem?' a voice suddenly called out.

It was Colonel Sparker.

'Look!' the Drookian pointed. The cargo-8 was listing to the side, the shredded tyre steaming.

Sparker stood between him and Minka. 'It appears you have a burst tyre. You're now impeding the road. Please remove your truck.'

The Drookian swore in response. It was a Drookian curse, and the Cadians did not know the words, but the meaning was clear.

Sparker had no time for nonsense. 'Breve!' he shouted and signalled the Chimera forward. 'Please move this rust-bucket off the road.'

There were shouts of alarm as *The Saint* shunted the cargo-8 forward, dumping the Drookians off the side of the road.

Minka clambered aboard. She felt the Drookians' hatred as they stared up to watch her pass.

'I remember you, Cadian!' their captain called out. 'We'll see how your Cadian superiority manifests itself on the battlefield!'

Minka lifted her hand in mock friendship. 'Not until you get that truck fixed, you won't.'

The Cadians pushed onwards through what was left of the night. The bleak penal camps were gradually replaced with increasingly cramped cities of flakboard pre-fabs, field-chapels and field-latrines.

Sunrise found them deep within the siege camp. In the grey light of dawn of their second day they passed neatly laid-out munition dumps, watchtowers, sunken armament silos and lifters loading hulking locomotives.

The air was chill, the sky grey. Lyrga passed about a sack of hard-slab. Minka wasn't hungry. The scale of the military camp reminded her of Cadia in the months before her planet's final battle. Those memories brought a melancholy air to the scene about her. Then, they had all been doomed. She drew in a deep breath. This time, she told herself, it was the Imperium and not the traitors who were the besiegers. But still, a niggling doubt remained. You never knew what any battle might bring.

Over each gatehouse flew the colours of the resident regiment. They were gaudy emblems from planets with no great reputation, proudly emblazoned with battles that Minka had never heard of. The troopers stood as sentries at the gates of their compounds. They were dressed in a motley assortment of armour, camo and braid. Minka did not recognise many of their regiments, but she had seen their type many times before. Ill-fitting uniforms and scavenged boots gave the troopers a dirty and downtrodden look.

They were the rank and file of the Imperium. Men, women; black, white and every colour inbetween, drawn from feral worlds, hives, industrial forges, deserts, jungles, ice worlds, vast agri planets and orbital colonies circling gas giants. A conscript rabble. Underfed, poorly turned out, lacking discipline, semi-feudal, ill-trained. The cannon-fodder class of the Imperium of Man. They were mediocre forces raised from little-known planets to fulfil Imperial tithes and obligations. These troopers' bones were the foundations upon which Imperial generals made their reputations.

While she looked upon them with disinterest their expressions showed anything but. The sight of the convoy of Cadians, the famous emblem of the Cadian Gate fluttering from every pennant, electrified them. For most it was their first ever glimpse of these famous warriors. Heads turned. Hands pointed. Some ran closer or just stood dumbstruck, while others pressed up against the wire fencing that lined the sides of the broad metalled service road and made the sign of the aquila.

41

'Cadia stands!' a voice shouted.

There was hope in that phrase. It was a celebration of an indefatigable spirit. A resolute and unwavering courage in the face of utter defeat.

Minka lifted her hand in answer. 'Cadia stands!' she called back.

Even now, those words woke fierce within her. She remembered crouching in the rubble of Kasr Myrak, listening to Creed's speeches cracking over the vox. The lord castellan had given them hope of victory when there was none, but now even he had been taken from them. Everything was taken from them.

She stopped.

Not everything, not yet. She was still here. As long as she still fought, then Cadia still stood.

Thirty hours after planetfall, the Cadian 101st finally entered their assigned camp: ZV-332, in Sector 7 of the Malouri Front. It was three hours before sunset of their second day, a grey, cloudy affair, punctuated by the distant thunder of yet another artillery barrage.

The camp was template Munitorum pattern, replicated a million times across the Imperium. In the centre, within its own perimeter fencing, was the command depot. Hab-blocks made up of flakboard sheds and converted metal containers were set around it in neat lines. There were rows of tented accommodation, latrines, workshops, ammo stores. There was a flakboard Imperial chapel, a command office, medicae pre-fab, Munitorum warehousing.

Lumens had already been lit. They showed the earth was chewed up by tracks. The pre-fab huts that the labour-corps had constructed had a slapdash, temporary feel. About the camp was a ditch and bank perimeter with loops of wire screening it.

The advance party had already started work. Sentry towers were being erected from lengths of rebar and corrugated flakboard. Land-movers were digging underground bunkers and using the rubble to fill sandbags. Work teams were already out repairing the thirty-foot fences and triple concertina wire. By dawn, this camp would be a fortress.

Minka was exhausted. She lay back and rested her head against the rough canvas of the turret. The Chimera's headlights were bars of light in the gloom. But despite the Cadian energy, the camp had a tired air to it, as if the place was already weary of the siege that was taking place upon its soil.

Troopers with lumen wands and hand-held vox-horns directed them to their quarters.

Seventh Company were sent to the armpit of the camp, next to the latrine huts. The powerful scent of counterseptics hung in the air.

Orugi looked about. 'Won't be long till that stinks,' he said. 'Baine! Did you screw someone over in logistics?'

Dreno stood and looked about him. He rolled his eyes as he caught Minka's eye. 'This is Sparker's fault,' he said.

'Speak about your commanding officer with respect,' Minka told him.

Dreno put his hands up. 'Sorry, sarge. Listen, he's good on the battlefield, but camp after camp is a wreck.'

Baine yawned as he followed Jaromir down the ramp. He looked about, his pack thrown over one shoulder. He slapped Dreno's back. 'Don't worry. We won't be here for long.'

Minka's squad pulled their packs down from the luggage nets. Breve let the engine run for a minute while he checked the power plant, then let it judder to a halt.

A team of tech-priests were making their way along the line, mechadendrites plugging into the cog-sockets, communicating with each machine-spirit. Breve was already feeling defensive. He stood back as an adept came to his Chimera.

The adept was largely human with just a single mechadendrite coming out of one of his sleeves. He plugged it in and there was a whirr of data reels. Breve stood rigidly, waiting for the priest's diagnosis.

'This tank's service is incomplete,' the adept said at last in a thin, high-pitched voice, before listing the problems found. 'Suggestion – increase frequency and thoroughness of maintenance routines.'

Breve couldn't stop himself. 'I know all that. But you tell me where I can get the parts from! Don't you know there is a war going on up there?' He waved his hands at the sky, but really he was talking about the galaxy. Or what was left of it.

It was a rhetorical question, but Breve sensed the adept was going to answer. There was a brief pause as the adept brought up secondary data banks. 'There is always war. However, systemic incoherencies within the Munitorum supply structure increasing exponentially due to the fall of the Cadian Gate and surrounding systems are causing major logistical challenges in Segmentum Solar. Do you want me to list the affected forge worlds?'

'No!' Breve said. 'But that is why this Chimera is suffering so many problems. It's nothing to do with poor maintenance!'

There was a pause. The adept's expression was blank. 'In lieu of suitable replacements, recommend increase frequency and thoroughness of maintenance routines,' he said at last.

Breve sighed. The Adeptus Mechanicus was full of adepts who were losing the ability to navigate human communication. He started to explain, but the adept interrupted, 'Action is imminent. Increased frequency and thoroughness of maintenance routines is vital.'

FIVE

Minka shouldered her pack up the flakboard steps of the pre-fab barracks. At the top, Sergeant Barnabas had a clipboard in hand and an irritated look. 'Lesk,' he said and checked the paper before him. 'Fourth squad. At the end. Right-hand side.'

Minka couldn't stand him. She made no response, turned right and led her squad down the corridor. There were shouts and complaints from each dorm room as troopers bagged the best cots. Everyone was pushing back and forth as they found their rooms and bunked down. Minka shoved through them all. The gap was so narrow her pack scraped along the wall. At the end of the corridor, Sparker's aide, Kavik, was already sticking notices up on the board.

The first one was the Thought for the Day. This long into service, they all started to sound the same.

'*Every Cadian is a spark in the darkness,*' she read. 'Wasn't that yesterday's?'

'Was it? I guess there are only so many,' Kavik said, but the truth was officers like Kavik all worked from the same thumb-eared *Book of Daily Thoughts*.

'They've made a complaint,' Kavik called after her.

'Who?'

'Those Drookians.'

Minka made a rude gesture. 'That was Sparker, not me.'

'Tyson is on the warpath,' Kavik warned her.

Minka had already turned into her room. It was long and narrow, lined on both sides with bunk-cots. She was sharing with the other women in her squad and a couple of others from the rest of Seventh Company. The bunks by the window were already taken.

'You take that one,' Minka told Karni and Lyrga. It was the better one. 'I'll take the one by the door.'

Karni nodded. She was a tall, quiet woman. Lyrga took the bottom bunk. Karni took the top.

Minka had grown up in a world built and maintained by the drab-clothed Cadian labour corps. They'd taken their work as seriously as the rank and file of the shock troops took their military prowess. Of course they could fight as well, though that was not their primary training. They built barracks, fortifications, pontoons, trenches, dug-outs – anything that the army needed – to the highest specifications.

This new-build already had the look of a shabby old construction. The walls were unpainted flakboard. Raw nail heads ran in lines from floor to ceiling. There were straight graphite stylus marks, scrawled workings out in plain Gothic by semi-literate labour corps workers.

Minka gave the door a kick to make it close, then threw her pack down, puffed out her cheeks and looked about. She needed to sleep. She kept her boots on and lay down. The cot was a hard board with thin sheets and a colourless scratchy blanket with a faded Munitorum stamp.

'Don't wake me,' she said to no one in particular, and lay back and put her arm over her face.

It seemed that no sooner had she fallen asleep than she was woken up by the distinctive note of a breakfast truck arriving outside – the squeak of the brakes, the back ramp swinging down.

Minka was up in an instant. She shook Lyrga's bunk as she sat up.

'Come on. Ration time! If you're not quick, Baine will have eaten everything!'

Minka was almost first in line for food. The cooks had been up all night and they were in a foul mood. Nothing was ever right when you first arrived. The local Munitorum staff were always an unhelpful lot. It was an arm of the Imperium that seemed to attract the worst sort of incompetents, crooks and extortioners. Supplies were missing, mislabelled or stolen. It was a knot of corruption, and the canteen officers were on the front line of this internecine little war.

'This is all you're getting,' the cook said as he stirred a thick lumpy green slop with his ladle.

Minka held out her bowl. The slop landed heavily. The next cook was handing out biscuits of hardtack. One each. No more. No less.

She took her breakfast to where *The Saint* was parked in line, and climbed up. The tank's thick plating was cold from the night before and slick with beads of condensation. Its weight and armour were reassuring. She sat high on the turret so she could look out westwards.

Dawn was starting to bleach the western sky as the canteen staff lowered more vats of slab off the back of their cargo-6. Clouds piled up on the horizon. The camp was waking to the clink of cheap press-steel implements and the scent of hot food.

Orugi was next. He joined her on top of *The Saint*. 'Morning, sarge,' he said as he lowered himself down.

'Where's Baine?' she said.

Orugi pointed with his chin across to the line where Baine was craning his neck to see what was on offer. She laughed as she shovelled more food in. Across the wire, in the neighbouring camp they could see a group of irregular soldiers staring towards the Cadians.

'Who are they?'

Orugi put a hand up to shade his face. 'Not sure.'

Minka shovelled in another mouthful, kept looking. No doubt they'd be one of the local regiments.

Baine came up. 'Look at this!' he said. 'What do they think I am?' He clambered up and took his place and then fell silent as he started eating.

One by one, their platoon members left the canteen queue and made their way over, sitting on the ground or climbing up for a place on their Chimera. Dido had been talking to the canteen staff and came over with the air of someone who knew something. She pointed across to the neighbouring camp.

'Drookians,' she said.

Minka suddenly felt everyone's eyes on her. 'Same lot we ran into yesterday?'

Dido shrugged. It was hard to tell. Either way, Drookians had a reputation for theft and disorder. 'Better set a guard,' Dido said. She slapped Minka on the arm. 'Your squad can start.'

'Well done, sarge,' Dreno said.

Minka didn't pause. 'Pleasure. You and Orugi are first up. Off you go.'

'Now?' Orugi said.

'Now.'

The rest of Minka's squad watched them move off to the

perimeter wires. They sat on *The Saint* as the sun rose, scraping out the last of the slab and chewing their hardtack.

The sun lit the sky a pale blue and green. Silhouetted against it, Minka could see a distant forest of Earthshaker barrels, stretching out to either horizon. 'The poorer the infantry, the more artillery you need,' she said.

Beyond were the great piles of clouds. But something was not right with the way the light fell on them. Someone pointed. Another cursed. Minka put her hardtack down, suddenly understanding. They were not clouds.

That was the island fortress – Crannog Mons, rising up like a lonely mountain into the blue sky.

'Holy Throne!' Baine said.

It was one thing to hear about it, but another to see it in the flesh. No chart or pict-image could convey its impregnable nature. Golden slanting sunlight struck the island and threw its many crags and statues and bastions into sharp relief. It filled the horizon before them.

From the Cadians about her there was awed silence.

It was Viktor who broke it. 'How long has this siege been going on for?'

'Four years,' Minka told them.

'They've barely scratched it,' Viktor said.

Minka paused. But even she was shocked at how little damage the besieging forces had done. How many of the people stood around her now would still be standing when the fortress fell?

Orugi and Dreno walked up to the edge of the camp. It didn't take long for a squad of Drookians to take up position across from them.

'What's your regiment?' the Drookians shouted.

'Hundred-and-First,' Orugi shouted. 'Hell's Last.'

There was a pause. 'We are Clan Boskobel.'

Orugi and Dreno had never heard of them. They took little interest, but started moving along the wire.

'Cadians!' the shout came again. 'You have wronged us.'

Dreno made a rude sign.

'By the Emperor, we shall have our honour returned!'

'What do you think they'll do?' Orugi said.

Dreno was dismissive. 'They'll steal a truck or a delivery of slab.'

The day wore on with routine jobs as everyone settled into their new camp and the regimental supplies and armour began to trickle in from Starport. But that evening, as the sun set over the blackened land behind them, there was activity in the Drookian camp facing the Cadians.

Baine had the auspex raised to his face. He watched four Drookians carrying something heavy between them. They fixed something to the end of a pole and then lifted it up and set it in the ground.

Baine wanted to laugh. 'It's a grox,' he said. 'They've skinned it and lifted its head on a pole.' It was so tribal. Typical of a world wreathed in superstition as much as it was in mists.

The grox stared blindly towards the Cadian camp. The rest of the skin draped down on either side.

Lyrga shuddered involuntarily. She put her hand up to her face to see better. It looked particularly eerie in the half light. She shivered again. 'It's creepy,' she said.

Baine looked at her as if she were simple, but then he felt it too – a chill that went down his back. He looked about. Nothing was there.

'We'd better tell Minka,' he said.

* * *

Everyone felt it. A strange chill in the air as soon as they turned towards the Drookian camp. It didn't take long before news of the ritual insult started to spread. Colonel Sparker summoned Minka to his office.

'You've seen the curse-pole they've put up?' he started.

'Yes, sir. Feral world superstitions.'

Sparker nodded. 'Maybe. But I don't like it. The captain you ran into was nephew to the commander of the Boskobel chieftain, or whatever he calls himself. The whole clan has taken it as an affront to their honour.'

Minka nodded. She noted how Sparker had used the word 'you' in describing the run-in on the highway. She felt the weight of regimental disapproval bearing down upon her. She had started this, the attitude was, so it was she who had to end it.

'I could challenge him to a duel.'

Sparker shook his head. 'No. Killing him won't help anything. But at least get rid of that thing.'

'Yes, sir.'

Sparker nodded. 'And most importantly, don't get caught.'

Minka saluted. 'Understood, sir.'

SIX

Major Luka had lost his leg so long ago he could barely remember what it was like to have four functioning limbs. He'd retired from the Cadian Eighth decades past, and he had followed the natural course of a Cadian's life and returned to his home planet to supervise the training of Whiteshields.

He'd already been training Whiteshields for twenty years when the war for Cadia began. The loss of his home world had thrown him into a deep depression. Not just for himself and his fellows, but also for the loss of a role that he had felt great pride for: taking young Cadians and sharpening them into deadly weapons of war.

For Major Luka, the loss of Cadia meant many things, not the least of which was that the Whiteshields were no more. For the Cadian High Command, no Whiteshields refreshing the ranks meant that the existence of the Cadian Shock Troopers was at threat.

A solution had to be found before the Imperium of Man was robbed of its finest fighting force, just at the moment when it needed it most.

And it was as part of this proposed solution that Major Luka was one of those summoned to El'Phanor and given the mission, by Lord Militant Warmund no less, of ensuring the continuation of the Cadian Shock Troops as a viable fighting force within his warzone.

A variety of solutions had been proffered by the lord militant's staff. On some warfronts Cadian commanders had recruited cadets from suitable planets.

'Find me a new Cadia and I will agree to that,' Warmund stated. It was clear he thought that no such planet existed.

There was a pause. 'We could recruit veterans from other regiments...' another adjutant suggested.

'No!' Warmund's voice enhancer kicked in automatically and made loose objects in the room rattle. He lowered his voice. 'What is the best of another regiment next to a true child of Cadia?' He strode up and down the vaulted chamber they were meeting in. 'It's impossible! They will bring their own habits and traditions in. And so dilute the Cadian spirit! The steel that runs through us all.'

There was a scrape of metal as Dowding, his senior aide-de-camp, stepped forward. Dowding was a grizzled veteran of a thousand warzones, with the wounds to prove it.

'The only way we can instil the Cadian spirit is through taking suitable candidates to elite training bases. Moons. Asteroids. Ice planets. Places where we can raise children as we were raised. Cadian fashion.'

Warmund nodded. 'I agree. Have the Munitorum draw up a list of suitable locations. But such a scheme would take a generation to reach fruition, and meanwhile my Cadian regiments are being obliterated. We are facing a Black Crusade. Whole regiments, with their names and histories, lost in some of the heaviest casualties we've ever recorded. In this sector, without reinforcements, the Cadians as a fighting force do not have twenty years to wait.'

He felt his rage building once more. At moments like this the volume of his battlefield-augmented voice threatened to break glass. He stopped himself and drew in a breath. When he started to speak again it was in a more controlled fashion.

'In the meantime we need to plug the gap. There must be thousands of children within Cadian baggage trains, those born to fighting regiments. Gather those of a suitable age and by the Golden Throne, put them through the wringer. They will not be to the standard that we expect, but they will keep our regiments alive until our other plans reach fruition.'

There were nearly twelve thousand enlisted into the first Whiteshield training course. The hopefuls gathered upon the surface of El'Phanor. Terraforming had been going on long enough that life had just started to return to the long-dead planet. There was a thin atmosphere at least. And above they could see the steady twinkle of the Ramillies-class star fort as it hung like a moon.

Urae Yedrin was one of those recruited. He was the only child of a Cadian captain and a naval rating. He'd lived an odd life following his mother's regiment, being both Cadian and distinctly not Cadian.

'It's your eyes,' his mother explained sadly. 'They're blue.'

During her career Yedrin's mother had tried many times to have him transferred back to her home world, but the Imperium had better things to do than ferry lone children across the galaxy. Even if they were Cadians. What would later turn out to be named the Thirteenth Black Crusade had already begun, and the frenetic tension of war was starting to take hold.

His mother's regiment had been on garrison duty in the Centaurus Arm, far in the galactic north, when he found his mother that night, in her barracks, looking fretful. 'There's an immediate recall of all Cadians,' she said.

Her face was filled with dread as she lifted the order and read it to him. It came from Governor Primus Marius Porelska. Urgent recall: all Cadian regiments to return to their home world with all speed.

'Do you think they will let me come too?' he said.

She looked at him. 'I do not know,' she said at last.

At first there were not enough available transports. They managed to get a transport as far as a nondescript world named Formund, where there was already a backlog of Cadian regiments barracked in hastily refitted orbital facilities.

The waiting was terrible. Month by month the rumours grew steadily worse and the Cadians, stranded on the other side of the galaxy, had greeted the reports with gathering concern.

Their impatience grew. All every Cadian wanted was to be home, facing whatever dangers that brought.

'If Cadia falls, then I fall with it. If the spirit of Cadia dies, then I die too,' was the phrase that summed up the spirit of those Cadians stranded far from home. But they never really believed that Cadia could fall.

Ultimately their recall had come too late. By the time they left Formund's system and set a course for the Cadian system, Cadia was about to fall.

The loss came whilst they were still in warp transit. Their void-craft was buffeted like a cork in the storm, the passage the worst that anyone could remember. Yedrin himself had spent the whole journey tormented with nightmares and visions, vomiting with warp-sickness. It turned out that they were one of the last regiments to escape out of what was to become Nihilus, squeezing through a narrow gap in the roiling warp storms that would make up the Cicatrix Maledictum.

They had exited the warp in the Agripinaa System and met forces that had escaped from Cadia. They were greeted with the awful news that Cadia had fallen just weeks before. It was almost an impossibility. But each survivor told similar tales. Cadia was gone.

'But,' as General Bendikt had assured them all, 'Cadia still stands.'

For Yedrin, the loss of Cadia sparked a maelstrom of emotions. Furious denial, grief, recrimination and then a gnawing sense of guilt.

With Cadia lost, Yedrin's chance of becoming a real shock trooper was gone. In the lower hab decks of the ageing troop transport, *Sanctus Invincible*, he found an old janitor's storeroom and locked himself away, and wept.

When he came out, he apologised to his mother. It was clear from the look on her face that she had been weeping as well. He had never seen his mother show weakness before. It was like watching water welling up from a crack in a stone.

'You will find another way to serve,' she said, and swallowed back her pain.

In the following months, as they were thrown about by the tumults of war, Yedrin sensed a growing distance between him and his mother. The future she had envisioned for him had been ripped away. He felt as though he was a constant disappointment to her. Whenever she looked at him he saw the well of sadness in her eyes.

So when, years later, word came of a new cadet programme, Yedrin enlisted immediately. His mother had been too overcome to speak, but she had gripped his hands and embraced him, and managed to whisper, 'The training will be ruthless. But have faith. You might so easily have been Cadian. Do not fail in this. Understand?'

'I promise,' he told her. He would either succeed or die in the attempt.

Now, as Yedrin stood to attention in a giant square of twelve thousand others on the solid ground of El'Phanor, he felt more relief than joy or pride or exultation. He had made it this far, which was further than he had ever dared to hope.

He watched the distant Lord Militant Warmund stride up to the podium and make a short speech about how the future of the Cadian Shock Troop depended on them all, before leaving by personal lighter for the Ramillies star fort in orbit about the planet.

Yedrin had soaked it all in like a sponge. It was the closest he would ever get to Cadia. It was like catching the echo of a song that would never be sung again.

There had been other speeches, of course, by other Imperial dignitaries. Cadet Yedrin couldn't remember everything that had been said. It had been momentous. *You are the first, an exciting new programme, a great honour, ten thousand of resistance, a refusal to ever be defeated.*

He remembered the pride. The thrill of hearing those words and believing them. The immense honour that he had been given, from the untold billions of young men and women within the Imperium of Man, to enter this programme.

And then they were led off into their training company, twelve thousand hopefuls, chests swelling with pride as the wringer started to squeeze about them.

Day by day, hour by hour, the hopeful recruits were given the full Cadian treatment. It was more demanding than any of them thought they were capable of enduring. They trained until they could not go another step. They rehearsed mock attacks and deployments at all hours of day and night and without regard to food, shelter or hunger. And at the end of their days they fell into bed and slept in their clothes. They were asleep before their heads hit the pillow.

Their Cadian trainers were relentless. Each day they expected more of the troops, and to their own astonishment, the cadets found that they were achieving things they had not thought possible. Everything they did, their trainers did with them. When the recruits were bent double, the Cadians were barely out of breath. When the end of day came and the recruits crawled back to their barracks, the Cadians strolled about, seemingly unaffected.

They worked in teams of a hundred, at first. They were driven to extremes of heat and cold, hunger and exhaustion. They were woken in the middle of the night, left stranded on the dark side of asteroids with only a few hours to reach safety. They trekked across hi-grav jungle worlds that sucked them deep into the putrid mud. Each night they pulled off their boots and removed bloated leeches from their skin. They staged mock attacks on polar defence silos, trudging across ice plains and glaciers that creaked and groaned like tortured beasts.

Their instructors drove them incessantly. Over the three years of training their numbers were steadily whittled down through dismissal, execution and accident, until they numbered only a few thousand.

Yedrin was sure it was a hell that would never end, but one morning after yet another trooper had dropped out, their trainer, a no-nonsense Cadian named Larsk, suddenly walked in as they were shovelling down their brief morning meal. 'Congratulations,' he said. 'You have passed the initial training. Finish your breakfast. Pack your bags. We're moving out at oh-eight-hundred hours.'

Larsk started to walk away. It was Yedrin who put his hand up. 'Sir, what do we do between now and then?'

They had never seen Larsk smile, but he did now. 'You get some rest. You'll need it. This afternoon we're moving into phase two of the training.'

Phase two proved to be much like the first, only the tasks and challenges set for them were harder. The training intensified yet again, and Larsk came to look like a doting uncle by comparison.

The one benefit, Yedrin noted, was that the chaff had been winnowed out. There was a sense of achievement in just getting this far and knowing everyone about you had done the same. In crossing the featureless plains of El'Phanor, building rope bridges across the fissures, or a night drop in the ice and snow of Yuddson's Glacier, you could rely on the grit and knowledge and determination of the other cadets as you clawed an ice-cave till your bare hands stained the snow red with blood.

Failure became less commonplace. They worked as teams to carry each other through the hardest challenges; it was the only way of getting through alive. Powerful personal bonds made each squad stronger than ten individuals.

By the time they returned to their base camp, nearly a year after their initial induction, another intake of fresh-faced recruits had arrived, a thousand strong, parading to hear the same kind of speech.

Yedrin looked at the newcomers as if they were another species. Only then did he realise the transformation that had been done to him. He was separate now. His mind knew calm and focus and the power of decision. His body was lean and tireless. There was only one thing left: phase three.

They were handed over to a new instructor team. One, so the rumours went, that had trained Whiteshields before. On Cadia. The instructors that arrived that morning did so in the back of a Centaur. The first thing Yedrin noted was their age. Each one was greying or bald, and their faces were masks of scar tissue and grim looks. The second thing he noticed was that each of them was wounded. A missing finger. A limp. Metal plates drilled over holes in their skulls.

Last came their leader, a major, with one augmetic leg. He stepped forward to introduce himself.

'My name is Major Luka. I served with the Cadian Eighth. I knew Ursarkar E. Creed when he was just your age. I have trained thousands of Whiteshields. You have almost reached the culmination of your training. I have been following your progress.'

There was a long pause as he seemed to look at each of them in turn. 'Emperor willing, you will all make fine additions to the Cadian Shock Troop.' In his hand was a Cadian tridome helmet. He held it up in the air for them all to see. It had the distinctive white stripe from forehead to neck. 'There is another test awaiting you, the deadliest you will face. Pass this third and last phase of training and you will be honoured with one of these.'

Yedrin felt his eyes suddenly start to water. He could not believe that he had got so far. He imagined his mother's reaction. The joy. The pride. The immense sense of achievement.

He turned to the cadet next to him. It was Zweden. They'd known each other long before they'd been inducted into the Whiteshield programme. They'd shared many things. Zweden's mother was also Cadian, though he'd already been orphaned by the time Yedrin had met him.

'Think your mother is watching?' Yedrin asked.

Zweden had a thoughtful look. At last he said, 'No. I do not think so.'

'No?'

Zweden shook his head. 'I wish she was. But I cannot feel her. When I try to remember her I cannot even see her face.' He paused. 'But I do remember the scent of her webbing as she held me. I do remember that.'

Yedrin nodded. He thought of his own mother. Last time he had seen her, two years ago, she already had shots of grey in her hair. Her regiment – the Cadian 1123rd – was being broken up and reassigned to others.

Throne-knew where she had ended up. Throne-knew if she was still alive. And if she was dead, if her soul was with the Emperor, would He pass on the news?

Yedrin strove to impress Major Luka as the old man supervised the last phase of training. Luka was not the same kind of barrel-chested, vox-horn voiced drill sergeant he had become used to. He was, if anything, a little indulgent.

'He can afford to be,' a fellow cadet told Yedrin after a day's training. They were drenched in sweat as they strode back across a dusty plain towards their camp. 'Look about.'

Yedrin did.

'He's got two thousand of the best.'

Yedrin laughed. He'd never thought about himself as one of those. But it was true.

'Think of it like this,' the other cadet said. 'Their job was to take rough ore and beat out the impurities, and then smelt us into steel. It's Luka's job to sharpen us into a blade.'

The metaphor seemed apt. Luka's job was to turn Yedrin and the others into Whiteshields, and then to bring them to battle so they could kill or be killed.

Only then would they be fit to join the shock troopers.

* * *

Six months after Luka had taken command of them, they had drilled, marched, manoeuvred, camped and practised all manner of military assaults and defensive actions. Almost all who had arrived graduated as Whiteshields.

There had been another ceremony, this time in the shadow of the ruins of the great Kromarch. Major Luka's voice had broken as he announced their graduation. One by one they filed up to shake his hand and receive their tridome helmet from him.

'I am proud of you all,' he declared. 'Make what farewells you need to. You are all to be transferred to the battlefront within days.' There was a great cheer. 'We are going to a planet named Malouri. Yes! Your last test is upon you all. You are being sent into battle. Those of you that survive will be graduated from Whiteshield to Cadian Shock Trooper!'

A stunned silence greeted these words. Yedrin felt a wave of fear and joy surge through him. He thought of his mother, and tears choked him up, and he prayed that he could meet this last test with all the courage and grit of his forebears.

SEVEN

They had been on the lower decks of some troop transport when they had first been given their orders to end the siege on Malouri. Bendikt had promised his regiment they would at last be returning to El'Phanor, where the real fighting was, but Lord Militant Warmund, it seemed, had not quite forgiven Isaiah Bendikt for killing the Praetorian general, Reginald de Barka, in a duel.

Duels were disapproved of within Cadian ranks, but the Praetorian had insulted Cadia, and Bendikt did not think he had any choice. Warmund disagreed, of course, which was why they were here, fighting border wars.

'Another pointless conflict,' Bendikt stated with fury as he slammed the parchment down onto his desk. The broad oak timbers splintered under the impact.

Bendikt cursed. His augmetic arm was a masterwork of the Departmento Bionica, indistinguishable from a human hand but augmented with steel-rod tendons and a grip that could crush plate armour. Or a table. And he was still getting used to the power within it.

'We should be returning to El'Phanor!' Bendikt growled. 'On the front line! Not here. A second-line army could break this fortress. We are Cadians!'

Prassan looked away as Bendikt shook the fragments of table from his fist. The trooper standing guard by the door winced. Six months ago, when they had arrived on the ice world of Crone B9, Prassan had been assigned to the command staff. When he received his orders Prassan could hardly believe his luck.

It was Colour Sergeant Tyson who had given him the news.

'Don't go getting excited, Prassan,' the blunt officer of Second Company had snapped. 'You'll be back in the line soon enough. We don't leave anyone in HQ. They get *soft*. And when a trooper gets soft they get themselves *killed*. And worse than that, they get *others* killed as well!' He had lifted a scarred finger in warning. 'When you do come back, I'll be waiting, and if you've turned into one of those smooth-handed pen pushers I'll have you leading the next charge with nothing but a *bayonet*. Understand?'

'Yes, sir!' Prassan had saluted and then run to get his dress uniform in order. He couldn't stop grinning.

But now Bendikt was starting to erupt and Prassan didn't know where to look.

Bendikt took a moment to calm himself down. He sucked in a deep breath and puffed out his cheeks. 'Apologies, gentlemen,' he said at last, clearing his throat. 'What were we discussing?'

Mere stepped forward with the discarded files. They were the honours lists of the regiments currently serving on Malouri.

'These all seem the run-of-the-mill sort. Apart from the Mordians, of course.'

It was true. The forces were drawn from local militias and

regiments from the Gallows Cluster, with a few main-line regiments to add a little backbone to them all. Mostly mediocre warriors given mediocre training and officers with mediocre expectations made of them. They could garrison, or fill a trench and shoot in the right direction, but show them a fort and order them to take it and you'd come up short.

One of the named regiments stood out. 'Potence Mountain Infantry,' Mere read aloud.

Bendikt turned. 'Didn't we fight alongside them on their home world?'

Mere nodded. 'Yes, sir. General Dominka. Died at the cathedral.'

Bendikt nodded and carried on through the list. There were a few regiments of note drawn from the planetary elites or from wild tribes. The Drookian Fenguard was both of these. The regiments had official numbers, but the truth was they simply came from one of the many clans that inhabited the benighted swamps that made up their planet.

'Clans Kharr and Boskobel.'

Bendikt didn't know them. Mere explained. 'Boskobel are led by their clan master, Dunelm. His family have a century old feud with the leader of the Kharr.'

'Have they been stationed well apart?'

'Yes, sir.'

'Good!' Bendikt didn't know a unit who loved their feuds more than the Drookians. They liked killing each other almost as much as they liked to kill the enemies of the God-Emperor. 'When the time comes I think we should field them alongside each other. A little competition will go a long way!'

Mere nodded. 'I will make sure of it.'

Bendikt arrived at Malouri seventy hours earlier than the 101st, his lander bringing him down onto the planet at night. There was a welcoming committee of senior military staff. Mere stood at the general's side as the joints of Bendikt's augmetic hand grated against each other.

Mere scanned the assembly. 'No Praetorians,' he commented.

Bendikt nodded briefly. 'Good.'

An hour later General Bendikt was at the command headquarters to meet and greet the commanders of his army. The adepts of the Munitorum were building a small city for the Administratum staff, with hab-blocks, sunken bunkers and a magnificent palace with dining rooms. They were also constructing a prayer chapel, libraries filled with military histories and broad gardens featuring aquila-shaped parterres of neatly clipped box.

Bendikt took the place in at a glance. His metal hand flinched with irritation. The Munitorum were clearly preparing habitation sufficient for decades of siege.

That number was ringing in his head as the palace staff led him along the gravel paths. There were broad steps up to a double set of high windows, and a pair of cherubs hovered above the doorway to the great hall. The planetary dignitaries were gathered there to welcome him. He saw a line of stiff dress coats, velvet lapels, embroidered shakos and long white gloves.

The planetary governor-general was a thin and youthful man, with a high starched collar and prominent Adam's apple. He had the air of a man newly appointed to the role and spoke platitudes about his arrival being a ray of hope for their planet, the indignity of having traitors upon their home world and what an honour it was for Cadians to die to free his planet from heresy.

'We have already started the foundations for a mausoleum fit for such heroes,' he said.

Bendikt nodded. 'Don't make it too big.'

The humour was wasted upon the other man. He appeared

overwhelmed by the reputation that Cadians brought with them. 'If you have time, perhaps I can show you the architect's plans.'

'Thank you,' Bendikt said. 'Let me win your war first.'

Bendikt did not trust his augmetic hand yet, so he shook their hands with his left, spoke some encouraging words, and passed on. The greeting line of planetary dignitaries led him through a wood-panelled entranceway. Inside, a broad marble staircase swept up under a line of crystal chandeliers. At the bottom of the stairs stood a fervour engine, with pseudo flames guttering from its open grates and three servitor skulls chanting hymnals on loop through snout-shaped vox-grilles. Another line of dignitaries stood at the door of the great hall. From within he could hear the distinct note of the military welcoming committee. He had been to many such meet-and-greet events like this. A room full of generals and their aides, typified by clinking glasses of amasec, politely mixing commanders, and a general air of how-long-do-we-have-to-stay-until-we-can-leave.

But they were important nonetheless.

He remembered how Creed managed such situations. Stiff and awkward until he'd had a glass or three of amasec, and then he had slipped into his own particular gear, which had mixed utter self-confidence with a brusque humour.

There was a brief flurry as Bendikt turned to the fervour engine. It was on a loop of sayings of Saint Ignatzio. Bendikt lit a votive candle. So far, the Mordian, General von Horne, had been in charge of prosecuting this war, and his arrival meant von Horne's demotion.

The residual spine of a passing servo-skull brushed Bendikt's shoulder. Someone took his augmetic arm. 'This way, please, general.'

Bendikt paused at the entrance to the main chamber. A bell

rang and a master of ceremonies announced his arrival, 'General Bendikt of the Cadian Hundred-and-First.'

Bendikt felt the cold and hostile atmosphere within and took a deep breath before stepping inside the hall. He noted that the Mordian commanders of the 17th Field Corps stood apart. Their dress uniforms were so starched Bendikt imagined they could stand up by themselves. Under the peaked caps were faces dark and hard as Mordian granite.

Their commander stepped forward. 'General Otto von Horne,' he said, introducing himself.

'Greetings,' Bendikt said, and he used his augmetic hand to shake the Mordian's hand. He heard the grate of gristle and bone, but the Mordian man's face showed no trace of pain.

'My men and I are honoured to fight alongside you,' the Mordian said. There was no warmth to his words. They were cold and clinical. But Bendikt had prepared himself for something less worthy and he took the Mordian's words at face value. From his experience, Mordians did not open their mouths to speak unless they believed what they said. They were prone neither to flattery nor dissimulation. And as a general rule for life, he always thought it better to assume the best motivations in others.

'Thank you,' Bendikt said. 'Likewise. You have achieved much already. Your efforts have been noted in my dispatches to Cadian High Command. With our steel and conviction there will be nothing we cannot achieve here.'

The Mordian's pale cheeks coloured a fraction. 'Please do not flatter us. We live and die only to serve.'

Bendikt greeted each of the Mordian's command. None of them spoke. They were a culture that valued actions, not words. Clearly their commander had said all that needed to be communicated.

Next in line were clearly the largest contingent, the divisions of Rakallion who boasted an entire field army with six infantry corps, artillery divisions, and a brigade of sappers and other ancillary units. Their commander was a tall man with a feather-plumed brass helmet, long waxed mustachios and a double-breasted kossack jacket. He bowed stiffly and introduced himself as Klovis Plona-Richstar.

Klovis' aide stepped forward quickly. 'General Klovis is the highest ranking Richstar upon this planet.'

'I am honoured,' Bendikt said. 'Though, as for your status as senior Richstar upon this planet, I fear that will be an honour you will soon lose.'

Klovis looked bewildered as Bendikt moved along the line.

The void-miners of the Crinan Fourth stood out in their bright yellow fatigues with royal blue flak armour and tattoos up their arms and necks. The fierce-looking warriors were led by a dark man with a broad, black beard jutting out from his chin like a trenching shovel, and the badge of his regiment tattooed under his left eye.

He wore the yellow asteroid miner's void-suit with enamelled blue flak breastplate, and his barrel chest gave his voice a deep resonance. 'General Bendikt, I am General Waqani of the Crinan Fourth. We are deeply honoured to serve under the command of a general of Cadia. It is His will. We shall die gladly.'

'I hope you live to do His will longer.'

'We fight without hope,' Waqani declared proudly, 'for hope leads the soul onto the road of disappointment.'

Next were the Gilgamesh Rifles, the Besite Chasseurs and then General Folau of the Potence Mountain Infantry. Bendikt shook his hand. 'I fought with General Dominika. Did you know her?'

'She was my cousin,' the other man replied.

'A fine warrior. She died well.'

'So I have heard,' Folau said.

At the end, one of the Drookian Fenguard chieftains stood with his tribal Thanes and selected Fianna. No two Guardsmen were dressed alike. Each wore the odd mix of Munitorum-issue and homespun, and bedecked themselves with trophies – plundered and purchased equipment and armour.

They greeted Bendikt with deep solemnity.

'I am honoured,' Bendikt said.

The Drookian pulled him close and whispered, 'I am Chief Dunelm of Clan Boskobel. The other,' he said, nodding towards the opposite side of the room, 'is of Clan Kharr. They are liars and thieves!'

Bendikt nodded. He somehow knew that the commander of Clan Kharr would tell him the exact same thing.

Last of the groups were the local Malouri Uhlan. Their commander was a woman, a stout, heavy-set wrestling type, with hair cropped short and a uniform of Munitorum surplus field-grey fatigues. Her name was Major Brera. She and her command corps looked as though they were wearing hand-me-downs two sizes too large for them.

But she breathed excitement to have a Cadian on her home world. She took his hand and bowed low. 'We are deeply honoured,' she said. 'And we pray that you will purge our home world of the taint of rebellion.'

'There is no doubt,' Bendikt told her. He felt no hesitation in stating this. He was Cadian. The enemy would be shattered.

Once Bendikt had given each commander their due he stood in the middle of the room and took in the atmosphere. He'd heard Creed speak, and somehow he always managed to find the right words.

Bendikt took a quick swig of amasec. It was at moments like this that he felt the gulf between himself and Creed. He wanted to say, 'There are great battles being fought today. Far from here. Some of the greatest battles ever seen in the Imperium of Mankind. Millions of banners carried aloft. Each warrior holding the love of the Emperor in their hearts. Driving back heresy, treachery, faithlessness. Those are the wars *we* want to be fighting. Far away from this world where those who should be fighting at our side have turned their faces away from the Light of the Golden Throne. Reserve your hatred for them. Hold them in contempt. There is nothing as contemptuous as a traitor!'

But he could not.

Instead, he said, 'Greetings all! I am honoured to be your commander for the rest of this battle. I pray I will not hold this position for long. The Munitorum are preparing for decades of siege. Decades! Major Brera, this is your home world. I am sure that you and your brave Uhlan want nothing more than to purge the stain upon your planet. For the rest of us, a campaign of that length would be the death of too many. No mausoleum would be fit to honour the blood of all the Imperial troops that would be shed upon this world. No. The Munitorum have this wrong. You will instil within your troops the conviction of imminent victory. The heresy upon this planet will end within months.' He let the word settle upon them all. 'Months! Be assured of that. Months! Not decades.'

'Impossible,' a voice stated clearly.

Bendikt turned slowly. From Clan Kharr a wild looking chieftain stepped forward. He had the appearance of an old wolf with his ceremonial headdress hanging down the side of his face. 'I, Major-Chief Rittonic of Clan Kharr, say it is so. We have thrown ourselves time and again against the enemy rock, and we have gained less ground than this room contains. You, Cadian, do not know what we are against. Crannog Mons is

75

impregnable. Every foot of mountain is a fortress – an endless barrow of murder holes, barracks and artillery. Curtains of withering defensive fire. The dead of my clan lie piled in heaps before our trenches. *I* say it is impossible.'

Bendikt was grateful to this man for speaking out. Fighting was what Bendikt had been bred for since he was a child. Since he had been lifted in his father's arms, forced to stare into the Eye of Terror and swear his hatred for the Emperor's enemies. He smiled. 'You speak like a man who has not seen Cadians fight,' Bendikt stated calmly. 'And when you have done so, I promise you that you will change your mind.'

The Drookian sneered. 'How can we have faith in those who lost their own planet?'

A sudden chill went through the room.

Bendikt paused before speaking. 'My home withstood ten thousand years of trial and we remained resolute. When the Archenemy came, I was there. His fleet was so numerous that it turned the skies of Cadia black. Heretics rained upon our planet for months. Sorceries raised armies of the dead. Battalions of unspeakable horrors. Waves of the insane, harvested from a thousand worlds and spawned upon ours like cancerous spores.

'I was there and I tell you this. Kasr by kasr, the forces of Cadia soaked up the enemy's assault. And then, under Creed's leadership, we counter-attacked and drove the enemy back in confusion. It was not Cadia that broke, but the blockade of the Imperial Navy who let the Planetkiller into our orbit. That is a fact. I was there. I saw this all happen.

'But I am not here to squabble about such petty matters. There are many of us whose home worlds have been devoured by the enemy. They are lost battles, and those we cannot fight again. But there are many others that we can yet win. And there are some here, among you, whose worlds are now threatened not just by the enemy, but also by traitors from within our midst. The cowardly. The infirm of purpose. Those of little courage and little heart, who rather than coming together have chosen this moment of pause to put the knife into the back. These are the enemies we face here. Let us put down the line. Here and no further. No more worlds lost, no more armies orphaned, no more once-proud regiments dwindling to old men.'

He looked at them all from face to face. The silence stretched on, but it had a different feel now. He sensed that with these words he had won them over at last.

Even von Horne, of the Mordians, allowed himself a nod of assent.

Bendikt smiled and took another gulp of amasec. 'The line is here. The faster we can break this – this *rock* – the faster we can take the fight back to our enemies. The faster we can put our vengeance where it belongs – into the flesh of our foes.

'By that day, Crannog Mons will have fallen back into Imperial hands. Major Brera, that is my promise to you and all the people of Malouri.'

Bendikt turned to Mere. 'How long until the Feast of Sanguinalia?'

'Fifty days,' he stated.

Bendikt paused. The amasec was doing its work. He felt some of Creed's bluff confidence, and buoyed up by it he declared, 'By the Feast of Sanguinalia, Crannog Mons shall be ours!'

EIGHT

As commander-in-chief, Bendikt was assigned the principal suite in the commanders' wing of the General's Palace. The rooms came with their own household staff, all locals. They had the haunted look of a people years into a bitter civil war. They bowed and fawned and appeared terrified of the slightest mistake.

By the time Bendikt had finished talking to Mere and his personal staff, they had already turned his bed down and stocked the cast-iron stove with fresh fuel.

'Anything else, sir?' the servant asked. He was an old man, short and round with bowed shoulders, and wore a preposterous outfit of black hose and ornate brocade waistcoat.

'No. Thank you.'

The man bowed and, remaining so, paced backwards towards the door. Bendikt looked up. 'Wait. One more thing,' he said. 'Tell me your name.'

'Servitore.'

'Servitore,' Bendikt said and waved his hand. 'Don't do that again. None of that frippery. From any of the staff.'

Servitore bowed, and stopped halfway. 'I understand. The Mordians…'

'I am not Mordian. I am Cadian. Do you understand what that means?'

The old man nodded. 'Yes, sir. I shall pass on your command. Would you like breakfast served here?'

'No. Thank you. We shall be out early.'

'Will you be back for noon meal, sir?'

Bendikt sighed with tired irritation. 'Servitore. Assume I will always be here. If I am not then I am sure there are many mouths who will be glad of the kitchen's services. But I am here to win a war, not to eat your meals.'

Servitore bowed even lower. 'Understood, sir.' There was a pause.

It was clear that the servant had something else on his mind. 'Is it true, sir, that you will free our planet of these heretics?'

'Yes,' Bendikt said, a little short. 'That is true.'

The old man rubbed his hands together. 'Forgive me. But it is said that you will take Crannog Mons by Sanguinalia.'

Bendikt's temper was immediately soothed. He drew in a deep breath. His head hurt a little from last night's drinking, but now he had said the words, he knew he had to be held to them.

In truth, part of the reason for announcing a deadline was exactly this: for word to spread. It would keep the Imperial troopers honest. No doubt the traitors would hear it too, and the sapping seeds of doubt would be sown.

'Yes,' he said at last, 'Servitore. I promise you. Crannog Mons will fall before Sanguinalia.'

The old man fell to his knees in thanks. Bendikt had to help him up.

Fifty days, he told himself as he lay down to sleep. For a moment he felt that stab of self-doubt. *Did Creed ever waver?* he wondered.

Surely not.

Bendikt and his staff were out long before dawn to see Crannog Mons with their own eyes. The night was still dark. Searchlights spread bars across the sky as he made his way to the landing platforms on the rear of the palace.

The lights of three Vulture gunships and his Valkyrie were flashing in the gloom. As he came closer he could see that they were outfitted in black livery, with flames about the mouth, the pilots' masked faces uplit as they exchanged hand signals with the ground crew.

Bendikt bent as he climbed inside, his boots ringing out on the metal flooring. There were fold out seats. A few hours ago this craft had been ferrying Guardsmen to the front lines. Now it held the commander of Imperial forces on his way to see Crannog Mons for the first time.

He had a shot of amasec for breakfast these days, and already he could feel the warmth and the confidence spreading through him.

It was an hour's journey, flying low over the ground with the Vultures flying point and wingmen. Below, Bendikt saw the neat camps of the siege army spread beneath him. Classic, solid, predictable.

Ten miles from the front line the pilot brought them down at a landing zone sunk beneath ground level. Sandbagged walls filled their vision, then they touched down.

An hour later Bendikt's convoy of Centaurs and Chimeras was

winding through the acres of artillery dug-outs. To either side were forests of raised Earthshaker barrels with an army dedicated to manning them all. Each gun was dug in and sandbagged. Each Basilisk platform was attended to by a team of gunners – two to carry the next shell into position, one to screw the fuse into place, another to sight the gun, and two more to close the firing chamber and one to pull the firing pin.

Dawn was starting to pale the sky when the nearest Earthshaker batteries began to fire. Firing chains were pulled. Shells were flung in ten-mile parabolas. Hydraulic pistons cushioned the recoil. Breeches were thrown open and new shells slammed into them as locking pins were pushed into place. Again, the chains were pulled, accompanied by a fiery snort as the forty-ton guns recoiled against the stacked dampers. It went on like this for the entire hour of the journey until the air was thick with clouds of black fyceline and the gun barrels glowed red with the heat of firing.

An onshore wind blew the hot air, rich with the combined scents of superheated metal and fuel, back over the sprawl of Militarum camps. Discarded gun barrels hissed and steamed within puddles.

Bendikt's convoy drove through it all, right up to the cliff-top, where the Chimeras slewed sideways and came to a halt fifty yards from a rockcrete observation post dug deep into the tus-socky grass.

A supplies official was there to meet him. He had the look of a Munitorum pen-pusher. Bendikt nodded. At an unseen signal, the bombardment suddenly stopped. Bendikt strolled out to the cliff, pen-pushers and officers in tow, and stopped an arm's width from the edge. Wind flattened the grass. He stood rock-still, staring towards the island bastion he was here to take. Five miles of choppy steel-grey sea divided him from it.

'How long does the bombardment usually go on for?' Bendikt asked.

'Four hours each morning,' one of the Munitorum staff told him.

Bendikt was resolute. 'That is not enough,' he said. 'We have fifty days. From now on, the bombardment will continue without cease. All day and all night.'

'We do not have enough munitions–' the man started.

'You have stockpiled for years' worth of shot, in line with the projected fall?'

'Yes, sir. In ten years' time.'

Bendikt put up his hand for silence. 'Crannog Mons is falling in fifty days.'

The man's mouth opened to object.

'Silence!' Bendikt snapped. 'The bombardment will not cease. It will run continually until we have broken *that* rock!'

The accompanying generals stopped and stood with monoculars pressed to their faces.

Crannog Mons rose, blue with distance, straight up out of the mists that lay over the water. The island fortress was a masterpiece of Imperial manufacture. Its rugged cliffs gleamed in the morning light with a dull-grey shine like beaten steel. The cliffs were studded with pillboxes fashioned from the rock and reinforced with rockcrete and ferrosteel girders. The natural stone blurred with the smooth buttresses, barbettes and casements. Everywhere was pockmarked with gun slits and stepped embrasures. Over each bastion crackled the thin blue light of void shields.

Bendikt turned to his right. 'And that is all that remains of the bridge?'

'Yes, sir,' an aide said.

Bendikt had studied the plans during the warp-transit. Before the heresy, a suspension bridge had provided a vital link between

Crannog Mons and the mainland. Columns of rockcrete had punctuated its length, holding the great steel wires from which the roadway was slung. A tongue of road stuck out from the mainland, but two miles out to sea the heretics had blown it up behind their retreating forces, and now the thick steel cabling hung twisted and loose. A few scraps of rockcrete still clung to the single span that had not yet fallen into the water.

The Munitorum ambassador hesitated. 'And that is the causeway that von Horne commanded to be built.'

Bendikt had already shifted the auspex to where Imperium siege engineers were driving a vast causeway of shattered boulders out towards the island.

'A magnificent endeavour,' he stated.

'Thank you, sir.'

Von Horne's original plan had been to surround the whole island. Bendikt favoured a simpler, more direct thrust straight at the nearest fortress of Tor Tartarus, and had issued orders before landing on the planet. Now the causeway led straight to the island before breaking into three prongs, like a vast stone trident laid out before them, aimed at the heart of the enemy.

'As you instructed,' the aide went on, 'the causeway covers a series of assault tunnels, which can transport troops and armour right up to the front line.'

'Good,' Bendikt stated. 'How long until we can attack?'

'The construction teams are building at the rate of a hundred yards a day. This is starting to slow as we draw closer and the depth of the water increases rapidly. Work teams inform me that there is an ocean shelf where the drop-off is precipitous.'

'You have not answered my question.'

'No…' the Munitorum ambassador said. 'Of course, we had hoped to finish it for your arrival. But the terrain has slowed our approach considerably.'

Bendikt watched the progress of the other moles. 'How long do my troops have to wait?'

'Three months,' the Munitorum ambassador stated.

'Impossible,' Bendikt told him.

'But...' the ambassador started.

'I do not care,' Bendikt snapped. 'With all due respect. I cannot wait that long. We *must* accelerate the attack. Those traitors are sitting on that rock and mocking us all. I have declared that traitor rock must fall by Sanguinalia!'

The ambassador's cheeks coloured. 'I will relay your command.'

'Thank you,' Bendikt said.

The ambassador bowed before leaving.

Bendikt paid him no notice. He stood for a long time, field-auspex lifted to his face. He had studied the plans of this bast-ion many times, planning attacks from all directions, and the consequences of each. But this was his first opportunity to see it all for real, to take in the awesome impregnability of this ancient defensive work.

Crannog Mons was roughly diamond shaped. The cathedral of Saint Helena Richstar lay at its central point, and from it the four quadrants reached out. Commanding each quadrant were four massive fortresses of squat rockcrete tiers, one stacked on top of the other, bristling with thick-barrelled guns.

At the far end of the island the smallest of the fortresses stood, the narrow tower of Ophio, with the low volcanic cone of Tor Kharybdis just off its shore. Linking these two was a cableway.

Margrat was the southernmost fortress. Domes of orbital defence silos were trained up into the sky. Opposite, at the northern corner, lay the ruins of Baniyas. Its destruction was the chief victory the Imperial forces under von Horne had achieved.

'Its void shields collapsed under sustained bombardment,'

Mere briefed Bendikt. 'The Imperial Navy's warships reduced it to ruins within a few hours.'

Bendikt nodded. He studied the jagged ruins of Baniyas and did not like the thought of attacking it head on. The supply lines were too long, the cliffs there were too precipitous, and though the fortress appeared ruined, he had no doubt the rubble would provide the defenders with foxholes impossible to spot.

No, his intent was to take the largest and nearest fortress, the one that glared at him from across the water, the gatehouse of Tor Tartarus: a grim construction of pillboxes and rockcrete redoubts.

There was a time, not so long distant, when he had held the rank of captain, that the loss of a whole squad of his troopers would have been shocking. Now he was general, he was considering an action that would cost the lives of millions, and it left him, to his surprise, entirely unmoved. He focused his field-auspex. 'Ambassador,' he called out.

The Munitorum official came forward.

'What is the current strength of your labour corps?'

The man hesitated. 'Combining penal and indentured… we have enough, sir. For the construction of the siege camp, extensions to Starport, and the causeway.'

'Good. We will need to make a requisition for military service.'

The ambassador hesitated. He wanted to sound willing, but his voice betrayed his concern. 'How many, sir? Ten thousand… a hundred thousand?'

Bendikt lowered the auspex. His face was set as hard as rockcrete. 'Ambassador. I want all of them.'

NINE

When Bendikt returned to the General's Palace, Colonel Baytov, commander of the Cadian 101st, was waiting for him with the captains of his First and Second companies.

Baytov and Bendikt had spent many years together as young captains. There was no need for formalities between them. Bendikt strode straight towards the group and shook their hands warmly. 'When did you land?'

'Yesterday,' Baytov said. He was a broad man with a barrel chest and a resonant voice. 'The regiment has just made it into camp. We came ahead.'

He gestured to the two figures next to him. Bendikt knew them both. Captain Ostanko of First Company was one of Baytov's favourites, a true son of Cadia: handsome, lean, with a roguish manner and an unruly mop of glossy black hair. Captain Irinya Ronin, commander of Second Company, was one of the most respected officers in the regiment. She had metal joints in her left arm, and a short buzz cut of steel-grey hair. In earlier times she would have retired from front-line service and transferred to a Whiteshield training programme, but there was no retirement now, and there was no weakness or infirmity about her as she returned Bendikt's handshake.

'Welcome to Malouri!' Bendikt said to them all. He led them into the palace. The fervour engine was singing beatitudes of hatred: hatred of the weak, hatred of the xenos, hatred of the unclean, hatred of the cowardly.

A few officers were hanging about, hoping to catch Bendikt for a quick word. Mere intercepted them. Against this eventuality they had carefully inscribed their petitions on parchment, and he gathered them all under his arm. 'I will make sure these are all screened and, if necessary, seen to personally by the general and his staff,' he said.

Once they were out of earshot Mere handed them to Prassan. 'Deal with these.'

Bendikt led them into his private suite. Servitore had just finished tidying the room, and he began backing out as the Cadians entered. Bendikt took no notice. He strode to the side table where a freshly refilled bottle of Arcady Pride stood next to a set of hand-polished crystal glasses.

Bendikt unstoppered the bottle and poured each of them a healthy shot.

'To Cadia!' he said as each took their glass.

They upended their glasses and set them down on the table, then Bendikt took off his cap and tossed it aside. 'Sit,' he said.

The Cadians looked incongruous amidst the opulence of the General's Palace, with its damasked cushions and fine Namian carpets spread upon the floor. They were lean and hard, with battle-worn uniforms, and old scars of blade and shot upon their flak armour plates.

But they had work to do, and they focused immediately as Bendikt gave a brief summary of his morning's expedition. 'I trust that you have seen the island?'

'Yes,' Baytov said. 'We asked the Valkyrie pilot to take us out to the cliffs. It's impressive.'

'Good, then you have a sense of it. I have declared that it should fall by Sanguinalia.'

Baytov made no comment, but Bendikt could tell the other man thought this was a tall order. 'You think that is impossible?' he said.

Baytov shook his head. 'If that is our orders then that is what we shall achieve.'

Bendikt nodded. 'Good!' He spread the charts on the table. 'Come,' he said. 'Have a look at these and tell me what you think.'

They all stood, looking down. Baytov leafed through the data-slates before handing them to Ostanko and Irinya.

Bendikt couldn't hold himself back. 'I'm not going to mess around here. Taking this place by Sanguinalia will be a real challenge. But it can be done. Von Horne was meticulous, but unimaginative. Mere says he was trying to bore the traitors to death. Munitorum estimates state that the expected completion of the siege, at current rates, is over fifteen years away!'

They knew this, of course. Ostanko laughed, Irinya was impassive, Baytov nodded slowly.

Bendikt gestured about him. 'The Munitorum have already built us a palace. They'll build a city here before the end. Sanguinalia! *That* is when this battle ends!'

'So what is the plan?' Baytov said. 'Have they tried Termites?'

'Yes. And they have been thwarted by a combination of stiff opposition, porous strata and flooded tunnels.'

'Not a lack of determination?'

'Possibly,' Bendikt said.

Baytov glanced through the sheath of reports. 'And then there is the causeway.'

'Yes. Assault pipes are built into the structure, beneath the surface. We'll be able to bring our forces right up to the front, unharmed,' said Ostanko.

'Yes. But once ashore there's Tor Tartarus. Any who assault there will be slaughtered,' added Irinya.

Bendikt listened to them and took a swill of his drink. 'You're all on the wrong track.' He stood, glass in hand, thinking aloud. 'The key to victory is Holzhauer and his Elnaur Chasseurs. They're the steel in the fist of our foes. Once we break them the rest will crumble.'

Irinya knew her old commander well enough. 'Sir,' she said to Bendikt, 'you have a plan?'

Bendikt smiled. Of course he had a plan. But first he looked to Ostanko.

The captain of First Company lifted the map of the island and stared at it. 'If the substrata really is impossible for subterranean attack then there are two other options. One is via aerial drops. The second is a waterborne attack.'

Bendikt smiled. 'If I put you in command of a waterborne assault, how would you do it?'

Ostanko paused. His forefinger briefly tapped the map as he ran through all the possibilities. 'The obvious would be the gatehouse of Tor Tartarus. But the enemy are expecting that. Baniyas?'

'The cliffs are half a mile high.'

Ostanko nodded slowly, considering. 'Then the only other option would be to attack Ophio at the far side of the island. But first you would have to mount a major amphibious assault to take the island of Tor Kharybdis.'

Bendikt listened carefully. When Ostanko was done Baytov raised a cautionary note. 'If our landings were opposed in force, then it would be very challenging. Do we have the transports for such an endeavour?'

'We have Chimeras,' Irinya put in. 'They are amphibious.'

Ostanko's cheeks coloured. 'They are amphibious if you are crossing a marsh. Or a river. But there is no way they'd survive the journey to the island, across an open channel. Working against the waves would swamp them, and they'd be floating in the surf for the defender's artillery to pick off. Few would make it.'

'Can we lessen the load on them?' Irinya asked.

'No. Even if we stripped out the secondary ammunition, and sent them in bare, the powerplant is not strong enough to push forty-odd tons of metal through that ocean. One swell and they'd all be washed up twenty miles down the coast.'

Bendikt had stopped listening. He drummed his fingers on the table. His enthusiasm was almost bubbling over. 'Ostanko, Irinya, Baytov – thank you all. I feel better having heard you.' He jabbed a finger into the air. 'Holzhauer's strength is his Elnaur Chasseurs. He is a proud man. He will want to test their mettle against Cadians, so we have to give him that opportunity. We have to present him with a series of impossible choices. First we will take the island of Tor Kharybdis. He will have to commit. And when he does, we bleed his Chasseurs white!'

As Baytov, Ostanko and Irinya left, the Munitorum ambassador arrived accompanied by a flurry of what Bendikt liked to call 'bureau-rats': thin, sickly-looking scribes and bean-counters who only ever seemed to spill grit into the administrative wheels. They shuffled in about their master. 'Sir,' the ambassador announced, 'I have brought the chief logistician to aid you in your plans.'

'Good,' Bendikt said.

The chief logistician stumped in, walking laboriously. Short neck, round head, deep-set squinting eyes, he was a ball of a man, as wide as he was tall. He was draped in voluminous robes of a heavy red felt, embroidered across the waist with a golden aquila. Everything the rotund man did was with great effort. A distinct odour of sweat accompanied him. He spread his ink-stained fingers in a simple greeting. 'General Bendikt,' he said, breathing heavily through his nose. 'The Blessings of the Holy Emperor upon you. I have heard your plans and I will do all I can do to assist them.'

Bendikt nodded. 'As primary representative of the Munitorum upon the planet, I shall need your active involvement. While in transit, I already started communications with forge worlds that had close links to Cadia.' The truth was he had gone much further, establishing contact with the foundry, forge and supply worlds throughout the system, as far afield as Makkan, Rhana and Armageddon. 'I am awaiting the arrival of a craft from the forge world of Rhana.'

The chief logistician did not appear augmented, but if he was not then his powers of recall were impressive. 'Yes, sir. Their craft is currently awaiting a landing berth. They have sent three Leviathans with full complements of skitarii.'

'Facilitate their landing as soon as possible.'

'That is already under way. I will ensure they have all the support they need. My enginseer teams are also constructing suitable roadways for them from Starport to the causeway.'

Bendikt's impression of this man improved. He seemed on top of his brief. 'And the other requests?'

The chief logistician nodded. 'Yes, my lord. The new rotas for bombardments are in place. We have had to bring our supply dumps forward. There is much to do. Our resources are stretched.' He paused. 'There was a time when I could have sent a request and I was guaranteed its delivery. But with times as they are, I can assure you that we are doing all that is possible. We are working around as best we can.'

Bendikt grunted in approval. The sheer logistics of maintaining an all-out bombardment had occurred to him, as well as a possible solution. 'If we asked the Imperial Navy's gunners to maintain the bombardment for a certain period each day...'

'That would give us a few hours grace.'

'Excellent. Mere, petition the Navy to take over bombardment schedules. That will allow the chief logistician some leeway. The sooner we finish this siege, tell them, the sooner we can move off from this backwater world.

'Now, quartermaster general,' Bendikt turned to the smaller man standing beside the chief logistician, 'the amphibious craft?'

The quartermaster general met Bendikt's gaze. 'Yes, sir. We received the instructions you sent via astropath and have already started work procuring the vessels you requested. We have searched the STC files and come up with this.'

He motioned to one of the clerks, who carried over a holo-projector. A vision appeared in the air before him: a blunt, blocky craft, with a command tower set two-thirds back along its length and a landing ramp at the front. The quartermaster general made a circular motion with his hand and the image spun slowly. There was a low hush. The quartermaster general's manner seemed immensely smug. 'For your situation, sir, this is my recommended solution. Each can carry ten Chimeras.'

'Good. I need hundreds of them.'

The chief logistician allowed himself a wry smile. 'General Bendikt. We have already started work.'

TEN

Dido pulled her collar close, but still she felt a strange chill in the air as she stood in the watchtower and watched Minka lead her two chosen troopers out into the no-man's-land between the Cadian and Drookian camps.

Feral world scum, she thought, as she considered the Drookians. She'd fought with them on Cadia and didn't have a high opinion of them. They'd caused as much trouble for the Imperial forces as they had for the enemy. And now they were camped right next to them.

As Minka disappeared into the darkness, Dido scanned the Drookian camp. The curse pole still stood staring towards the Cadian camp. She felt that chill again. A mist was rising.

'Throne!' Orugi said, blowing onto his fingers. 'I thought this was supposed to be a temperate planet.'

An hour later Dido saw the three forms crawling back towards the Cadian camp. They had cut a small hole in the wire beneath the watchtower where Dido stood and once back inside they repaired the holes. It had taken little more than two hours.

Dido stood waiting as Minka clambered up to the watchtower. When she came through the hatch she had a broad smile on her face.

'All set,' she said. She waited for Baine and Maenard to clamber up.

Maenard was the demo expert. He held the detonator in his hand. 'Now?' he said.

Minka nodded. In the darkness there was a sudden gout of fire, followed by a loud crack. In the light of the flames they could make out the curse pole in the moment that it was blown to pieces.

Shouts of alarm carried across from the other camp. They could see the lights of lumens hurrying to the spot where the curse pole had been. Its remains lay scattered in a wide circle, burning from the heat of the explosion.

They stood up to enjoy the alarm of the Drookians. 'What do you think they're going to do in revenge?' Minka said.

Dido shrugged. 'I don't think they'll have the chance. We're moving out tomorrow morning for field exercises.'

Ten minutes later, Minka stepped inside Sparker's office.

She felt a weight off her shoulders as she reported, 'It's gone, sir.'

'Any problems?' he said simply.

'None.'

'Good,' he said and almost smiled. 'Well done.'

True to Dido's words, they were out after breakfast, in a long convoy of Chimeras and Leman Russes. The air had turned warm. They pulled open the tops of their Cadian drab uniforms to allow a little air to circulate as they drove inland for nearly two hours, into the charred remains of an old battlefield.

Mechanicus crews were busy gathering the debris of armour

and transports. The Cadians camped amidst the tank grave-yards and left-over trenches. All about them were the towering mounds that marked the mass graves of Imperial dead. Regimental banners flew from each one. The largest mound rose like a hill from the flat plain, the foundations of a stone mausoleum marked out with Imperial flags. A temporary chantry chapel stood alongside. It had been built of flakboard and appeared to be staffed by a lone Rakallion minister, who stumped about, chainsword over his back, in a clinking suit of armour made from the ID tags of dead troopers.

He stood at the door of the chapel as the Cadians filed past. His look was not friendly.

They returned his gaze with resolve.

But he was like a spectre. This is how many of you shall end up, priest and mound seemed to say. Bones in a field on some forgotten planet.

For weeks the Cadians practised voxless night assaults, bunker clearance and trench defences. All the time the great mass of Crannog Mons reared up in the western sky over the mass graves.

When, at last, they returned to their camp Colonel Sparker summoned Lieutenant Dido. She entered and closed the flimsy door behind her. He was still in combat gear, camo stripes across his face. He shoved a piece of paper towards her.

'Ceremonial duties,' he said. 'Bendikt has asked for your platoon.'

She said, 'Does this have anything to do with the Drookians?'

Sparker appeared to have forgotten about all that. He waved a hand. 'No. You were specially selected. High priority. Local aristocrat. Get your lot cleaned up and head out. You've got to be on the road by midnight.'

* * *

Dido found each of her sergeants and handed out the shower chits. 'Dress duty. Out by midnight.'

Minka passed the orders on, handing each their metal chit. She found Breve. He had spent the week coaxing *The Saint*'s machine-spirit to full working order and was looking forward to a period of rest where he could strip the engine down and soak the pieces in holy unguents.

He took the news badly. 'Throne! Driving back to Starport? You have to be kidding.'

'Dido has asked the tech-priests to minister to all our Chimeras.'

They could see the lumens of the tech-priests and their servitor entourages, making their way across the camp.

'Great!' Breve said, with mock pleasure.

There were six shower blocks set about the camp – long flakboard buildings with a boiler at one end and a pair of chambers set with naked metal hoses. An attendant sat in the antechamber, his pinched face staring out. There was a small gap at the bottom of the window through which shower chits could be swapped for clean, dry towelling.

Minka got to the shower as Lyrga and Karni were leaving. 'Sarge,' they called out cheerfully as they towelled their hair dry. Warm water had an amazingly restorative effect. There was no trace of the weeks of accumulated grime on them.

Minka handed her chit through the window. The attendant wordlessly handed her the towel.

She pushed into the women's changing room. It was a plain, damp space, with rows of metal hooks hammered into a cross beam. Dido had arrived just before Minka and was stripped down to her military issue vest and underwear. She pulled her vest over her head and hung it on a peg.

Her arms and face were tanned dark, but her torso was pale and lean and hard, her contours shaped by the tight knot of muscle and the scars of battle. Minka knew Dido's scars as well as her own. She had helped treat some of them. On Dido's left arm was a raw and puckered scar where she'd taken a glancing hit from a hard round. Her abdomen was marked on both sides with entry and exit scars courtesy of a pair of stubber slugs. There was also a long, slanting scar from her ribcage to her navel where the medicae had needed to open her up and stitch her back together.

Minka undressed as well and hung up her clothes. She laid her boots under them, peeled her socks off. They were stiff with a week's wearing and stood up by themselves next to her boots.

Blocks of hard soap with the strong carbolic stink of anti-lice chems littered the benches. She grabbed one and threw her towel over her shoulder as she walked into the shower chamber. The air was warm and foetid. An open drain ran along the middle of the room, long lines of exposed metal pipes along either side. The showers were plain open pipes that spouted water at a set temperature. Dido turned the handle and stepped in. Minka took the hose next to Dido.

If the water had ever been warm, it had been used up. Now it was icy. Minka's skin shrank at its touch, goose pimpling against the cold water. This was going to be a perfunctory bath.

Dido was already done. Minka finished only a few seconds later. Maintaining combat effectiveness was one of the first duties of a Cadian. There was no lingering. Once she was clean, Minka stepped out. The towel was stiff with Munitorum detergents. She rubbed herself down and grabbed her pack. She carefully opened the bag, took each item of her dress uniform out and laid them down on the wooden benches.

When she was dressed she ran her fingers through her hair, checked her uniform in the single mirror, rubbed her boots with a dirty cloth.

'What's this mission we've been given?'

'No idea,' Dido said. 'But we're specially requested.'

It sounded ominous. Dido misread Minka's expression. 'Nothing to do with the Drookians.'

Minka laughed. 'Oh, I'd forgotten about them.'

When they were ready to leave, Minka found Breve inside the Chimera's driver cabin. There was cursing and the sound of metal being dropped as Minka clambered up onto the roof decking.

She called down. 'How's it going?'

'Well. It's been blessed,' he called out from inside the driver's cabin. 'But now the batteries are overheating.' His head appeared at the open driver's hatch. 'I've adjusted the wiring. The problem was Crone B9. So many parts went wrong there. I've replaced them but the stuff coming out of Ryza...' He pushed himself up from the cabin. 'Half of the parts are substandard.'

This was an increasingly common complaint. War had flowered across a thousand systems, and to compound the crisis, demands for materiel had risen exponentially. The Munitorum, least glamorous of the pillars of mankind, had passed the point of crisis. Even though forge worlds like Ryza might still be churning out war-materiel on industrial scales, their gear was often inferior.

It was the story of the Imperium of Man: a slow collapse and decay, made dramatically worse by the fall of Cadia, which had sundered ten-millennia-old supply routes. Forge worlds were deprived of ore as the mining worlds upon which they depended were lost in warp-storms. Hive worlds starved as agro-planets went suddenly silent, their mountain cities shaken by the death throes of riot and war.

'Wulfe has taken it apart,' Breve said and puffed out his cheeks. 'But it's basically shot.'

The gunner, Wulfe, appeared from under the Chimera, rolling

out on a mechanic's trolley. He was a compact man, a little deaf after so long spent close to a heavy bolter. He spoke too loudly as he said, 'I've rigged up a rough coolant system. I've drenched it in unguents and said more prayers than a Holy Sister, but it's just a field repair. We'll need to find a replacement if this old lady comes into battle with us.'

Minka nodded. There wasn't much she could do. She'd sent in repeated requests, but the quartermaster's office had been inundated with similar requests. None of them could magic up a replacement. 'Listen, I've just heard. We're heading out at midnight tonight,' Minka said.

'Where to?'

'Not Starport. We're going to the General's Palace.'

'How far is that?'

'Five hours.'

'I'll say a prayer,' said Breve.

They set off half an hour early.

They were starting to get used to the constant bombardment. It was a non-stop drone that rose and fell in waves as rotas brought various batteries into play. *The Saint*'s powerplant was humming nicely above the noise outside. Minka clambered forward to congratulate Breve. He had his ear defenders on, but got the gist and raised his hands up in the sign of a prayer.

She climbed back and dropped in through the open top hatch. The week of trench training had worn them all out. Their eyes were closed, their heads in their hands, resting against the walls, or on each other's shoulders. Baine was lying between their legs, head propped on a rolled-up camo net.

Minka found a place to sleep. It was a rough and uncomfortable night.

* * *

By dawn their convoy of Chimeras had arrived at the designated landing zone. They woke, bleary eyed, stretching in the tight confines.

Breve had not slept. He parked the Chimera and, still sitting in the driver's chair, pulled his helmet down over his face and put his feet up, folding his arms about himself.

'Wake me when it's done,' he said. Minka nodded. They still didn't know what 'it' was.

There was an hour's wait by landing pad 74-B9. A grav-pallet of ordnance was being loaded onto one of the low funiculars that supplied the Earthshaker batteries. The two Sentinel lifters stalked back and forth as the Cadians waited.

Nikloaz brought the platoon banner out of Dido's Chimera. It was a light pennant carrying the symbol of the 101st, embossed upon the Cadian Gate. The pole was set with a steel aquila. The pennant flapped lazily in the breeze.

Nothing else moved, except the winding white contrails that tracked each lighter ferrying supplies from orbiting warp-craft above Starport.

When the lighter appeared there was nothing of the Munitorum about it, nor any of the brute functionality of the Astra Militarum. It was a sleek, personal craft, with sweeping lines and ornate bas relief of gold and bronze.

They kept well back as it was waved onto the rockcrete landing pad. Its engines wound down. Coolants vented. The plating panels were still buckled from the heat of re-entry. Steam rose from it. The Cadians took up their positions. Dido strode forward and waited by the access ramp.

There was a long wait before the hatches were opened with a hiss of equalising pressures. Within seconds a flock appeared, each one chanting Psalms of Unification. But they were metal, not flesh, and they flapped out with wheezing pistons.

As they lifted up into the air, a woman appeared, dressed in silver power armour with a boltgun clamped to her thigh. Her helmet was cradled in the crook of her arm, her face tattooed with a chalice.

She was one of the Adepta Sororitas, the military fist of the Ecclesiarchy.

'Hear me! In the Name of the Emperor! I am Superior Melissya of the Order of the Argent Shroud. Upon this planet of Malouri, I shall mark the sacrifice of my wards!'

She was not addressing the Cadians. She was addressing the heavens, like a shaman announcing her presence to the spirits of the world.

To Minka she looked much like the Sisters she had seen before. Pinched cheeks, hair cropped close behind the ears and a light in her eye that had all the sparkle and hardness of a carefully faceted diamond.

Minka turned to Dido. 'It's not...' she said, but Dido shook her head.

'No. Different order.'

There had been a Chapter of the Adepta Sororitas on Potence. But those Sisters had worn black and this woman was armoured in silver, her cloak of white fur lined with embroidered red damask.

As the Sister spoke, a band of warriors strode out around her as if they had been summoned. They did not wear armour, but were clothed in rags like penitents begging outside a holy shrine. Yet there was nothing of the mystic or mendicant about them. Some wore belts of chain, some leather. Half wore gags. Many had lost an eye or a hand. Tied to each of their bare limbs were prayer pennants that fluttered as they stalked forward. All were armed with eviscerator chainswords, some almost as tall as the women themselves. They were not looking for charity; they were looking for a means of redemption.

Next, four lifewards stepped out. They wore bronze muscled breastplates and tall velvet shakos pinned with voluminous ostrich feathers. Their visors glowed with augmetics and they carried power lances in their hands. The lifewards took up position outside the door, waiting.

Minka heard the voice before she saw their master.

'Careful!' said a woman's voice with an imperious accent.

The old lady that stepped out had been through so many rejuvenat cycles it was hard to pinpoint her age with any degree of accuracy. She could be anywhere between a hundred and eight hundred years old. Despite this, she had a lithe and dangerous look.

This was Lady Bianca Richstar, Gerent of Tokai – a world that had been lost to the forces of heresy. But since the death of her cousin, the Patridzo, on Potence, she was the highest ranking Richstar within the Gallows Cluster. In light of the system's precarious politics, she had thrown her lot in with the forces of General Bendikt. Her chief strengths were her ancestry and her noble status, and she was well aware of this. For her entrance on Malouri she wore a golden ruff, a bodice of black vitreous glass and skirts of silken lace.

There was a long pause as she cast an imperious eye over the whole of Seventh Company's Second Platoon, standing below.

Dido strode forward until she was between two of the lifewards, then stopped and saluted. Minka couldn't hear what Dido said, but the Lady Bianca's response carried for a distance. 'Where is General Bendikt?' Her voice had been augmented.

Dido went on at length. Minka wondered what she was saying.

She couldn't tell from the body language. At last, Gerent Bianca seemed content, though her words carried to them all, 'I shall present my thoughts to General Bendikt.'

She descended the steps of the lighter, then paused. 'Of course, there is one far greater than I.'

At that moment, a golden grav-palanquin floated out of the lighter, its occupant screened by ancient curtains of embroidered silk. Censers trailed incense. The praise birds circled over the palanquin.

'Lieutenant Dido,' Lady Bianca continued, 'I put myself and my honoured forebear, Saint Ignatzio Richstar, within your care. Now. Escort me to General Bendikt!'

ELEVEN

Bendikt was stood on the stairs of the General's Palace with a committee of Astra Militarum grandees to greet the Gerent Bianca. He had clearly just come straight out of a planning meeting with the Munitorum ambassadors and looked exasperated. He had a map rolled up in his hand, and he patted it into the other hand as he waited.

Gerent Bianca's lifewards followed behind her as she walked to the palace steps. The palanquin bearing Saint Ignatzio was brought forward. Already, a crowd that almost numbered a hundred trailed behind in a state of religious awe. They were menials, mainly, and kept a respectful distance.

The guards waved them back, but Gerent Bianca intervened. 'They are with me,' she said, 'and they are with Saint Ignatzio. You shall let them through.'

Bendikt came down the steps to greet her. 'Welcome,' he said. 'I have issued instructions for you to be given full honours. As befits your rank.'

He had ordered that the palanquin be lodged in his private chapel, while he himself gave up his suite for Lady Bianca.

'I could not,' she insisted.

'Please,' he said. 'I would be honoured, and it is important that you and Saint Ignatzio are kept somewhere where your safety can be ensured. I am moving all the general staff closer to the front. It is not healthy for them to be pampered in the rear while our troopers are in trenches at the front.'

As Lady Bianca and her entourage continued up the steps, Bendikt approached the Sister of Battle who had followed in their wake.

'Superior Melissya,' Bendikt said.

Her face was as hard as carved marble and it did not soften when she saw who addressed her. 'Yes, general.'

'I wanted to thank you.'

She stared at him as if he was an idiot. 'For what?'

'The honour you pay us in joining this warzone.'

Despite her finely cut face and almost fragile-looking cheeks, the suit of power armour gave her both bulk and height that dwarfed him as she turned full square onto him, the pistons within her armour giving off a low, menacing whine.

'Our presence here is no honour to you or your men. My charges gave up all chance of honour long ago. Now there is only shame and disgrace. Only their deaths can mitigate their sins.'

'Well,' Bendikt said. 'We are honoured nonetheless.'

'All I ask is that you allow us the chance to give up our lives in battle.'

'I will do that,' he said. He paused. 'Tell me, superior. You speak of your wards, but what about you? Are you here to die as well?'

'I am not a penitent.'

'I did not mean that…'

'In the years that I have been fighting I have seen many defeats. Some military, some personal. But I have never felt the need to become a penitent,' she said.

Bendikt nodded. 'My question is, when is your mission complete? Do you die with your wards?'

Superior Melissya's eyes were hard as she stared back at him. 'That is not for me to say. The place and manner of my death is for the Emperor, alone, to decide. Either way, I do not fear it. Death is welcome for warriors like us.'

Minka and the other Cadians stood and watched the exchanges. As Bendikt led Gerent Bianca to the house where she would be living, Dido and the others filed away.

Minka saw Prassan within the officers surrounding the general. She had to double take. He had grown. Command staff rations. She smiled and lifted a hand. She caught his eye, but he remained standing stiffly in place.

When he was not needed any more, he peeled off and came forward to greet her. He was a little earnest at times, but they'd fought together, and that was a tight bond that was hard to undo.

'How's life up here?' she said.

He laughed. 'Long meetings. Ceremonials. It's a little boring.'

'I don't believe a word of it. You must be learning all kinds of things.'

Prassan's face lit up. 'That's true. But I can't talk about it.'

'You sound very mysterious,' she said.

He forced a smile and nodded. 'You'll find out soon enough.'

Minka was about to speak when Dido called out. She'd managed to acquire meals from the palace canteen before they set off.

Baine and Orugi were first in line. There was meat, fried slab, the best food the Imperium of Man could offer. The cooks were stocky, their white aprons stained where they had cleaned their hands. 'Go ahead,' they laughed, 'this is all left over.'

Second Platoon piled their plates high. Minka could not finish what she'd taken. Baine looked expectantly at her. 'You done?'

She nodded.

'Can I?'

She pushed the plate across the table. 'Take it.'

Minka filled her flask with recaff. It was the best stuff she'd tasted since Potence. She walked out into the courtyard, passing a young man in Cadian garb, a white stripe over his helmet.

She went straight by him before she realised what she had just seen. 'Hey!' she shouted, spinning on her heel.

The other man stopped and turned and saluted. 'Sir.'

'What the hell are you wearing?'

He paused. 'A helmet.'

Minka could have punched him. 'What is your name and unit?'

'Cadet Yedrin. First Whiteshields.'

'What the hell do you mean, "Whiteshields"?' Minka grabbed him by his collar and shook him. 'You're not even Cadian!'

There was no Cadia, so there could not be any more Whiteshields. To suggest there were was a transgression against the memory of their planet. It was an *affront*.

Minka dragged the boy into the canteen. The sight of the Whiteshield uniform struck the Cadians dumb. Minka barely needed to speak.

The cadet was bombarded with the same questions from the rest of the platoon. The sight of him was like a whizz of frenzon. In an instant they were all furious.

Dido pushed them back, but she was as angry as the others. 'What the hell do you mean that you're a Whiteshield?'

Yedrin held up both hands. He stammered as he tried to explain. But there was no reason he could give.

'I'm not alone,' he said.

'There are more of you?'

'A whole company.'

Sure enough, in the drill ground behind the palace a whole company of Whiteshield cadets was lined up in the courtyard. Hundreds of them, all with the white stripe over their heads.

Minka took the steps slowly. An order was barked out and the Whiteshields snapped to attention and saluted with the shout, 'Cadia stands!'

'Throne,' Minka cursed. Her last statement was a cry of hurt and confusion. 'Why has no one told us?'

The drive back to camp was quiet.

Baine scratched a basic grid into the panel at his feet, and he and Karni played three man standing. They used credits as the counters, trying to outmanoeuvre each other in an attempt to get a straight line. It was a simple game, which Minka found both irritating and strangely compulsive. Karni kept beating Baine, but he didn't seem to lose any of his enthusiasm.

At last Minka couldn't stand it any more. She fell asleep, and dreamt of Kasr Myrak, Rath Sturm always with her – cocky, calm, defiant. When she woke they were still playing and Baine was still losing.

She watched for a while, then remembered the Whiteshields and that soured her mood. She clambered up to the top of *The Saint*. They were riding in file. Dido's Chimera led, followed by Elhrot, Barnabas, and then Minka's squad. They were about ten minutes from the camp. Minka could see the watchtowers.

She leant back against the turret. Breve had his head out of the driver's hatch. He seemed happy.

Minka's gaze turned towards Crannog Mons. It was blue in the distance, under the pall of black smoke that hung over it. Her mind wandered. She was trying to visualise forcing a landing there. It was coming, she knew, and all she could do was put her faith in her commanders.

A flash and boom blew from beneath Dido's Chimera.

The shock waves punched Minka backwards before she realised what was happening, stinging her skin with a spray of earth. Picking herself up, she looked to Dido's tank. It had shed a track in the explosion, which now unwound behind it as it slewed to a halt.

Minka ran forward, her laspistol drawn. Dido's Chimera was burning. A large hole had been blown through the side armour and flames licked up the side, turning the Cadian drab black.

Elhrot clambered out of the turret cupola of his own tank. 'What the Throne happened?' he demanded.

Minka pointed. There had been a buried demo charge. It had carved a crater into the road. She jabbed the release stud on the access ramp, which slammed down, and the command squad tumbled out from the smoke-filled interior.

None of them appeared hurt. Dido came last. 'I'm fine,' she was saying but it was clearly not true. Her nose had stopped bleeding, but the blood was clotting about her nostrils and smeared across her cheek. She stumbled forward and Minka caught her. She put her arm under Dido's armpit, taking her weight. 'Come!' she said. 'Sit!'

By now the Cadians had formed a protective perimeter, but there was no one in sight. They left a guard on the burning tank, bundled Dido and the others into another Chimera and raced off towards camp.

'Traitors?' Minka asked, looking towards Crannog Mons.

'I'd say blame lies closer to home,' Sergeant Barnabas said, nodding towards the Drookian camp.

When they got back to their camp it seemed that everyone had seen the smoke and was on full alert. Baytov had sent a platoon out to investigate. They came out of camp, engines roaring, multi lasers and heavy bolters primed and ready to shoot.

Minka signalled that there had been no fatalities. They swung into camp, emptied out of the Chimera and headed for the medicae station. People swarmed around them as they walked, all wanting to know what had happened.

Banting was not at the medicae station, thankfully, but one of the nurses cleaned Dido up, shone a light into her eye, examined her ears, and passed her fit. After a large mug of recaff, Dido claimed she felt better.

'So what about these new Whiteshields?' the nurse said.

Minka started. 'You've heard?'

'Announcement made last night,' the nurse said.

'What did they say?'

The nurse paused. It clearly wasn't of as much concern to her as it was to Minka. She repeated some line that she had heard about them all being drawn from the Cadian bloodline.

'What the Throne is that?' Minka said. 'Cadia's been cleared and resettled countless times!'

Dido was still catching up. 'They're baggage brats?' she said, meaning children born within the entourage that followed regiments about the stars.

Minka was blunt. 'Exactly! So they're *not* Cadian!'

Dido looked at her. 'Well, they're Cadian blood. Isn't that good enough?'

Minka looked at her lieutenant as though the bomb had

shaken her brain. There was a blood clot in one of Dido's eyes that was slowly spreading. It reminded her, horribly, of the Eye of Terror. She thought she was going to be sick. She turned away and breathed deep. It took a long moment, like dragging herself up from deep water.

It was them against the galaxy, and Cadians were a dying breed.

'No,' she said. 'It's not!'

Later, in the dorm, Minka had thought through what she wanted to say. 'It's like another death,' she said at last. 'They're destroying what we were. Who we are. We stared into the Eye of Terror. We lived under its shadow. We never forgot our duty. We could never forget!'

Dido cradled her head in silence. She had nothing to say against this.

Minka went on. '*That* is what it means to be Cadian. It's a state of mind. It's a duty. Not a bloodline. There is no bloodline! How many times has Cadia been left lifeless? Each time we were resettled with veterans from across the Imperium. It was the planet that shaped us.' She kicked the wall. It was so flimsy she left another hole in the flakboard.

'I know,' Dido said at last. She looked exhausted by the day.

Minka looked about at the others in the room. Siku and Doxa had both come in. They sat silently as Minka ranted. They were all agreed. Another insult to the memory of Cadia.

Minka paused. 'You know what's worse? When I saw that cadet this morning I thought he was my brother.'

Dido was silent. Minka felt compelled to go on. The last time she had seen her brother was in the muster yards of Kasr Myrak, standing tall and proud in ill-fitting military cast-offs, his helmet too big for his head, his cheeks hairless and soft.

'His name was Tarli,' she said. 'I always hoped he'd made it. I always told myself that I would have felt it if he was dead. But, of course, if he lived then there's no way he'd still be a Whiteshield.'

Dido pulled a bottle of amasec out from under her bed. Her eye was dark with the blood clot.

'Here,' she said, pouring a pair of heavy shots. One for her and one for Minka. 'I think we both deserve one of these.'

TWELVE

As a youth Minka had spent months out in the arctic wastes of Cadia, trekking from pylon to pylon, camping in the shelter of the vast graveyards – keeping out of sight of the priests as they made their way from headstone to headstone.

Their route was predictable. They bent over each tombstone and then moved onto the next one.

'What are they doing?' Minka had once asked one of the older cadets. 'Are they looking for someone?'

The other cadet had shaken his head. He had pointed to the tombstone they were hiding behind. The wind had scoured it of name and rank and date of death.

'When all the names are lost, then there is no need to honour their memory,' the other said. 'The graves are emptied, the bones taken to the ossuaries, and the graveyard waits for the next lot of martyrs.'

Minka had spent many hours in the ossuaries. They were

cold, vaulted chambers, silent and reverential, heavy with the weight of death that pressed down upon them. Broken panes hissed with the wind. The walls were stacked with long bones and punctuated by row upon row of mouldering skulls. Aquilas of thigh bones hung on the wall, chandeliers of ribs, and here and there was a complete body of some ancient hero, the bones held together with threads of sinews and skin, all stained brown with age and lit by the light of a flickering candle.

Keeping their age-long watch, skeletal fingers held aloft banners that had long since mouldered down to a see-through gauze.

In their first year, each cadet in Kasr Myrak had to spend one night a month alone in an ossuary, praying for the departed. Minka had been fearful the first time among the decaying remains of the ancient heroes – thousands of skulls with their blank eye sockets and jawbones missing, the dust of the long dead in her lungs.

But with time, she had learnt there was nothing frightening about the massed graves. There was melancholy, yes, but the longer she maintained her vigil, the closer she felt to these lost generations. And the greater the weight of expectation she felt in the empty eye sockets.

The last night Minka had been in an ossuary was a month before the Black Crusade had struck. She remembered the night with a chill of fear. The Eye of Terror had been livid with unspeakable colours, vomiting up plumes of warp-energies as they swirled back into its heart and there were howls in the night outside, as if the world itself was being whipped up into a state of eldritch torment.

Shadows had crept up the walls, their long arms ending with clawed fingers, their heads little more than a circle of mist, the elongated jaws fanged with gloom. She knew these were just apparitions. The Eye of Terror had a baleful influence upon their world, but she was not so weak-willed as to be scared by shadows.

Surrounded by the dead of ages, she took strength from their remains.

We died to preserve Cadia, the silent bones stated. Our lives were brief and violent, but in that sacred duty we did not fail.

Of course, not all young Cadians could bear a night alone. Drill and training and punishment dominated every hour of life and any who failed the exacting physical and mental standards were mocked and beaten, and subject to public opprobrium.

Others lost the will to fight, and pledged themselves to the war effort in other ways. Some died. Those whose failure was absolute were blacked out and expunged from the records.

It was brutal, but Cadia had been a military state. War was its past, its future, its religion and its function. A Cadian had one duty in life, so people liked to joke: to die for the Emperor.

The memories of her childhood kept coming up as Minka lay on her bed.

Her home city of Kasr Myrak was a fortress. Each hab was a bunker, each street a kill-zone where any enemy intruders could be gunned down. Each dawn began with drill. Each night ended with the *Cadian Prayer*. Not a supplicant's prayer, but a soldier's appeal to the ultimate high commander.

Before Minka was born, her mother had birthed five children already, their fathers either killed or sent off-world. She had still had one more child to raise before she fulfilled the quota she had given herself. She had shown her zeal by producing two: Minka and her little brother, Tarli.

Her parents' coupling had not been a result of a love-marriage, they had not believed in that. Just two young healthy and fertile warriors breeding the next generation.

119

Minka's father had manned the southern polar defence station and been called up for off-planet service in one of the Imperium's many wars when she was young. He was now just a vague shape in Minka's mind: a restless, lean-faced man who had taken her out to learn field-craft.

Minka had been ten when she was put into the draw for which Whiteshield unit she would join. Like everyone else, she had wanted to join the 17th – the Kasr Myrak elite. When she had been given her token stating her enrolment with the 76th instead, she had locked herself away and wept. A posting like that wasn't worth half a credit.

Her mother had come up with many reasons why the indignity of the 76th was not the worst thing that could happen to her, and on the day of the Gathering Minka had refused to cry. She would not show emotion. She would join them and better them, and make sure that they came top in the next year's annual assessment.

The night before her posting had been her cousin Jorden's Living Wake. He was six years older than her. He had gone away to military camp a boy and come back a man with strong jaw and broad shoulders. Minka was hungry for his calm, his experience, the studied look in his violet eyes. He had been toasted many times that night, and had held his drink down well. When it had been her time to salute him, he had poured her just a drop of spirits, and clinked his glass to hers.

'Which unit are you joining?' Jorden had asked.

She almost cried when she had to admit it. 'The seventy-sixth, but I'm going to ask for a reassessment. No one reassembles a lasrifle faster than me. I come first in every race and can do more press-ups than anyone else. I push myself. I train without food. Run without water. I run barefoot in the snow. I endure and never complain. In the annual ratings I came second in my barracks. I thought that would be enough.'

'You think that because you are among the best cadets you should be sent to the best Whiteshield unit?' She saw a flicker of disappointment in his eyes. 'If they put all the best cadets in the best units, what would that achieve?'

Six months later, Jorden had died suppressing an uprising on St Josmane's Hope. When she next came home from Whiteshield camp, his helmet hung from the wall, the seal of completion stating the time and place of his death. She would never forget what he had told her that afternoon.

'You should be grateful. They put you in the weakest unit *because* you are the best. You have an opportunity to show your worth. Be a leader. It is only through the hardest trials that we grow and learn and prove ourselves.' His violet eyes had been determined. 'The very hardest trials.'

Minka armoured herself with her cousin's and her mother's words the day she left her parent's hab-cell in the lower buttresses of Kasr Myrak. She stood ramrod straight, silent with shock that she was leaving home. Her pack was light. It held her few possessions. Blanket. Ration tin. Water bottle. Cord. Thread. Needles. Whiteshield issue medi-pack: bandage, blood-clotting gel, counterseptic powder. A knife her father had given her. A copy of *The Uplifting Primer*.

Her suit of Militarum surplus Cadian drab was three sizes too large, the boots too big. She had punctured extra holes in her belt to get it to fit, bound the flapping ends of her trousers tight with Cadian drab puttees, but as she strode through the streets she felt like the lord governor primus, the commander of Cadia.

That winter, the 76th Myrak Whiteshields brigade were posted an hour north of the city in the round-topped hills that ringed Kasr Myrak.

'Have faith in the Emperor,' her mother said as the row of cargo-8s waited. 'If you do not like the standard of the seventy-sixth then ask yourself what you can do to improve it.'

Tarli was also there to see her off. Minka loved her brother. Of all her siblings they were closest in age. He wanted to be a shock trooper even more than she did.

'When you go, I will be all alone,' he said. The thought was unbearable to him.

'Put in for an early transfer,' she told him. She had heard the best ways of demanding this. It was a matter of drill-ground gossip. 'I can send a request as well. You can come to my unit and help improve them. If the battle demands are high then they accelerate processing.'

'I will,' Tarli promised.

'Have faith in the Emperor and your lasgun,' her mother told her as farewell. When her mother stepped forward with her arms out, Minka stood stiffly and refused to embrace. Instead she snapped smartly to attention and saluted her.

She was not a child any more; she was a soldier.

The last time Minka had seen her brother was on the seventh day of the Black Crusade. The skies had been filled with the hulks of the Despoiler's warships. They blocked out the sun, but even in the darkness she could see how proud he was as he stood to attention, his lascarbine hanging from his shoulder, as the instructor spat fire and fury into their faces. He had kept his gaze resolutely fixed forward. He did not look at her, even as his troop of a thousand children marched past. His chest was swelled up, shoulders back, chin out. That was the last time she'd seen him. A proud little Cadian, who had disappeared in the confusion of war. Lost, like so many other things, into the clutches of the past.

These were just some of Minka's experiences of her childhood on Cadia. Her home world had shaped her, its rough hands forming her into a physically tough, mentally ferocious warrior.

How could these baggage-brats match real Cadians?

When Minka woke next morning, Dido had already come from a check-up at the medicae station. 'I'm fine, apparently,' she said, but the blood clot had spread and now covered half her left eye. Minka could barely summon the energy to sit up.

'You all right?' Dido asked.

Minka was lying on her cot, one arm thrown over her head. She was exhausted by the memories, but also by the shock of Dido's close escape.

She paused for a moment. 'I'm fine,' she said. 'Honest.'

A full dress parade was called at 0800 hours, giving them just half an hour to be ready. The 101st formed up at a run, and were in place when Colonel Baytov took the podium.

He had a ream of regimental business to get through, speaking in his deep baritone. He went on for nearly an hour, and at the end he paused and looked over the ranks. 'I am aware that some of you have met the troopers of the Seventy-Second Whiteshields.'

The Cadians stiffened at the very name.

Baytov paused. If the words were unpleasant for him, he did not let on. 'I understand the concern that many of you have. But I expect no more dissent. Lord Militant Warmund has confided to me that at the current rate of loss the last Cadian regiments under his command will have been wiped out within seven years.'

He paused to let that fact sink in. Minka could not imagine the Imperium surviving without the Cadians.

'To replenish and revitalise, this is the purpose of the recruitment drive. To keep the finest regiments within the Imperium up to full fighting strength. I have spoken to General Bendikt and he assures me that only the very best have been selected for the Whiteshields. Throne-willing, they will soon be going into battle. Those that survive and show the requisite abilities – only they will be joining our ranks. And when they do, I expect you to welcome them.'

The silence that greeted his words was complete. Theirs was a mindset of service and sacrifice. If that was what Baytov ordered, then – like all things – they would honour his command.

THIRTEEN

The Imperial siege camp was a city of millions, geared to war. Beneath the blackened landscape were storage chambers, subways, munition trams, troop conveyance pipes, mine heads, Termite loading bays and rows of yawning assembly chambers with dimly lit troop pipes leading towards the front. It was a gridwork of camps and barracks linked by underground networks all funnelling towards the causeway that pointed to Tor Tartarus.

As the moment for the grand assault drew near, the whole landscape seemed to be seething with activity. Bendikt's staff had started work on this attack long before they had even arrived on planet. Neighbouring forge worlds had to be enlisted for aid, the proud reputation of Cadia exploited to facilitate emptying prisons and penal facilities. His team had worked round the clock to bring all this to fruition and now everything was to be thrown at the bastion.

But now he was on the planet, Bendikt worked hard getting to grips with all the aspects of supply and command necessary for victory. There were excavations to be completed, the finalisation of the great siege moles, the stockpiling of ordnance, the requisitioning of troops, and the logistical problems that millions of hungry mouths on a war-ravaged planet presented. For months, agri worlds that had not seen an Imperial tithe-ship for a hundred years suddenly found Astra Militarum units landing in force to accompany the Munitorum assessors who had a heavy tax to impose.

In order to finalise the causeway, Bendikt had accelerated the quarrying threefold by transferring some of the local regiments to the command of the labour corps. This move had caused a minor ruckus among the respective Astra Militarum commanders. A few regiments had refused, and he had the entire officer corps of each of the transgressing units transferred straight to the penal legions.

Let there be no mistake, the message went out, the Cadians were in charge now. Bendikt had no truck for argument and debate.

General von Horne's plan had been a little unimaginative. It involved the surrounding of the whole island with siege causeways before launching all-out assaults. It was a sound plan, but Bendikt did not have time for niceties.

He had studied Holzhauer's record. It was true, the traitor had never been defeated.

Until now.

Bendikt pulled in a deep breath. He outlined his plan to von Horne. The Mordian greeted it with silence, focusing instead on smoothing out the front of his tunic. When he finally finished, he said, 'I have seen the amount of penal troops you have gathered. I ask that my troops are not sent into battle alongside such rabble.'

Bendikt refused to be boxed in. 'I cannot guarantee that.'

Von Horne's face darkened. Bendikt patted the other man's arm. 'Do not worry. I have great faith in your troops. I see them marching alongside the Cadians for the final assault.'

Von Horne nodded. His pride had been mollified.

Bendikt spent the rest of that week negotiating with the ambassadors of the Adeptus Mechanicus – a succession of increasingly augmented humans until there was no flesh to be seen, just the sibilant hiss of well-oiled joints, the hum of internal batteries, and the monotonous drone of vox-grille voices.

The list of excuses was almost interminable. Bendikt batted them all away with increasing irritation. He set Mere on them full-time, and his adjutant slowly wore them down in a manner they found hard to counter: methodical and logical arguments.

It took an enormous effort of persistent and respectful cajoling for Archmagos Scarlex to give the Leviathans up. The Cadians' relationship with her forge world was critical.

'The archmagos is unwilling to let her children go,' her ambassador hissed. 'They are beasts of war. Their purpose and destiny is war. Each of them is condemned to die in fire and explosion. It is hard for her to let her creations go.'

'"Children",' Mere noted. 'It is strange that you should use this word. It is an oddly human emotion for a member of the Mechanicus to feel, though I understand it. But think on this. It is the duty of us all to die in battle. The legacy of her "children" will be measured not in lifespan, but in dead heretics. And I have no doubt, they will take an immense toll upon our foes.'

At last, the archmagos conceded.

In the end, Mere was forced to take a lighter to the orbital forges that hung in low orbit. He went with an honour guard of Cadians. His mission was to finalise the transfer of the Leviathans planetside.

They met a wall of plumed skitarii: deadly constructions of steel and flesh and gun barrel. From their midst skittered Archmagos Scarlex. There was nothing human left about her, except perhaps her maternal concern for her children. Her body was hidden in long robes fringed with the symbol of the cog. She moved on ten insectoid legs, and from the shadows of the hood a voice that was not human spoke, 'I calculate the chances of their survival to be minimal.'

Mere nodded. 'None of us can predict the moment that the Emperor calls us. I pray that they will have many years of battle before them. When they return to you, their machine-spirits will be full of the pride of achievement.'

There was a scrape of metal, like insectoid jaws grinding together. 'What do you know of the machine-spirit, *human*?' The last word was said with disgust.

Guilty as charged, Mere thought to himself.

The archmagos led him through the tunnels of the forge. At last he reached a window looking out onto the void-factorum, and the tech-priest lifted cold mechadendrites to the glaspex window.

'The *Hammer of Spite*,' the monotone voice hissed.

With *Hammer of Spite* came its Leviathan siblings, *Terra's Contempt*, and *Hatred of Iron*. They hung in their steel cradles, surrounded by the scaffold of the orbital forge.

The distance belied their size. They were machines designed to smite the enemies of the Imperium with terror: snub-nosed monsters, with tremor cannons jutting out from their chins, towering weapons of war and destruction with boarding parapets, siege towers and slabs of ablative armour.

Mere swallowed as he tried to think of something to say.

The archmagos stated simply, 'You are without words. That is a compliment.'

The truth was that the three Leviathans destined for this warzone were old tech, classified as sub-optimal and warehoused centuries ago. But they were perfect for the Imperium's needs, and after hasty refittings they had been prepared for transfer to Malouri.

The great beasts landed at Starport under cover of darkness, each one slung under a vast lander and accompanied by an army of tech-priests to minister to them.

There were always teething problems when void-forged beasts were transferred to gravity. The superstructures groaned; the inner core of welded rebar strained under their weight. But these were machines of siege and war, with secondary systems already kicking in to cover any localised failures. A week of finishing touches, and then the machines were ready for the final blessings.

When all was prepared, Archmagos Scarlex came planetside with a coterie of skitarii and magos-priests for a formal handover to Bendikt's command.

It was a strange ceremony, Mere thought, watching the insectoid archmagos caress each in turn. At last she withdrew her mechadendrites, and at an unseen signal the volcanic plasma engines kicked into life. Reactors roared, chimneys vented scorching fumes, gun loaders whirred with anticipation and the earth shook as they began to rumble ponderously forward, their quad tracks leaving impressions nearly three-feet deep.

News of the landing of the Leviathans spread waves of both gloom and excitement across the siege camp. Some soldiers wept, sensing their doom in the battle ahead. Others, like the Cadians, were glad that the long wait was over. The sooner they fought this battle, the sooner they could move on.

Whiteshield Yedrin saw them as he returned from a last month's intensive training in the abandoned trenches north of Starport. Zweden was with him. They were tired but they stood to see the Leviathans rolling towards them.

They had never seen anything so fitted out for war.

'Holy Throne,' Yedrin said.

Zweden let his breath whistle between his teeth. The fact that there were three of them only seemed to add to their monstrous power. They moved inexorably, like glaciers, or time.

Behemoths of war, with a sole purpose: to break Traitor Rock.

FOURTEEN

The same day the Leviathans landed, the Cadians were given the order to strike camp. Minka went to each of her squad to pass on the news. Each one took it according to their nature. Orugi looked blankly at her. The quiet girl Karni said nothing, but went back to her rosary of metal skulls.

Lyrga said, 'We're moving out?'

Minka nodded.

'Throne,' Lyrga said. 'I'd better get to the quartermaster.'

Dreno and Belus just nodded. Viktor was wearing his beret and was cleaning his carbine. Maenard was asleep. Allun was stripped down to his combat vest, going through his daily workout. His vest was stained with sweat from his pectoral muscles and the small of his back. He wiped his forehead and nodded.

Baine had his feet up. He was retelling one of the tales of his Whiteshield training, but it wasn't clear anyone was listening to him. He stood up when Minka entered.

'Yes, boss?'

'Tomorrow,' she told him.

'Tomorrow?' Jaromir said, as if not quite remembering the meaning of the word.

Minka put a hand to his shoulder and squeezed. 'Tomorrow.'

He nodded slowly. He looked up and said, 'Will you come with me?' He was not looking at anyone in the room. He was looking into the air above his head. 'Be with me,' he said again.

Minka did not really understand who he was talking to but she replied anyway. 'They'll be with you,' she said.

Minka's backpack stood in the corner of her room. She hung her grenades from the webbing, oiled her war-knife, cleaned the excess away and wiped down the sheath.

By sunset Minka wanted to clear her head, so she set off to the western guard tower, stretching her legs along the newly laid mat roadway. From each barracks-block came the sound of carbines being cleaned and put back together, the low, serious chatter of warriors about to go to war, the occasional burst of black humour. But it was good to walk away from it all.

The sentries had marked her approach and were alert. She lifted a hand to them and indicated which way she was heading and they nodded, but kept watching as she passed by.

The bombardment rolled on. She stopped at the westernmost guard tower. It was standard pattern with a rebar frame and elevated viewing platform, heavy stubbers mounted on each outer facing and steps zig-zagging up beneath.

When she approached the top a voice called out, 'Halt!'

She had to give the password before they would let her through the hatch.

'Sergeant Lesk,' the officer on duty said as she clambered up.

His name was Sacha, a man from Fifth Company. He had a wistful air when he said, 'When are you going in?'

She gave them some details.

He nodded. 'We've been assigned guard duty,' Sacha said. His tone said it all. Minka looked about. The faces of the other troopers were just as frustrated as their commander.

Minka felt for them. To come all this way and to be forced to sit it out! She strained a smile. 'Don't worry. We'll leave some for you.'

She strode to the seaward edge of the platform, where Crannog Mons filled the western horizon. It reminded her of the view of Markgraaf Hive. Its bulk rose high into the air, blue with distance. Dwarfed in the foreground were the Leviathans, the angular metal armour glinting in the slanting light of the setting sun. They looked like children's toys under the shadow of the mountain bastion.

As she stood there she could see the flash of long-range fire arcing in from the batteries on Crannog Mons. One of the sentries offered her the auspex, then they went back to their duties and left her to it. The Leviathans were already attracting a storm of long-distance fire. The mountain was all bastions and gothic statues and bristling gun platforms.

Minka felt herself prickling with anticipation. Hatred was rising within her. She could almost feel her pistol in hand, the weight of her war-blade, could almost smell the blood of her enemies. Her reverie was broken abruptly.

'Sergeant Lesk.'

She turned. It was Chief Commissar Shand, the senior discipline officer within the regiment. He was a good foot taller than her, with lean, scarred features. He was both feared and respected and now here he stood looking down on her, his face inscrutable behind the mask of scar tissue.

'May I?' he said, and took the auspex from her hand. He held it to his face. 'I hate this waiting,' he said. 'It is always a relief to be back in the front lines. Do you feel that too?'

'Yes, sir.'

Shand handed the auspex back to her. 'I hope your squad understand the depths of our foe's treachery.'

'Yes, sir. They have thrown off their love for the Emperor. They have put their faith in false prophets.'

There was a long pause. Minka had questions and the presence of the chief commissar seemed too good to miss. 'Sir,' she started, 'I am concerned. I am sure General Bendikt knows what he is doing, but I do not understand. The enemy know exactly where we're planning to attack. They can mass their own troops to defend it. Anyone attacking will be slaughtered.'

With other units this was a dangerous thought to voice aloud, but within the Cadians there was a degree of tolerated doubt. A hint of a smile played upon Shand's thin lips. 'Go on.'

Minka understood that her line of questioning was safe. 'If it was another Imperial commander then this would be what I expect. But Bendikt is in charge. And we know he is no fool. So there has to be a plan.'

Shand smiled. 'There is a plan. Don't worry about that, Sergeant Lesk. Make sure you're ready for battle when the call comes.'

She saluted. 'Yes, sir!'

As she spoke one of the Leviathans fired. The shot impacted on the void shield that protected Tor Tartarus and the energy dissipated in a kaleidoscopic burst of colour.

A dull *boom* rolled back towards them. Minka turned towards the battlefront. That first shot was like a signal to all the Imperial batteries. Night became day as the coastline Earthshaker batteries fired as one. The roll of sudden thunder made the watchtower vibrate.

The three Leviathans rumbled forwards, their own massive siege guns adding to the tumult. The shells were so large they moved in low parabolas, hitting the walls with earth shattering explosions that threw immense clouds of dust up and set off landslides of shattered permacrete. And then from the heavens lightning strobed down as the Imperial Navy ships in low-orbit entered the fight.

The white glow side-lit Shand's face. He smiled grimly. The battle for Crannog Mons had begun in earnest.

FIFTEEN

The thunderous artillery battle went on through the night and the Leviathans pushed forward under the smoke and flame of battle. As they drew closer to Tor Tartarus the mountainside glittered with the muzzle-flash of counter-fire. A hailstorm of las-bolts and shells flared against the void shields. For the last mile of the attack the Leviathans suffered withering defensive fire, their own void shields crackling and sparking as they deflected las-bolts and armour-piercing shells.

The *Hammer of Spite* got within five hundred yards of the causeway's end when its void shields overloaded. The crackling blue nimbus shell suddenly blinked out. A terrible race began between the reactor crews struggling to find the fault and fix it, and the traitor artillery batteries scrambling for a kill.

The vulnerable war machine looked small and insignificant in the shadow of Crannog Mons as shells rained down like hailstones. Three times the void shields flickered to life and three times they failed again.

The generators were just starting up once more when a lucky warhead penetrated the plasma reactor chamber. The fifty-strong boiler corps died within seconds as fires roared through the colossal beast. Hatches were slammed shut and coolants poured into the plasma reactors. But too late.

A succession of detonations tore through to the magazines. Fyceline explosions ripped out of the encased chambers. Infernos howled through the guts of the behemoth, seeking an escape route with all the force and fury of magma escaping from a planet's core. A fountain of fire and sparks erupted like a geyser into the air before *Hammer of Spite* was ripped apart in a series of cataclysmic explosions that flung debris out in all directions.

The death of *Hammer of Spite* was felt throughout the Imperial forces. Her wreckage burnt for hours as her two sister craft *Terra's Contempt* and *Hatred of Iron* trundled forward, guns blazing until the barrels glowed red.

Shells screamed overhead and the lightning of Navy lance shots strobed the night. The traitors worked furiously, desperate for another kill. The void shields of *Terra's Contempt* and *Hatred of Iron* held – just.

As they reached the lower circuits of Tor Tartarus, assault teams gripped their weapons and prepared themselves for the furious attack. The great tracks ground on as the Leviathans pushed out across the last hundred yards.

At last they were in position, staring up at the rising walled circuits of the fortress.

Tor Tartarus had not escaped unscathed. The massive ferrocrete walls and bastions were pitted and scarred. The sober statues that had adorned its walls were fractured and broken, and in places the cliffs had given way and great landslides had carried away whole swathes of defences.

But despite the damage, it was clear the fortress and its void shields were intact. Its kill-zones and death-traps lay ready for the inevitable assault.

Bendikt stood to watch the Leviathans make their way towards Traitor Rock. His face betrayed no emotion at the fiery death of *Hammer of Spite,* but the command staff felt the tension rise. Prassan relayed vox-reports from the remaining Leviathans. The tension ratcheted slowly up, until at last the Leviathans were in place.

'Ready, sir?' Prassan queried.

Bendikt gave the command.

At his words the boarding ramps at the front of each Leviathan slammed down like drawbridges, explosive barbs burying themselves into the rockcrete skirt of Tor Tartarus. A hailstorm of assault grenades drove any defenders back. Then whistles were blown and the first Imperial troops roared their war cries and charged.

Bendikt had given the Honour of Immolation, the glory of making up the first wave, to the penal camp who had worked hardest. The position was given to the ten thousand men and women of the Seventh Kallic Penitentiary.

Their war cry was St Burri's Psalm of the Condemned.

Forgive us, oh Emperor,
We who go into the pit.
Beyond hope of redemption.
The slain in the grave
Cut off from your hand.
Grant us redemption.

Their charge was an act of suicide. None of them got to the end of their prayer. The Seventh Kallic Penitentiary were cut apart by a blinding salvo of las and hard round fire. A reeking mist of blood and viscera rose into the air, and from the eviscerated bodies sheets of blood slewed from the sides of the boarding ramps like waterfalls in the mountains, and stained the sea beneath red.

Next came the 17th Crone Penal Guard, then the 104th Scarus Sinners, both regiments charging forward as soon as they could be brought to the top of the boarding ramps.

Tens of thousands of penal legionnaires were torn apart by the withering defensive fire. The slaughter was shocking, even to members of the Commissariat who witnessed the bloodshed.

Priests and commissars drove the troops forward with a terrible mix of terror, encouragement, exhortation and example. Bodies fell so thick that they made hills of the dead such that the warriors following used them as sandbag barricades. Bit by bit the walls of dead crept forward like the high-water mark of a murderous tide.

After an hour, the wall of bodies had reached the end of the boarding ramps. At this moment ogryn shock troops were unleashed. Each carried a triple-barrelled ripper gun and an ablative shield. Marching behind the wall of iron, they held on under the torrent of close-quarters fire.

The metal began to smoke. The ogryns clung on until their shields glowed red. As their hands burned, the dumb brutes threw the shields down in pain and they died by the hundred.

But they had done their job. They had acted as cover for the entrenching squads who fanned out with shovels and tube charges in the rubble skirts of Tor Tartarus, scraping out foxholes and establishing points of defence.

In the opening hours of the battle, Bendikt threw waves of chaff at the enemy.

All previous attempts by the Imperial Navy to bomb the island had been driven back by a rising crescendo of flak and hard rounds, but now at last, as the weight of ordnance drove the defenders into their bunkers, Bendikt gave the Navy the go-ahead.

Behind Tor Tartarus the batteries of Margrat added supporting fire to defend the gatehouse. Puffs of white smoke speckled the air and tracer fire swung upwards in long bending lines. One of the lead Marauders – *Black Rose* – began to trail white smoke. It listed to the side like a sinking boat, and then the smoke turned black, and within the darkness they could make out the lick of flames. One after another, Marauders were blown out of the sky. Some disintegrated in the air, the shapes of crewmen spiralling out from the wreckage. Others caught fire and plunged down into the sea where they were shattered by the force of their impact.

Nose lascannon gunners pinpointed anti-aircraft emplacements. They managed to lessen the hailstorm of fire being directed towards them, but the amount of flak from Hydra platforms was blinding. The first flights dropped their payloads early. Water fountained up in lines before they banked up and away. But the following pilots pressed home right up to the lip of the escarpment. Their payloads exploded in the shallows and then up the cliff face in a necklace of explosions. As they banked away their rear gunners raked the bastions.

Flight after flight added their ordnance; the thousand-kilo colossus bombs seemed to fall in slow motion.

They hit the battlements of Tor Tartarus with a blast of low-spreading white smoke. Each hit the ground like a meteor flung with the gravitational force of a star. Whole segments of the bastion broke and plunged into the waters below. Glacier-sized landslides of rockcrete thundered down and set off tidal waves that lashed the rocky causeway or buried the attacking troops.

As the Marauders distracted the traitors, Bendikt had battalions of bombards brought inside the void shields of Tor Tartarus. The crews quickly dug into the rubble, and then they started to fire. The armour-smashing stubby barrels ripped into the massive defences. Huge cracks opened up while frag rounds kept the heads of the defenders down.

Hidden under the causeways were a series of parallel pipes through which troops could move forward to attack. Long files of weary penal legionnaires had waited in position, the pipes vibrating with the tumult of the battle raging above them. On the landward side of the causeway, marshalling halls were filled with regiments of desperate reinforcements. As the Leviathans' garrisons were exhausted, they were herded forward in a constant stream, shuffling through the pipes. The terrified troops were fed up into each Leviathan, commissars hustling them forward until they suddenly found themselves on the assault ramps in the face of the enemy.

The slow died almost instantly. The quick and the lucky managed to scramble into the trench system that was spreading out from the bridgehead. Where there was open ground they made trenches out of the dead – a stinking mass of bloated bodies, pools of gore and rotting guts. They were piled up in low walls of hollow eyes, tongues hanging out of slack mouths, lifeless hands clutching those who passed.

The traitors clung on tenaciously, but they had been driven back, trench by trench, until the Imperials were right at the bottom of the defences of Tor Tartarus. With bodies and with picks and shovels, Imperial forces established dug-outs and bridgeheads that went right up to the skirts of the bastion.

On the second morning, fresh assaults were launched. Some were driven with frenzon, others with religious zeal or a guilt that had been whipped into a hatred of all life, especially their own. They hurled themselves into furious cross-patterns of las-fire.

Bendikt was impassive as he reviewed the reports of death and slaughter. At the description of the barricades of bodies he nodded slowly. 'See, Mere! I told you so. Even after death, the penal legions serve a function. They keep the living alive.'

By noon on the third day the supply of reinforcements slowed, as the chief logistician's plans began to take the strain. The attacks had faltered and the defenders sallied out, driving the desperate penal legions back onto the guns of their overseers.

As evening on the fourth day fell, each side scrambled to reinforce their front-line trenches, and renewed flights of Colossus Marauder bombers pounded the upper defences with bunker-buster shells.

Bendikt did not like to waste words. He paced up and down over the map of the battlefield. All about Prassan the command staff were intent on their jobs, some marshalling counter-attacks, others directing artillery fire or liaising with troops on the ground, while Prassan was responsible for recording casualty figures.

'Please confirm that,' Prassan said as the number of fatalities was relayed to him.

The vox-officer for the first penal division was at the front. Prassan could hear the rumble of explosions in the background.

The numbers were apocalyptic. Even for a Cadian they seemed impossibly extreme. 'You are sure?' he said after a long pause.

'Yes, I'm damned sure,' the penal officer responded.

Prassan added the total to his list. The next vox-officer was another penal legionnaire. Every second word was an expletive. Prassan was sceptical until he saw pict-images flickering on the dataslates that showed piles of the dead, lined up like sand-bags across the boarding ramps, squads being mown down by withering defensive fire, torrents of blood filling the drainage channels along either side of the assault ramps.

He felt somehow responsible. His hands were covered with sweat and they stuck to the papers. He felt sick as each hour rolled past and he marked lists of regiments as effectively destroyed.

He stopped questioning the figures.

One by one, each of the penal and guard divisions relayed their casualty lists. At last he compiled them all and took them to Mere.

'Sir.' Prassan's voice cracked as he handed the sheet to Adjutant Mere. 'The casualty figures you requested.'

Mere nodded without speaking and Prassan kept his concerns to himself.

As the fifth day wore on, the penal troops made progressively less and less ground. Fox holes were enlarged, joined together, dug deeper, until trench networks spread across the ridges and high points. Desperate fights erupted as trenching teams struggled to take the best land. In some places they were so close that the occupants could throw grenades into each other's trenches.

In the early hours of the sixth day the two sides had reached an impasse. Bendikt needed something to break the enemy's defence line. Mere presented him with a list of available troops.

Bendikt shook his head.

'Shall I send in the Cadians?'

'No,' Bendikt said. He paused, considering. 'Send my regards to Superior Melissya. Tell her that the Emperor has granted her wards their moment of redemption.'

The two hundred Sisters Repentia had spent their last night alive in the corner of the low-ceilinged 17th Assembly Chamber waiting for this moment. Superior Melissya was leading her charges in prayers when she received the news.

She let out a long breath and closed her eyes, taking a moment to give her thanks to the God-Emperor. Lifting her hands, she related the joyful news to her wards. 'The Emperor forgives the virtuous dead,' she announced. 'Our moment of redemption has arrived.'

There were shouts of approval and delight from the wards. Even those that wore gags to mark their oaths of silence let out low moans of release. They had lashed themselves, both mentally and physically, with the sins of their former lives. The only release from this torment would be their own deaths. Only then would their service to the Emperor be complete.

They were quickly led up into the lower levels of *Terra's Contempt*. The muzzled women knelt on one knee as Superior Melissya reminded them of their oaths and their sins. They moaned and cursed as she whipped them up into a fury of righteous anger.

They could smell the battlefield through the echoing corridors. They sang as they marched towards the battlefront, stained chainswords resting on their shoulders, flesh exposed to the cruelties of the enemy, their expressions of grim aggression covered for the moment.

Their attack was reinforced by a battalion of ogryn storm troops and storm squads of Mordian veterans armed with flamers.

As the sun broke the horizon on the sixth day, Bendikt gave the order for attack.

Superior Melissya made the sign of the aquila and, screaming her war cries, she charged.

The sudden switch of strategy, from smothering waves to elite troops, punched successive holes through the traitors' lines that were enlarged into gaping tears. Traitor troops already worn down by five days of fighting were unable to face the vicious ferocity of the Sisters. Rumour of ogryns spread terror through them, and fleeing traitors clogged the reserve trenches, the elite flamer squads massacring whole sections of trenches.

The Sisters carved their way forwards. The traitors poured reinforcements into the front lines but three complete trenches fell before the last of the Sisters Repentia breathed their last.

As that attack petered out, the 47th Rakallion Grenadiers were unleashed into the left flank of the enemy. The veteran troops were fresh and determined and forced a sudden breakthrough, taking the ruins of the first redoubt.

The rest of the day was a series of local raids as both sides attempted to consolidate their meagre gains. Twenty feet in one. A mere few in the next.

That evening, summary reports were compiled. Prassan double-checked the casualty figures. When he was done he took in a deep breath and marched smartly to where Bendikt stood, and held the paper out with a trembling hand. Mere took it and lifted his eyebrows, then handed it silently to Bendikt.

Bendikt handed the paper back to Mere. The adjutant appeared entirely unmoved, although he said, 'Less than we had expected.'

Bendikt paused. 'Send word to Major Luka. I think his White-shields were blooded. Let them know that I shall be there to personally watch their assault. We'll see how he has managed to put some Cadian soul into them.

'Oh, and send my congratulations to the surviving front-line troops. Let them know that due to their efforts it has taken us only six days to break the outer fortifications of Tor Tartarus.'

SIXTEEN

Major Luka's Whiteshields had been moving forward for days, a river of humanity with tributaries across the camp. Warders shouted and waved them onwards.

The assault pipes were broad enough for twenty to walk abreast. Sheaths of power cables and foil ducting ran in ropes along the ceiling of plain grey rockcrete. Along alternating sides of the tunnel, oval bulkhead lumens lit the chamber with a cold blue light. The Whiteshields marched quickly. There were tremors, and in places the ground shook violently.

At each intersection arrows pointed forward. Yedrin had only a rough idea of where he was, somewhere under the causeway. But with each step the roar of battle grew louder until they were so close to the front they could make out the shriek of individual explosions.

Their last night was spent asleep in a side chamber. It had been full that morning; there was evidence everywhere. As they arrived labour corps teams were sweeping up the piles of half-eaten ration packs, and the wax-paper wrappings, personal possessions and abandoned military gear were stacked where each regiment had been. They were being bagged up in giant nets to be loaded into cargo crates by teams of Sentinel lifters with flashing yellow lights.

The chamber now bare, the Whiteshields lay down to sleep. They were silent with the weight of expectation pressing down upon them. The breeze carried the stink of ash and death, and the lumen above Yedrin's head rattled with each rumble overhead. Each of them lay down knowing that by the time the next day fell, many of them would be dead.

I made it, Mother, Yedrin thought. *I will serve the Emperor as a Cadian Whiteshield.*

In the morning, Major Luka made a short speech. The Whiteshields gathered round in the half-grey light. Yedrin put his shoulders back as he listened to Major Luka's words.

'We, your instructors, shall accompany you on this, your last training exercise. One final task faces you all – the ultimate challenge that all Cadian Shock Troopers have fulfilled.

'For many of you this will be the end of your career. Your remains will be given the greatest honours the Imperium can bestow. Your bones will be gathered and interred within holy shrines with chantry chapels to pray for your soul until the end of times. However, those of you who survive this battle will be elevated to the finest body of warriors within the Astra Militarum.

'For those of you who pass this test, you will remove the white stripe from your helmet and you will be transferred to the Cadian Shock Troops.'

The Whiteshields marched for an hour. Someone started singing. It was a man's voice, low and strong. It was Major Luka singing *Flower of Cadia.*

Yedrin's skin goose pimpled. He had grown up listening to his mother singing that song. The words came back to him in an instant and he joined in. The song rippled out, back through the line. Soon it was ringing from a thousand voices in that mix of grim nostalgia and fierce determination.

It spoke of a world they had never been to. A world they would never visit. A planet lost in the warp. The fortified kasr, the hab-blocks, the monumental squares, bath houses, barracks-blocks, training camps, the smells and emotions of home. And the people. Mothers, brothers, fathers, sisters.

A long rockcrete gallery led to a wall of open lifts. Major Luka stood to supervise as the cadets of the 72nd Whiteshields loaded in their fifty-strong squads. They were quiet and pensive.

'For the Emperor!' Major Luka called out to them all. Some nodded, or forced a smile, or saluted.

Yedrin's emotions were getting the better of him. His teeth rattled and his fingers shook so hard he could barely hold his lasgun.

Zweden was next to him. His friend had come first in the most recent round of training and as a reward had been assigned the platoon's flamer. The thick strap was slung over one shoulder, the tank at the small of his back. 'Excited?' he said.

Yedrin nodded, but the truth was he was terrified. He forced a smile as they pressed up into the lifts. Each stood nose to jowl with the others. They started with a mechanical jolt, then set off upwards at a steady pace.

It was at least a minute up to the surface tunnels. The higher they went, the stronger the scent of promethium smoke and dust, the louder the thunder of artillery. By the time they reached the surface the noise was so loud they needed to shout to be heard.

'Light ahead!' someone yelled.

Light *was* glimmering, yet it was not the light of day but the blazing fires of an inferno.

'Keep down,' Luka called out, 'or you won't last long.'

Bendikt and his command staff stood on the cliffs facing Tor Tartarus, field-auspex lifted to their faces. Even here the stench of death was overwhelming.

'How good are these Whiteshields?' Bendikt asked Mere.

'They have been through a training regime close to what they would have had before the fall as we could achieve within the timescale.'

Bendikt nodded. A lot went unsaid. Cadians had always been the best, the product of planet, society and training. They would have to be Cadians without Cadia.

'Do you have a lho-stick?' Bendikt said.

'Yes, sir,' Mere said. He always kept an unopened packet in his breast pocket for rare moments like these. He tore the lid open, removed the aquila-printed foil, and slid a lho-stick out for Bendikt to take.

At the same time he took a lighter from his back pocket and held it up, cupping the flame in his hand. Bendikt drew the flame into the end of the stick, then stood and exhaled the long plume of blue-grey smoke out into the cool night air.

'A bad habit I picked up as a sergeant,' he said. Mere nodded. 'Well,' he said at last. 'We shall see how they perform today.'

There was a long pause. The vox-officer was checking his chronometer. Bendikt kept tapping the floor. Mere could tell he hated this waiting.

'Are they ready yet?'

Mere knew exactly who he was talking about. 'Yes, sir.' He paused. 'They're going to go over the top any moment...'

* * *

The Whiteshields filed out of the Leviathan straight into the trench network that had been scraped out of the rubble and rock. Sagging clapboard walls held the earth back. Troopers here were dusty and dirty. Everyone stood as if bracing for foul weather, their heads tucked in low.

Yedrin saw a hundred deaths before he reached the front lines. A signals officer crawling forward to fix a trench wire was blown apart by a shell. A medicae officer was hit by a sniper as he crouched over a dying man. A stray lump of shrapnel. A pair of Whiteshields picked off by marksmen. There was no time to help them. No one paid them any attention. They lay where they fell and bled out their last as their comrades followed orders, taking their place and waiting for the command to attack.

Yedrin felt cold as the deaths mounted up. It seemed that there were as many slain as there were living. In some places where the fighting had been fiercest, cadavers formed a carpet two or three bodies deep. The fallen slumped against the trench walls. They sprawled on the floor. They sat curled up in the foetal position. They were a constant warning.

Yedrin had to bend almost double in places as they picked their way to the front-line trenches. These were full of traitor dead – a poorly turned out lot with patchwork uniforms and ill-fitting boots, or no boots at all, just raw and bloody feet wrapped in thick clogs of sackcloth and leather.

Finally they were in place. Yedrin gripped his lasrifle. It was a beaten old object, already passed through dozens of hands. He pressed it to his heart as they were waved into position. It was a mark of all he had struggled through.

Major Luka was making his last rounds along the lines. 'General Bendikt is personally watching this attack!' he whispered to each.

He had drawn his sword. His pistol was clamped in his fist. His face was drawn.

When he reached Yedrin, Luka paused. All the Whiteshield eyes were turned towards him, waiting for his instruction.

As Major Luka's sword descended, whistles were blown and the Whiteshields surged forward.

Bendikt stood watching as smoke shells shrieked overhead. The trails of smoke were small at first, but soon the white clouds settled thick over the ground. And through it the first waves started to move.

The traitors clung to a precarious line of defence, scrabbling out of the ruins. The morning's objectives were to take the front trench line and then push onto the redoubts on either wing.

It was to be a three-pronged attack. The Rakallions were on the left, distinctive in their long trench coats. The Drookian Fenguard were on the right, small teams pushing forward before their tribal leaders.

But his concern was mainly in the middle, where Major Luka's Whiteshields were seeing combat for the first time.

Even from where they stood, Bendikt could hear the shrill blast of whistles. He lifted the auspex and watched as the attack began. The traitors' heavy weapons poured fire down into the Imperial lines.

Yedrin was third on his ladder. The first trooper breasted the top and was immediately shot dead. She tumbled back onto Yedrin and slumped to the trench floor.

He did not even look back. He felt no fear. Or perhaps he was so terrified he felt nothing else.

The next Whiteshield was hit as well. And then it was Yedrin's turn.

He scrambled up the ladder, and as he reached the top shouted, 'Cadia stands!' and threw himself forward. The tight confines of the trench suddenly fell away and he felt utterly exposed.

He was standing on an open rubble slope, with lines of wire and craters all around him. It was a world lit by fire and las-bolts. A world of silhouettes firing, falling, dying.

Yedrin ran forwards. He could see Major Luka away to his right, stumping resolutely forward with his augmetic leg, shouting out encouragement as the Whiteshields were mown down.

There were dead bodies everywhere. Yedrin flung himself down next to a dead ogryn. Its great, ugly face was turned towards him; it had been dead long enough that its eyes had already started to sink into the skull, its tongue beginning to blacken.

Yedrin's heart was hammering, but Major Luka was still walking forwards, head bent, as if marching into a storm.

'Forward!' he was shouting. 'Cadia stands!'

Yedrin was elated to still be alive. He saw other Whiteshields rushing forward. It was vital to maintain momentum. He took in a deep breath and pushed himself up.

'Cadia!' he shouted, to give himself courage.

Major Luka kept onwards up the rubble slope as hard rounds ricocheted about him. By the time he reached the enemy trenches his laspistol was already hot in his hand.

It was a hasty construction, crudely dug out of the rubble. The footing was uneven, and it zig-zagged around great blocks of rockcrete that had been too large to move.

Traitors roared towards him, and there was a vicious struggle as he held his place. Within moments his chainsword was splattered with gore. To either side Whiteshields were locked in furious hand to hand battle with the enemy, widening the breach.

Major Luka's voice was hoarse as he stumped along the trench. They were sweeping the enemy back. He paused at an intersection. A wounded traitor was sitting propped up against the trench wall. 'For the Emperor!' the traitor hissed.

Luka shot him in the face. 'For the Emperor,' he muttered.

A shell landed nearby. Luka ducked instinctively as shrapnel ricocheted off the rocks above his head. Rockcrete dust filtered down as he lobbed a grenade into the opening of a field latrine.

He risked a quick look over the top. The next trench was about fifty feet higher up the incline. The no-man's-land between was a scree slope.

He stumped back to the communication trench, as Whiteshields swarmed past their fallen cohorts. Each corpse had been killed by a wound to the front. He was proud of them. It was just how a Cadian should die.

SEVENTEEN

By lunchtime the Whiteshields had cleared the first two lines of enemy trenches. As soon as they had done so, they worked their way sideways along the line, taking out each heavy weapon emplacement one by one, dug-out by dug-out, until the Drookians on the right could finally move up and secure their objectives.

By this time the Rakallion troops had also taken the second trench line, and they held the line against repeated counter-attacks. The fighting did not die down even as night fell.

The Whiteshields crawled through no-man's-land, bypassing the front trenches and working their way deep into the enemy's rear where they mounted daring attacks, panicking the traitor troops.

Later that night, the traitors launched a series of counter-attacks. They rose up without warning and came on down the slope with a terrible speed.

'Fix bayonets,' Major Luka was shouting along the line. 'Ready for the counter-attack. Make sure you know who is standing next to you, and who is manning the heavy weapons. If you only have your rifle your job is to aim and fire faster than the trooper standing next to you. Grenades ready! And once they're in range give them hell!'

Yedrin and Zweden fought together, Yedrin taking out any threats with his lasrifle as Zweden hosed the main body down. The traitors stumbled forward, clothes and hair on fire, some of them shouting curses as they fell on their faces and kept burning long after they were dead.

The two young troopers fought until their promethium canister ran dry. Yedrin found a fresh one in the trench and again the pilot light was hissing gently. All he had to do was let them get into range.

Zweden was almost ecstatic to still be alive. 'We've got to live through this!' he kept telling Yedrin. 'We've got to survive.'

Yedrin nodded. To be honest, he'd never really thought he'd ever get this far. He'd heard stories from his mother and her comrades of troopers running out of powercells, so he'd scavenged more than he could carry. Even now he had a handful of them lying on a rough rock ledge just before him at hand height. A belt of frag grenades lay beside them.

Throne! If he was going to go down then he was going to go in style.

Major Luka was standing in the trench behind them. Counter bombardments were starting to rain down on the ground about the trench. Stone and shrapnel were hissing in the air above their heads. Yedrin already could tell the difference between a bombard and an Earthshaker shell. The dangerous ones were the mortar shells that went too slowly to be heard. But they were a hit or miss thing. Either they landed outside the trench or inside. And if they landed inside, it didn't matter whether you heard them or not. There was no way you were going to survive.

The trooper on the other side of him was a small girl named Blanchez. She was a tough little camp brat. An orphan, as far as she knew, and a survivor. She'd taken three of Yedrin's power-cells and swapped her lasrifle for a long-las that she'd found abandoned in the trench, a sniper's weapon with long barrel and heavy stock. It looked taller than her. But she'd already racked up an impressive kill-rate.

She was treating this like a game.

'Gotcha!' she hissed as she ducked back down, flipped the spent powercell out and took another from Yedrin's pile. 'Come on, you bastard. Gotcha!'

Yedrin's mouth was dry. He took a quick sip from his water bottle, unscrewing the lid one-handed so he could keep the other on his rifle. He just wanted to be the best. And he wanted to do everything right.

'Here they come!' Major Luka shouted.

The Whiteshields put up a furious fusillade. Major Luka laughed. 'They think they're facing mere cadets. They have no idea who they're up against. Shoot them down! Aim, fire, reload!'

The world went silent. If the enemy artillery were still firing then Yedrin was oblivious. His cheek was pressed against the butt of his rifle. All he could hear was the hiss of his las-bolts and his own slow breaths. He could smell the overheated rifle barrels. Then he could hear curses and laughter from Zweden and Blanchez, Major Luka's metal foot scraping on the rocky trench floor.

His cheek bone throbbed. His trigger finger ached. Each time he pulled the trigger the dull pain grew a little worse.

Major Luka's voice was hoarse by the time the last traitor assault petered out. Yedrin's shoulders and back were stiff. He rolled his shoulders to loosen them.

The day was almost upon them. Voices were shouting for more ammunition or powercells, or a medi-kit.

'Well done! Get some water. Get some food,' Major Luka was telling them all. 'They'll be back again soon enough.'

Yedrin looked to his side. Zweden wasn't moving. He put his hand out. 'Ready?' he said, but his friend fell sideways and slid down the edge of the trench. Zweden had been shot in the face – a burnt hole where his left eye should have been, blood streaming from his mouth and nose.

Blanchez pulled Yedrin away. 'He's gone,' she was telling him, over and over.

He couldn't believe it. It was Zweden who had said they had to stay alive during this, and there he was lying dead.

'He's gone!' Blanchez told him, again. There was dirt smeared across her face. It was ash, he realised, and he saw that the butt of her gun had singed about the barrel. She was surprisingly strong. 'He's dead. Let him be. He's at rest now. It's the living you've got to worry about. Which means you. And me.'

Two more attacks came in the following hours.

Major Luka seemed to be everywhere. He had a cut on his cheek from the second attack, but his ragged features were refreshingly unchanged.

Star-shells spiralled slowly down, and Yedrin had to close his eyes as he fired to stop the glare from his own las-bolt temporarily blinding him. Zweden's body was stacked against the back wall with the other dead. There was no time to do anything else with them.

All this time, runners were coming forward with water and ammunition. They came in gangs of three or four, each there to take the load if the first was shot down.

As the morning wore on a company of Rakallion Chasseurs joined them. Their officer was a tall and lean-faced warrior, who somehow managed to scramble through no-man's-land and the tortuous twist of the trenches and still look impeccable.

'Major!' he said, saluting Luka. 'Your cadets have done well, but I have been commanded to strengthen your position.'

'We don't need strengthening,' Luka told him. The other man started to speak but Luka cut him off. 'And these are not cadets. These,' he said, gesturing along the line, 'are Cadian Shock Troopers.'

Yedrin was so exhausted he started laughing. He was too tired to savour that moment, but he did allow himself a second to close his eyes and send a prayer of thanks to the God-Emperor of Mankind for allowing this honour.

The 72nd Whiteshields were in the front lines for three more days before being relieved by a company of Crinan asteroid miners. Their distinctive yellow void-suits and enamelled blue void armour were grey with dust.

'The faithful man never dies,' their priest chanted as they made their way into Yedrin's trench. 'The faithful heart is a shield against heresy. The faithful mind is armour against the lies of our foes!'

The priest was a bulky man with a black eyepatch and a wild grey beard. His robes were splattered with blood and mud. Over his shoulder he carried an eviscerator chainsword, as long as he was tall. He wore holy pennants on his void-suit armour. He glared at the Whiteshields as if he saw a lack of faith or conviction in their souls. As Yedrin passed he put out a hand.

He had a thick accent that Yedrin took a moment to catch. 'Did you kill traitors?'

'I did,' Yedrin said.

'How many?'

'I lost count,' Yedrin said. 'A hundred. Maybe more.'

The priest nodded. 'Good,' he said at last. 'I shall kill more to prove my faith in the Golden Throne. And while you kill with the gun, I shall kill with this…' He patted the double-handed hilt of his heavy chainsword. 'That is my oath of battle.'

Yedrin nodded. 'The Emperor Protects!' he said.

The priest smiled slowly. A chilling look. 'So he does.'

It took half a day for the Whiteshields to return to the access tunnels that led down into the assault pipes. The tunnels were now lined with field medicae facilities, rows of wounded warriors lying on the floor, and teams of penal legionnaires assisting the medicae staff with plasma and cleaning wounds. A preacher was moving along the line saying prayers for the dying. The dead were being piled up for disposal.

Moans echoed down the tunnels towards them. It was like listening to a wounded grox: inhuman sounds of pain and incomprehension. As they stumbled forward they saw the cause, a wounded ogryn being held down by a team of medicae and penal legionnaires.

Half the ogryn's face was missing and he was thrashing about like a giant child. He had already killed one of the medics. The others were struggling to restrain him.

Major Luka stumped forward. 'Back!' he shouted as he drew his pistol. 'Stand back!'

The major put his pistol to the ogryn's temple and said, 'Your service is done!'

It took three shots before the beast let out a long sigh, his massive torso sliding gently onto the ground.

'Thank the Throne!' Blanchez hissed.

And they passed on, utterly weary.

At last the surviving Whiteshields found an empty space along the side of the tunnel.

'Rest,' Major Luka croaked. His voice did not carry very far, but it was enough. There were only a few hundred left. Yedrin found a patch of wall to lean against.

He had no strength left in him, and slid down until he was in a seated position.

He was asleep before he hit the floor.

EIGHTEEN

In the following days the attack on Tor Tartarus ground on with catastrophic loss of life. Imperial troops had taken the lower levels. Fighting was going on within the fortress as well as on the outside, through tunnels and guard chambers and access shafts. It was murderous battle fought at close quarters, with blade as much as shot.

The traitors were forced to block all access points. They mined some and drove tanks into others, Leman Russes plugging the larger corridors and filling the confined corridors with furious fire.

At the base of the fortress, like a high-water mark, the dead now lay in mountains and yet still both sides were forced to pour increasing numbers of troops into the quagmire.

At the General's Palace, Imperial commanders grew increasingly unhappy with the tactics of General Bendikt. After one planning meeting, von Horne stayed behind. He was a blunt man even for a Mordian and he was not a man to beat about the bush.

'Sir. With due respect. Is this progress? The rate of attrition...!'

'Less than anticipated,' Bendikt said.

'But how much longer can this go on for? Will Tor Tartarus fall?'

Bendikt put the chart down and let out a long sigh. 'General. I am not trying to take Tor Tartarus.'

Von Horne paused. He did not understand. 'No?'

Bendikt stepped forward and brought him to the maps pinned to the wall. 'No. The attacks on Tor Tartarus are a trap. I offer Holzhauer no choice. Either we take the gatehouse or he has to commit more troops. And yet more troops. As he does, we bleed him dry.'

'But we must be losing twice as many as he,' von Horne started.

Bendikt almost smiled. 'Yes. But it is not an equal swap. The majority of our losses are penal legionnaires while Holzhauer is forced to spend the lives of his troops. Even if we lost three to each of his, it is a trade that he is losing. We have many more lives to spare than Holzhauer.'

'But will this bring about the fall of Crannog Mons before the Feast of Sanguinalia?'

Bendikt shook his head. 'Alone, no. But while Holzhauer struggles to hold us back at Tor Tartarus, my attack there is just a feint to lure him into a deadly barter.'

Bendikt pulled a sheet from his charts and pointed to the other end of Crannog Mons, to the volcanic cone of Tor Kharybdis. 'My real intent is to strike the rear. Tor Kharybdis is currently held by reserve troops. The Hundred-and-First have been training since their arrival on the island. They will launch an amphibious assault and then Holzhauer will have to defend himself on two fronts!'

PART TWO

ONE

The last time the Cadian 101st had undertaken an amphibious assault was eighty years before. That had been a limited water landing on the flooded world of Thuja, part of a combined air assault that had been launched in conjunction with the Elysian 74th. But that had been on nothing like this scale.

No, to find the last time the whole regiment had been committed to a water attack the savants had to go back five hundred years to the Ettan Crusade, when they were involved in the largest battles on the swamp world of Tuqiri. Unfortunately, that attempt had been a disaster.

The Chimeras' engines had become clogged in the fine mud, and once stuck they had been sitting ducks for the enemy forces. Regimental tomes of fine vellum reported it all in neat, painful detail. The Cadians had been trapped. Squads that tried to dismount and attack were either sucked down into the mud or unable to move.

The archives reported that it had taken twenty years for them to return the regiment to full strength. A century to wipe away the shame.

Colonel Baytov had the salient points distributed to each company for further dissemination. Each of them felt the shame of that ancient defeat.

'Shame never killed a man,' Colonel Baytov declared. 'It will serve as a goad. I want us to outdo our forefathers in this at least.'

The truth was that the conditions, and dangers, for this landing were very different to those on Tuqiri. Here the Cadians would be crossing a wider and more treacherous body of water, and once landed it would be hard for the Cadians to be resupplied.

That meant they could not afford to be bogged down. This would be an attack that would rely on the Cadians' famous esprit de corps. They would have to take the island within a matter of days, or risk being exposed on the beaches and headlands, and so massacred.

The difficulty of the task did not intimidate the Cadians. It excited them, and drew on their martial spirit. Ever since they had landed, the Cadians had been preparing relentlessly for this.

Throughout the planning process, Colonel Baytov and his senior aides studied all the material that Bendikt's office had supplied to them. Command staff rehearsed every possible setback and misfortune. Picts were analysed. Scenarios planned. Possibilities assessed. Factuals and counterfactuals were run through calculators.

There were seven suitable moments when the tides were low and when climatic conditions were within the acceptable range of danger. Bendikt picked the first and issued the necessary orders, and within minutes the well-oiled wheels began to turn.

* * *

Sparker wanted to brief his subordinates. He stood before charts of Crannog Mons, a sheath of papers folded in his fist. He spoke in a tired sounding monotone as his orderly, Evrind, stood at his side, ready to clear up any queries. She was a vicious little fighter, and had been the regimental champion in unarmed combat in her youth. She had the broken nose to prove it.

'First major casualty!' he said, pointing out the ruins of *Hammer of Spite*. 'Void shields failed in the opening attacks. The other two Leviathans are immobilised, but their void generators are still functioning and they are in position. This is Tor Tartarus,' Sparker said, pointing to its position on the chart. 'The former gatehouse. There used to be a bridge connecting the island to the mainland, but it was demolished in the early days of the war. The upper storeys are now host to a withering amount of ordnance. They're making it hell down there, in the trenches. Whiteshields went in the opening days.'

Dido called out the question everyone was thinking. 'How did they perform, sir?'

Sparker checked with Evrind. She spoke quietly and he turned to answer them all. 'Heavy casualties,' Sparker reported. 'As expected. But they reached all their first-day objectives by lunchtime. They were in the front line for a number of days. I think high command are pleased.'

'Will they be joining us?'

Sparker consulted Evrind again. She didn't appear to know.

'The Hundred-and-First has been tasked with taking Tor Kharybdis.' He flipped the chart over to display a map of the island. It was a low cone of black volcanic rock, topped by a hexagonal fortress. 'Nicknamed the Lone Redoubt,' Sparker noted. 'Standard STC template.' He traced out the six long ridges that tumbled down from the peak. The end of each was fortified with massive rockcrete redoubts, their heavy guns overlooking the black-sand beaches. 'Again, they're all STC design. First Company will be landing on the three narrow beaches of Faith, Marius and Josmane. Between Fourth and Fifth Redoubts is the long straight stretch of Tyrok Beach. That is where the majority of Cadians will be landing.'

He tapped the map with his wooden pointer. 'We're here. Tyrok Beach.'

Evrind distributed maps of the beach. Minka stared intently at hers. It was a wide and shallow bowl with headlands rising up at either end, defended by standard rockcrete pillboxes with void shield generators.

Dido nodded and took the plans to her sergeants. They were expected to memorise these, to know the main access tunnels, the genatoriums, the water supplies. Everything.

'Our attack relies on swift and intelligent decisions by you all. I expect everyone to know this off by heart,' she told them.

Secrecy was of primary importance. Intelligence reported that Tor Kharybdis was currently held by second-rate regiments. Any hint of an impending attack could mean the defences were drastically upgraded.

Finally, Dido went over the particulars of this engagement. There were ten seconds to get out of a tank if it floundered. Commissars would consider it cowardice if any stopped or retreated during the landings.

Next morning General Bendikt arrived in an unmarked Valkyrie for a personal visit. He had been the 101st's commander for so long he knew most of the troopers by sight and name and he strode along with a measured gait, shaking hands and trading words with every veteran he knew.

'Like the new arm, sir!' some called out and Bendikt lifted his clenched fist in a silent salute. The Cadians mirrored the gesture.

'For Cadia!' they shouted.

Each time Bendikt paused he was surrounded. At last he went into a meeting with Colonel Baytov and when he came out two-thirds of the regiment were waiting for a glimpse of him.

He stood before them and lifted his hand in salute again. They did not want to let him go, but at last Baytov came out and issued an order for them to stand aside. The Cadians did so reluctantly. Bendikt passed along the line, still shaking hands. He was loath to leave them, and he stood in the doorway of his Valkyrie for a long moment before his flier lifted up from the ground and turned for the General's Palace.

After he had left, the Cadians were all shown a short vid-pict. There was no music at first, just an image of a Warlord Titan striding across Tyrok Fields, silhouetted against the lurid glare of the Eye of Terror. Cleansing the sky from the horizon up was the yellow stain of dawn. The dawn grew brighter, and then *Flower of Cadia* started to play. Soft at first, but growing in volume until it was a rousing chorus.

Throughout this were images of Cadia that they all knew. The high walls of Kasr Tyrok as a Valkyrie flew over it, the zig-zag patterns of the streets beneath. The high mountains that ringed the great landing fields. Bleak highlands in snow, and aurox grazing beneath a pylon that, as the pict-imager panned backwards, rose needle-thin into the air.

Frame by frame their home world of Cadia was alive to them again. There was not a dry eye within the whole regiment, and at the end the last notes of *Flower of Cadia* faded, and the screen went to void-black.

Afternoon was spent running through various planned scenarios. Then long hours of waiting and sleeping or playing cards.

At one point Minka noticed Dido putting her hand to her ear.

'Are you all right?' she asked.

Dido forced a smile. 'I wish it would just start. I hate the waiting more than anything.'

TWO

Early on the morning of the upcoming attack, Chief Commissar Shand stood in the half-light with three of his commissars, their black leather greatcoats flapping about their legs.

Shand kept his hands behind his back. His face was shaved, angular and hard.

'They're coming,' Commissar Knoll noted as a file of transports turned off the main thoroughfare towards the Cadian camp. It stopped at each checkpoint, and then moved into the camp proper.

Six cargo-8s pulled into the camp and turned towards the centre of the base, where Shand and the others stood. As they came to a halt the back flaps clattered down.

'Shall we?' Commissar Shand said as he led them forward.

Shand had read Major Luka's after-battle reports. The major claimed that these new recruits were the match of any other unit of Cadians. Shand was wary of Luka's enthusiasm. He had met the major a number of times at official occasions, and the old man seemed to love his students a little too dearly.

Major Luka stumped forward. 'I confer three hundred and thirty-six Cadian Shock Troopers to your care, chief commissar. I can confirm that they have all seen battle and killed in the Emperor's Name.'

Shand stiffened. 'Thank you,' he said as he returned the salute.

He stood before the recruits. The youth of the Whiteshields struck him first, although whether this was because there had been no new recruits from Cadia for five years, or whether he was just getting old, he could not tell.

The second thing he noticed was that these troopers had the haunted look of those who had just been in a ferocious battle. There were bandaged heads, arms in slings, a couple with crutches and stumps where a foot had been, awaiting the next round of crude military augmentation.

There was something else. He couldn't put his finger on it.

'Their eyes!' Knoll whispered.

That was it! None of them had the distinctive violet eyes that were a token of life under the Eye of Terror. They had not been lifted up to stare into hell, and spit in the Archenemy's face.

Shand beckoned Commissar Knoll forward. He unfurled the banner in his hand. 'This is the regimental standard of the 101st,' Shand declared. 'It bears the emblem of the Cadian Gate, and the honour names of the great battles that this regiment has fought in the name of the Emperor. Learn those names. Commit them to memory! Let their deaths be an example to you all. Hold yourself to their standards. Try to make your deaths as glorious as theirs!'

As he spoke, Commissar Knoll lifted the banner. The pole was of a hard, dark wood, and at the top was the golden laurelled skull signifying the God-Emperor. He unfurled the banner. Its image was hidden in the darkness, but they could see the glint of golden thread.

This was a sacred object before which, for centuries, all new recruits to the 101st had sworn their allegiance to Cadia and the God-Emperor. But there was a newer addition, hammered just under the skull that topped the pole.

It was an icon that showed the face of the great hero of Cadia, Lord Castellan Ursarkar E Creed. His face stared out, as if assessing the new recruits.

'Repeat after me,' Shand declared.

As the words were read out, the Whiteshields repeated them word for word, and saluted.

Shand nodded. 'Welcome. You have now joined the Cadian Shock Troopers – the finest body of fighting men the Imperium has at its command!

'Today you will be sent into battle once more. It has been decided that you will fight as a body. My Commissariat staff shall accompany you into combat. Any of you who survive will be assigned to units if your performance is deemed suitable.' Shand paused to wet his lips. 'I should add that many Cadians, myself included, do not believe you should be allowed to wear the Cadian badge. There are many others who are wishing for this programme to fail. Which means that you will have to prove your worth. You will have to be above and beyond reproach.'

They greeted his words with stony silence.

Shand turned to the toughest disciplinarian he had. 'Knoll, when we go into combat, I want you to accompany this lot.'

Knoll's eyes were already narrowed. He had a hard face. He nodded – a brief, simple movement, like the chop of an executioner's axe.

'It will be a pleasure, sir.'

* * *

As dawn broke, an Imperial Navy battleship started to fire on Crannog Mons. A few shots hit the void shields. The energy crackled out across the void-domes. But most of the shots veered wide. Where the lance strikes hit the sea, plumes of super-heated water erupted. This went on for hours, until the air became thick and soupy with humidity, and then, at last, the battered naval ships pulled back to a safe orbit.

Dreno had been watching the whole thing. 'Well, that was a waste of time and effort,' he said. 'What is wrong with them? They couldn't hit the side of a kasr. Lieutenant! They're not supporting our attack, are they?'

Dido pulled a face. She had no control over this but she appeared confident. 'Not a chance.'

An hour later, the whole regiment moved off.

Minka spent some time in the Chimera's cupola. In the distance a bombardment was hammering Tor Tartarus. She lifted the auspex to see one of the shots hit a section of roadway that clung to the old bridge. Section by section the surviving rockcrete slabs fell away. The column remained standing. Minka could just make out the old suspension cables, dark against the sky. Above she could see the diamond pattern of a high-altitude squad on morning patrol.

That battle was far away. Hers would be on the island of Tor Kharybdis. She found it through the auspex. The outline of the island's defences was just visible on the horizon. It appeared quiet and unsuspecting.

Not long now, she thought.

The wiring had been coming loose on the secondary battery pack. Allun had soldered it; Minka flipped the spray covers to make sure the solders had held. She flicked the switch and it lit up with a low but solid green light. She shut it down again, pushed herself up into the cupola and sat on the lip, turned fully round so she could see behind them.

This was the worst part of battle. The waiting to go in. She had all the worries of a sergeant about to go into combat – concern that she would let the Cadians down, let herself, her planet, the legacy of the whole Cadian Shock Troop down.

Minka puffed out her cheeks and let the tension out. Whenever she was assailed by worries she went back to basics. She was Cadian. She had been prepared for battle since the moment she was born. Whatever she faced, it could be killed with las-bolt or blade. Whatever happened, she would be ready. And if her time was up, she would go to meet the Emperor with her head held high.

Minka looked about. She loved the sight of the regiment on the move. For a moment the view reminded her of being a girl, when the Whiteshields returned from the Myrak Hills after their winter training. They had processed in long columns of Chimeras, each squad sitting on the turrets, eager to be home. It was a view as symbolic as the turning of the year.

She sat there for nearly half an hour. It was good to feel the breeze on her face. At last she slid back inside but left the hatch open for air.

Her squad had checked and double-checked their kit.

'Any news?' Jaromir said.

Minka shook her head. 'None.'

He nodded, and yawned. At last he put his head forward and rested it on his knees.

She slid into place next to him. They rattled about in the back of the Chimera. Dreno had already stretched out his feet and closed his eyes. Maenard was checking through his detonator pack. Wires. Explosives. Detonators. Melta pack.

They kept heading south. Cool damp air drifted in through

the vision slits and the open hatch above. There was the distinct ozone smell of the sea and rotting seaweed. The rhythm and drone lulled the others to sleep.

Only Karni and Minka were still awake. Neither of them spoke. Karni had a far-away look in her eye.

At last, they reached a wide pebbly bay. Flat-bottomed war-arcs were beached all along the shore. The file was being quickly loaded. Their metallic shapes were dark against the dull beaten glimmer of the sea. Squat gun rigs stood out further to sea, silhouetted against the pale sky, guarding the entrance to the harbour.

Breve swung the Chimera round and waited to load. Karni caught her sergeant's eye. 'So this is it?' Karni said as they mounted the ramp of the landing craft and came to a halt.

Minka nodded. This was it.

THREE

It took a few minutes until Breve had the Chimera in the right place. The loading crews were intent that each vehicle was loaded precisely, and Breve had cursed a number of times before the officials were happy. 'We don't want the ship capsizing!' the crewman called up, as if in apology.

Breve was still cursing, but Minka put her hand to her helmet. She agreed with that.

One by one, each Chimera was loaded and stowed. When the vehicles were all aboard, the ship's smoke-stack let out a great gritty cloud and shunted off from the beach, the water churning white as its blunt snout slammed into the waves.

Medic Banting was going in with them. His Chimera had red turret markings and the back was open. Inside, Minka could see everything needed for a field hospital. Banting was in full officious mode as he had the medics check off the barrels of blood plasma, boxes of stimms, metal tins of field dressings and hanging plastek sheaths of field tourniquets.

He was furious with anyone stupid enough to go near him. He'd seen the bloodbath at Tor Tartarus. 'I don't know why Bendikt has agreed to this. It's going to be a massacre,' he snapped to Minka. 'They should be sending penal troops in!'

Minka was calm. 'They want the job done properly.'

'It'll be a disaster. They're not making any more of you, you know.'

'Apparently they are,' Minka said. 'Haven't you seen them?'

Banting grunted something in reply. Minka didn't bother answering.

Dido's command squad were dismounting. They had a new Chimera, a reserve tank with freshly painted squad and company markings.

'How is she?' Banting asked.

Minka guessed he meant Dido. 'Fine,' she said.

'Good.'

Minka paused. There was something in the way that he had spoken. 'Is there something I should know?'

Banting brushed past her. 'Lesk. You're one of Dido's sergeants. If there is anything wrong I'm sure you'd be the first to know.'

The first two waves were a mix of landing craft and Pegasus Amphibious Assault Vehicles. The Pegasus were lighter variants that forewent the front guns in favour of assault ramps and flotation tanks. They would be leading the first wave into the tight coves of Faith Beach and then Creed Beach. Seventh Company were going in to Tyrok Beach. Their attack there would be in the third wave. Each had their own specific objectives.

Minka readied herself. Her pack was almost as big as she was, and the Chimera was loaded with sheaths of razor wire, entrenching tools and materiel to supply the squad for weeks.

Breve was looking pale and his forehead was clammy. He hated boats. He pursed his lips as he patted the tank.

'Think she'll make it?' Minka asked.

'Well. She's never let us down before, has she?'

Minka laughed. She could think of a number of times when the Chimera had not been there for them. But there didn't seem any point in bringing it all up again. 'No,' she said. 'Never. The Emperor Protects.'

Breve wiped his upper lip. He looked green. 'So he does.'

Minka stood in the turret hatch as they pulled away from the shore. She was not someone who could sit still. She paced up and down the decks. They were flat and featureless, except for the bridge tower, a low, squat turret two-thirds of the way along the craft, with heavy plates of riveted armour on the front facing and a pair of light gun turrets at its waist. The autocannons were loosely covered against sea-spray. Compared to the defences they were going up against, these armaments were paltry.

The first trails of sea-mist were starting to form as they pulled out into the bay. By the time they were past the headland and had turned north-west, the mist was a thick fog. It obscured almost everything, except the white wakes that widened behind them.

Within an hour Crannog Mons was an island in a sea of mist.

'Ha, Dreno!' Baine called out. 'I think the Navy did that on purpose!'

Dreno was with Minka, running over plans of Tyrok Beach and the targets in order of priority. He looked up and laughed. 'You give them too much credit.'

When Minka had briefed all her squad she walked out onto the deck. The mist hung like a pale ghostly wall over the black water, the waves beneath choppy with flecks of foaming grey. She wiped the splashes from her cheeks. They smelt vaguely sulphurous. She couldn't tell if it was the water or the bombardment.

Now the mist was so thick it was condensing on everything. The inner compartments of the Chimeras were filmed with gleaming beads, like cold sweat. Soon they began to drip from the roofs. Dreno cursed as a drop went down his neck.

As they came around the headland of Tor Kharybdis the sea turned wild and a whipping gale shredded the fog. Through it they caught glimpses of the island, before the curtains rolled over them again.

The enforced waiting left them cold and wet. But they had suffered worse as children. The only safety lay in crushing the enemy.

At one point they were thrown about so violently they feared that they would be washed overboard. Minka bounced along the guide wires as the landing ship pitched and rolled. She clambered up the hand rails to the side, half-drenched as water rushed over the deck. She was sure they would be lost, when to her astonishment their craft tipped and righted itself again.

She struggled back to her Chimera. Spray was pouring off *The Saint*'s sides. Breve climbed up to clamp the hatches shut. He looked drenched too. 'Holy Throne!' he spat.

'All good?' she called.

'I hope so,' he said.

Wulfe was already checking that none of the systems had suffered water damage. The front gunner, Bergen, started to line up his rolls of heavy bolter shells. The multi-laser whirred with anticipation.

'They're good!' he said.

For the next hour the sea tormented them all. 'How long is this going to take?' Breve asked, wiping vomit from his chin.

'Two more hours,' Minka said.

'Throne!'

* * *

Evening was coming on when the bombardment began hitting Tor Kharybdis. Above it the void shields crackled with a fluorescent blue light in the gathering shade.

'It's void shielded?' Jaromir said.

'Of course it's void shielded,' Dreno told him.

Jaromir looked concerned. 'They're going to destroy that, right?'

Dreno gave him a withering look. 'That's the plan.'

There was a long pause. No one really shared Dreno's confidence. Minka certainly didn't. She expected the void shields to be in full working order when they landed, and the defences essentially untouched.

Jaromir thought slowly. His expression revealed his confusion. You could almost see the question forming on his face before he asked it. 'If they don't…?'

'Then you'll lose the rest of your brain,' Dreno said, and turned to the others, who looked at him disapprovingly. 'I just can't stand his stupid questions.'

'Let it rest,' Minka told him. She put a hand to Jaromir's arm and the big man turned and locked eyes with her. 'Whatever happens,' she told him, 'the Emperor Protects.'

Jaromir nodded very slowly. 'The Emperor Protects,' he repeated.

'Unless He doesn't,' someone said.

It was Baine. He was grinning. Minka gave him a withering look, but Baine held up his hands and imitated Father Keremm's sermonising manner. 'The Emperor protects *the virtuous*.' He sat back. 'I'm not virtuous. Nor is Dreno or Belus. No! Don't pity us. We're used to looking after ourselves.'

* * *

After some time spent out on deck, Minka went back to *The Saint.* She clambered inside. It was good to get out of the wet.

'Lesk! How are you?' a familiar voice said from outside the open ramp.

'Good, sir.'

Dido smiled as she clambered inside and sat down next to Minka. The two of them stared out of the open ramp towards the waves. 'It was hard,' Dido said after a while, 'seeing Cadia again.' There was a long pause. 'I was from Kasr Tyrok.'

Minka knew that, it was obvious from her accent. There was another long pause.

'What would you give to have Cadia back?' Dido asked.

A gust of sulphurous spray caught Minka in the eye. She wiped it away with the back of her hand. 'Everything,' she said, instinctively. She paused to consider the implications of this. 'I'd give up everything for Cadia. Throne, I'd give up all ten thousand of us just to have Creed back with us.'

Dido nodded. 'Me too. Tonight we have a chance to make sure the name of Cadia is never forgotten. Every time we go into battle we do that. Some of us will die. Some will keep on fighting. We'll all die somehow. Better to go out in style, don't you think?'

As darkness fell on the convoy, the rest of Minka's squad returned to the Chimera. Jaromir was rubbing at a stain in his left palm. Viktor had his eyes closed. Belus and Baine began a game of Black Five and had found an unscuffed corner to scratch the scores.

'Want to play?' Baine said to Minka.

Why not? Minka thought. 'Sure.'

Baine dealt her cards.

She looked at them without expression. It was a bad hand,

but that was exactly what she had wished for. She didn't want her good luck going to waste on a game of cards. Only Belus seemed happy. He had a pile of credits between his boots.

Belus was one of those troopers who couldn't stand silence. He kept talking. 'I hear the Whiteshields are coming in with us,' he said.

'Chief Commissar Shand has said that they're no longer Whiteshields,' Minka told him. 'They're shock troopers now.'

Dreno laughed. Baine pulled out his flask and unscrewed the top. The smell filled the Chimera's chamber. 'Recaff, anyone?'

He filled a tin mug and passed it round. Everyone took a mouthful before passing the mug back to Baine. He sieved the dregs through his teeth, swilled it out with some water.

There was a long pause. Baine made his recaff strong enough to keep them all awake.

Allun sucked in his breath. 'Throne,' he said, rubbing his eyes. 'What's in that stuff?'

Baine laughed. 'Stimms.'

Minka put her cards down and Belus held out his own hand. Minka nodded to Baine. He scratched the tally onto the floor of the Chimera.

She'd lost a small fortune, but she was content. There you go, she thought to herself as she stood up. That's my bad luck done with.

As the mist thinned they began to make out the shadows of the other landing ships about them, each butting through every wave that swelled towards them. For a moment they saw the whole convoy – three miles of landing craft carrying ten thousand Cadian Shock Troopers, a thousand tanks and a single point to prove: that the Cadians were the toughest bastards the Astra Militarum could put onto any battlefield, and that a sea crossing had put them all in one hell of a bad mood.

Smoke poured from the chimney stack as they approached Tor Kharybdis. The crossing turned yet wilder, and a fierce current slammed into them from the port side. The pilots had been pushed sideways, and the first sight of land had shown how far off track they were. Now they were struggling to resume their course.

The swells lifted the crafts up and threw them down. The blunt nose of each assault ship slammed into the waves, sending sheets of water splashing over everyone. Stomachs lurched as the craft tossed and yawed.

Darkness had fallen when Breve shouted back into the troop compartment. 'First Company are already landing on Faith Beach!'

They could hear the chatter over the vox as First Company went in. Across the water noise travelled far. In the stillness of the storm came the sporadic patter of hard calibre guns, the deep, persistent *thud-thud* of autocannons, the higher-pitched staccato boom of the heavy bolters and the tin-rattle sound of stubbers. From this distance the las-bolts were silent, but they made a lightshow of flashing fire, striping the night, dwarfed by the explosions.

Minka looked up through the top hatch, which had been left propped open. She had a rough idea of where they were supposed to land. They were too far out. There was no way they were going to take part in the first wave of landings.

Dido was standing out on deck. Minka shouted her concern to the lieutenant.

Dido already knew. 'The engine is failing,' she called back. 'The tech-priest is working hard.'

As if to reinforce this fact a wave tilted them dangerously. They righted suddenly, as another wave broke over the side of the craft that was alongside them.

Minka clung desperately onto the hatch as their craft was tossed back and forth by the swell. Finally, the engine gasped and powered through the flood.

It appeared that they were back on track for the broad shelf of rock under what was labelled as Bastion 4. Dido ran to her Chimera.

A moment later the voxed orders came, 'Prepare for landing!'

All across the landing craft ramps were closed and secured, protective covers were removed from gun barrels, knives were checked, powercells engaged.

Minka's squad had an intense air about it. They just wanted to land now. If their deaths were waiting then it was time to get them over with.

'All ready?' she said.

They nodded.

She climbed forward to the command cupola and flipped the multi-laser battery on. The pilot light turned green.

Full charge.

They were about four hundred yards from the shore when Minka could make out the defences. They looked just as they had on the map, rising up before them. There was wire, mine fields, pre-sighted fields of fire.

The traitors must know, she thought, but as yet, the traitor guns were silent. It was as if they were holding everything back.

Black smoke poured out above her head as her landing craft turned straight on into the swell. Spray fountained up and water swilled over the deck.

They were two hundred yards off shore when a flare rose into the sky and then the traitors opened up with every gun they had. Lines of tracer fire and the hissing flashes of las-bolts lit up the night. The waves glittered with each shot that was fired.

The light show was terrifying; it was one of the most beautiful displays Minka had ever seen.

FOUR

By the time Minka was landing on Tyrok Beach, the landings were already well under way. The first kill-teams, made up of First Company veterans, had been inserted by a flight of Valkyries just after sunset. To avoid the traitors' auspex they had flown so low their landing gears had cut through the tops of the waves.

Only as they reached the beaches did they climb. One Valkyrie caught the cliffs and tumbled out of the air, bursting into flames. The remaining pilots struggled to retain control. They dropped their squads at the top of the cliffs as they were buffeted by winds that swirled up from below.

It seemed the surprise was complete. A few alarmed traitors fired into the air as the Valkyries hovered just above the ground. But they were poor quality troops, easily startled, and within seconds the elite veterans of First Company overpowered them.

Their target was the large winchhouse that powered the aerial cableway that linked the island to Crannog Mons. The void

shields over the Lone Redoubt threw a blue light on the under-
side of the low clouds, and a low breeze made the taut wires
hum above their heads.

Captain Ostanko, commander of First Company, led them
off at a low run over the tussocky scrubland. Bendikt had personally given Ostanko his orders. The captain had brought
his finest warriors with him, and they moved forward in staggered bursts, snipers scanning the ground ahead through their
scopes.

The void shield distorted the view of the wheelhouse within.
The mists had been blown against the bottom of the void shield
and caught there, like flotsam on a beach. It gave the Cadians
perfect cover as they waited until all were ready.

On Ostanko's signal the veterans moved cautiously through
the void shield. There was a brief shock, like touching a bare
wire, then they were on the other side. A puff of mist followed
each trooper through.

The wind was lessened inside. It was strangely quiet. Before
them was the winchhouse, a Guardsman outside, dressed in the
padded greatcoat and criss-cross puttees of the Ongoth Jackals.
There was a low flicker of light and the guard stood, hand to
mouth, the glow of a freshly lit lho-stick in her mouth.

If she had heard about the imminent attack she was displaying what, for the Cadians, would be criminal neglect.

Ostanko moved forward cautiously. His instincts told him
this was a trap. He stopped about twenty feet away. The Jackal
sucked the end of her lho-stick and then let the stub drop. It
lay at her feet for a moment, the end of the paper still glowing.

She coughed, a rich, phlegmy sound. The gobbet landed with
a wet slap. She sniffed, and spat again. Her boots scrunched on
the grit. She paced up and down and then turned to go inside.

She stopped a yard short as Ostanko caught her in a murderous embrace. Hand over her mouth, knife into her kidneys, then up inside for her heart.

The Jackal was surprisingly strong. No one died easily. He wrestled her back as he drove the knife in deeper. It took a long time until she stopped struggling. There was a smear of blood as he let her slip to the floor.

His troopers were already at the door of the winchhouse.

They were in. Now all they had to do was fight their way into the tunnel network beneath, find the void shield generator and blow the thing into fragments.

As Ostanko's kill-teams were landing on the clifftop, Colonel Baytov was leading the first amphibious landings in Pegasus Amphibious Assault Vehicles towards the shore.

They had been given the most difficult landing zones. Their beaches were narrow and rocky, with shoals stretching out into the waters, which would shred any landers that strayed off course. Hitting the designated beach was like hitting a bulls-eye blind.

The Cadians maintained vox-silence, signalling only with hooded lamps. A hundred yards out, even these lanterns were extinguished.

In the cupola of the lead Pegasus stood Colonel Baytov. The sea lapped dark and glossy below him and the cliffs rose up ahead, a wall of black. Water swirled about the Pegasus with a dull red phosphorescent light.

As the amphibious tank drew closer, Baytov could make out the steel hedges of razor wire, tank traps and pillboxes. He had absolute faith in the troopers with him, from one-eyed Diken to Aaron, and the metal-jawed Flynt and Balchin. They were scarred and grizzled veterans, toting a fearsome array of flamers and grenades. But their real weapon was secrecy.

'How far?' Diken asked as Baytov dropped down into the crew compartment.

'A hundred yards.'

Each made themselves ready. Flynt fired up his flamer. The wire coil igniters glowed a dull red in the half light of the cabin. The smell of super-heated metal mixed with the scents of lubricant and unguents, sweat, salt-water corrosion and wet boot leather.

The Pegasus grounded twice before a wave finally slammed it up onto the beach. It roared forward, hitting wire and scraping through. They were thrown about as the tank careered up the beach, and then suddenly it skidded to a halt. The front ramp crashed down.

The black volcanic sand glittered in the night. Black cliffs rose up around them like an amphitheatre, the low rockcrete bastion of Second Redoubt glowering from the clifftop. All about him the transports were disgorging their troops.

The quickest were already clambering up the cliffs. They were horribly exposed. If this attack was to succeed, every moment counted.

As Colonel Baytov stormed the headlands above their objectives, the first waves of Fourth, Fifth and Sixth companies landed on the wide bay of Creed Beach.

The traitor forces there were led by Colonel Skall of the Swabian Fusiliers. Alerted by the las-fire around the island, he hurried from trench to trench, galvanising his troops by sheer force of personality.

The Cadians faced a broad, gently sloping beach ringed on both sides by rocky outcrops and low headlands pock-marked with pillboxes and razor wire. But worst of all, they faced a determined opposition.

The beach was covered with tank traps that made any advance with the Chimeras almost impossible. To make matters worse, the lead Cadian Chimeras ploughed straight into a recently laid minefield that set four of the vehicles ablaze immediately.

Their crews tumbled out in desperation, bent under their loads of charges and wire and detonators, but were soon cut down by withering heavy calibre fire.

Arcs of interlocking fire made the assault up the beach a murderous venture. Hard rounds ricocheted off tank traps, while missile silos returned fire at the approaching fleet of Gorgons. Wayward bullets sprayed the ground, kicking up sand into the faces of the advancing Cadians, as stray las-bolts fused sections of the beach into lumps of dirty glass.

One flamer-trooper led the assault, gouts of flame hissing out up the beach. He got as far as the first dune before a round hit his gas canister. The resulting explosion catapulted him a hundred yards back down the beach, his burning remains coming to rest near the surf.

The gunners on the landing craft did their best to support the ground teams. They tried to return fire, but their ships' thin hulls were no match for the beach's defences. Within minutes most of them were reduced to burning husks, the disembarked troopers now trapped between a sea of flames at their backs and a wall of las-fire before them.

The burning craft had also blocked others from reaching the shore. Panicked crews ordered the tanks to disembark too far out. Leman Russes rolled off the barges, hit the water and sank straight to the bottom. Chimeras struggled. Some sank, while others were hit by missiles that lit the water a vivid red.

All were conscious of what had happened to their forebears on the swamp world of Taqiri eight hundred years before. They had become pinned down and they had been slaughtered.

There was no choice. The Cadians pushed forward in tight bands, throwing themselves behind any scrap of cover they could, hitting the enemy so hard the survivors reeled back in stunned confusion.

The second wave landed on Creed Beach before the first had barely made it off the beach.

Major Luka and his former Whiteshields were part of that wave. Yedrin had tied his boots and webbing tight. It made him feel secure, as if he were wearing armour.

They were three hundred yards out from landing when a heavy howitzer shell hit the water twenty feet behind them, then another. The sea fountained up and soaked them all.

'They're bracketing us,' Yedrin hissed. Sure enough the next shell landed right next to their port side. The ship listed immediately, and the Cadians clung on as the helmsman struggled to drive them to shore.

The assault craft behind them was not so lucky. It turned turtle.

Yedrin saw the flames and slaughter and it chilled him. Equally chilling was the presence of the brooding Commissar Knoll. As they approached land, the commissar repeated the threat he had given them already, 'Anyone stopping or retreating on the beaches will be shot.'

Yedrin's Gorgon disembarked from its landing craft fifty yards from the shore of Creed Beach. It was a short drop for the giant tank. It ploughed bluntly into the water, throwing everyone inside off their feet. A great wave of freezing water splashed down into the open cabin and swilled about, drenching everyone again. There were shouts of alarm that the Gorgon would sink, but its giant tracks found the sea floor and they roared forward as waves slopped over the side.

Yedrin struggled back to his feet. Over the crowd of reeling troopers only one man had remained standing. Commissar Knoll.

The commissar met his gaze with cold contempt. You are no Cadian, his expression seemed to say.

Yedrin had a brief view of tank traps submerged in the water before the Gorgon slammed ashore. Yedrin held on tight as the craft went a little way up the beach before hitting a tank trap and lurching to a stop. For a moment all was smoke and confusion, then the assault ramp slammed down and the troopers paused in shock.

The Gorgon was supposed to carry them right up to the enemy defences, but had instead stranded them here, at the far end of hell.

'In the name of the Emperor – out!' Commissar Knoll shouted. He fired his bolt pistol into the air.

Waves smashed a half-sunk Chimera against their Gorgon. There was a screech of metal as the tank started to rip apart. The crews were already struggling to reverse.

Knoll was barking out orders. Yedrin started to the top of the assault ramp. Bodies were already falling before him. He tripped over one, and only just managed to keep his feet.

A shove from behind threw Yedrin off the Gorgon. He fell onto all fours, holding onto his lasrifle, his mouth now full of foul, oily water. He had to get up or he would be trampled into the surf or crushed by the tank being carried on the waves.

The trooper before him lifted a fist and shouted. 'Forward!'

A second later he fell dead. Yedrin did not stop to check on him. The water clung to him as he struggled through the hissing surf. Heavy bolter shells kicked water and black sand up all around them. There was no shelter before them, just bodies everywhere, burning tanks, the whistling hiss of hard rounds ricocheting all about him, and broad sloping sand that rose up to the headland.

'Forward!' Knoll roared.

To their right a Leman Russ fitted with mine-clearer chains struggled ashore. The chains threw up sand and dirt and exploding fragments as mines erupted before it.

Yedrin stumbled after it. 'Forward!' he shouted, though it might have been, 'For the Emperor!'

He did not know; he did not care. There was no choice now, Yedrin told himself as he sprinted up the beach. It was do or die.

FIVE

The day before the landings, commissars had reported dangerous levels of discontent among some of the local units.

'They're petitioning me to impose stricter discipline,' Bendikt said to Mere. 'I think it would be better to raise their spirits a little.'

After visiting the Cadian camp, Bendikt spent the day in his Valkyrie, touring the front line to assess the attitude of the troopers. They started with the Potence Mountain Infantry, who had suffered a mauling in the trenches about Tor Tartarus.

The mood was hostile at first, but when Bendikt dismounted from the Centaur to walk among the local units, the troopers met his appearance with awe. The aura of the Cadian general cast a kind of magic upon the troopers. Just his presence seemed to electrify them.

He thanked them for their efforts and sacrifices, and assured them that, 'You will be part of a great victory! For the Emperor!'

They answered his words with a great cheer. 'Cadia stands!' he shouted and they answered his shout louder than before.

By the time Bendikt left he had turned them around.

'Excellent, sir!' Mere said at the end.

Bendikt nodded. He was exhausted. He needed a drink. 'Yes. But there isn't enough time to do this with every regiment under my command.'

As evening fell they had visited more than twenty regimental bases, and Bendikt had performed the same magic of giving faith and hope and confidence to the local troops.

As night fell they returned to the General's Palace. Praise birds were perched along the roof of the chapel where Saint Ignatzio lay. The saint's presence had noticeably enlarged the camp of penitents. They were singing psalms of hatred. Each time one of the praise birds took off and swooped down over the crowd there was a gasp of excitement.

Gerent Bianca was also buoying up spirits. She was hosting a meal, and as they arrived, a series of military dignitaries were trooping inside.

Bendikt nodded. 'I suppose we are obligated to attend.'

'It would be fitting,' Mere said.

'Any news of the landings?' Bendikt asked.

Mere nodded. 'Ostanko and his men have already landed,' he reported.

Bendikt nodded. 'Let me know as soon as there is any news.' He turned to the rest of the command staff. 'I expect you all to engage with other officers.'

Gerent Bianca was just inside the doorway. She clearly enjoyed each officer's attention. The fervour engine was chanting mantras of the Emperor. The Cadians listened to them as they approached the front of the line.

Bianca did not seem to notice Bendikt until he was upon her, when she lifted her hands. 'General!' she said. 'I am delighted! I did not think you would be attending.'

'How could I refuse?' he said.

She lowered her voice. 'Is all well?'

'So far,' he said.

In the dining room a buffet had been laid out with chafing dishes along a side table. The candles gleamed against the polished silver trays. Each one was embossed with the Imperial aquila and the Richstar coat of arms.

Prassan could feel the air in the room taut as a wire. The officers who had come in already were standing about in conspiratorial groups. The serving staff stood stiffly along the side of the room while a few fussed at the arrangement of spoons and lids and condiments. A bell rang outside the room and a butler came in balancing a tray of amasec in cut crystal glasses.

Bendikt took one and downed it in one shot. He replaced the glass on the tray and took another. After the third drink, Prassan noted that Bendikt's stiff composure seemed to soften. He smiled for the first time in days. But there was little humour in his expression, rather the grim satisfaction of a job well done.

No one dared eat until Bendikt had done so. Prassan watched him down at least another five glasses before he moved over to the chafing dishes. Officers took their meal in strict rank order which meant that Prassan would have to wait.

There were a few other officers of the same rank as Prassan, but it was a matter of pride to them that they should go before him. Three of them sported the tribal weave of the Drookians. They were taller and more heavily built than Prassan, and vicious-looking – the kind of thugs who would think nothing of slitting a man's throat at a moment's notice.

One of them shoved Prassan. It was a clumsy effort, ill disguised. Prassan did not move.

When the Drookian shoved once more Prassan stamped on his foot. 'I'm sorry,' Prassan said, but his tone was about as unapologetic as it was possible to be.

Within a moment Prassan was surrounded.

'Get out of the way, Cadian,' the shortest of his foes said.

'It's always the smallest,' Prassan said, picking up a fork.

'Get out of the way,' the big one said.

'Tradition says that the staff of the same regiment of the commanding officer have precedence.'

'You can stuff your tradition, Cadian!'

Prassan toyed with the fork in his hand idly, watching. The big man moved to take a plate, and Prassan moved so quickly it was a blur. He pinned the big man's hand to the table.

The servers looked on appalled as blood began to stain the white tablecloths. 'Oops,' Prassan said, and turned to take a plate. He moved along the line and scraped up the last of the fried slab.

Someone took his shoulder and spun him about. It was the short guy. Prassan stepped in close and put the edge of his knife to the other man's throat.

'I don't think your commanding officer would like it if I killed you here. Would you like to step outside?'

The other man blanched.

'Is there a problem?' a voice said.

It was Adjutant Mere. He addressed Prassan.

'No problem, sir,' Prassan said.

Mere looked at the Rifles officer, and the other man stepped back and smiled. Mere nodded. He saw the man with his hand pinned to the table. He addressed the butler. 'This gentleman seems to have had an unfortunate accident. Can you assist him, please?'

Mere stood watching as the Drookian was led away. The other two backed off, and left Prassan standing alone.

'Sorry, sir,' Prassan started, but Mere put up a hand.

At that moment, Bendikt called Mere over. A second later the adjutant called for silence.

The Munitorum officer made the announcement. 'Officers! I have some good news to share. This month our casualties were five per cent less than we had predicted. We also estimate that the enemy lost ten per cent more than we had hoped.' He went through the figures that he had been given and at the end he paused for dramatic effect. 'And this means that the completion date for the siege has been reassessed by the adepts of the Munitorum. I am pleased to say that the projected date has changed from fifteen years to only seven.'

There was a begrudging round of applause.

Bendikt put his hand up. 'Of course, the Emperor cannot wait that long. There are other wars that He wants us for. In the morning your troops will advance back into the attacking trenches. We need to wear the enemy down. We need to pin him down. Hold his attention before we strike him where he least expects it. I am happy to share with you all the news that even as we speak, the Cadian Hundred-and-First have forced a landing upon the island of Tor Kharybdis!'

There had been a complete black-out as far as the landings were concerned, but an air of excitement now spread through the room. There was a cheer and then a round of applause.

The resentment that had built up over the previous weeks turned to relief and joy.

The battle would surely be over soon, the listeners thought. The Cadians were taking the field!

SIX

The organ mountings of dedicated rocket ships opened up in rippling salvos as Seventh Company roared towards Tyrok Beach. The chain of projectiles blasted towards the enemy and lit the mainland with yellow flames.

Minka and her squad were like ducks in water, paddling slowly to shore.

'Two hundred yards!' she called down as the landing craft to their left took a direct hit amidships. The impact broke its spine and it split in half, gouting thick, roiling flames. One half capsized, the other veered sideways and then, as the armoured tanks within slid down into the water, it righted itself for a moment before taking on so much water that it sank.

Minka watched appalled as three Leman Russes went down like stones.

A shell landed just at their bow and a column of water leapt up before slamming down on the decks.

'Mines!' someone shouted. Minka had a brief image of a round black shape just breaking the surface.

The landing ship to the other side flew fifty feet into the air as the water beneath it erupted. The explosion of surf blocked Minka's sight, but when it cleared there was no trace of the boat left, only floating wreckage.

'Steady,' Minka shouted as she flipped her multi-laser on and pumped out a salvo of red bolts to where the enemy fire was coming from.

There was still a hundred yards to go. The weight of tracer fire increased, bending towards them. She fired back once more.

The engines of the landing ship roared as the pilot accelerated for shore. Explosions bracketed them, the third one hitting the port side. The whole craft shook. Minka was thrown violently against the hatch rim. There was blood in her mouth.

A crewman was running along the line, gesticulating with both arms. 'Off! Off!' he shouted.

'It's too deep!' someone answered, but there was nothing to be done.

'Go!' she shouted to Breve.

The Saint lurched forward. They splashed into the sea and spray bucketed over them all. Minka was soaked.

The swell was too strong for them. The Chimera's engine screamed as it strained through the water.

'I'm trying!' Breve shouted.

Minka clung on as they edged towards the shore, then she felt the sudden grate of land beneath the tracks. The next wave lifted them up and threw them further up the beach. The tank slammed into the sand.

Breve gunned the engines.

* * *

Dido's Chimera hit the beach first.

It led the charge up through the gap and behind it came the other tanks of her platoon. They had gone nearly twenty yards before Barnabas' Chimera hit a mine and shed its tracks, slewing sideways and coming to an abrupt halt. The troops were out within a moment, piling out of the rear ramp and charging forward.

Seconds later a shell hit the tank and it erupted in flame. Minka saw the turret spinning up into the air.

The next Chimera was hit by a salvo of autocannon shells that punched narrow round holes into its side armour and shredded those inside.

She had a glimpse of Sergeant Elhrot crouched double, running forward as the beach erupted with mortar shots.

Dido's own vehicle plunged forwards up the right-hand side of the beach, beneath the headlands. The squat bulk of Fourth Redoubt rained fire down on them. They were nearing the lower slopes when Dido's tank slammed into the lines of razor wire.

There was a screech of tortured metal as the wire scraped a thousand sharp nails along either side. The note of the engine rose as it took the strain and then its weight and power and momentum drove it forward.

Breve aimed *The Saint* at the gap that Dido's Chimera had made, but another tank had got there first. It caught on a half-buried tank trap and snagged, one side of its tracks spinning helplessly in the air.

'Go around!' Minka shouted down to Breve.

'I can't see!' he shouted in reply.

A line of tracer fire hammered the stricken tank. Deep red sparks sprayed off into the night.

'Get out,' Minka willed, but the Chimera remained stuck, the troops still inside. Breve was slamming the gears as he spun *The Saint* round. 'Forward!' Minka shouted. 'Now!'

Breve spotted a place where the tank traps had been laid too wide apart, but they didn't have enough of a run up to crash through the barrier.

'I'm going to have to back up,' he cursed.

'No!' Minka shouted, hammering the turret with the butt of her pistol. 'Forward!'

Breve cursed as he revved the engine until the machine-spirit was screaming hatred, and the Chimera jerked violently forward.

Minka clung on. They hit the next line of wire with a scream of metal. The razor wire did not give. Through the corner of her eye Minka could see the immobilised Chimera was attracting a huge amount of fire.

There was no time to hesitate.

'Dismount!' she ordered, and in a moment her squad were piling out and running up the beach into a hail of death.

On Creed Beach, armoured units that were supposed to have landed in the first wave brought vital momentum. Lines of Hellhound variants were fed straight into battle, clambering up from the beach and cresting the lip of the cliff, then roaring out towards the low tower of the main bastion, which was strangely quiet.

The commanders of these tanks had a reputation for insane courage, and they showed all that and more as they roared forward, their turret-mounted guns spraying gouts of burning promethium and toxic chems.

Yedrin threw himself sideways behind a Hellhound, his fingers scrambling for a fresh powercell. As he ejected the old one he caught sight of Blanchez, away to the right, pausing to kneel, her sniper rifle braced against her shoulder.

He heard the clang of the fist-sized rounds hitting the armour of the tank. He felt the vibrations through the metal hull.

Knoll was not far behind. Yedrin was up in a moment, dashed forwards. He fell in behind another tank. He kept so close to it the exhausts splattered his cheeks with the hot gritty fumes.

Yedrin couldn't see where Blanchez's squad were. Where she had been were now just bodies. For a moment it seemed everyone was dead, except for Commissar Knoll, pacing behind.

He followed the Hellhound a hundred yards up the beach before it hit a tank trap and jammed solid. Its tracks spun as the commander tried to push forward, and then tried to reverse, and then desperately spun each of the tracks in turn.

The whole attack had now broken down into small squads and the dead were littered all the way back to the shore, where bodies lapped back and forth in the surf.

A missile streaked towards the Hellhound he was sheltering behind. It exploded against the front armour, spraying the sand with shrapnel but failing to penetrate. A second missile arced towards them, hit the turret and ricocheted up into the air.

Long bursts of hard rounds raked the sand about him, while above his head a blizzard of las-bolts was raging.

Yedrin paused for a moment. He could not stop. He glanced round, hoping to see Knoll lying dead, but the commissar was coming relentlessly onwards.

'We've got to keep moving!' Yedrin shouted.

The others with him nodded. They did not want to die.

'I'm with you,' Trooper Dargin said. He had been issued with a meltagun. He held it like an heirloom. 'Just get me close enough,' he hissed. 'I'll fry them!'

Another rocket roared overhead. The tank crew tried to go backwards. Its tracks spun in the loose stones and threatened to run them all down.

'Let's go!' Yedrin shouted, and sprinted round the side of the tank. The beach levelled out about fifty yards before them, then sloped steeply up in sandy banks. The trenches were dug into these. They could see the line of them, just below the ridge, by the flash of lasrifles.

To his amazement he made twenty yards. It seemed impossible that no one had shot him. He flung himself down. Dargin and Noord were still with him.

Yedrin paused for a moment, then he was up again. He reached the first dunes and threw himself to the ground to fit his bayonet. Of the fifty troopers who had boarded his Gorgon, there could be no more than fifteen left. He looked back. The tank they had sheltered behind was burning. From the flames he could see a long trail of dead bodies.

Above him, on the crest of the headland was a network of pillboxes, tank turrets set into the rock, and communication trenches. Every minute, the gunners raked the dune they were sheltering behind.

Three more troopers threw themselves down next to him. And a fourth. Yedrin had never seen them before. 'The heavy bolter is there!' one said, pointing. 'I'll go first,' he said. 'You cover me.'

A thrill of delight went through Yedrin. They were Cadians. *Real* Cadians.

'I'll cover you,' he said, and he put his lasrifle to his shoulder and fired as the Cadians moved forward.

Blanchez ran forward, threw herself down and rolled to the side. There was a pile of bodies scattered at the bottom of the dunes. 'Throne!' she cursed. She was lying right beneath a rockcrete pillbox. Heavy stubber fire was raking the ground before her. She put the sight of her long-las to her face, and looked for a target. It was hard to see anyone inside and this angle was no good. She had to get a shot through the narrow opening and hope she would hit someone.

She waited until she thought she saw movement and fired.

The return came instantly in a hail of stubber rounds. Trooper Apraksin was hit right next to her.

'You all right?'

'No,' he said.

Apraksin had been hit in the leg. She could see the entry wound. It had torn a hole in his trousers and there was bare flesh beneath, blood as well, soaking his trousers.

She crawled over to him. She had a medi-pack on her hip. She tore it open and her fingers searched for the tourniquet. She could hear the heavy tread of booted feet coming up the beach.

'Forward in the name of the Emperor!' a voice shouted.

Blanchez pulled the tourniquet out and used her teeth to rip off the ties.

'Up!' a voice commanded. She heard the click of a bolt pistol.

'He's wounded,' Blanchez said but Commissar Knoll aimed his pistol and fired. The shot went right through Apraksin's chest. It punched him back into the sand.

Blanchez scrambled forward and dived down next to Yedrin.

'That bastard shot Apraksin!' she hissed.

Yedrin turned. Sand was kicked up all about the commissar as he stalked up the beach. The pillbox was twenty yards ahead of them.

'Cadia stands!' he hissed and scrambled forward.

He grabbed the demo charge from one of the dead Cadians and kept running. Blanchez was right behind him. Incredibly they reached the rockcrete base of the pillbox and slammed themselves against it.

'Ready?' he said.

She nodded.

He set the time, counted to five and then flung the charges through the opening.

SEVEN

The repetitive hammer of bolter fire was making a dreadful mess of the Chimeras on Tyrok Beach, shredding the roof armour and the bodies within. Burning tanks and assault craft lit the black sand as Lieutenant Dido's Chimera hit the base of the scree slope and slewed to the side to protect the troops as they dismounted. The gunner and commander began to lay down withering fire from the turret-mounted autocannon and the nose-mounted heavy bolter.

Right above them, on the top of the headland was Fourth Redoubt. They could not see it, which was good, as the troops inside couldn't see them either. But they knew it was there. The tracer shots and las-bolts gave its position away.

'Right,' Dido said. 'Let's blow these bastards to smoke!'

She ran out with her command squad in close support. Kristian and Raske carried flamers, Mohr and Pietsch had a pair of demo charges each, hanging from their belts.

The black sand of the beach gave way to a shale cliff. Dido led her troops up a dry creek that had carved a narrow cleft in the scree slope. They were so close she could almost taste it. This was what Second Platoon did. They piled in and took names.

Dido was halfway up when a fist punched her in the back.

She cursed, thinking it was one of the men behind her running into her, but then she found herself on the floor. She tried to get up, but there was no strength in her legs.

She started sliding back down the way she had come. She felt stupid. She imagined what Colour Sergeant Tyson would say. *Dido, we're supposed to be going forward!*

She hit the bottom and rolled three times, coming to rest with her face in the sand.

'Throne,' she cursed, spitting grit from her mouth. She put her hands under her and pushed herself up.

Except she didn't. She was still lying there in the dirt.

'Dido!' a voice said. It sounded like someone she knew, but she couldn't tell. There was so much going on about her. The noise, the fire, her face in the sand.

Keep going, she signalled. 'Take that damned pillbox out,' she ordered, though no one heard her words.

Minka's legs pumped as she powered up the steep slope. Raske lay at the top. Part of his face had been blown off. She grabbed the flamer from his hand and tossed it to Orugi who was right behind her.

There were a pair of foxholes. She had a brief glimpse of a traitor rifleman and then she felt the punch of a las-bolt as it hit her flak armour.

She was knocked back for a moment, but her armour saved her. She closed the gap with three strides and fired down into the foxhole, killing both men inside.

Orugi reached the lip of the cliff and crawled to the base of the pillbox. It was only twenty feet, but Minka had never seen someone cross ground so fast while lying on his belly. He reached the bottom of the pillbox. He crouched and thrust the hose of his flamer into the mouth of the pillbox, then fired.

Smoke gouted from the loopholes. Asko was right behind Orugi. He lobbed two grenades in.

The central loophole was big enough for firing a heavy calibre gun. Just big enough for someone as small as Karni to slither through. Asko held her legs as he pushed her inside.

Moments later she had the back door open and the Cadians were in.

The ground floor was littered with the dead and the dying. They didn't bother to dispatch them. The pillbox had two more levels. They sprinted up the press-steel staircase. There was vicious hand to hand fighting as they took the second level and then the third.

Within a minute the trickle of Cadians hurrying up that defile was turning into a steady flow. From the top of the pillbox they started firing down into the traitor trenches and foxholes.

The Jackals fell back in astonished panic. They did not understand how their position could be overrun so effectively.

The Cadians thrust onwards, cutting down astonished reserve troopers hurrying forward, or the supply troops, sweating and laden down with rolls of ammunition. Only Minka paused. 'Viktor!' she shouted. 'Keep them moving!'

'Where are you going?' his expression said.

She pointed down. 'I need to check on Dido!'

Minka slid down the scree slope. Dido was lying face down, one hand flung out, the other hidden beneath her. Her face was pressed into the sand.

It was the stillness that struck Minka. She looked like she was dead.

Minka shouted her lieutenant's name, but there was no response. She only had a few moments to spare. She checked her body and quickly found a wound in the middle of Dido's back, just below her flak armour. Her uniform was soaked with her blood. Minka ripped open her medi-pack in her thigh pocket and fumbled for the needle of stimms, then stuck it into Dido's arm.

'Talk to me,' she said as she worked.

Dido did not speak. A hard round whistled overhead. Another hit the ground next to her. Black sand sprayed into her face. Minka blinked it away as she cut open the clothes and stuffed gauze into the wound, pressing it tight.

She turned her lieutenant over. Dido was still breathing. That blood clot had almost filled her left eye. She loosened Dido's chin strap, fumbled for her tongue brace and fitted it into Dido's mouth. 'You're going to be fine,' she hissed.

A shell screeched overhead. An answering salvo from the Imperial gunships lying off-shore landed short and tore up the bank fifty feet ahead of her in a necklace of explosions. Minka shielded Dido's body with her own. Once the explosions died away Minka pushed herself up.

'It's just a scratch,' she told Dido. 'The things you do to get out of battle! Don't you dare die on me!'

At that moment Dreno appeared. Minka didn't need to ask the question. He showed her his hand. She could see right through it.

'Las-bolt,' he said. Las-bolts cauterised, but already the wound was thick with sand and starting to ooze gore.

'She's alive,' Minka said. 'Banting is down on the beach. Get her down there. Can you help carry her?'

'I can,' Dreno said.

Minka cursed. Someone had to take command. She looked about. Sergeant Barnabas was nowhere to be seen. No Elhrot. There were no stretcher crews either. Minka did not hesitate. She scrambled back up the defile. 'Belus!' she shouted. 'Get back here. Go with Dreno. Get Dido back to the medicae!'

She went back down the slope with Belus. Dido's eyes were wandering. It wasn't clear if she could hear anything. 'Keep talking to her,' Minka told the two troopers. She pressed Dido's hand. 'You stay with me!' Minka told her.

Dido's eyes were closed, but Minka imagined that she mouthed the words *Cadia stands.*

And then she was gone. And Minka had a platoon to lead.

EIGHT

The air within Bendikt's command bunker was tense as the first reports started to come in. Ostanko had landed. Baytov had secured a bridgehead above Faith Beach. Things were looking grim on Creed Beach. The landings on Tyrok Beach were facing tough resistance.

All evening the vox communication had been quiet. Half an hour after Ostanko's reported landing on the headlands by the wheelhouse, the vox-traffic was loud and chaotic. Across twenty channels came the clipped chatter of a regiment locked in a deadly battle. Troopers pinned down. Troopers desperate for counter fire. Curses as friendly fire hit their own troops. Commanders reporting progress. Sergeants demanding support.

The reports from Creed Beach sounded increasingly dire.

'They're trapped,' Mere observed.

Bendikt stood over the map of the island and stared down. Creed Beach was a gentle curve. Contour lines showed the sloping gradient of the beach and the two headlands. It shouldn't have been this difficult. But the map showed none of the dangers that the Cadians were facing: The hail of fire they were enduring as they were trapped on the beach, and the stalwart resistance from a handful of Ongoth Jackals.

The vox-chatter from Creed Beach made it clear they were suffering terrible casualties. Bendikt could not bear to listen to the shouts and demands for air.

'Throne above!' he snapped. 'What have we got that can help?'

Mere went through the lists of resources. They had no reinforcements. There was a squadron of rocket ships but their weaponry was deadly but indiscriminate.

'How about Seventeenth Squadron?' Bendikt asked.

Mere checked his lists. Seventeenth Squadron was on a bombing run against the batteries of the Lone Redoubt. 'They're supposed to knock out the defences there. They're armed with colossus bombs,' Mere stated.

Bendikt nodded. 'Order them into Creed Beach. Is the void shield down?'

'Not yet.'

Bendikt cursed. Ostanko was taking longer than he had expected. 'Get onto the Navy.'

'The shields aren't down yet.'

'We can't wait.'

'It's dangerous for Marauders...' Prassan started, but Bendikt gave him a withering look.

'I don't care about the Navy!' he snapped. 'Those are Cadians on the beaches!'

Prassan was suitably chastened as he relayed the orders to the vox-operators.

'Two squadrons diverted from primary bombardment,' Prassan reported. 'Yes,' he snapped, as tense as Bendikt. 'Now!'

* * *

In the command centre the Cadians stood watching the squadron's course. The bombers approached dreadfully slowly. Prassan didn't know that it could get worse, but it sounded like the troops on Creed Beach were being massacred. He could feel their gathering desperation. After dreadfully long minutes the Marauder squadrons came down a thousand feet to make their attack runs.

Prassan listened to the vox-chatter of the bomber crews amongst themselves. They had a calm detachment that the Cadians did not, as gunners, bombardiers and pilots prepared for the bombing run. Disparate voices were speaking in tense, clipped tones.

Bomb doors open.

Bombs going in a minute.

Can you see him, rear gunner?

Flak coming at me.

Don't shout all at once.

Turn onto zero-eight-one.

Then the shout, *Bombs away.*

Yedrin saw the black shapes of the colossus bombs as they fell in a ragged line, their tail fins emitting dull screams. Then the first of them hit, but it did not go off. As did the second, and the third.

'What the hell is wrong with them?' he hissed. He could not believe that they were being left to die out here, and that the Navy could drop so many duds. Then suddenly he leapt a foot from the earth. Or rather, the earth dropped away beneath him.

For the next twenty seconds it was all he could do to cling on.

At last the string of detonations came to an end. 'Throne above!' he hissed.

He'd never seen Blanchez looking so shaken. Her face was pale and she'd dropped her long-las.

'Throne above!' she echoed him as she scrambled to reclaim her gun.

The blasts had even knocked Commissar Knoll from his feet.

Where the bombs had hit pillboxes or trenchworks they had broken the defences into fragments. But most of them had fallen harmlessly into the sandy earth, leaving great craters in the soil.

One had landed so close to Third Redoubt that it caused a collapse in the cliff-face and threw the redoubt sideways. The whole rockcrete edifice was now hanging precariously over the drop to the beach.

For a few long seconds there was a moment of stunned shock, then a Marauder destroyer squadron came in, low off the sea, twelve strong, each wing-mounting loaded with racks of krak missiles. The squadron fired as one, a series of *whooshes* as the missiles were sent off in punishing salvos.

The roar was audible over the vox-chatter in the command centre. The Marauders wheeled round as they came in to strafe the beaches with autocannon and tail-mounted assault cannons. And on the beach Yedrin and Blanchez pressed themselves into a crater and tried to shield each other from the fury of the bombardment.

Then Blanchez heard a familiar voice and, looking back, she saw the black-coated figure of Commissar Knoll pushing himself to his feet.

She dragged Yedrin up. 'Come on!' she hissed. 'We've got to keep going!'

NINE

It was nearly midnight when Prassan leapt up with the news that Bendikt had been waiting for. 'Void shields are down!'

Bendikt's face showed all the long hours of stress. He spun round and clapped his hands together. 'At last! Get onto the Navy!' he told Mere, while to Prassan he said, 'Get onto the spotters. I want precise bearings!'

It took long minutes for the Navy ships in orbit to bring their massive batteries to bear. When they did, a sudden lightning storm erupted as lance strikes hammered down on the ridgeline above Creed Beach.

Precision shots tore through the rockcrete fortifications. Magazines detonated, setting off a series of explosions. In the many galleries of the fortress, defenders fell stunned to the floor, their hands to their ears as ships and aircraft poured their fire into the defences.

For a brief moment the defenders got the void shields working again on a reserve power supply. The blue light crackled back to life. But seconds later a series of explosions deep within the fortress caused it to blink out once more and the next salvo threw chunks of rockcrete into the air.

As the Imperial Navy lance strikes hammered down on the Lone Redoubt, on Tyrok Beach signals officers were trying desperately to set up command and control bases close to the front. They were dealing with vox-traffic from the supply barges, Imperial Navy, high command and the ground troops. As each craft came in it was a race to get their provisions off-loaded. Logistics officers were tasked with maintaining a steady flow on and off the beach while teams of commissars herded fresh units straight towards the battle.

'Which way?' one sergeant asked and the commissar pointed up the beach.

'Just keep moving forward!' he snapped.

There was never enough. Non-essential supplies were getting in the way of desperately needed ammunition. As one Cadian support unit landed and started to try to organise the landing craft carrying cargo that was desperately needed, a mortar shell landed in the middle of them, and within seconds the black sand was littered with dismembered bodies.

'Get them out of the way!' a commissar ordered. 'Quick! Load them onto the landers! Move them!'

Medicae Banting had landed with the first wave. He'd followed the troopers up the beach, stopping every few yards to minister to one of the wounded. As soon as the battle had passed forward, Banting had set up a field hospital in the burnt-out ruins of the central pillbox.

The wounded were stacking up. Not all of them would survive

evacuation. He had some tough choices to make. This battlefield had it all – mines, shrapnel, abdominal wounds, catastrophic blood loss.

The priorities were clear. Stabilise those who could be saved. Get as many onto the boats as could survive the journey. Make those who were going to die comfortable.

He'd spent hours binding wounds, splinting shattered limbs and cauterising open lacerations. He'd already worked his way through the pale faces of troopers in shock. They had been through gallons of blood plasma. In the crude operating theatre – little more than a clean sheet spread over a wooden table – there were pools of blood that the medi-matting could not soak up.

Banting saw the rank markings first and waved the carriers forward. He knew the troopers by name. Dreno and Belus.

But Banting wasn't interested in them. He had to check the name badge. 'Now, Lieutenant Dido,' he said, with rehearsed calmness, in what passed as his bedside manner. 'Looks like you've been in the wars.'

Dido was deathly pale. Her eyes had rolled up, but from her throat came a dreadful sucking sound. Banting didn't know if he could save her. The nurse passed him a field dressing. 'Hold it there,' Banting said, 'and press hard.'

As Banting worked on Dido, Dreno was pulled aside by one of the nurses. He took his hand and washed away the dirt.

The nurse was named Vasily, a severe-looking young man. He sprayed carbolics on the open wound and Dreno cursed.

'Throne above!'

Vasily worked quickly to bind the wound up. He blurted out commands – turn your hand, hold this there – and then he used a pair of long, thin scissors to cut the bandage, finally wrapping the wound in tape.

'What is your name?' he said at the end.

'Trooper Dreno.'

'You will have to see the Commissariat,' Vasily told him.

Dreno lifted his hand up. 'Because of this?'

'Possible self-inflicted wound,' Vasily told him. A Commissariat cadet was standing at the end of the tent. It was the young lad, Commissar Salice, a recent graduate.

Salice stepped forward and motioned for Dreno to follow him.

Belus protested. 'He's just carried a stretcher all the way down the beach. With a wounded hand.'

Salice gave him a cold stare. 'Did you see the action?'

'Yes!' Belus said.

Salice said, 'Good. Then come with me as well.'

Belus shook his head. 'I'm not going anywhere. I've got a battle to fight!'

As Banting struggled to save Dido's life, Minka led her squad up the steep cliffs before her. Sappers had hung ropes down the slopes from the top of the headland and Minka hauled herself up, legs and arms pumping as she angled against the slope. She could hear the shouts of battle above, voices of alarm, voices of fury, the screams of the dying, as she landed in one of the firing trenches.

The trenches had been excavated from the bedrock, the hard rock still grooved with the teeth of the excavator. The floor was strewn with dead Jackals. The shrapnel was vicious in a space as tight as this.

One by one Minka's troops caught up with her. As they looked out to either side, they seemed suddenly to be above the battle. Creed Beach lay on their right, Tyrok Beach to their left. Both were lit with flames. Both were a mess. And before them the Lone Redoubt waited.

Minka had nearly twenty troopers with her, and while the sight of Cadians pinned down and being massacred appalled them all, 'Our orders,' Minka reminded them, 'are to push onwards with all rigour.'

They understood what she meant.

'Right,' she said. 'Let's go!'

The supply trench followed the crest of the long ridge that climbed steadily up to the hexagonal fort of Tor Kharybdis. Minka gripped her war knife and pistol as she sprinted to the supply trench entrance. It ran away at a forty-five degree angle, then switchbacked again in a zig-zag. She paused as her squad caught up, then led them forward, running at a half-crouch. At each switchback she went more slowly, alert for the sounds of the enemy.

She risked a glance, then waved her squad forward. Traitor reinforcements hurried into view. They were running towards the battle, heads down, their rifles slung over their shoulders.

Minka let them come almost upon them before she leapt up from the shadows and charged, firing with her pistol. It was a brief battle. The traitors were too startled to put up much of a defence, and in less than a minute the Cadians had killed each one, dispatching the wounded with knives.

Minka pushed on. She could hear voices round the next corner and signalled to the others to get ready. As soon as she rounded the corner she knew something was wrong. As one of the troopers swung round Minka kicked the rifle from his hands and caught the young warrior in a neck lock, the pistol barrel pressing to his forehead.

'Who the hell are you?' she snapped.

'Cadian Shock Troopers!' the young man hissed between gritted teeth.

'Impossible!'

She was about to put a las-bolt into his skull when a distinctive black shape stepped forward. 'Sergeant Lesk,' a voice said. It was Commissar Knoll. 'That is Trooper Urae Yedrin! He is from the Whiteshield programme.'

Minka let Yedrin go and sat back against the trench wall, slamming her pistol into its holder. 'Your eyes!' she said, and then shook herself and put her hand out. 'Welcome to the Hundred-and-First!'

Minka led her troops up the supply trench at a run. They twice met supply troops running down the trench towards them. The Cadians fell on the unsuspecting reinforcements with knives and fists and the heavy butts of their guns. The sound of breaking bones, spurting blood and strangled curses filled the trench for a few long, sickening seconds. The struggles ended with Minka pistol-whipping the officer across the face. He was flung against the trench wall. She kneed him in the gut, then slammed the butt of her pistol down upon the back of his neck.

There was a sharp crack as his vertebrae broke. He fell like a butchered animal.

They grabbed the Jackals' overcoats. 'Let's go!' Minka said.

The second time, the coats were enough disguise in the darkness. The results were the same: death to the traitors.

Minka's squad were fearless; they aimed to do what no other troopers wanted – to become cut off and encircled deep within the enemy.

TEN

The Lone Redoubt dominated the whole of Tor Kharybdis. For military purposes, it *was* the island. It was a fastness of a massive angular construction, with a deep, dry rockcrete moat, covered at each corner with heavy bolter cupolas.

The fortress had clearly been struck a number of times, but it had been built to withstand just such bombardments. While the rockcrete casement had been cracked and fractured, the fortress was to all intents and purposes intact.

A hundred yards off from the outer perimeter, Minka crouched down and the other troopers knelt behind her. She felt a low dread in her stomach. She had thirty troopers and one melta-gun and a whole bastion to take. To make matters worse, she had thirty troopers and one commissar and that happened to be the butcher, Commissar Knoll.

She led them right to the edge of the dry moat. The metal drawbridge had been pulled up, and the sally port lay across the fifty-foot trench, ten feet from the ground.

Loopholes stared down: black, ominous holes in the massive walls. Minka felt a cold chill. They had to get close enough to that doorway to blow it away. She puffed out her cheeks.

'It's a death trap,' Baine said.

She glanced back. Knoll still had his bolt pistol in his gloved fist. She ignored him for a moment so she could think this through.

He gave her a few bare seconds. 'Do not forget your orders, Sergeant Lesk,' Knoll called out.

Minka nodded. 'Yes, sir.' She turned to the others. 'Right, I need two of you.'

They all volunteered.

She picked Baine and Jaromir.

'Orugi,' she called out. 'Give me the melta.'

He was reluctant to hand it over, but she was insistent. She took the weight of it in her hands and gave her pistol to Viktor. 'Here,' she said. 'Take command if anything should happen to me.' Talking to the rest of them she said, 'We're going to blast that door open. When we rush forward, cover us. Understand?'

They nodded.

Minka took a deep breath, and said a few words to the God-Emperor. Half prayer, part apology, part appeal. Private stuff. Between her and the Emperor.

She didn't know if He had heard or not. 'Cover us,' she mouthed.

They nodded again.

Minka began counting down from three. At two, she started running.

The trench was faced with a steep, smooth fall designed to tip any attackers into a deadly killing zone. Minka slid down the facing, leapt the last few yards into the bottom of the dry moat, bent double.

The moat had been kept clean and empty. She got to the other side and threw herself against the foundation wall of the bastion. Baine and Jaromir were right behind her. There was no cover, of course. Baine pointed out a loophole looking down at them.

She could see the dark round muzzle of the gun. 'Quick!' she hissed. The Cadians were already firing at the gun ports as Baine and Jaromir made a stirrup with their hands and lifted her.

She scrambled up, aimed the melta, and fired. The air rippled before her and she had to look away as the backwash seared her face; the pinpoint beam was thousands of centigrade. And then the gun whined down as the charge was spent.

Minka opened her eyes. The gun had melted a fist-sized hole, but there was an inner door beneath it. It remained untouched. She felt her heart sink.

But there was something odd.

They were still alive. No one had shot at them.

She couldn't believe her luck. 'Try the window!' Baine pointed. Above her was a narrow observation window, set deep in the rockcrete wall. There was a metal grille screening the opening. She fired at that, and the beam cut through the heavy metal bars easily. Gobbets of molten iron dripped down. One landed on Jaromir's arm and went straight through flak armour, cloth and flesh.

He did not let out a sound.

Minka had just enough room to get her foot into the hole and kick. She rammed her heel against the steaming iron. On the third kick one side came away. She scrambled about and stripped off her flak armour to squeeze through the gap.

She had to wiggle her shoulders to get through, but then she dropped inside. Stone galleries ran away on either side. If there were any defenders, they were occupied elsewhere.

Minka found the sally port and threw the door-bolts back. The door was heavy. She put her shoulder to it and shoved. The Cadians rushed through.

It was an hour after midnight, and the Cadians were inside the Lone Redoubt.

ELEVEN

Commissar Cadet Salice had to record all the details in the regimental log. He worked slowly, but neither Belus nor Dreno seemed in a hurry. Salice took down their statements, then demanded, 'Can you fight?'

'If I had a hand, then yes. But as it is...' Dreno held his hand up. 'No.'

Salice turned to Belus. 'You are fit?'

'Yes, sir.'

'And you are here...'

'Because I was a witness to Trooper Dreno's being shot in the hand.'

Salice knew all that. 'You have given your statement. Now, you need to re-join your unit.'

Belus grabbed his lasrifle, checked it and put the strap over his shoulder. 'Any idea where it is, sir?'

Salice felt he was being taken for a ride. His cheeks coloured. 'Follow them up the beach,' he said.

Belus saluted.

As the two men walked away, Dreno said, 'Did you do that on purpose?'

'What?'

'You know. Get yourself pulled in to get away from the front line?'

Belus was furious. 'Are you mad? Who the Throne would want to get pulled in by the Commissariat?'

Dreno's eyes narrowed. 'I'd be careful if I were you.'

'It's you in trouble with the Commissariat,' Belus snapped. 'Not me!'

Minka led her troop into the deserted corridors of the bastion. Two troopers from Barnabas' unit, Ilina and Petrov, were at her shoulder. Between them they manned a heavy flamer unit. Ilina went first, Petrov behind, carrying the heavy promethium tanks on his back.

'Where the hell are the traitors?' Minka demanded.

There was no sign of them.

Each room or intersection they came to was deserted. Here and there the lumens had been knocked out. In the sporadic lighting they could see places where sections of roofing had fallen in. The rockcrete walkways were littered with rubble, the stink of ozone hanging in the air.

'Think the Navy knows we're in here?' Baine whispered.

Minka cursed. She should have reported their presence. There was nothing for it now. They kept moving forward.

At the top of a stairwell they heard the rumble of many voices coming from below. Minka signalled to her troop to stay hidden. They backed out of the flickering light of the stair lumens as a platoon of Jackals came tramping up the stairs.

They had the air of troopers who had been sheltering from the bombardment in the basements and were only now returning to their posts. Their lack of discipline was disgusting to the Cadians. The Jackals went against all that the Cadians stood for. Not only were they traitors, but they were also a rabble. Not even fit to wear uniforms.

Silently the Cadians steeled themselves. This treacherous scum had to die.

The stairs wound out of sight below them, the platoon spread about thirty feet down. Minka had to wait until the foremost were almost upon her.

She held up her fingers and counted them down from four. On her command the Cadians leapt around the corner.

The cries of the Jackals filled the air. The note in their howls was at first startled, then appalled, and finally they cried out in fear and pain. The Cadians gunned them down with a ferocious salvo of las-fire on full auto. The Jackals did not get a single shot off in reply. They tumbled back down the stairs, knocking each other over and coming to rest on each of the landings, their heaped bodies crumpled against the walls.

Minka held her hand up for silence. Far down the stairwell someone called up in alarm.

'What is happening up there? Heh!'

The Cadians did not move. Step by step they heard someone advancing up the stairs. Minka started to slide down the side of the wall, looking to get a shot off, but the dead Jackals had tumbled out of sight, and as the investigating trooper came to the first dead body there was a low curse, and then shouts of alarm from the bottom of the stairwell.

'Right,' Minka said. 'They know we're here. No choice now. We have to keep up momentum!'

Minka went first. While the external walls of the Lone Redoubt were heavy cast rockcrete, inside the bastion the internal partitions were fashioned from carefully dressed stone. They passed long side chambers with triple-bunked cots set end to end along the wall. Mess halls were filled with mattresses, stacked weapons, ammo crates.

They could hear the shouts and screams of battle in the levels about them. They had no idea whether the traitors were holding the Cadians back, or if their fellows had forced an entry.

At the next chamber Minka scanned the piles of clothes and bags for any hiding inside. The young trooper, Yedrin, fired bursts into each of the rooms. The bedding kept burning as they pressed on.

Baine was first round the corner. A wide flight of stairs plunged down. Minka slid over the banisters, landing in a crouch, pistol ready. She pulled a grenade off her webbing, slid her finger into the loop, put her back to the wall and slid along. Baine and Asko were with her, carbines raised.

There was a door at the end of the corridor. Minka stopped at one side of the doorway and signalled for the other two to be ready. Baine kept his eye on the trench while Asko stepped up behind Minka. She lifted the latch and pulled.

The door creaked open, and Minka fired three shots into the darkness. It took a second for her eyes to become accustomed to the gloom inside. There was a ladder leading straight down, a table of wooden ammo crates, a heap of discarded clothes.

The Cadians rushed forward. Shouts echoed up from stairwells and ventilation shafts. Sirens were sounding deep within the great bastion.

The Cadians plunged deeper. They could hear the sound of batteries up ahead, the persistent *thud-thud* of an autocannon. They went straight towards it.

The conversation of the artillery crew did not sound like the chatter of the Jackals. This had the crisp, efficient tone of well-drilled troops.

As the Cadians gathered, readying for a charge, there was a

sudden shout from behind. A supply squad had come up behind them. Minka spun about. She could make out the sight of troopers in smart uniforms jogging down the corridor.

There wasn't a moment to lose. 'For Cadia!' Minka shouted and charged.

As Minka battled inside the fortress, Colonel Baytov led the elite of First Company up to attack the northern side of the Lone Redoubt.

They could see the damage done by the orbital barrage. Smoke was already rising from its air-vents and loopholes, but as they approached the dry trench, determined defenders responded with accurate las-fire.

Baytov put his hand up for a pause. His squads had pushed on, as they were trained to do, finding weak points and smashing through them.

He signalled them to either side. The Cadian kill-teams picked their way around the walls of the redoubt, looking for a weak spot. Along the next face of the hexagon they found it. An orbital strike had sheared off the front of a ground floor gallery. The rockcrete wall lay shattered on the floor, the arched ceiling of the chamber revealed within.

'I'll lead the attack!' he ordered, and hastily divided the forces into three. One to attack, one to cover, and the other to attack the same point from the other side.

In the tight confines of the Lone Redoubt, the discipline of the Swabian Fusiliers showed. They worked without any of the shambolic attitude of the Jackals. They did not panic, but shouted their own war cries. Las-bolts stitched the air between them as the two bands closed at speed.

Ilina crouched and started to hose flaming promethium into

the narrow space until a well-aimed las-bolt hit her full in the face, and she fell back with a groan of pain.

Out of the corner of her eye, Minka saw Yedrin grab the hose from Ilina's hands. He engaged the firing handle and a flaming gout of promethium flared out. There was a furious hand to hand battle. The Cadians outnumbered the Fusiliers and the element of surprise weighed in their favour.

The Fusiliers fell back into the hab-zones of the fortress. Scattered and furious battles erupted through the outer galleries. The las-bolts were so intense that they set off fires among the heaps of bedding. Yedrin stayed close to Minka, clearing side-chambers with gouts of flame.

'I feel like we're being herded,' Orugi hissed.

Minka had the same feeling. It was as if they could sense the enemy all about them, hurrying to isolate them.

They moved forward into a large storage chamber. It was filled with crates and bedding.

One of the troopers shouted, 'They're behind us!' She dropped to her knee, firing rapidly.

More Swabian Fusiliers had followed them down. At the same moment a body of thirty Jackals came at them from the other side, suddenly full of courage and screaming treacherous war cries. Vlada was hit in the throat. Yedrin was too slow in getting down. Minka had to grab his legs and wrestle him to the floor as a spray of las-bolts occupied the place where he had just been.

'Block the doors!' Minka shouted. 'We'll make a last stand here!'

Baytov had been fighting with the Cadian Storm Troopers for thirty years. The 101st relied on their armour. It was a long time since he had been required to mount a foot assault of a position like this. But he, and all the other Cadians, had drilled incessantly for exactly these kinds of situations. One thing Cadia did not lack was the ruins of defensive fortifications. The landscape was dotted with deserted bastions and kasrs, wrecked or abandoned in long-forgotten wars.

Some had been sites of heresy, declared excommunicado by the Inquisition, others retained exactly for training purposes. So this assault was like a training mission.

Assess the strength of the defences. Lay down suppressing fire. Charge.

As Baytov prepared the forces, Diken came forward. The one-eyed veteran had carefully watched the fire.

'It is not held strongly,' he said. 'I assess no more than fifty defenders. And they do not have much heavy weaponry.'

'That doesn't make sense,' Baytov said. 'Why wouldn't this position be held more stoutly?'

Diken paused and took in all the evidence he had seen from the fighting so far. 'I guess that the last thing Holzhauer expected was this push. All the troops we have fought so far are the Jackals. Those, and a handful of Swabian Fusiliers. And whoever was commanding here appears to have been as third-rate as their troops.'

Minka's troops were desperately resisting an attack on all sides. Only Yedrin and his flamer kept the enemy back. And within a few short minutes, the pressure on his flame thrower began to slow, the fire coming in spluttering spurts. 'We're running low!' Yedrin cursed.

'Anyone find another tank?' Minka shouted.

Baine scrambled about the storeroom, yet he found nothing but case after case of hard slab.

As the flame thrower gave a last gasp, Minka tossed Yedrin one of the Fusiliers' lasguns. 'Here!' It was a triplex variant. Minka kept her head down behind a crate of slab and briefed him quickly. 'There's three settings. Standard. Precision. Hot shot.'

He nodded. Minka looked about. There were twenty of them left. They were surrounded and out of grenades. The Cadians used the crates as cover and kept up a furious fusillade to fend the enemy back.

Minka's laspistol was starting to overheat and she had to grab another triplex pattern lasrifle from the floor. She left it on standard, but after a few shots the enemy learnt from their mistakes.

There was a brief lull. 'They're getting ready to come from both sides again,' one of the new troopers – Blanchez – warned.

Minka flipped her gun onto hotshot.

In ten shots she had exhausted her powercell. Rather than wait to reload, she tossed the gun down, pulled out the power sabre she had plundered and engaged the power-stud. She prepared to charge. 'Stay with me!' she ordered.

Minka's Cadians were once more assaulted on three sides. The Swabian Fusiliers officer came straight for Minka, hoping for an impressive kill. He was a tall man, with a lean face and long black moustaches waxed down like fangs. In his fist he carried a pistol and power sabre. Blue lightning crackled along the curved blade.

'Traitor!' he roared at her, and brought his blade down in a long sideways swipe.

She had no choice but to parry with her own power sabre. Eldritch light crackled around the impact. She held against the blow for a moment, then her blade started to come apart in her hand.

She let go.

'Traitor!' he shouted again, as he shook the remains of her sabre from his blade. But Minka was already moving inside his guard, pistol in hand. She fired into his face at point-blank range. The las-bolts hit true and slammed him backwards.

TWELVE

Dawn was breaking when Colonel Sparker clambered up the last slopes towards the looming fort of Tor Kharybdis. He had fought up through the trenches, which had been held by Swabian Fusiliers. There were bodies lying in the dry moat. But as the light began to spread, it was clear that they were not Cadian dead, but traitors.

The guns were silent. Above, the fort flew a banner.

'They're not firing,' Colour Sergeant Tyson commented to his colonel.

Sparker nodded. He had better eyesight than the old veteran next to him. 'And damn me if they're not flying a Cadian flag,' he said.

They stepped out onto the lip of the moat.

Colonel Sparker stood with his hands on his hips. 'Throne!' he said, as a figure climbed out of one of the gun emplacements.

It was Colonel Baytov who met them. He had a broad grin as he said, 'Sparker. Where have you been?'

'Clearing the trenches,' Sparker said. He'd taken Fifth Redoubt as well. He looked at the bulk of the Lone Redoubt. 'Well done, sir!' he said and put out his hand.

Baytov laughed. 'Don't thank me. It was your lot who got here first.'

'My lot?'

'Sergeant Lesk. Found an unguarded sally port. Apparently the defenders were sheltering from the naval bombardment. She forced entry and ploughed straight into the guts of the foe. True Cadian style! We found them barricaded in a storeroom five levels down.'

Sparker whistled to show his appreciation. He'd always thought well of Lesk, but this was something new.

He turned to Evrind. 'Find Lesk and bring her here.'

His orderly nodded.

It didn't take long for Evrind to find Minka. She was sitting on the walls of the Lone Redoubt, recounting her story to each officer that came up.

'Sparker wants you,' Evrind said.

Minka pushed herself down. They retraced the way that Evrind had taken.

'Ah!' Sparker said as he turned full on towards her. 'You've done something quite remarkable, Sergeant Lesk.'

She saluted. 'Thank you, sir.'

'I hear you're responsible for the fall of the Lone Redoubt.'

She laughed. 'Not really, sir.'

'Take the compliment,' Sparker said. 'And not only did you take the Lone Redoubt, you did it right under the nose of Colonel Baytov!'

'It was a group effort. We had two of the Whiteshields with us. They did well, sir. I take back everything I've said about them. I was impressed.'

Sparker considered this for a moment. 'Good. I'm pleased. I'll let Colonel Baytov know.'

There was a pause before Minka said, 'Colonel Sparker. Any news of Lieutenant Dido?'

Sparker's face darkened. He shook his head and spoke in a low voice. 'No, sorry. I've heard nothing.'

PART THREE

PART THREE

ONE

Official regimental histories recorded that, due to the courage and fortitude of a Cadian sergeant and a band of new White-shields, Tor Kharybdis had fallen by lunchtime on the first day. While the troops on the ground knew the fortress was taken by Sergeant Minka Lesk of Seventh Company, it suited the politics of the time to exaggerate the contribution of the new White-shields. The histories focused long on the struggles of Creed Beach and how the Cadians were pinned down, until the White-shields cleared the trenches on the ridge – how those troops earned their place within the regiment.

There was no mention of the stubborn last stands by the trai-tors. Nor that some of those units were from planets that had once stood shoulder to shoulder with the Cadians. Those were the bitterest battles as local rivalries were inflamed by the different choices that each unit had made. Each blamed the other for the loss of their home worlds. No quarter was given or expected.

The rabble of Jackals who did surrender were turned straight over to the Commissariat. In a matter of days they had been screened by confessors, ring-leaders turned over to the Inquisition, officers executed, and the rest pumped full of frenzon and sent into battle against their former allies.

The Cadians barely had time to dig themselves into the polygonal fortress of the Lone Redoubt before traitor batteries on Crannog Mons began to bombard it.

The creaking old fortress, which the Cadians had stormed only hours before, was now their shelter. Minka's squad found a serviceable chamber in the lower circuits and poked through the belongings of the former garrison. Heretical texts were handed over to the Commissariat. Anything else that seemed suspicious was burnt.

From the provisions stores, food was handed about. It was hardtack. Imperial issue. It gummed up their mouths. Asko found some serviceable water tanks. They were stale, and had a strong chem-flavour, but at least they were clean. An hour later water came round as well. They passed canteens along the line. Minka took just what she needed to swill the last of the sticky hardtack from her mouth.

A familiar figure appeared in the doorway and Minka stood up.

'Belus!' she said.

The other man came forward.

'So you're all right?'

He nodded and held out his hands as if to say, 'nothing wrong with me.'

'Where's Dreno?'

'Medicae. Probably off-island by now.'

'And Dido?'

'Well. She was alive when we got her to Banting.'

'She was?'

He nodded.

'And any idea what happened?'

Belus shook his head. 'Dreno got reported. We had to go and see Salice and make statements.'

Minka nodded. The bats were pretty strict on these things now. She paused, thinking of Dido, then said, 'Well, good to see you again.' Her words sounded false even to her. 'Get some rest,' she told him, then turned to the rest of her squad. 'That stands for all of you,' she called out. She went around, checking on each of them. Some had minor wounds, cuts, burns, grazes.

At last Baine called out, 'Sergeant. You should get some rest too.'

She nodded and took a seat. Asko was rolling a lho-stick. He offered it to her. She took it as he rolled another before handing it to Baine. They waited until he had rolled a third, and then Baine passed about a light.

Minka rarely smoked, but sometimes it was what she needed. She sucked the acrid smoke in deep and let it out in a long plume. 'So,' she said. 'We took the island.'

Asko grinned. Baine nodded. 'Yes, we did,' he said.

Minka savoured that. In a few hours of fierce fighting the Cadians had taken more territory than the Imperials on Malouri had taken in the previous three years. It was a morale blow, but they had not landed on Crannog Mons, and the island fortress appeared no closer to falling than before.

'What next?' Asko asked after a while.

'Next we attack the island,' Minka told him. She paused. 'And we fight the Elnaurs.'

Minka found a clean enough bed and lay down as the thunder of the traitor bombardment roared on. Dust sifted from the roof above them. The lumens flickered and went out. At some point the bombardment stopped. The sudden silence startled Minka. She sat up and looked about.

Asko was lying with his hands behind his head. 'They've got the void shield working again,' he said.

She puffed out her cheeks. She could feel the hum of the generators in her bones.

Her mind wandered as she started to sleep, but it kept returning to the sight of Dido lying still in the black sand as fires burnt about her.

TWO

In the command centre, the tension had been slowly ratcheting up throughout the night. The battle for Creed Beach had been so much fiercer than they imagined that Prassan began to harbour doubts. Maybe Bendikt had overreached himself with this attack, a voice in his head whispered, beyond any hope of immediate support. The prospect of the Cadians then having to assault the Lone Redoubt filled them all with unspoken worries.

News that the Lone Redoubt had fallen came with the first light of dawn. There was stunned disbelief, and then shouts and cheers and self-congratulation.

Bendikt seemed to show the most relief. 'I knew they would do it!' he laughed and as if to make his point he smashed his augmetic fist through the table.

The sudden joy within the command centre spread. The praise birds flapped into the air and sang a paean of victory, and the pilgrims who camped in the gardens outside the chapel woke and lifted their hands in wonder, not quite knowing what had happened, but sensing the change in the air.

'A drink!' Bendikt called, and Mere found an unopened bottle of Arcady Pride. They gathered a motley collection of tin mugs and shared the bottle about the room.

Once Bendikt and Baytov had had a long conversation, the general allowed himself some time to rest. 'The fort was taken in the early hours by a sergeant of Seventh Company!' he said at the end. 'Arminka Lesk. That girl from Kasr Myrak.'

Mere couldn't place her.

'The one who came off the planet with the Space Wolves. With that kasrkin. Sturm, was it?'

Mere suddenly remembered. Those two were the last Cadians off the planet alive. He nodded. 'Excellent news.'

'And she did it with the support of some of Luka's Whiteshields.'

'They're not Whiteshields any more,' Mere said.

Bendikt waved a hand dismissively. 'You know what I mean.'

At that moment word came that a high-ranking prisoner was being brought in for questioning.

Mere gave Prassan the duty of assessing their strength, deployment and morale. Prassan took a staff Centaur to the landing zone.

The prisoners came in aboard Valkyries, with armed guards. Prassan was among those waiting for them to land with a unit of intelligence officers and a platoon of Mordians. He had learnt all the uniforms of the rebellious Guardsmen and he screened those that dismounted. There was a mix of second line regiments, but primarily they wore the drab uniform of the Ongoth Jackals.

He saw the prisoner he was looking for – a colonel in the uniform of the Swabian Fusiliers.

'Bring him with me,' he said.

Two Mordian troopers brought the man into Prassan's Centaur.

The traitor had been handsome once, with well-manicured moustaches and a patrician set to his jaw. But now his nose had been broken, his upper lip split. There was dried blood crusted about his nose. He looked beaten. Prassan nodded to say that the Mordians could leave now.

He did not fear this man. He had been disarmed, his hands were bound, his spirit broken. Prassan took him in. 'What is your full name?'

'Colonel Skall. Swabian Fusiliers.'

Prassan checked the name against the dataslate before him. The man appeared to be telling the truth.

He questioned him about the units on Tor Kharybdis. Their morale.

The colonel answered all of his questions with a fierce pride. 'We are defiant,' he announced. 'We will prevail. It has been foretold. Your days are over!'

Prassan wanted to shoot the man himself, but he had to turn him over to the Commissariat.

'Any Elnaur Chasseurs on Tor Kharybdis?'

'Why?'

'Answer the question.'

The Swabian started to laugh. 'Is that who you fear, Cadian?'

'Answer the question.'

'Holzhauer has never been defeated, you know.'

Prassan couldn't help himself. 'Until last night, you mean?'

There was a moment's pause as the colonel held his tongue, and it was Prassan's turn to smile.

The Centaur arrived at the designated depot. It was a nondescript building a mile from the General's Palace. He could hear the singing of the pilgrims and hangers-on. In their words he could hear the name Ignatzio repeated over and over.

Prassan accompanied the prisoner to the cell in the basement of the command bunker. Two burly Cadian intelligence officers were ready for the questioning. They were a scarred, mean-looking pair. They seized the man by the arms, slapped him about and then, when they were done, they threw him into a chair, lashed him down and hit him about some more, swearing and cursing.

The colonel took the beating well. But to Prassan's dispassionate eye there was a practised, ritual element to the violence. The atmosphere changed when the door opened and a figure in a black leather coat entered. Even the intelligence officers paused. He was tall, his face a mask of scar tissue.

Prassan was amazed that he had returned from the front so swiftly, and that he looked so vigorous.

The newcomer spoke quietly. 'My name is Chief Commissar Shand.'

He took off his gloves. Then he removed his hat and put the gloves inside it before laying it upside-down upon the counter. As the chief commissar turned, Prassan saw the back of his head where a section of his skull had been replaced with polished steel plate. His hair was combed over it badly, as if it could hide the metallic shine and the thick knots of pink scar tissue where it fused with his skin.

He turned and took in the look on the prisoner's face. 'Yes,' Shand said as he stepped closer. 'I have faced many foes on behalf of the Emperor of Mankind.'

Even Prassan felt fear then.

Shand motioned for Prassan to stay in the room. The two intelligence officers stood back against the wall. The chief commissar's metal skull caught the light as he stood preparing himself for the interrogation.

He loomed over the captured traitor. An air of murderous disappointment flowed from him.

He did not need to look at the notes in his clenched fist. 'Colonel Skall. Swabian Fusiliers. Commander of the troops on Creed Beach.'

'Yes.'

Shand's hand whipped out. The speed and strength of the blow was astonishing. Prassan winced. Blood started to flow from the colonel's nose. He seemed to take a moment to catch himself.

'It seems that during your time on Crannog Mons you have forgotten the correct way to address a commissar of the God-Emperor.'

'You are the spokesman of a corrupt and heretical organisation,' the traitor spat. 'An Imperium that has become mired in superstition, abuse and heresy. I believe in the Holy Emperor, the Imperium of Mankind, and I believe in the Holy Temple.'

Each time the man spoke Shand struck him. The commissar was going to beat the man to death. By the time Skall had finished his declaration, one eye was swollen shut and his broken nose was now just a bloody smear on his face. Blood-flecked drool hung from his broken lips as he hissed, 'I believe in Father Bellona. I believe in the cleansing fire of *reform*.'

Shand's judgement was as quiet as a hiss from a punctured tyre. 'You are a traitor to the Imperium of Man.' His breath was short and sharp, taken in through flaring nostrils. The last blow whipped the man's head right round and it hung limp on his neck, chin resting on his chest.

Prassan thought for a moment that the commissar had killed him, but after a long pause his head came up and he stated his creed once more.

'I believe in the Holy Temple. The reform of the Imperium of Man,' he whispered.

Shand did not strike him this time, but took his bolt pistol from its holster.

* * *

The shot was still ringing in his ears when Prassan came out of the interview chamber. The smell of blood was in his nostrils, and when he closed his eyes he could still see the face of the dead man. When Prassan returned to the command centre, General Bendikt was sitting at a camp table with a glass of amasec.

A whole team of adjutants were sitting looking earnest, with notepads in their hands, and a pair of savants were in the corner working through order sheets with surprising speed.

A servo-skull hung in the corner, its anti-grav units giving off a low hum. An unlit lho-stub lay in a small pressed tin bowl. Mere was pacing up and down before him.

Prassan tried to sneak in, but as soon as he entered, Bendikt's attention seemed to be done. The general appeared glad of the chance to shift the focus.

'Prassan!' Bendikt said. 'Any sign of them?'

'None,' Prassan said. 'Only second line troops. I am told that most of them are ill-educated and poor. Some of them renounced their heresy before the end. Those that did not were suitably punished.'

Bendikt nodded, but kept his thoughts to himself. 'Well, we've dangled the bait before him now. Let us see how he reacts.'

Once the amasec was done, each of the Cadian officers retired to bed leaving Prassan, as the least senior officer, on station, just in case.

The only other people in the room were the savants of the chief logistician. The binharic data streams were just audible from their ear-pieces as their fingers played over their counting beats.

They appeared to be assessing how much the Cadians had captured, and how quickly they could be resupplied and reinforced. Prassan shoved the papers and stencils aside and put his head down on the desk before him, laid his head sideways and just shut his eyes for a moment as sporadic vox-traffic played in his ears.

It was a mix of lists of dead, wounded, missing, techseers asking for long lists of replacement parts, and self-congratulatory stuff as units compared each other's performances. Seventh Company were the loudest. It was one of theirs that had taken the Lone Redoubt.

Prassan had been asleep for about four hours when the wall alarm rang out. He sat up immediately.

His vox-headset had come askew. He straightened it and started recording the details. Within seconds he was through to Baytov's command centre, in the upper circuits of the Lone Redoubt.

He was on the line to the First Company captain, Ostanko – something of a legend within the 101st. Prassan had never spoken directly to him before. He felt trepidation as he took down the message.

He paraphrased Ostanko's words. The details were chilling.

'The traitors have launched a massive amphibious landing,' Ostanko reported. 'Throne knows. That rock must be full of materiel. I counted at least a hundred Gorgons, and they're crammed with troops.'

Within the minute Mere burst into the room.

Prassan leapt to his feet and saluted.

'What is happening?' the adjutant demanded.

Prassan almost shouted out his reply. 'The traitors have launched a massive counter-attack. Ostanko expects landings on the northern beaches of Tor Kharybdis within thirty minutes.'

Bendikt returned to the command centre just as the first traitor landings began.

Mere briefed him quickly on the latest situational reports. Bendikt stood listening. To Prassan's amazement, the general appeared unflustered. In fact, Prassan thought, he seemed pleased.

'Get reinforcements onto the island.'

'Already under way,' Mere said.

Bendikt paced up and down as the usual hubbub of crisis command filled the room about him. Prassan had the vox-receiver pressed to his one ear. He was tracking contacts on the map before him. He could immediately point out where the enemy were pushing forward most strongly.

Bendikt continued his pacing. 'Any sign of the Elnaur Chasseurs?'

Prassan shook his head. 'Nothing yet,' he said.

THREE

On Tor Kharybdis the Cadians were scrambling down the supply trenches. Their task now was to hold the trenches they had been attacking just hours before. Seventh Company were given the beaches between Fifth and Sixth Redoubts.

'Lesk!' Colonel Sparker shouted. 'You are in command of Second Platoon!'

'Thank you, sir!' Minka saluted. She was strangely calm as she led her squad along the headland.

The smouldering ruins of Fifth Redoubt were still strewn with the charred bodies of dead Jackals. Minka had the best part of three squads left. Viktor had taken command of her old squad and Barnabas and Elhrot took the others.

The beach beneath them was broad and flat. It was one of the beaches that had escaped assault by the Cadians, which meant the beach defences, at least, were largely intact.

Minka risked a quick glance above the trench parapet. She

could see the hastily thrown together flotilla coming towards them. It was flotsam. Disorganised. Haphazard. The waters were cluttered with amphibious craft.

It was less than a mile between Traitor Rock and the volcanic cone of Tor Kharybdis. The packed traitor craft were dark against the afternoon glitter of the sea. The counter-bombardments had achieved little effect on the trenches, except where there was a direct hit and the blast had chewed up the duckboard footing and torn the walls of the trench down.

The front-line trench, beneath Fifth Redoubt, was set halfway up the sand dunes. The sandy ground was held back by sheets of flakboard, nailed in place with iron bars driven deep into the ground. The firing step was a series of ammo crates, filled with sand, lined up along the front of the trench.

The first thing Minka had to decide was where to position their heavy weapons.

There was a pair of heavy stubbers rigged up at either end of the trench and Orugi found a heavy bolter under a dusty tarpaulin at the back of one of the crude dug-outs. It was Accatran pattern, with front tripod and belt fed at the side. He and Baine worked together to get it ready.

'How many rounds are there?' Baine said.

Orugi dug through the discarded equipment and pulled out two crates of Munitorum issued heavy bolter rounds. Each one was as long as his forearm.

'Know how to fire that?' Minka said.

Orugi grinned. 'Marksman, first class, remember?' he said, and tapped the steel plates in his skull. 'Even with a few bits missing.'

Minka put Baine and Orugi in the centre of the line, nearest to the supply trench that zig-zagged back up the dunes.

'If we have to pull out, make sure that gun comes with us,' she told the two men.

Minka sent Breve and Wulfe running back to see if they could get some anti-armour weapons. 'If nothing else, then krak grenades!'

She pulled out the island charts from her thigh pocket. She watched the enemy assault coming slowly nearer. She estimated their position and voxed in the coordinates to Sparker.

Asko, Allun and Maenard were in the middle of the line, next to Baine and Orugi. Minka had found a store of powercells and gave each of them a handful. Sergeant Barnabas' squad were ranged along the left-hand side with a pair of flamers. Sergeant Raske was on the right with the other heavy stubber and a plasma gun. Kristian was missing. Elhrot had the rest of Dido's command squad with flamers ready.

'Enough canisters,' Elhrot said, 'though not much use if they get up here with armour.'

'How are you doing, Karni?' Minka asked as she reached the end of her section of the line. Karni and Lyrga were together, propped up against the flakboard. Lyrga had her face pressed up into a trench periscope, her grenade launcher in her fist. There was a case of grenades next to her, the top cracked open.

'Ready when they are,' she said. Minka passed along but Lyrga stopped her and put out her hand. 'Congratulations, sir. I'm very pleased to serve under you, Acting-Lieutenant Lesk.'

Minka laughed out loud. It was not a title she had ever expected. 'Well, let's make sure that we make this a successful start to my career.'

The Cadians hunkered down as they called in artillery bombardments from the Earthshaker batteries on the mainland. White gouts of water rose high into the air. Minka was on the vox immediately with corrections. The next salvo came almost as soon as she had finished. There were more white splashes but out in the bay there was the flicker of fire. A few moments later black smoke began to billow up.

'That's a hit!' she reported. She checked with the auspex. 'Confirmed. A hit!'

As the artillery crews got their bearings, the Earthshaker bombardments rose to a storm. Soon the water ahead of them was erupting with plumes of smoke and spray.

The traitor counter-bombardment started a few minutes later. The guns of Tor Tartarus targeted the Imperial batteries, while those of Margrat and Ophio turned to face Tor Kharybdis.

The first shots were surprisingly accurate. Minka kept her head down, but she risked a few glimpses and saw the beach erupting with fountains of sand.

'Spectacular, but wasteful,' Elhrot said.

The sergeant of First Squad had always considered himself superior to the other sergeants of Dido's platoon. Minka noted she would have to handle him properly.

They held tight, watching the lead Gorgons steaming forward through the swell. The sheltered straits between the islands were much calmer than the swells they'd faced, but even so, the Gorgons were low down in the water – harder to hit from the shore but easier to swamp – and true enough, one sank when the pilot got the angle of approach wrong.

The Cadians held their fire until the first Gorgons roared ashore, slewing water from their armoured flanks. The giant tanks dwarfed the defences. Their engines howled as they ploughed forward, smashing through the first lines of wire and tank traps. The lead behemoth hit a mine halfway up the beach and it threw a track. It skidded to the side before its armoured prow slammed open, bridging the wire.

Traitors spilled out. They wore the brown greatcoats of the Swabian Fusiliers. As one, the Cadians of Seventh Company opened up. The heavy stubbers and heavy bolter barked out and a lightning show of las-bolts streaked down the beach.

Minka aimed the lasrifle she had found and pumped shots down into the enemy. It was glorious. Two more Gorgons disgorged their cargos of traitors. The whole of Seventh Company seemed to be rapid firing, and the traitors fell in their hundreds – some as they ran down the ramps, others shot dead where they stood, waiting their turn. The beach was a charnel house. Half-drowned men were taken out as they staggered from the water, and their bodies hung on the wire, like a warning to the others.

The Cadians held on for the rest of that day as waves of attackers crossed the narrow waters separating it from the island of Tor Kharybdis.

Holzhauer piled more and more troops onto Tor Kharybdis: Swabians, Ongoth Jackals, all manner of second line regiments – feral, hive-world, Gallows Cluster conscripts.

All this time the Cadians were isolated. After a week, reports came back of dawn landings by a new force. The first sightings confirmed the news. Black carapace, visored helmets, and officers wearing grox-skin capes. The Elnaur Chasseurs had landed in force.

As soon as Bendikt heard he poured himself a mug of amasec. 'Excellent!' he declared, raising his mug to the symbol of the aquila on the wall. 'Holzhauer gives us what we need.'

FOUR

The Elnaur Chasseurs were impressive. They came on fearlessly with a rolling bombardment only a hundred feet before them, shrugging off the hail of las-bolts as they marched forward.

Sparker appeared as the enemy did. 'You have to hold!' he ordered Minka. 'There is no retreat!'

Minka nodded and looked at her section of the trench. She understood what this meant. She would die in this action if necessary.

Orugi held onto the heavy bolter with both hands as he engaged the firing mechanism. Each salvo sent judders down to his toes. The recoil made his whole body shake. He kept having to dig his boots in as Baine fed the belt of bolter shells in. Spent shells rattled as they started to pile up. Baine swept them to the side when they got in his way.

Each bolt tore a Chasseur apart, but the rate of fire was such that the gun kept overheating and the massive bolt shells jammed in the mechanism.

Each time this happened, Baine cleared the breech, burning his fingers and swearing profusely.

A ricocheting bolt broke Belus' middle finger. He held it up as it swelled up to twice its size.

'Well, you can't go to the medicae,' Asko told him. 'Not after last time. They'll have you down for suspicion of cowardice.'

Belus cursed as Asko strapped the broken digit to the next finger.

'There!' he said. 'Can you still fire?'

Belus demonstrated and Asko slapped him encouragingly on the back.

It could have been moments or hours later when Sparker came back along the line. There was a splatter of blood across his face and he had a breathless air about him. 'How are you doing?' he demanded.

'Good,' Minka stated.

Sparker paused next to her. 'Petr's lot have been hit hard. I need ten of your troopers.'

Minka slapped every third trooper on the back and sent them along the line.

Moments later, Colour Sergeant Tyson appeared, chin thrust out in a defiant pose. He stepped over the dead bodies of the foe now settling into pools of their own blood. 'For Creed!' he shouted. 'For Cadia!'

He was there when the next wave of enemy troops charged, and immediately behind them another wave, and then a third. The Cadians fired until their fingers ached. There was no way they could kill all the troops that were landing. The enemy were so thick that they fell in drifts, like snow.

Hundreds reached the Cadian trenches. A ferocious battle

was taking place all along the front lines – hand to hand, in the manner of ancient warriors, death so close you could hear the last curses of the dying, feel the caress of their last breath upon your cheek, their hot blood spill out over the hand that plunged the knife into their throats.

Elnaur officers fired their pistols at point blank range as their troopers smashed about with spiked trench-clubs. One of Barnabas' troopers was hit full in the face with a swinging blow. There was an explosion of teeth and blood and spittle that arced across the narrow defile. Another was hit on the back of the neck by a blunt trench-club, not much more than a length of iron with a heavy bolt screwed onto the end.

It was enough, however. There was an audible crack as the trooper's neck broke. He went down like a dropped sack. Minka fired her laspistol, but the carapace protected the traitor.

Minka had taken the power-sabre from the Swabian officer. It was a beautiful sword with a basket hilt embossed with the marks of the aquila – the kind of weapon handed down from father to son. A blade that had been forged and fashioned in the Emperor's name, reclaimed from the corpse of a traitor. She roared, 'For the Emperor!' as she thumbed the power stud and swung. It crackled as it cut the traitor in two.

She moved along the line, exhorting them all with a voice hoarse from shouting. Baine had a bulge on the side of his face that was already livid and purple. Six of her platoon had been killed. Seven more had broken arms or legs. They were stretchered back, or walked, according to their injuries, while the survivors flung the enemy out of the trenches.

As the battle raged along the headlands, a fresh wave of Chasseurs landed, specialised assault troops rushing forward with flamers and grenade launchers now that the Cadian lines were blooded.

Sparker returned as he worked his way along the lines. He'd taken shrapnel in his upper arm during a terrible firefight to clear the trenches. His flak armour breastplate was pockmarked with scorch marks. A shot had burnt a line across his cheek. It had been vicious fighting, and he'd lost two of his command squad and another one had been injured.

Minka could see in his face that he was worried. He caught her eye. 'All right?' he said.

She nodded. She was worried too, but they were still alive and there was still a fierce fight within them.

'Got enough powercells?'

She nodded. 'For the moment.'

Sparker moved through the ruins, continually assessing the dangers, offering encouragement and support. The longer they held on the better their spirits.

That night, urgent supply ships landed on Creed Beach and unloaded before taking away the wounded. The equipment was carried up to the front lines. At the same time convoys of Sky Talon Valkyries came in under the cover of darkness and dropped metal containers of ammunition, weapons, medicae kits and desperately needed food and water.

But the traitors had also dropped fresh troops and supplies under cover of darkness, and next morning the assaults began again.

Each night they heard long convoys of transports arriving, but it seemed they were always short of everything, and the quartermasters shrugged their shoulders. 'If I had it I would give it to you.'

Even Orugi lost his temper. 'Throne above! How can we hold out without powercells?'

* * *

The orders for each day were for the Cadians to hold every inch of ground with their blood. As the Cadian lines were thinned and reduced, the gaps were filled out with fresh Rakallion and Drookian reinforcements.

Bit by bit the Imperials were forced to give ground under a relentless bombardment and repeated assaults. They pulled back, trench-line by trench-line, until, after three days of furious fighting, the Cadians were pulled back to hastily laid out defensive lines that ran roughly parallel to the rockcrete contours of the hexagonal fortress behind.

Cadian engineers had been preparing this line of defence ever since the traitors started landing. And the wheelhouse was one of the strongpoints.

It was where Ostanko's First Company had managed to break into the generatoriums in the bowels of the island, and so take down the void shields, but the Adeptus Mechanicus repair teams had long since cleared away any traitor dead.

The ceremonial arch of the wheelhouse's entrance displayed an aquila held aloft in the hands of two sober-looking Guardsmen in archaic Rakallion greatcoats. The doors had been removed, and now the archway stood open to the wind.

Minka inspected the rest of the building as her troops made themselves as comfortable as possible. Baine was frying slab, Karni was boiling up a pot of recaff and Asko had pooled all their lho and was rolling sticks with the paper he had left.

The wheelhouse had once powered a giant air-conveyor between the two islands, and while the massive wheels were still there, the steel cables had been cut and now the waist-thick ropes of plaited steel trailed out into no-man's-land and down into the water.

The wheelhouse roof had been hit. It had partially caved in, as had the walls, but the more the place had been pounded the stronger it became, defensively.

Their orders were to hold ground and minimise casualties.

'No counter-attacks,' Sparker ordered. Minka hated passing that order on.

The Cadians looked crestfallen. 'We just sit here? We're not pushing back?' Baine said.

'You're welcome to go yourself,' she told him, 'just don't let anyone catch you.'

The traitors came in under cover of darkness. Minka was lying in a low dug-out, Allun next to her. He spotted them first and pointed. Minka saw the dark shapes scurrying forward.

Firing started immediately. Minka had scavenged a carbine, which she now slid into her shoulder and bent to fire. After an hour she had to slam in a fresh powercell.

Mortar rounds started to fall among them. One landed so close it showered them in flakboard and masonry debris.

They called in artillery support. As the traitors charged, a forest of explosions erupted before them.

When the air had cleared, the land was strewn with bodies. A few of them were twitching. One raised his hand as if to ward off a blow. Minka was distracted; she watched his movements slow and become more sporadic.

By the tenth day the Cadians were starting to be withdrawn. In Minka's section of trench line, hers was the only Cadian unit left. On one side were Rakallions and on the other, Drookians.

When Minka went to greet their captain she saw with horror that it was the man she had met on their first night. His name was Captain Midha.

'Look! Some valiant Cadians in need of help,' he said. 'Give me your name and rank, so I know who I fight beside.'

'My name is Acting-Lieutenant Arminka Lesk.' She had hoped

the dust and dirt had made her unrecognisable, but he looked at her slantwise.

'I know you,' he said. 'You're the petulant child that shot up my convoy!'

There was no point in denying it. She bit her tongue but his blood was up. 'How have you been coping fighting things that shoot back?' he sneered and reached out to pat her head in the manner of an adult disciplining a wayward youth.

She caught his arm. He tried to hit her with the other, but she knocked him back with an open-handed blow to the sternum that started in her right ankle and moved up through leg and hip and core, through her arm.

He fell back, sprawled in the mud.

'You dare?' the Drookian spat and leapt forward.

Minka braced herself, but suddenly she was pushed aside. 'Now then. What's all this?' Colour Sergeant Tyson demanded.

'Your acting-lieutenant struck me,' the Drookian stated. 'She shot and damaged Imperial equipment!'

'Have you made a formal complaint?'

'Yes!' the Drookian snapped. 'But she also struck me, a senior officer. Have you dogs no honour?'

'I think you should make another complaint,' Tyson said. His words were conciliatory, but everything in his manner and attitude said the opposite. The Drookian's cheeks coloured but Tyson was formidable, even when he was feigning politeness.

'Cadians,' Captain Midha spat, and turned his back in disgust.

Tyson held Minka back.

'Don't get involved,' he warned her.

FIVE

Tyson reassigned Minka's troops to the other end of the line. She was in a dug-out along a ridge that overlooked Josmane Beach.

The next few days were quiet, battle-wise, but each night they heard the scrape of metal and the rumble of heavy machinery from down on the traitor beaches.

'They're massing for an all-out attack,' Belus said. 'And we're stuck here.'

'You should have stayed with Dreno,' Baine told him.

Belus held his hand up. His broken finger was starting to turn purple. 'If it wasn't for him I'd be out of here already.'

As night fell, Tyson came with news to say that the Rakallions were being pulled back to the beaches. That night the Cadians could hear the tramp of feet as the Rakallions moved along the trenches.

Asko and Orugi stood to watch them go. Asko was sucking

on the half-burnt end of a lho-stick. The Rakallions had the look of condemned men given a reprieve. They were laughing as they marched back to the beaches.

'That's the fastest they've moved since they got onto the island,' Orugi said.

'Bastards,' Asko said.

The Rakallions grinned. They shouted and waved. 'Good luck, Cadians!'

Minka sent Elhrot with Baine to coordinate with the Drookians. 'It's Midha,' Baine said.

'You're sure?'

He nodded. 'Sure. He mentioned you a few times.'

Minka rolled her eyes. This was all she needed.

Tyson came round with the news that the whole Imperial force on Tor Kharybdis was being evacuated.

In answer to her questions, he said, 'Bendikt doesn't believe we're capable of holding the place in the face of sustained opposition.'

'Bendikt? After what we did on Potence? Nonsense,' she told him.

He wasn't here to argue. 'Orders are orders. Of course, we can't let the enemy know. It's got to be done in complete secrecy.'

She understood.

'We're going out platoon by platoon. You're the last, with your friend, Captain Midha.' He gave her the time. 'You pull back then, no earlier. Understood?'

She repeated the time. He nodded. 'Fine,' she said.

The Cadians hastily packed whatever they were taking with them. Sentinel guns were brought up and Baine and Orugi worked hard to set up the heavy bolter in automated firing mode so it would appear that their lines were still held.

The front-line troops began to thin out along Minka's section of the trench. They sat waiting for the order, listening to the other troops depart. Sporadic firing sounded all along the front.

'Sentry guns,' Orugi said. But it wasn't. It appeared that the enemy were mounting night raids.

Minka's platoon were spread as thinly as they dared. They scanned the darkness for any sign of the enemy, las-bolts pumping out into the darkness.

Minka kept moving along the lines. Belus was re-strapping his finger. 'Shouldn't we be pulling back?' he said.

'Not for another half an hour,' Minka told him. 'The Drookians and us are to withdraw together.'

At that moment, a day-flare was fired up into the air. It cast an eerie phosphorous white light over the battlefield. Minka could see dark lines of Elnaur Chasseurs marching towards them. The light glinted off their armour and guns. There were thousands of them moving together as one.

Her troops started shooting, but there was nothing coming from the Drookian trenches.

'Blanchez,' she called out. 'Get back and find Midha, see what is happening over there. We need to fall back at the same time.'

Blanchez appeared a few minutes later. 'Lieutenant. The Drookians have pulled back. All of them.'

Minka realised that something had gone terribly wrong. The Drookians had abandoned them, and now there was a platoon of Cadians facing an all-out attack by the Elnaur Chasseurs.

She ran along the lines bundling each of them out of the trenches. 'Pull back now!' she ordered. 'Back to the beaches!'

As Minka paused to check she had everyone, a carapace-armoured Chasseur appeared in the trench to her left. He got three wild shots off at her before her power-sabre plunged through his breastplate. There was a crackle of blue, eldritch light, a thread of smoke from the armour and then the stink of burning flesh. She pulled the blade out and shot her pistol into the face of the next.

It was worse than she had thought. The whole position had been compromised.

Baine tried to bring the heavy bolter with him. 'Leave it!' she shouted.

'Throne I will!' he hissed. He ripped it down from the firing step and held it waist high, and fired. He staggered under the weight of it. Minka ran with him, pistol ready.

Both sides of the trench were already overrun. Las-bolts flared red about them as they took the tracks that led towards the beach. The lie of the land meant they had to clamber up the ridge before they could drop down, their backs exposed as they did. Two of Elhrot's squad were shot. Minka tried to get them up, but they were both dead.

All the time they could feel the Chasseurs gaining on them. 'We're going to have to fight,' Minka said.

She and Baine stopped at the end of a trench and fired, but the truth was the Chasseurs were on either side of them. The pressure of numbers was starting to tell. There was no way she and Baine could hold them all off.

SIX

By the time Minka got to the edge of the cliffs the last evacuation boats had already pushed off. They were a quarter of a mile away by now, the wakes behind them widening, already diminishing. 'Hey!' Minka shouted and waved her hands. It was still ten minutes until their scheduled evacuation time.

A sniper's las-bolt flared over her head.

She ducked. They had to get off the clifftop. They were sitting ducks here.

Below them were the beaches where Second Company had come ashore. Their scaling chains were still hanging down the cliff face.

'Down!' Minka ordered. 'There might be a boat or something down there. Quick!'

She crouched as she bundled the others down before her. She risked a look back the way they had come. A squad of Chasseurs were running forward. They were giddy with victory and had not seen her. Minka hurried the last of her platoon down the chains, and then slid over the edge herself.

In the command centre the air was quiet. The darkness seemed to press in. They were all watching the clock hands tick towards zero hour. When at last the hour struck, Bendikt said, 'Are all our troops off?'

All eyes turned to Prassan. He nodded. 'Yes, sir,' he confirmed. 'The last boat has departed Tyrok Beach. Withdrawal is complete.'

Bendikt let out a sigh. 'Start the fuses,' he commanded. 'Holzhauer is about to learn the cost of victory.'

Prassan's mouth was dry. In the days since Tor Kharybdis had fallen, the magazines under the Lone Redoubt had been stocked to the ceilings with explosives. All they needed to do was blow the island up and take half of Holzhauer's Chasseurs with them.

The countdown began. When the moment came, Mere offered the detonation button to Bendikt. He made the sign of the aquila and then pressed it. There was no reaction.

Nothing.

Prassan felt his heart skip. The demolitions officer frowned and stepped forward as if to check the device, but as he did so he fell sideways as an enormous *boom* rolled out over the planet, and a plume of rock and debris lifted into the air, mushrooming up like a volcanic eruption.

Sheets of flame raced along the corridors of the Lone Redoubt as mega-tons of explosives caught fire and erupted. For those unfortunate enough to witness the event, it was as if the whole fortress had shrugged its shoulders and lifted hundreds of feet into the air. It was not just the Lone Redoubt. The whole volcanic cone of the island blew and then collapsed down upon itself, shattering into ruin.

The first initial explosion was followed by a number of further blasts that shook the ground and sent a gathering cloud of dust and smoke into the air. They ran around the island in a necklace of detonations, each one setting off further landslides. The volcanic plug that had long since held the elemental forces of the planet at bay was gone. Fountains of molten rock glittered yellow in the gloom of ash and destruction.

As the centre of the island collapsed, the sea rushed in, resulting in yet more explosions of superheated steam. Cliffs of black rock slid into the water, sending out a tsunami of boiling water in the direction of Crannog Mons. It smashed against Traitor Rock, where it curved around the island towards Tor Tartarus and the Imperial troops still fighting there.

The wave was half as high as the Leviathan *Terra's Contempt*. The beast of war and her crew had no chance of escape. The wave swept it from the island.

But there was worse to come. Once the Leviathan had been torn free, the assault pipes buried within the causeway were exposed, and millions of gallons of boiling water rushed in to fill the void.

Thousands of Imperial Guardsmen were caught in the torrent. The lucky ones died instantly.

It was only through the timely intervention of one warrant officer that the blast doors were shut, saving the troops further behind. He himself did not survive, however, and his act of selfless courage went unnoticed, unrecorded and unknown by all whose continued existence relied on it.

For those traitors who did witness the explosion, it was the last thing they saw. They were buried by landslides, crushed by Baneblade-sized fragments of rock, burnt by fountains of magma, scalded by hissing blasts.

* * *

Minka was halfway down the steel grappling cable when the mines under the Lone Redoubt went off. She had no idea what it was. There was a sudden roar in her ears and the chain she was hanging from lashed up and down like the tail of a thrashing grox.

She clung on until she thought her shoulders would be ripped from their sockets. Dust and debris rained down upon her and got in her nose, her eyes, her mouth, down the back of her neck.

But she knew she could not let go. She could not fall, because Baine was right beneath her and she could hear his grunts to stay on.

Asko was thrown against the cliff face as the cable shook. He clung for dear life even as the steel rope stripped the skin from his palms, half-smoked lho-stub clenched between his teeth. Next was Maenard, but the demo expert couldn't maintain his grip. As the cable thrashed in his hand he was thrown clear. He tumbled silently, arms and legs spread like a child's rag-doll, disappearing into the darkness.

Near the bottom of the chain, Allun was the fastest to react. He held on, one arm locked through the cable as Karni slid ten feet to land on him. Allun held both of their weights as Karni struggled to pull herself up and away.

She was almost there when Orugi slammed down onto her.

Allun felt the weight and grunted in pain. 'Up!' he hissed. 'Wrap it about your arm!'

Karni did as he said and it gave her purchase. She used the tension to pull herself upwards.

'Good!' Allun hissed through gritted teeth. 'That's it!'

It was impossible. Aftershocks were jolting them all free. Above Orugi, Baine would not let go of the heavy bolter but it slipped from his grasp anyway, and then his other hand gave way and he could do nothing to slow his descent.

He hit Orugi with the force of a dead grox. They both slammed into Karni. The chain shredded the fabric of her uniform, flaying the skin from her forearm. She saw it come away in shreds but she didn't feel any pain, not even when she saw tendon and bone. She was in such a deep state of shock.

As all three of them crashed down into Allun, there was no way he could hold their fall. The weight snapped his arm, and sent him careening free and away from the others. He bounced off the rocks before hitting the water.

Below the spot where Allun had clung on moments before was Viktor. He saw Karni and the others sliding towards him and caught the loose end of the cable, wrapping it about his waist like a belt as the others thudded down into him.

Even about his flak armour the cable squeezed him so tight he thought he would pass out. But he stopped their descent. The four of them hung in the air, twirling in pain, each one pressed into the other.

'Throne,' Orugi said at last.

No one else could speak. Baine's hands were a shredded mess. Karni was moaning. Viktor was struggling for breath. 'I've got you,' he hissed at last. He had to grind the words out as the weight of all three of them tightened the cable about his waist. 'I've got you.'

Baine looked at his hands and saw the burns, the flesh flayed away. As soon as he saw the dreadful damage it was as if someone had turned his pain circuits on. The agony seared through him.

'I've got you,' Viktor repeated, trying to adjust the cable. The buckles of his flak armour were pressing into flesh. They felt like they had been stapled into him.

He was grunting with the effort. It was a hell of a job keeping all four of them up. He looked down. They were hanging from a single wire cable, three hundred feet above the beach, turning slowly on their axis.

'It could be worse,' Orugi said.

Karni made a weeping noise. He had never heard her sound like that before. Above her Baine was struggling to hold on without his hands. His efforts sent them into another spin.

'Hold still!' Viktor hissed. He tried to slow their revolutions. 'Can you pull yourself up?'

Baine tried, but his hands were lacerated and there was no way he could get purchase.

'Wrap your hand into the wire,' Orugi told him. The muscles in his arms were starting to tire. 'Wrap it round twice, and pull.'

Baine did so. It was agonisingly slow work while keeping his wounds away from the cable, but inch by inch he managed to lift his weight off Orugi. Then Orugi did the same.

Viktor felt the weight ease. He managed to adjust the cable. It hurt a little less. 'Karni?'

She didn't answer. It was clear that she was not in any state to pull herself up. He could see the silvery tendons in her forearm moving her fingers, but there was no strength in them, and she was so deep in shock that her reactions were hopelessly slow.

Viktor had been in worse scrapes, he told himself. 'Right, Karni, I'm going to try to shove you up. Then I need you to hold yourself up. I'm starting to slip.'

She moaned, and he took this as assent and twisted the end of the cable about his hand. She slipped and fell back into him, the weight of them both yanking the wire tight. It had shifted beneath his flak armour, about his waist, and now the cable was starting to cut him. He could feel the blood pooling in his fingers. 'Karni,' he said. 'I need you to hold yourself up. Orugi, reach back to pull Karni up.'

Orugi did so, hauling her up by her webbing.

'We're going to make it,' Viktor assured them all as he slowly lowered himself down the three hundred feet of cable.

SEVEN

The eruptions lit the night as the Imperial troopers were carried back to the mainland. The air was warm and thick and sulphurous. A stink of ash hung about them all. The days of close quarter fighting had been easier than enduring the waves and the explosions. The terror of being aboard these craft had worn many of their nerves to shreds. They lay down and closed their eyes and prayed for dry land.

Colonel Baytov was there on the beach, ready to welcome his regiment ashore. The landing craft came back throughout the early morning, in dribs and drabs, like exhausted men.

Some were half empty. Others were overcrowded or crammed with wounded. They landed where they had embarked, in the wide pebble bay south of the camp.

Baytov strode down to catch ropes, pull men ashore. It looked and felt like a different place entirely. Maybe it was just because they were changed. They'd lost their bull-headed eagerness.

They were now blooded, scarred and many of them were more than a little seasick.

'Well done!' Baytov told each and every trooper of his regiment, and he meant it.

In the blackened plains of the tank graveyard, Breve stepped down from the cargo-8 and looked about. Tanks painted in the distinctive colours of the 101st stretched away as far as he could see. The Cadian armour had been salvaged and carried off by the Adeptus Mechanicus reclamation squads. There were tanks, Chimeras, support vehicles, Sentinels, all parked neatly in rows with all the obsessive thoroughness of the Munitorum's savants.

'I wonder if they're parked in platoon order?' Breve said as they approached the row before them. The first tank had the markings of First Company, First Platoon, First Squad.

Breve and Wulfe looked about. 'Throne,' Wulfe said. 'They are!'

Breve cut through the line, aiming for where he guessed Seventh Company's tanks would be. Looking about, much of the armour here was junk. There wasn't just shell-fire, but water damage as well, which had fried some of the wiring.

His heart began to race as they passed through the tanks of Fifth Company.

Breve had not seen *The Saint* since they'd been forced to abandon her halfway up Tyrok Beach on the night of the landings.

As they passed along the line they found the tanks of Sixth Company. A number were missing. Breve steeled himself as he saw two crewmen pulling a body out of one of the Leman Russes. The inferno inside had turned the corpse into a calcified black husk. The crewmen had to break the spindly arms in half to get it out.

Breve looked away. He'd seen dead crewmen like this many

times. They always seemed to have grinning teeth. It was always the teeth that survived, he thought.

Wulfe had gone on ahead. 'Look here!' he called out. Breve clambered down the side of an Executioner-class Leman Russ, and was amazed to see *The Saint* standing there, as if waiting for him.

'Look at that!' he said and clambered up to pat the turret emblem that gave the tank its name.

Wulfe, the gunner, had drawn the turret-art, but the inspiration had come from Minka herself. A winged golden figure, flying over Kasr Myrak.

Minka had been very specific about the details.

Wulfe checked the Chimera's exterior for damage as Breve clambered in through the open hatch. There was a hell of a lot of sand and grit on the floor, but otherwise, it seemed that the machine had survived. 'She'll be right as rain when we get back,' he yelled from the cockpit. 'And if she isn't, then I'll have words with them.'

He tried the engine. It turned truculently.

Breve climbed back up the hatch and poked his head out. He looked to Wulfe. 'Know what I'm thinking?'

'Time for a new powerplant?'

'Exactly,' Breve said. He pushed himself up. The tank graveyard stretched inland for acres. 'There has to be one out there that will do.'

It took Breve an hour to find a suitable donor. It was a Rakallion Chimera with the name *Ignatz* emblazoned on the side. They had to get the powerplant out before the Adeptus Mechanicus priests found it and salvaged it themselves. Wulfe kept a lookout while Breve went in and started unscrewing the hatches.

It took both of them to manoeuvre the thing out.

By the time they returned to the camp that night, Breve was so happy he went to Minka's cabin.

The door was open. He knocked as he stepped into the doorway. 'Guess what!' he said, but the words died on his lips.

The bunks were empty.

He checked next door.

Empty as well.

He found Kavik, pegging up a fresh thought for the day.

'Where's Minka?'

Kavik spoke through the pins in his mouth. 'You haven't heard?'

'No.'

'She didn't make it.'

'She didn't? What the hell happened?'

Kavik shrugged. 'None of them made it.'

Breve fell back against the wall. It was as if he had been punched. 'You're kidding,' he whispered, but Kavik wasn't one for jokes.

Tears came unbidden. Breve sniffed and wiped them away. His heart ached.

All of them, he thought. I'm not supposed to be here. I should have died with them.

Breve turned his back as Kavik pinned the thought for the day onto the noticeboard.

Death is Honour, it declared.

Breve wept outside on the steps of the barracks-block. Everywhere he looked he saw Minka or Baine, or even quiet Karni. His throat ached. He pursed his lips and he started crying again.

You fool, he told himself, and sniffed and wiped his nose on the back of his sleeve.

He'd never liked Kavik.

Breve found Colonel Sparker in his office with Colour Sergeant Tyson and medic Banting. Banting had just finished daubing Sparker's grazes with iodine and was now packing his kit up in his leather satchel when Breve knocked on the open door.

Sparker looked up and Breve stepped in. He was too grief-stricken to go through formalities.

'Sorry, sir,' he said in a rush. 'I just heard that Sergeant Lesk did not make it off the island. Is that true?'

Sparker nodded. 'Afraid so.'

He was clearly busy. Breve swallowed. 'Do you know what happened?'

Sparker shook his head. 'She never made it to the evacuation vessels.'

'How could that be?'

Sparker knew a hundred reasons, but there didn't seem much point in listing them all. She was the rearguard and that was a dangerous place to be. 'War,' he said simply. 'People die. It happens.'

Prassan was another who could not believe that Minka was dead.

It was one of his duties to go through the casualties list each day, highlight any consequential losses to Mere, and then go and visit the wounded and pass on the compliments, best wishes, or commiserations of the general. He'd spent three days visiting all the medicae facilities with wounded Cadians within them, and in the three days since the evacuation he'd seen all the casualties and ticked them off his list.

On the fourth day, in Medicae 27, he made his way to the canteen for a drink of water and was greeted at the end of Ward 17 by a grey-haired medic with bright eyes and a slight stoop.

She was reading a chart as he approached, but she heard his

boots on the flakboard floor and looked up as he approached. 'Cadian?' she said.

He nodded.

'There's one of yours down here,' she said. She nodded into the ward she'd just come out of. 'Don't think any of your lot have been in to see her.'

Prassan's heart leapt. 'No?'

The old medic nodded. 'No.' She looked to the other medics for confirmation. They all shook their heads. 'Of course, she should have died,' the old lady said, and her eyes seemed to twinkle with hope. 'One of the Emperor's little miracles.'

Prassan said a prayer as he approached the bed. As he saw the occupant he felt that small hope within him die. He pursed his lips and stood smartly.

'Lieutenant,' he said, and saluted.

Dido lay with tubes up her nose. Her eyes were bruised and swollen, her legs held up in the air, and one of her eyes was red with a blood clot.

She gave a brief nod and Prassan cleared his throat. 'General Bendikt sends his regards,' he started.

Dido's eyes squeezed shut in what he guessed was a forced smile. 'Cut the crap,' she said.

Prassan took that as an order. He pulled out a chair and sat down next to Dido, and went through all the usual things an orderly would when faced with his old lieutenant. Dido was not in a chatty mood. She'd never much liked Prassan, and he knew that and spoke for both of them.

'You're not telling me something,' she said at last. There was a pause as she winced. 'Is it my injuries?'

Prassan shook his head. 'No,' he said briefly. He looked uncomfortable.

There was a long pause.

'You had better tell me because I can't get out of bed and shake you,' Dido said. 'And I'm too pissed off to play guessing games.'

Prassan dew in a deep breath.

'What is it?' she demanded.

Prassan didn't know what to say. After a longer pause, she said, 'It's bad?'

He nodded.

She closed her eyes. 'Tell me.'

Prassan coughed to clear his throat, took another deep breath and let it all come out at once. 'We lost Minka.'

Dido stared at him. 'What happened?' she said at last.

Prassan sighed. 'No one knows exactly. Minka was made acting-lieutenant. Her lot were rearguard.'

'Why the hell were they rearguard?' Dido snapped. 'That damned Sparker! Always wants someone else to do the dirty work.'

Her sudden outburst drew concerned looks from the medics at the door.

'The mine ripped the island apart. It started an eruption. It's a mess.'

'Throne,' Dido said, her expression guilty. 'If I hadn't got wounded I'd have been in command of her platoon, and I'd have made damned sure she didn't get left behind.' She swallowed. 'Not a chance they survived?'

Prassan slumped forward. He shook his head. 'The Navy have been over the island. They say there are no signs of life.'

Dido nodded. 'I understand,' she said. There was a pause. 'I hope it was clean.' She looked at the ruin of her own body. 'Not like this.'

Prassan nodded. That's what troopers wanted. A glorious life and a clean death.

Dido turned her face away. He could see tears starting to well in her eyes. As they began to fall he made as if to speak but she waved him away.

Just go, her gesture told him.

EIGHT

Colour Sergeant Tyson was on his morning rounds as he stood to watch a flight of Marauder destroyers returning from a raid. It was four days since they'd been evacuated from Tor Kharybdis, but the sight of the magma, fountaining red, was still mesmerising.

It reminded him of a warzone he had experienced his first real battles on, years before. They'd all been kitted out in hazard suits as they hunted for xenos. He'd never seen any, but he'd seen a number of his comrades consumed by the lava. It was a good lesson, he'd thought at the time.

Listen to instructions. All those who had died had failed to do so.

Tyson sniffed. The Marauders had clearly suffered a pummelling. A number of them were trailing smoke, the ragged holes in the squadron formations giving them the look of shredded cloth. A long way back he could make out a lone Marauder, white smoke billowing from the right wing, limping back. It looked like only one engine was still functioning.

They're not going to make it, Tyson thought.

True enough, the high-pitched whine of flagging engines cut through the drone of the others. The bomber was losing height rapidly, its white pennant of smoke following it down. It plunged, and hit the water far out, past the old bridge supports.

He felt the explosion – a distant tremble in the air.

He drew in a deep breath and remembered where he was going. The signals office was in the central square of the camp, a half-buried bunker reinforced with sandbag walls and sunken stairwell.

Tyson walked quietly wherever he went. He never wanted to be expected. Always wanted to find misbehaviour. Always wanted his appearance to be a shock.

It kept the troops honest because none of them wanted to cross Colour Sergeant Tyson.

He was a little disappointed to find that inside the dark, monitor-lit interior of the signals depot, everyone seemed to be hard at work. They all had their headsets on and were staring intently into their monitor screens. Tyson looked about. There was a servitor desk in the corner, eye sockets and mouth each plugged with neural inputs. At its waist was a roll of parchment. The remaining arm had been replaced with a steel quill. It remained stationary as it waited for input. Every few minutes it scratched and the parchment unrolled.

Kallio, the officer on duty, took a look at the parchment, before finally noticing Tyson's arrival.

'Sir!' he said.

Kallio was a thin man with a narrow neck, round face and a pair of wire-rimmed round spectacles balanced halfway down his nose. He was quiet and thoughtful, unlike the typical Cadian.

'I'm glad you're here. I have something I want your opinion on,' he said and motioned Tyson forward. 'Here. Come look at this.'

Tyson sniffed as he stared at the parchment read-out. He didn't expect much. 'What am I looking at?'

Kallio pointed, gathering up the folds of parchment. 'Here,' he said. 'If we screen out the other chatter, then look.'

Tyson picked the paper up between thumb and forefinger. At last he saw what the signals officer was talking about. Irregular signals spiking the feed.

Tyson frowned for a moment and then Kallio tapped out the sequence so Tyson could hear it. The colour sergeant started smiling. 'That's clever.'

Kallio grinned. Cadia had been a militarised state, with all the military frequencies on constant use. In order not to inter-fere with these, Whiteshields had had their own set of special dummy codes for children so that they did not interrupt the military channels. They communicated simply – things like *Danger, Stay alert, We're here.*

'Whiteshield training code,' Kallio said.

'I'm not so old that I've forgotten,' Tyson snapped.

'It's not a vox-set. Look. It's coming from the direction of Tor Kharybdis. It's across all these channels. It's crude, but if I had to hazard a guess, someone is sparking powercells.'

Tyson nodded. 'It's not something to do with the eruption?'

Kallio shook his head. He turned to his assistant, Trooper Stal. 'What does it say?'

The young man coughed to clear his throat. 'Sir. It's a series of numbers – one-zero-one-seven-two.'

'Cadian Hundred-and-First.' Tyson frowned. 'But what about the others?'

'Seventh Company. Second Platoon.'

'Dido's lot?'

Kallio slapped the tabletop. 'Yes!'

Tyson was impassive. 'It could be a trap.'

Kallio looked at him. 'It could be. There's only one way to find out.'

Tyson was secretly elated, but he was wary of joy like he was wary of hope – both were illusions that left the plunge of disappointment deeper than before.

But once Kallio had pinpointed the origin of the signal as coming from the area of Faith Beach, he went to Sparker with the news.

Tyson presented the information to him in a straightforward manner. 'There's a chance that the enemy know the same codes. Identical equipment. The same bandwidths. If they look through their data-library deeply enough, they will also have the Whiteshield codes, somewhere.'

At the end he said, 'What should we do, sir?'

'That is the best news all day!' Sparker said and almost broke out the grog. 'Get a crew out there! If there's one Cadian left we bring them in. Go get them. Now!'

It took an hour to get through to and persuade a suitable Imperial Navy officer. 'They've agreed,' Tyson said at last and Sparker leapt up from his chair and strode to the door. A plume of black smoke showed the location of the remains of Tor Kharybdis. 'It's a tough call,' he said.

Tyson nodded. That's what the Cadians were for.

The afternoon was wearing on by the time the Valkyries and Vultures were being filled with promethium. Only then did Tyson relay the developments to Colonel Baytov.

'You think there are survivors left behind?' the colonel asked.

Tyson maintained his flat demeanour. 'It is a possibility. Worth investigating.'

'I agree,' Baytov said. 'Well done.'

Tyson took the compliment and then said, 'It was Signals Officer Kallio.'

'Good. Congratulate him too!'

Valkyrie A-786 lifted off from Phaeton Airbase X-94 as the light was failing. Captain Uleg was in the pilot's seat. Jimal was co-piloting. The waist gunners were already swinging their heavy bolters out as the evening klaxons started to ring. The air rippled with the heat of the droning engines. He had an escort of two Vultures that rose into the air from neighbouring pads, their noses swinging round. Uleg saluted the other pilots. Vultures packed a serious punch, bristling with nose-mounted heavy bolters and missile pods underslung from their wing mountings.

Jimal ran through the basic checks as Uleg established vox contact with the Vulture pilots, and then said, 'Let's go!'

The three noses dipped low as they accelerated forward, flying low and hard, pilot lights flashing as they roared out towards the sea.

Each crew knew that as soon as they crossed the cliffs and were over water, they would be picked up by the sensor stations on Crannog Mons. And then it would be a desperate scramble to locate the missing Cadians and pick them up before a fighter response or anti-aircraft fire could take them out.

'We'll copy the routine cargo-shuttle routes, make this look as ordinary as possible,' Uleg told them. 'Then make a dash for it.'

The atmosphere in the lead Valkyrie was tense. Jimal kept a constant check on the augur. That 'dash' was only a ten-mile run, but it was ten miles straight into enemy territory. 'We get out there, see if anyone is alive, and then we get the hell back as quick as possible,' Uleg voxed.

'What about the eruption?'

'Nothing we can do about that.'

'Five minutes to objective,' Jimal stated.

Uleg nodded. Life in the Imperial Navy had taught him that if anything could go wrong, it would.

Colonel Sparker didn't do well when there wasn't much to do and now he paced up and down his office. The flakboard floor creaked under his feet.

Long ago, in his officer training academy, Sparker had been presented with the relevant sections of the *Codex Exercitus*.

'That is a copy of the original tome that sits on Terra!' the man had told Sparker, as if to instil the gift with extra weight.

In his time with the Astra Militarum, Sparker had heard a hundred facts about the Holy Palace, half of which contradicted each other. But he'd certainly heard that the *Codex Exercitus* was stored in its many leather-bound chapters that filled multiple floors of the palace library, where hexagonal rooms with statues of Imperial saints and heroes abutted one upon the other.

His copy was a paperbound and now dog-eared condensation. He picked it up and thumbed through it. It was all predictable stuff, restating the basics for savage world tribesmen. Ten troopers to a squad. So many squads to a platoon. So many platoons to a company. But there was always something that he'd forgotten.

He riffled through the pages a while longer and then tossed it down onto the desk.

He loathed the admin side of his job. He was a fighter, not a clerk. He hunched over it and screwed his nose up. Waiting was worse than going into combat.

After an hour or so, there was a knock on the door. Evrind put her head around the doorway. Sometimes the close combat expert resembled an oversized ratling with her wiry mop of curly brown hair.

'The Valkyrie has taken off,' Evrind said.

Sparker nodded. 'Good. Keep me informed.'

Uleg's flight kept low to the sea. The black mass of Crannog Mons rose to their right. It seemed impossible to know where they were to head for.

Uleg scanned the remains of Tor Kharybdis. The fountain of magma boiled up from within the crater, roiling black smoke billowing towards the tower of Ophio. He hoped it would scramble the traitor auspex.

As they swept towards the narrow coves of Faith, Josmane and Marius he lifted the nose and gave a flash of his front lumen. A code word. Another flash.

Uleg and Jimal stared at the hillside, straining for any sign of life. Nothing.

'Let's go closer,' Uleg voxed. He was in charge of this mission, and they were going to do it right.

The headland rose steeply ahead of them. Uleg cursed and banked to the right. He checked his bearings, matched up visuals to the map on his data-screen. He kept flashing the lumens as they flew over a narrow inlet. Nothing.

It was hard maintaining a safe distance from the cliff. He was about to call off the search when there was a crackle in his earpiece from one of the waist gunners. 'Contact!' he stated.

The word came so loudly and confidently it made Uleg jump. Jimal gestured to the right.

'There's a signal,' he confirmed. Uleg checked. Sure enough, there was a light flashing up from below. He swung the Valkyrie down. Landslides had created a defile from which the signal came.

'It's too narrow!' Jimal warned.

The flash came again; the same signal crackled on the vox. They were in broadcast mode. In irritation Uleg flicked his channel to that of ground troops.

'We're coming in,' he confirmed. 'Hold tight.'

The updrafts buffeted the Valkyrie, throwing it towards the cliffs as Uleg tried to bring it down into the narrow gap. He had to throttle back to descend, but it gave him less thrust to hold them straight. It was an exhausting descent, playing the thrusters with both feet, trying to balance out nature, wind, gusts and gravity.

He did not have time to check the augur but the sudden flash of green caught his eye as the tracking arm flared with contacts.

'We've got company,' Jimal stated.

'I've got it,' Uleg said. There was a pause as the Valkyrie descended. The Vultures were already swinging away. 'Three hostiles, nine o'clock.' There was a pause. 'They're coming in fast.'

'Lightnings!' one of the Vulture pilots reported.

Uleg could feel his palms starting to sweat. His helmet felt hot. It was better than Thunderbolts, he thought. He had a grudging respect for Thunderbolts. They were tough as rockcrete. He made a quick calculation as he pushed the accelerator handle forward. 'I can see them!' he said.

He was talking about the Cadians, not the Lightnings. There was a flashlight shining constantly now, waving him in.

There was a rattle as the waist gunners stowed the heavy bolters and swung the rappelling wire out into the darkness.

'Wires away,' the waist gunner told him. It took all of Uleg's skill to keep them off the rocks. He felt the weight of each Cadian being hauled up. 'Got one,' the waist gunner voxed.

One by one they were pulled aboard. The green blips moved nearer and nearer.

Uleg wiped the sweat from his lip.

'All aboard,' the report came at last.

'Right!' Uleg voxed. 'Let's get the Throne out of here.' He backed up slowly, riding the wind.

Once he'd crested the headland, he could see the crater that was all that remained of Tor Kharybdis, and the spraying fountain of magma. He could feel the heat as well.

There was no time to enjoy the wild beauty of it all. Alarms were ringing inside the cabin. Those Lightnings were almost upon them.

He swung the Valkyrie round, dropped the nose and pushed the accelerator forward. 'Heading for home!' he voxed.

Uleg's Valkyrie skimmed so low that its engines ploughed a straight white furrow through the water. He risked a glance at the augur. The enemy Lightnings were closing. His Vulture escorts had fallen in behind him in wing position.

The Lightning pilots flew over their position once, then doubled back, using that furrow as their guide. The Vultures peeled off to either side. One of the enemy circled round, while the other kept the Valkyrie within visual contact.

'They're starting their attack run,' Jimal reported.

'Engaging,' one of the Vulture captains reported. There was a distant flash as its missiles exploded. The other Vulture fired off a salvo of hard rounds.

'One down,' the confirmation came.

Uleg could hardly believe it.

The Vultures fired again.

'Second Lightning is pulling out.' There was a pause. The Vulture captains were giddy. 'He's disengaging.'

'You sure?' Uleg hissed.

There was no answer. 'Third Lightning coming in.'

There was a flash of red las-bolts, then the third Lightning roared over Uleg's head, the fiery blue disc of its afterburners visible as it swung up and round again for another pass.

'One man down,' Jimal reported.

Uleg nodded. He'd seen the blip of his right wingman disappear.

The other wingman was more serious now. The Lightning was making a great loop above them and coming in for another attack run. 'This bastard is keen,' Jimal stated.

At that moment the other Vulture disappeared off the auspex.

'What happened?' Uleg called out. Jimal tried to contact the Vultures, but both of them were silent. He tried them again. Nothing.

'I can't see them,' Jimal stated.

Uleg felt cold. It was a state of utter terror controlled by logic and training. He kept the Valkyrie running low and hard as he watched the green blip of the Lightning slow and then come round in its great loop. Uleg voxed to the waist gunners. 'See if you can scare him off.' They could hear the tension in his voice. He pressed the pedals to the floor.

The dark water below glittered with the refracted light of the sky. It was choppy down there. The swell rose up to meet him as they skimmed the surface.

'He's coming in,' Jimal reported.

'Hold on in the back!' Uleg voxed.

He watched the flash of the augury as it traced the attack run of the Lightning. How many times had he sat in the mess hall and theorised this move? It was all about perfect timing. Move too early and you were easy prey. Too late and you were dead before you'd even started the adjustment.

'He's coming,' Jimal said, as if Uleg's whole focus was not on this moment. Uleg's hand got itchy. It was not yet time, not quite.

'Holy Emperor,' he prayed as he pushed the thrusters forward, yanked the control gears up and backwards, and the Valkyrie's steel frame creaked as it climbed up and to the left in a steep loop.

Red flashes lit along the cabling glaspex. Uleg felt the world start to darken. His chest was too tight for breath. He felt the Valkyrie's welded joints begin to pop and cut the thrusters back. The craft slowed and then hung in the air, and for a moment it was as if they were going to stall.

Blue afterburner streaked overhead. Uleg pulled the nose round and hosed off a salvo of opportunistic multi-laser shots. They streaked heavenwards and were lost in the darkness. He didn't appear to have hit.

He checked the augur; the Lightning had peeled off to the left and was coming round for a third time.

'Are we in range yet?'

'Another mile.'

Uleg cursed. The Lightning would have one more chance to blow them out of the sky. And he couldn't pull that trick again.

Suddenly the flier disappeared from the auspex. 'Did it hit the water?' he shouted, looking about for sign of an impact.

'I can't see!' Jimal responded.

Uleg twisted uncomfortably in his seat. Where had the bastard gone? His auspex showed nothing. Then it came to him in a sudden moment of dreadful fear. The auspex had a blind spot directly above.

He looked up, saw nothing in the darkness, but he knew that the enemy flyer had to be there.

But as he searched the skies above, the Valkyrie rattled as hard rounds slammed into it. He threw the Valkyrie nose down and flung her to the side as the Lightning swept past her right wing, the turbulence forcing them further sideways.

Alarms sounded. The dashboard was full of flashing lights. Uleg silenced them and took a moment. The fuel tanks were hit and leaking fast. He could smell smoke within the cockpit. It could be a fire or just wires burning out. He felt a wave of panic rising as Jimal cried out, 'He's coming in again!'

Uleg's auspex was empty. 'Where from?'

'Right behind!'

'Hold him off!' he shouted. He felt the heavy bolters start to fire.

There wasn't enough fuel to outfly the enemy. They were a sitting target unless they did something. Uleg began to scissor sideways. But even as he did so the alarms for the left engine died. It was all he could do now to keep them running flat and straight.

Sparker couldn't rest. He pushed himself up and strode outside.

He skipped down the steps of his office block to the flakboard-lined path below. The mud squelched as he turned towards the signals room. Two troopers coming off sentry duty straightened up and stepped aside to salute him.

He nodded to them. It was a five-minute walk to the signals office. He tried to distract himself.

In the signals hut he was surprised to see Prassan.

'Have they got bored of you at HQ?' Sparker said.

'Not yet, sir.' Prassan put up his hand. 'They've picked them up.'

'Who?'

Prassan signalled that he didn't know. He was listening to the vox-chatter, but they were on Navy channels and it was hard to get any sense out of them. There was a long pause, before confirmation came. Sparker watched Prassan's face. 'Both Vultures are down,' Prassan said.

Even Sparker could hear the affirmative.

Prassan kept his mouth closed. He looked down, tracing his finger over the aquila on the vox-unit. He coughed to clear his throat, and said, 'And the Valkyrie?'

There was a pause.

'They've been hit, but they're coming in!' Prassan said.

The Valkyrie staggered the last half mile towards the shore. The air inside the cabin was tense, Guardsmen packed close together, more than normal safe operation would allow. There was nothing worse than being reliant on someone else. The waist gunners yanked their sliding doors open and leaned their heavy bolters out.

The guns' deep-throated chatter competed with the rattle and wind of the Valkyrie.

'Looks like they spotted us,' Baine stated. His face was pale. He was clearly holding back the pain of his hands.

Minka nodded. She didn't like this any more than the others.

The Valkyrie lurched to the side, throwing them all against their restraints. Wind tore at them. Sparks flew through the cabin. Part of the fuselage had been sheared off.

'We've been hit,' Asko hissed. He still had that stub of lho-stick in his teeth.

The cabin was full of smoke. One waist gunner had been almost cut in two by a lascannon; his superheated flesh had exploded when the bolt went through him, splattering viscera across the inner panels and cabin door. His bleeding remains lay half in and half out of the doorway.

The other one was crawling across the floor to them. He had been hit by shrapnel. He was making an incoherent mewling sound.

Minka unwound herself from the harness. She was as shaken up as the others.

The Valkyrie was listing heavily. The engines rattled as if they were full of shrapnel. Even though they couldn't see outside, they could tell that they were falling fast.

'Get the door open!' Minka shouted.

Baine had Karni by the shoulder. 'Hold on!' he called out.

There was a loud bang in the engine above their heads, and the cabin was suddenly full of spraying hydraulics.

Staff in the watchtower of Phaeton Airbase X-94 saw the lights of the lone Valkyrie coming in low. Thick black smoke bled out from one engine while the other spluttered and coughed.

A fire response unit was already backing into place, its yellow flashing lights casting an eerie glow over the landing pad. The wind had fallen, just enough to ruffle the wind-sock.

They fixed their attention on that Valkyrie. It was losing height too quickly. Its landing lights seemed too distant for it to make it.

It was still a hundred yards away when there was a sudden bang.

Flames appeared along its fuselage and the Valkyrie dropped like a stone. It hit the ground belly first, skidding forwards and losing both wings in the tumble before bursting into flame.

Fire spread from the rear engine, flowing all along the fuselage as the fuel ignited. Bodies tumbled out of the waist doors. Jaromir and Lyrga dragged the wounded gunners out. Last of all came Minka, her face covered in blood. It was running from her nose and mouth.

'I'm all right!' She pointed to the cabin. 'We need to get them out!'

The flames engulfed the cockpit. The canopy had jammed and the pilot was hammering against the glass. His face showed panic as the catches refused to give. Belus and Orugi rushed forward to help, but the growing flames forced them back.

The pilot's mouth was open in a scream. Minka turned away as he started to cook. She did not need to see that.

NINE

The crews were putting out the last of the flames when a medicae van arrived. Minka had brought seventeen of her platoon off Tor Kharybdis, packed in tight. They were in good shape, considering. Except Karni, of course. Her arm had become infected and they'd run out of stimms. Minka stepped up straight away to make sure she got in first.

'Baine!' she called next.

'I'm fine,' Baine said, but it was patently untrue. His palms had been flayed down to the tendons. They'd done their best, dousing his hands in the seawater and bandaging them with strips of uniform, but they needed some serious attention.

'Viktor!' she called out. He limped forward, his face pale. She thought Viktor might have broken a rib.

The medics screened the others. Minka refused to go anywhere until they were all seen to.

'We'll get another van,' the medic said as he clambered into the front cabin.

It took an hour for the next van to arrive. Minka bundled all of her remaining platoon inside. Yedrin held back to the end. She pushed him in. 'Go,' she said. 'They'll want to check you out. And, hey. You and Blanchez – you did well. I was proud of you out there!'

Yedrin forced a smile. 'Thanks,' he said, and ducked into the back of the van.

'Lieutenant?' Blanchez said, making space for her to join them.

Minka shook her head. 'I'll come later. I have a few things to clear up first.'

The van had just pulled off when a Tauros arrived. Prassan was driving. In the other seat sat Colonel Sparker. Her immediate thought was, what are those two doing here? But at that moment, Sparker saw her and leapt out.

'Congratulations! We thought we had lost you.' He took her hand and pulled her into a fierce embrace. 'Was it just you?'

'No,' she said. 'The others have gone to the medicae.'

'Have you eaten?'

'I'm fine, thank you, sir,' Minka said.

Sparker went on regardless. He bundled her towards the Tauros. She found the sudden attention bewildering. She was in shock.

When they got to camp Tyson was standing on the steps. From his expression she assumed she was in deep trouble. She thought of those that she had not brought off Tor Kharybdis, and it hurt.

But Tyson came down and embraced her. 'Well done!' he said. 'Smart idea with the signalling.'

'That was Yedrin's idea. Fresh in his mind from the Whiteshields camp.'

Tyson shook his head. He and Sparker led her into the captain's office. A runner had been sent to bring food and water.

She felt almost giddy. 'What are you doing here?' she said to Prassan.

He found his clipboard, which he had left on Sparker's desk. 'I've been asked by General Bendikt to assess the performance of the Whiteshields,' Prassan said.

'Now?' she said. She could see the colour rise up Prassan's neck. He coughed and looked down to consult his notes. 'Yes. As you know, this is a trial programme, designed to ensure that Cadian regiments within this warzone continue to be a bulwark of the Imperium.'

'You want to know how they did on Tor Kharybdis?'

He nodded.

'I had two. Yedrin and Blanchez. They did great. Full marks all round. Both to the troopers and the training staff.'

Prassan made quick notes. From the way his pen moved over the form, it looked to Minka as though he was ticking a series of boxes before him.

'That's it?'

He nodded. 'Yes. Thank you.'

'Good. Listen. I have one other thing you might be able to help me with. I've been told that Trooper Dreno is currently under Commissariat investigation. Shot in the hand. Some bat thinks the wound was self-inflicted.'

Prassan had heard. 'Y-yes,' he said at last. 'I was aware that something had happened.'

'Dreno is a good trooper. Bit of a bastard at times, but there're worse. I'd appreciate it if you could have a word with the bats.'

'I can't,' Prassan said.

'No?'

His cheeks had turned a deep red. He shook his head. 'I'm just a trooper. You're acting-lieutenant, so if you vouch for him then I am sure the Commissariat will consider your input with due respect.'

Minka laughed. 'Right. I will. Anything else, sir?'

Sparker intervened. 'No! Not now. Prassan – put that clip-board away!' He reached into a drawer. 'Here!' he said and tossed something towards her.

She caught it one-handed. It was small and heavy. She opened her fist, and there were a pair of laurel collar badges in her palm.

'Pin those on. Baytov has approved your promotion to lieu-tenant.' He tossed the arm-badges as well.

She caught them in the other hand and saluted smartly. 'Thank you, sir!'

From the other side of his desk he pulled out a bottle of his second-best grog. 'Here!' he said. 'Have a drink.'

They drank and Minka felt the heat of the white liquid settle in her stomach. It filled her with a sense of ease.

Prassan fidgeted with his pen. 'Listen, Minka,' he started hesi-tantly. 'I don't think you will have heard.'

'What?'

'Dido survived.'

Minka leapt up. 'She did? Where is she? I have to see her.'

Minka took Prassan's staff dirtcycle. 'I only need an hour,' she told him. 'Promise.'

She swung out of the gates and accelerated along the access bahn. It took her twenty minutes to get to the right medicae facility. She slowed as she turned through the gates. Some Rakal-lion troops were on duty. They were sitting in the guard house, hats lying on the table next to them, a pot of recaff on the table.

They saw her lieutenant badge and waved her through.

Sloppy bastards, she thought.

She found the ward and hurried inside. Minka gave the nurse

on duty Dido's name. The nurse consulted her papers. 'This way,' she said.

She led Minka into a long ward lined with beds. The bedding was all stiff and starched. There were bandages everywhere, low voices and the constant sound of moaning. 'Don't mind them. That is the song of the dying trooper,' the nurse said, and smiled. 'They know that they will meet the Emperor very soon.'

The nurse left her at the end of Dido's bed. All Minka could see were bandages. She felt a strange reluctance as she stepped forward. 'Dido?' she called out.

Dido's face peered out over the sheets. Her arms were out on the bed. She lay on her back, but one of her legs was held up in the air.

Minka sat down. 'Hey,' she said quietly. The starched white sheets suddenly reminded her of how dirty she was.

Dido lifted a hand. Her whole manner and attitude seemed despondent. 'Hey,' she said. 'So. I hear you covered yourself in glory.'

Minka shrugged. 'I did what was necessary.'

Dido's eyes fell on the lieutenant pins on Minka's collar. 'And they've given you my job as well.'

'Acting-lieutenant,' Minka lied.

Dido gestured to her body. 'If they're waiting for me to come back it could be a long time.'

Minka nodded. She hadn't expected this. 'Is it serious?'

'Shrapnel. Big as my hand. Went through my spine,' Dido explained. 'I can't feel a thing down there.'

Minka took in a deep breath. She wanted to sound reassuring. 'They'll do something.'

Dido cursed. She seemed in a foul mood, but after a long pause she apologised. 'Listen. I'm sorry. You're the first person I've seen from the regiment. Apart from Prassan and Father

Keremm. He's here every damned day praying for me. I could throttle him.' Dido sighed. 'How did my lot do?'

Minka told her everything. The Whiteshields. How the others all managed. The injuries they'd suffered. 'Karni's arm is a mess. Dreno's under investigation. We lost Allun and Maenard. When the evacuation came they left without us.'

'Sparker should never have given you that job.'

'It wasn't that,' Minka said. She didn't like her competence being brought into question.

'What was it?'

Minka shook her head. She didn't want to explain it all. 'We were left behind. Fought some traitor survivors, but they were more messed up than we were. The eruption made it difficult. There was very little to salvage. No vox. No food. No water. We only got off the island today,' Minka said.

They talked a little longer but this had not gone how she had expected.

At last Dido said, 'Here I am, moaning at you. Throne! You should go and get yourself a shower or something.'

Minka had run out of things to say. 'Yes. I'm sure I have some reports to fill out. I'll come back as soon as possible,' she promised.

Dido reached up to take Minka's hand. 'Listen. I'm cranky. Sorry. But I'm glad you're leading the platoon. I wouldn't want anyone else. They're a great bunch. Remember. You can't do everything yourself. You'll know when your time comes. It's when the others are pausing. That's when you've got to put yourself at the front. You have to lead.' She gestured to her own body. 'Whatever the cost.'

Minka nodded. 'Thank you. I will remember that.'

Minka strode back through the wards, looking at the lines of wounded and dying, and thanked the Golden Throne that she was not one of them.

The Rakallion guards were still sitting around their pot of recaff. She accelerated away, the dirtbike weaving through the lines of military traffic.

Prassan was waiting for her by the camp gates. She pulled to a halt, left the engine still running as she handed it over to him. 'How was she?' he asked.

'Not good,' she said. 'Think she'll walk again?'

He shook his head. Unlikely. They didn't give spinal augmetics to lieutenants, and if they did it was hard to get up to combat effectiveness. 'Maybe she can come and work at HQ,' he said. He was trying to sound cheerful.

Minka nodded. She put out her hand. 'Thanks for the ride. Look after yourself. Don't go getting fat on us. You never know when Tyson will call you back to the front lines.'

Prassan saluted her. 'Is that an order, Lieutenant Lesk?'

She punched him. 'Get out of here.'

As he drove off she repeated the words 'Lieutenant Lesk' to herself.

She thought of Colonel Rath Sturm. She'd like to tell him that she'd made it. She wondered where he was now, and if he was still alive.

But first, she thought, she needed a shower.

TEN

Minka's sergeants were Raske, Elhrot, Dreno and Barnabas. Elhrot was the kind of officer who did what you asked as well as he was able. Minka had never had a high opinion of Barnabas, but she didn't like to go against Dido's opinion. Barnabas resented her appointment over him. But there was nothing she could do about that.

Dreno was her first appointment. The rank of sergeant was only the first brief step on the ladder for him. He clearly thought he was destined for much greater things. He'd take orders, but he had initiative. Better in a sergeant than a corporal, and Minka couldn't begrudge him for a quality she'd shown in spades.

Minka spread the surviving veterans of Dido's personal command squad into her other squads as corporals, and moved Yedrin and Blanchez to her five-strong command squad, with Baine – when he was declared fit – and Orugi.

She put it about that she wanted to keep an eye on the two

young troopers. Blanchez reminded her of herself as a younger woman while Yedrin was quiet, earnest, as eager to please as a lost hound. He reminded her of her lost brother, Tarli.

He was up first in the morning, first to stand when she entered a room. Minka appreciated the respect. Cadians had very high expectations of their officers. The doctrines were straightforward. Always put your troops first. Never eat until they had all eaten. And always keep the troopers up to a high standard of readiness.

Minka found life as a lieutenant a big change from that of sergeant – how she was suddenly responsible for four times as many troopers.

She kept special tabs on her old squad, though. She spoke to Commissar Shand about Dreno.

'Yes, I looked into that. No evidence of self-imposed injury,' Shand said. 'An over-zealous cadet.'

When she shared the news with Dreno he made no reaction. It was as if he had been só wounded by the insult that he had refused to acknowledge it. 'And I want to make you sergeant,' she said, 'of my old squad.'

Dreno's face betrayed emotion at that. 'Not Viktor?'

She shook her head. Viktor liked being corporal. She saw no need to move him.

Dreno put out his hand and shook hers. 'Thank you,' he said simply.

Of the others, Karni was responding well to augmetics. Baine's hand was healing nicely. Blanchez and Yedrin were settling in well.

One of the biggest changes in her daily routines was that now Minka ate in the officer's mess. It was a block set apart from the other buildings, with guards on the door and its own catering staff. The room had been decorated with a selection of the artefacts that the regiment had salvaged from Cadia. A pair of crossed flags hung at the far end of the room. One was the company banner, the other a golden aquila embroidered onto a field of sable.

Silver bowls and plates hung on the walls, each one engraved with the name of an officer or a battle or a planet where the 101st had served. There were strings of paintings with heavy gilded frames, displaying the commanding officers of the company stretching back hundreds of years. Each likeness showed the officer in dress uniform or camo, according to the passing fashions of the time. Some had chosen to be painted amidst the scenes of their greatest victories. There were ice worlds, flames, broken bastions, great plains filled with furiously contesting armour. A few showed images of Cadia. Minka paused before those, and she drank the images up, like a thirsty man given a glass of clear water.

Now she brushed shoulders with the company officers. Sparker sensed her discomfort and took her aside for a briefing. 'There's no need for formalities. Treat senior officers with respect. But don't be backwards in approaching them if you need advice.'

'Thank you, sir.'

Each morning there were company officer meetings. Tactics were discussed. The state of each platoon, the regiment, the entire war. Minka soaked it all up. She was cautious of speaking at first, but it seemed that the other officers not only accepted her, but were keen to hear her opinion. While Tor Kharybdis had been a success, it hadn't won the war. And there still remained the question of how to break Traitor Rock.

'I don't think it's going the way Bendikt wanted. We've bled them, but not enough. Either that, or they're more stubborn than he was expecting.'

'We could attack Margrat,' Lieutenant Petr suggested.

It made no sense to any of them. No. The attack had to come at Tor Tartarus.

'But any attack there faces terrible bombardment from above. It would be very costly indeed.'

Colonel Sparker went round each person, asking how they would take Tor Tartarus.

When it was Minka's turn she tried to appear calm and unhurried. 'We could launch another amphibious assault at Ophio?'

'Unlikely to succeed a second time,' Sparker said.

Minka stared at the fortress. 'So it's Tor Tartarus.' She remembered Markgraaf Hive. 'Is there a way of going in with Termites?'

Sparker shook his head. 'No. The island itself is volcanic but the archo-geologists state that the shoreward side is porous rock. Too soft for Termites. They're likely to get swamped. Or drowned.'

Good, Minka thought. She had no love of Termites. 'How long until Sanguinalia?'

'Twenty days.'

'So we need a knock-out blow. We can't just bleed them to death.'

'Yes. But how?'

No one had any breakthrough ideas, so the meeting dissolved without any resolution.

That evening Minka went back to the guard tower on the southern face of the Cadian camp. She scrambled up the ladder and pulled herself through the hatch at the top. Karni was on duty with Belus and Asko.

'Look who's come to say hello,' Belus called out. He and Asko had clearly been playing cards. Both hands lay face down on the floor.

'Maybe save the cards for later,' she said. Minka was here to look at Crannog Mons. She had brought her field-auspex.

Across the water the steps of Tor Tartarus were visible. The massive fortress had been reduced to a ragged rockface of chewed rockcrete and exposed tunnel arches beneath. It looked more like a cliff of caves than a fortress. At the very top were the upper batteries, unloading a weight of fire into the Imperial trenches. She could see at least twenty Hydra platforms. Any aerial assault would be doomed. Valkyries were slow, for fliers, and there was no cover for them on the long sea crossing. They could try a Naval bombardment, of course, but mists would make an aerial landing fraught.

Minka put the auspex down. She stared intently, trying to work this puzzle out.

If only they could take that top terrace, she thought, then any attacks might have more success. But there was no way she could see to do it.

She turned away. She'd consult the regimental histories to see if there was any precedent for a battle of this kind.

Minka went back to visit Dido. Her former commander had been moved into a fresh ward away from the dying.

'We're the convalescents,' Dido said, waving a bored hand down the line of bandages and metal cots. 'You can set your watch by that one,' she said, pointing to the end of the line. All Minka could see was a breathing tube sticking out of the place where the man's mouth should be. 'Every two hours he wakes up and starts screaming. He's going to start in about ten minutes. Then they dose him up with soporifics and he falls asleep again.'

Minka sat down on the side of the cot. The metal creaked. The mattress was hard, and the sheets smelt of carbolics.

'How is my platoon?'

'Good,' Minka said, but she suddenly felt wary of speaking too much. 'They miss you.'

'Good. None of them have visited me.'

'They're confined to camp.'

Dido rolled her eyes. 'All I see is Banting. He feels my pulse and tuts and then he gives me a syringe. *Nothing you can't fix with an injection.*' Dido laughed, and gestured at her body. 'How's he going to fix this?'

Minka made a little conversation, but it was hard listening to the tedium of Dido's life, and the irritation that came out of it. At last Minka had to go. 'Anything you want me to pass on?'

'Tell the bastards that if they get soft then I'll roast them,' Dido said.

Minka had reached the door when the bandaged man started to moan.

'Told you!' Dido called out. Minka turned and looked at her lieutenant, lying crippled in bed, and lifted a hand in farewell.

It was a week before Minka could make it back to visit Dido. She hitched a lift in Commissar Knoll's Centaur.

'How is the arm?' Minka asked.

The commissar had taken a las-bolt to his forearm. He regarded the wounded limb with a curious disinterest, as if it had somehow let him down. 'It's a clean wound. It went straight through. I am told it will heal well.'

She nodded. The commissar was not much of a conversationalist, and after a few brief stabs at getting him to talk they fell into silence.

This time, when she got to Dido's ward, she found Banting standing at the end of Dido's bed.

'Lieutenant Lesk,' he said. He had Dido's wrist in his hand. After a pause he let her hand go.

'Any change?' Minka called out.

'I'm still alive,' Dido answered.

'You are,' Banting noted as he bent over her and moved her paralysed limbs.

'And unfortunately I'll still be alive tomorrow,' Dido sighed.

Minka sat quietly as Banting went through his final checks. At last he looked up from the clipboard and hung it from the end of Dido's cot. 'Any hope?' Dido called out.

'There's always hope,' Banting said. 'Put your faith in the Emperor.'

Banting turned to Minka. 'I saw the mess you made of Karni's arm.' Minka winced at the memory. He didn't give her a moment to respond. 'How are those two cadets?' he said at last.

'Yedrin and Blanchez?'

He tucked Dido in and stood up straight. 'Are those their names?'

'Yes. They're not Whiteshields any more. They're full Cadian Shock Troopers now.'

Banting snorted.

'They were very slick on Tor Kharybdis,' Minka told him.

Banting made a contemptuous noise. He turned to Dido. 'This is it. The onset of the rot. Replacing troopers like you with cadets. Here,' he said and handed her a pair of pills. They were pink triangular lozenges.

'Suppressants,' Dido said as explanation to Minka. 'Knock you out.'

Banting handed her a glass of water to swallow them.

Dido pulled a face. 'I'll talk to Minka first. She hasn't come all this way to watch me drool.'

Banting nodded. When he had turned his back she made an offensive hand gesture. *Bastard,* she mouthed. To Minka she said, 'So. Tell me the news.'

'The big push on Tor Tartarus is coming,' Minka said.

'Have the batteries been taken out?'

'No.'

Dido nodded. 'What's the plan?'

Minka didn't know. She was just a lieutenant. 'Not sure there is one yet. We got the vanguard of the Elnaurs in Tor Kharybdis. But their reserves are intact. Bendikt wants to offer himself as the bait. He's going to personally lead the assault.'

'It sounds desperate,' Dido said.

'He *is* desperate,' Minka said. 'There's a war out there.'

Dido laughed. There was a bitter note to it. She had known only war. War was what she had been bred for; it was what she lived for.

And now she was medically unfit.

Minka filled her in on all the ideas, but she could tell that Dido hated hearing any of this second hand.

At the end Dido said, 'I'm delighted for you, Minka.' But her tone was flat. 'Throne! I lie in bed. All I want is for the shrapnel to have gone an inch to the left, or a foot to the right. A little higher and it'd have gone straight through my heart, apparently. And I'd be dead and with the Emperor. A foot to the right and it'd have hit Barnabas instead. Why the hell did you bother saving me?'

Minka didn't know how to answer.

'You should have just left me there,' Dido cursed. 'I could have died. It's better than this.' Dido held up both hands.

Minka sat for a long time. 'Sorry,' she said at last.

They were silent for a while. There was a little forced small talk, then Minka said, 'I'd better go.'

Dido watched Minka leave. The suppressants were still in her hand and she thought about taking them. But what was pain, she asked herself, for a warrior like her?

Medicae Banting finished his examination. 'Good,' he grunted and took scissors to cut the stitches. Using needle-nosed pliers, he tugged out the last stitches, then swabbed the raw pink flesh with counterseptics.

Commissar Knoll pulled his sleeve down.

'It's healing well,' Banting said. 'I'd recommend avoidance of strenuous actions with that arm. At least for a week or so. You don't want it to reopen. And keep it dry.'

Knoll nodded. He fastened the button closed, flexed his fist. The wound was stiff, the skin felt strangely taut, but he did not notice any loss of movement.

'Noted,' he said. 'Thank you, medicae.'

Minka retraced her steps through the medicae facility. At the end of the corridor she turned and saw a party of seven Drookians talking to a medic. She could have taken a side-corridor but she was damned if she was going to give way.

She strode forward. She was Cadian, and Cadians did not step back from any fight. One of the Drookians looked up. It was Captain Midha.

'You!' Minka shouted. 'You abandoned your position on Tor Kharybdis!'

Midha grinned. 'I followed my orders.'

Minka was charging forward. 'You left my platoon exposed.'

His thanes stepped before her but she went for him. She ducked the first blow and barrelled low into the next man's belly. An elbow slammed her in the back, but Minka was already coming up with her shoulder in Midha's gut.

There was a satisfying grunt as she connected. She kept driving through her legs. She felt Midha lift off the ground and landed on top of him.

She was outnumbered, but she relied on their confusion.

'This is for Allun!' she grunted as her knuckles connected with Midha's chin. 'This is for Karni!' she said with the next hit. She had bare seconds to do honour to Maenard and Dido as well. No mother could have been so ferocious on behalf of her children. She was a blur of fists, even as the retainers dragged her off.

'Crazy Cadian!' one of the retainers hissed as they slammed a knee into Minka's stomach. She had tensed, but the blow was so hard it drove the air out between her clenched teeth, like a burst tyre.

A fist hit her chin, another the side of her face. Instincts were to ball up and protect herself. But Minka was Cadian. She fought back. She kicked, punched, stabbed her fingers into soft tissue, scratching and clawing at the faces of her foes.

'Little bastard!' Midha hissed and punched her on the back of the head.

One of them caught her right arm. She swung with her left, lifted her foot and slammed her heel into the foot of her assailant. A blow hit the back of her neck this time. It was a well-aimed strike. She staggered for a moment, and her left arm was caught. She readied herself for another kick.

Midha stood before her. He drew his knife. 'We're going to teach you a lesson about starting fights you can't finish,' he hissed. 'I'm going to gut you, Cadian.'

Commissar Knoll strolled out into the corridor. It was quiet and empty. He turned left towards the exit. He was passing through an officers' wing, but even so, each ward was cluttered with beds, the cots pressed close to each other. Nurses went from bed to bed, tending those whose pain was returning.

The wards were filled with the low and monotonous groan of the dying.

Knoll passed along the corridor. The closer to the exit, the less perilous the state of the occupants. But here and there a voice called out in sudden pain or tedium.

The lack of self-control disturbed Knoll. Everything he had been taught had instilled in him a sense of cold and ruthless discipline. He found the cries of the wounded a declaration of weakness. He hummed a military tune to drown out the moaning.

At the end of the corridor was a T-junction. He turned left again, humming loudly to himself. To either side were posters that proclaimed Imperial doctrine.

He only needed to see the first few words to know what each of them said.

The Emperor Protects the Virtuous.

The stalwart might die, but their souls shall join the Emperor.

The Emperor is our Shield and Protector.

Blessed is the mind that knows no doubt.

Knoll kept humming to himself as he passed the last corridor. From his right he heard a grunt. It was loud enough to startle him. He spun about. The sound of the commotion was coming from a room halfway down the corridor.

Knoll paused for a moment. His tune faltered. Knoll had been trained and indoctrinated since birth to look for and punish misdemeanour. He was like a hunting feline, paused, alert, senses straining for any hint of what was going on.

There was a splatter of blood on the floor outside. Through the door he could hear muffled fighting.

He thrust the door open. Shock was not something that his face often showed, but as he took in the scene before him Commissar Knoll looked shocked.

'Lieutenant!' he said.

Minka's hair was dishevelled, her face bruised, her nostrils flaring with exertion, her eyes flashing with suppressed anger. His gaze went from the knife in Minka's hand to the five bodies that lay about her.

'Explain yourself,' Commissar Knoll snapped.

ELEVEN

Minka sat in the darkness of the holding cell as footsteps echoed outside in the corridor. They paused at her doorway. There was the rattle of keys, then the lock clicked, the heavy door handle turned and the hinges squeaked as the door swung open.

A light shone into her face. She turned away to stop the sudden glare from blinding her.

'Follow me,' the voice said.

Minka pushed herself up and hastily pulled her hair into a ponytail. She was led out and brought along the corridor to a guard chamber. The guards showed her inside. The room appeared empty.

'Lieutenant Lesk,' a voice said.

She spun about. Chief Commissar Shand looked down on her. His scarred face showed no emotion, but his violet eyes glittered with a baleful light.

He stepped towards her. 'I have now received two official complaints about your behaviour. The second is very serious. You have wounded members of the Drookian contingent.'

'Yes, sir,' Minka said.

'The accusation is true?'

Minka nodded.

He stepped forward. 'You understand the punishment.'

'Yes, sir,' she said.

'And is there any explanation for this behaviour?'

Minka paused. 'We were stationed alongside each other on Tor Kharybdis. We were ordered to withdraw together and cover each other. He abandoned his position. We were nearly overrun.'

'You are accusing him of cowardice in the face of the enemy.'

She drew in a deep breath. 'Yes, sir. I am.'

'You understand the penalties for a false accusation?'

She nodded.

Shand's cold eyes bored into her. She clenched her jaw and returned the look. She started counting back from a hundred. She had reached seventy-three when Shand looked away. His cheeks coloured.

'I will look into this,' he said. 'Meanwhile, I am deeply displeased by your behaviour. As a lieutenant I expect you to set a better example.'

Minka nodded. 'Sorry, sir.'

Shand considered the matter done. 'You had better get back to camp,' Shand said.

Minka made the sign of the aquila. 'Thank you, sir.'

'Oh. Lieutenant Lesk,' he said as she reached the doorway. She paused. 'Give the Drookians a wide berth from now on. I don't want to have to deal with any more complaints. Or even worse, I don't want to lose a promising young lieutenant.'

Minka strode to the guard chamber. She signed for her

weapons. The guard returned them to her and nodded. She felt an air of respect from him and as he nodded, he winked.

'Well done, sir,' he said.

Minka stepped out onto the front step of the confinement block. She paused and looked about. There was the distant rumble of artillery. A fire was burning on Tor Tartarus. It was a deep red colour, like freshly spilled blood. Above the siege camp the ruddy clouds were sliced with searchlights.

She could see the upper storeys of Tor Tartarus, with their massed artillery.

The bridge supports were silhouetted against the sky. She paused for a moment. A few scraps of the road bridge sagged on the taut wires.

When she got back to the flakboard barracks hall, Minka said nothing about her absence, but there was no disguising the bruises on her face. 'I fell,' she said.

She gave Baine a look that shut him up.

'How is she?' Dreno said.

'Dido? She's not good,' Minka said. The words fell heavily in the room. Minka paused. 'I told her she was lucky not to be in the next attack.'

'Any idea when that will be?'

Minka shook her head.

Next morning Minka went out with Baine and Dreno. They stopped at the base of one of the suspension bridge supports. Two towers rose up into the sky. A service ladder provided access to the upper levels. The roadway had been mined, but high up the cables were still intact.

Minka clambered right to the top. She put her hand to the top wire. It hummed in the breeze.

'What do you think?' Dreno said.

Minka paused. 'I think we should have a word with Colonel Sparker.'

Sparker listened to Minka's plan. He came out with her onto the steps of his office. She handed him the field-auspex. He looked for himself.

At last he said, 'Well. It's possible.'

'Would you like me to present the plans to Colonel Baytov?'

'Not yet,' Sparker said.

They spent the next day driving along the battlefront. By the end of that trip even Colour Sergeant Tyson appeared to agree. Only then did they go to Baytov's office. Minka's heart was thundering in her chest as she stood before the commanding officer of the 101st.

She set out the difficulties and then laid out her solution.

Baytov listened quietly. Minka knew some of the officers there. Ostanko was captain of First Company, Irinya captain of Second Company. Of the veterans standing about Baytov, Minka only knew Diken, distinctive with his black eye-patch drawn over his missing eye.

Minka's gaze kept going to the veteran's face, trying to read his response. At the end Baytov said, 'Bold.'

He looked to Ostanko. The First Company captain nodded. 'I like it.'

Irinya was less sure. She laid out the dangers and difficulties at length. They were all true. Minka felt her heat rising. She started to move uncomfortably as she waited to speak, but Baytov didn't give her a chance.

'Hear that? It's a big risk, Sparker. Think your company is up to it?'

'Yes, sir,' Sparker said.

'Good.' Baytov looked about. 'I say we let Seventh Company take on this challenge. What do you think?'

It was Ostanko who stepped forward. He held Minka's gaze as he said, 'Brave are they who know all and yet fear nothing.'

Her cheeks coloured. That seemed to be sorted. She made the sign of the aquila and backed out.

'Well done, Lesk, you bowled them over!' Sparker said. He slapped her on the back. 'I am sure you're eager to test your theory by taking point on this one.'

The date of the attack was set nine days hence. Minka and Tyson sat down to devise a training programme for the whole company. Her platoon spent the week training relentlessly. Each night they were exhausted. Each morning they were up early to train once more.

On top of this, Minka had another hundred jobs to do before the attack. Paperwork. Officer rounds. Reports. Pay chits. Stuff that made her head ache.

She made time to go and say goodbye to Dido.

It was after a long session rappelling cliff faces and everyone else was taking their shower chits to wash before dinner. Minka, how-ever, was getting her coat on. Baine paused. 'Where are you going?'

'The medicae.'

'I'll come with you.'

Minka frowned. 'You don't need to come.'

'That's true,' Baine said. 'But I tore my palm open again. I'm not missing this attack, you know. Besides,' he said at last, 'you're the only person I know who goes fit to a medicae and comes back cut and bruised.'

The medicae facility was quiet at night. They saw no other visitors, only nurses and medicaes and the occasional orderly pushing a bed, or carrying out a dead body.

As they turned towards Dido's ward they saw a familiar looking figure. It was Father Keremm. His beard was as unkempt as ever, but he wore a clean surplice under his flak breastplate, and his chainsword had been freshly oiled.

'Ah!' he said, looking up. 'Lieutenant Lesk.'

She was still getting used to the new rank associated with her name. 'Evening, father! We didn't see you on Tor Kharybdis.'

'Oh, really? I was there. On Creed Beach. Doing my job. Inspiring the troops and killing the enemy. And I hear you did very well. Everyone is talking about you now.' The priest went on, 'Who are you here to visit?'

'Lieutenant Dido,' Minka said as she made the sign of the aquila.

'Ah,' he said and looked at her sideways, from under one bushy white brow. 'One tormented soul. Not one to be with us very long, I fear.'

'No?'

He pursed his lips and raised his eyebrows. 'Without hope, what are we but flesh and bone?'

'He's cheerful,' Baine said as they strolled along the long corridors.

'This way.' Minka led the way to Dido's ward. The dying man had gone. Pale, new faces stared up.

'Hello,' Minka said.

Dido glared out from her cot.

Minka felt a sudden guilt.

'I thought you'd forgotten me,' Dido said.

'I've been training the platoon.'

'Oh yeah?' Dido said.

Baine paused. He didn't really know Dido and he didn't want to intrude. 'I'll be outside,' he said.

Minka nodded and sat on the edge of Dido's cot.

'I heard you met some Drookians last time you came,' Dido said. 'I thought that was why you were staying away.'

Minka laughed at the idea. 'No,' she said. 'The attack is coming.'

Dido swallowed her response. She pursed her lips and let out a sigh.

'We're going in tomorrow night.'

Dido nodded. 'Do you think it was that curse pole that did this to me?'

'Got you wounded? No. Of course not!'

'I've tried to think of a reason why I got hit with this. It could have been Barnabas.'

'I'd rather it had been.'

Dido laughed. 'Yeah. Me too. Giving you trouble, is he?'

Minka shrugged. Barnabas was just an ass.

Dido sighed. 'Sorry I'm such a misery. I've just had that damned priest lecturing me.' She paused and reached out a hand to take Minka's. 'On faith and hope and joining the Emperor. All that crap.'

For a long time Dido didn't speak, but squeezed Minka's hand. Tears started to well up. She sniffed them back. 'Lead from the front,' Dido said at last.

Minka nodded. She looked down and took in a deep breath. 'I wish you were leading us.'

Dido smiled. She couldn't bring herself to speak, but she mouthed the words, *me too*. Minka filled her in with the news from the platoon, the company, and the regiment.

Along the corridor they could hear the cheap metal rattle of the dinner trolley.

Dido closed her eyes. She looked in constant pain.

'Shall I get more suppressants?'

'No,' Dido said. The orderly with the dinner tray came into the room.

Minka stood. 'I'd better go.'

* * *

Night had fallen when Bendikt made his way to the chapel where the body of Saint Ignatzio was held. The praise birds had fallen silent. They swooped in tight figure-of-eight flight patterns. It was as if they could sense the import of the events happening inside.

Bendikt looked resplendent in his suit of finely crafted carapace armour. At his side was an archaic Mars-pattern las-pistol – an ancient model, lovingly cared for and immaculately maintained by Bendikt himself. It was the same model that Creed had once used. As well as a fine weapon. It was his lucky charm.

Captain Ostanko had his helmet held in the crook of his arm. He made the sign of the aquila and stepped forward to greet General Bendikt. Behind him stood his veterans in kasrkin carapace, rebreather masks already engaged, hot-shot lasguns held ready.

'Good evening, general,' he said, and shook Bendikt's hand. He turned to the garden, which was packed with pilgrims who had made camp on bedrolls and items of furniture pilfered from the palace. 'They are not in the way. The Gerent is inside with the saint.'

'Good.'

They followed Bendikt through the gateway. The garden was packed with the prone figures of men, women, camp follow-ers, beggars. Some were scavenging, some asleep. Others were sitting around in prayer circles. A wild-eyed man, naked to the waist and with a beard that hung down to his chest, was walking through the crowd, calling out threats and punish-ments to the traitors. They parted like water before the figure of General Bendikt.

He looked like a figure of legend as he led his command staff across the garden to the stone steps before the chapel. Gerent

Bianca's lifewards were standing at the door. Lights were on inside the chapel, illuminating the stained-glass windows with a warm, yellow glow.

As Bendikt put his foot upon the steps the doors of the chapel were flung open.

Gerent Bianca appeared, resplendent in a suit of finely crafted armour, moulded with exaggerated muscles, like a statue of the Emperor. In her hand she carried an ornate sword – a fine duelling foil with a narrow blade and hilt worked in gold and jewels.

She beckoned General Bendikt up the steps, then held the sword towards him.

'Its name is Paragon,' she told him.

It was the most beautiful blade he had ever seen. He drew it and engaged the power stud and the blade lit with blue traceries of energy.

'Brethren!' Bianca called out. 'The saint fights with you today! He will be with you all. He will smite your enemies. He will break those that defy his father, the God-Emperor. And the instrument of his wrath is General Bendikt!'

As she spoke, a praise bird landed on Bendikt's shoulder. Mere and Ostanko and the assembled Cadians drew their swords and raised them in salute. There was a cheer from the gathered troops.

The saint had spoken.

As this ceremony took place, Minka was quiet on the return journey to the camp. Baine didn't want to intrude.

He had a fresh dressing on his left hand. 'They think it's all right?' Minka said at last.

He looked at his hand and nodded. 'Yeah.'

The two of them stood in the back of the cargo-8 holding onto the metal bars as the vehicle bumped through the potholes.

That night, Minka summoned Second Platoon for a meeting. 'So,' she said, taking a sheet of paper out of her breast pocket. 'We're moving out tomorrow.'

'Can you tell us where we're going?' Barnabas asked.

Minka filled them in. They listened attentively.

At the end she said, 'I saw Lieutenant Dido today. She wishes you all well.'

The troopers nodded. She'd expected more of a response, but maybe it was just the way of the trooper. They did not speak too much of those who were missing.

Minka answered a few more questions. At last she said, 'Get a good night's sleep. It's going to be a long day tomorrow.'

PART FOUR

PART FOUR

ONE

The sky was still black when the Cadians loaded up in Chimeras and cargo-8s.

Blanchez and Yedrin were with Minka. Orugi had his shades pushed up onto his forehead, and he was grinning. His plasma gun was slung across his front. He had spent the days lovingly stripping and cleaning it.

This was a special mission and they had been armed appropriately. Minka had sorted that out for them at least. Blanchez had her sniper rifle over her shoulder. It was as tall as she was. Yedrin had chosen a flamer. As a lieutenant Minka had been issued with a sturdy little mauler-pattern bolt pistol to go with her power sabre. It had a twenty round barrel magazine. She wasn't sure she liked it yet. It had a lot more kick than the laspistol, and made a lot more noise. The bolt pistol fired a self-propelled mass-reactive bolt that was set to detonate just after impact, ripping through the target.

A hit was spectacular and it was powerful enough to smash through flak armour.

'I've never seen it in live combat,' Blanchez said.

'It makes a mess,' Minka told her.

Blanchez paused. 'Do they make bolter sniper rifles?'

'Not that I've seen,' Minka said.

They moved out before dawn.

There was a spiralling dogfight far out over the water. It looked like Thunderbolts, but it was hard to say whose side they were on. One began to dive. A thick column of black smoke billowed out behind it, silhouetted against the lightening sky.

Minka looked away. She knew enough about flames and death and pain.

The isolated towers of the bridge supports rose up before them. She remembered Dido's words, 'Lead from the front', and laughed.

This mission would probably be the death of her. There was worse, she told herself, and Dido's fate came to mind.

The Cadians were a precision weapon and Bendikt had spent hours planning how to deploy. He had given each of the ten companies of the Cadian 101st a specific mission.

Five miles from the assault pipe entrances, Seventh Company split off from the others. They dismounted for a briefing, while those that kept marching called out encouragement.

Colonel Sparker spoke to them all. 'The Elnaur Chasseurs have moved into Tor Tartarus in strength. It's our chance to finally break the enemy's finest divisions.' Sparker paused before explaining the part that Seventh Company was going to play in the battle.

'You mean we're rappelling in along a single wire?' Lieutenant

Salon of First Platoon said. He looked about for support. No one answered. But he could see it in their eyes that they were all thinking the same.

Sparker nodded. 'Yes. Under cover of darkness we will cross over using the suspension cables. They have been tested. The wires are still intact. We will use those to cross the water and assault the batteries in the upper terraces of Tor Tartarus. May I remind you, General Bendikt will be taking his place in the front lines. Our mission is vital. If we do not succeed then the rest of the regiment will be exposed to deadly fire. We're going in very light. Pare equipment down to a minimum.'

Minka made sure that everyone was sorted before she started on her own belongings. She had already stripped her equipment right back to the barest essentials, then tested the weight and set to it again. *Still too heavy,* she thought and started over.

Minka unbuckled the top of her pack, pulled it open and went through everything. This plan was asking the impossible, but they were Cadian. Impossible was their meat and drink.

A minute later her pack was on the floor, and her belongings were spread out next to it. She stared at them, trying to work out what she needed.

Around her, she could read the silent frustration in the troopers. Everyone was tense. Throne, she was tense as well, but all she wanted was for the mission to start.

She saw Blanchez staring at her kit and said, 'Rations.'

'Yeah?' said Blanchez, checking the pack. She held them up. 'Got them.'

'You won't need them,' Minka said. 'We're either dead or we're not. We're not heading over there for a picnic.'

Blanchez nodded. 'Fair enough,' she said, and called out as

she tossed away the water bottle and ration packs, 'No need for rations, apparently. Except you, Baine. I think you'll need a snack.'

Minka took the slab jerky from her ration pack, then tossed the rest out. She started chewing and took a swig of her water bottle, then screwed the lid back on.

In the end she had got rid of everything but her armour, webbing, grenades, powercells, laspistol and combat blade. *Done,* she thought. She felt lighter already. Truth was, it was good to get rid of possessions. All they did was weigh you down. She went along the line, helping the others.

She was ready. She went back to her squad.

Jaromir had hit a mental block. He was staring at his pack unable to decide what to get rid of next. He was trying to say something. He opened his mouth to speak but no words came.

'Want me to do it?' Minka said.

Jaromir looked blankly at her.

'Shall I do it?' she said again.

Jaromir looked up at her and then he looked back down at his bag.

'I'll do it,' Minka said.

'Thank you.'

She went through it with the same ruthlessness as her own but left the water bottle and ration pack inside. He would be strong enough to carry it and Jaromir's injury meant that he needed something predictable to soothe him. Food would be perfect, she thought.

'Can you come and sort my pack out?' Orugi called out.

'Sure,' Minka said, and she strode towards him and dumped a bunch of demo charges into his bag. 'Here!' she said, pulling the bag onto his shoulders. 'Take that.'

* * *

The grav-palanquin of Saint Ignatzio made its way to the assault tunnels where the other companies had already assembled in full battle gear.

Bendikt nodded. 'It will be like the old days,' he said to Colonel Baytov. There was a touch of wistfulness to his voice. There was a long pause. 'We did not fail, did we?'

Mere looked up. 'What do you mean, sir?' Baytov said.

'Cadia,' Bendikt said bluntly. 'At night, when I cannot sleep, there are voices in my head that tell me we failed. There were times a few years ago when it was very dark.'

Baytov nodded. He had suspected the same. He had felt it too. Every Cadian had to balance guilt within themselves. Their ancient duty had been to act as the buffer between the Imperium and the spawn of the warp. To shield mankind from the filth that vomited out from the Eye of Terror.

And they had failed.

'Get some rest,' Minka called out as the tram chugged slowly along the narrow rails. She couldn't sleep herself, however. This mission had been her idea and now she began to have doubts. She lay rocking back and forth as the tram rattled through the long rockcrete gallery.

Each time the tunnels branched apart, blank-eyed servitors were set into the walls. They controlled underground junctions. Time after time they took narrower tunnels and passed boarded-up platforms, until at last they reached a terminus and the carriages wheezed to a halt.

A whistle blew.

'Dismount!' the order was given.

Platoon by platoon, Seventh Company dismounted and moved towards the wall of wide lifts. Each platoon loaded up.

The grilled metal gates were shut, and then they started with a mechanical jolt, setting off upwards at a steady pace.

They could smell promethium, smoke and dust on the air. The thunder of artillery was loud enough to mean they needed to raise their voices to be heard.

The lifts halted, and opened. Broad troop tunnels led towards the front, but there were Cadian engineering staff who pointed them away from these, along what looked like service tunnels.

The tunnel walls were plain grey rockcrete. Sheaths of power cables and foil ducting ran in ropes along the ceilings. Along alternating sides of the tunnel, oval bulkhead lumens lit the chamber with a cold blue light. They marched quickly. The ground shook violently whenever the orbital bombardment struck the planet.

The closer to the gates they came, the louder the roar of battle. Larger explosions made the lamps rattle in their cages. Passing backwards, the word was it was nearly dark outside.

'I should hope so!' Dreno said.

No one answered. They were thinking of the mission ahead. It was weighing on them all. Not just the danger to themselves, but the responsibility they had to the other companies of the 101st, who were going in on the ground.

They marched on. Orugi started to sing. He had a fine bass voice. It was an old marching tune, the kind they sang in training camp on Cadia. It made a change from *Flower of Cadia*. The song rippled out, up and back through the line, from one company to the next, until the song was ringing out from ten thousand voices.

'You know it,' Minka said to Blanchez afterwards.

'Of course,' Blanchez said.

Minka smiled. Maybe there was a link between the old Cadians and the new.

* * *

The last tunnels were deserted. They saw no one, except for a pair of tech-priests, walking in the opposite direction with an entourage of limp-faced and dead-eyed servitors stomping stiffly behind them, and a storeroom clerk who was working through a list of netted cargo resting on pallets. He had a stylus thrust behind his ear and a board in his hand, to which was clamped a set of Munitorum parchments. 'No!' he was shouting at a gang of labour corps dressed in dirty white overalls. 'That is not acceptable!'

But he was the last person they saw until the light of day showed through the armoured doors standing wide open at the end of the tunnel. There was a platoon of Rakallion guards at the gateway. The warm breeze whipped at their greatcoats. They were a smart looking bunch. The men watched the Cadians with awe.

From the light that filtered down to them they could sense above ground that the afternoon was failing.

The order went out that they would wait here until sunset.

'This is it,' Baine said.

Minka nodded. She was too tense to speak. She could not fail this time, she told herself.

TWO

Each Cadian prepared for battle in their own manner. One by one they started to camo up: dark stripes on cheeks and forehead, green and brown on the rest of the face, then texture to break up the smooth reflection of skin. Viktor cleaned his carbine. Asko rolled a lho-stick while Belus strutted up and down, trading banter with other troopers. Baine ate his rations then he got his cards out and started dealing hands for Lyrga, Orugi and Dreno.

Minka wanted to sleep, but the truth was her mind was too active. It would not settle. For some reason the memory of her first Whiteshield camp came to mind. She thought of Jaromir and how he had survived battle after battle when her cousin, who was top of his class, had lasted barely six months. Luck was an unsteady mistress. But each battle they put their lives in her fickle hands.

* * *

When they finally came out into open air they found themselves a mile north of the causeway, with an old service road winding along the clifftops ahead of them. There was a sea breeze blowing and fine rain being driven in the air.

The cliff was to their left while Tor Tartarus loomed in the distance. Evening was falling. The air had turned cool. They were marching along a narrow rockcrete pathway that ran along the cliff top. The Cadians moved quickly; there was a lot left to do. Ahead the sky was ablaze with smoke and fire as bombardments raked Tor Tartarus.

After an hour's walking Minka could see a great shape looming before her. The shadow stretched upwards. It was a vast circular column, the ancient rockcrete now stained with long streaks of rust and patched with a local powdery growth on the seaward side.

A group of Cadian officials stood at the bottom, with orders from Colonel Sparker. The leader was softly spoken. 'Sergeant Minka. Here's a map, courtesy of HQ. Take your platoon left and secure the area, and Colonel Sparker will take his right.'

Minka nodded. She knew that already. They had discussed all this in the company briefing: which targets were being taken out by whom. They'd run through all kinds of scenarios. This was the type of high-risk attack that relied on precision work.

She turned to her command squad. 'Orugi, lead them up. Dreno. Follow up behind. Then Barnabas, Raske, Elhrot!'

Minka stood at the bottom of the steps counting her troops up the ladder. The column she stood at the bottom of was one of a pair. The northerly tower had been broken about two-thirds of the way up, but theirs was largely intact. While one set of wires now plunged down into the water, with scraps of steel cabling and a few desultory lumps of rockcrete hanging from them, the other looked intact.

It was an old service ladder, with safety loops set along its length. In places the iron rungs had been rusted right through. Even at the best of times they were worn dangerously thin. Where whole sections were missing or dangerous, Cadian engineers had rigged up rope ladders.

Every few hundred feet there were open platforms. It gave them a chance to catch their breath and look down. Each stage left the ground farther and farther beneath them.

By the fifth platform Jaromir started getting edgy.

Minka put her hand out to his forearm. 'It's fine,' she told him. 'You're going to be fine.'

Jaromir looked from one of her eyes to the other, then he looked down at her hand. Whether it was the sight of her hand, or the sight of the Black Dragon tattoo on his forearm, she didn't know. He nodded slowly.

Minka caught Dreno's eye. Look after him, her glance said.

They reached the top after half an hour of climbing. The original service platform had rotted away and a new one had been fitted by the engineers. Metal plates had been tied onto the old framework of crossed I-beams. Railings had once enclosed it, but these had now rusted away. A plain white rope replaced them, strung about the perimeter.

Orugi bounced. The metal floorplates felt loose underfoot. The whole tower felt like it was swaying under their weight.

'Makes you want to jump,' he grinned.

Yedrin looked pale.

Orugi grinned. 'Don't like heights?'

'Love them,' Yedrin said.

'Heights?' Blanchez said, as she walked to the edge and leant over.

Yedrin kept away from the edge. 'So why hasn't anyone tried this before?'

'It's too dangerous,' Blanchez told him.

'Good answer,' Minka said. Blanchez had the right mix of cockiness and bravado. But the truth was, no one had ever thought of it. Or if they had, they did not have the troops with the skills necessary.

Next to them a team of Cadian engineers were consulting some plans with a low lumen. One of them was animated as he pointed at the plans; the others were nodding. She went to join them.

'Last checks being made,' one of the younger men said. He looked upwards as he spoke. Above them she could see teams of engineers silhouetted against the sky. 'You're Lieutenant Lesk, right?'

'Yes.'

'Your platoon is going in first,' the engineer said. 'Attack is scheduled at 0500 hours. Colonel Sparker wants everyone in place by 0400.'

Sparker appeared, an unlit lho-stub still clenched between his teeth. He checked the strength of the welding. It was solid, and the engineers had reinforced it with extra cabling.

Sparker tested the I-beam. 'Secure?' he asked.

'I'd bet my mother on it,' the engineer's commander told them.

'Is she here?'

'No, sir. She was on Cadia.'

Sparker kept his hand on the wires. 'Well, that's Throne-all use. Got any children?'

'Not yet, sir.' Sparker muttered something but the man took no notice. 'We've been watching the enemy all day. They're keeping their heads down. As far as I can tell they're not expecting anything. There's a crap-ton of heavy weaponry embedded over there.'

Sparker nodded and looked about. He checked his chronometer. They were ahead of time. 'Let's get in there and sort these bastards out. Lesk? Let's get going!'

* * *

They set off.

The Cadian engineers had been working at night lashing each section of boards to the bridge suspensions and rigging up grilled metal duckboards to replace the footing where it was compromised. Where the walkway was missing they had suspended a narrow flakboard walkway with a knotted cord on one side for balance.

Very soon the land dropped away, and it felt as if they were twice as high as before. All Minka could see below her was the sea. The walkway swayed dangerously as the file walked along it, wires creaked, and the whole edifice felt as though it was about to break free and plunge them all a mile down into the sea.

Each pair of bridge supports were spaced half a mile apart. They were all of the same construction, a gothic tower on massive rockcrete footings.

When they were halfway to the gatehouse of Tor Tartarus the Imperial Navy bombardment began. Lance strikes exploded into kaleidoscopic flares that spread out over the void's domed surface. It was like being caught in the air in the middle of an electrical storm. Someone cried out as a lance strike hissed through the air not fifty feet away from them. Its glare was blinding. Minka had to wait for her night vision to return, then she started forward again.

After an hour and a half the last support tower loomed up all of a sudden and when Minka looked down she saw not sea, but the ruined steps of Tor Tartarus.

Dido lay in bed and watched the clock roll slowly through the night. At two hours the man opposite started to wake. 'Nurse!' she called out.

No one came.

After a few minutes the man's moans grew louder.

She added her voice to the call. This time footsteps came down the ward's permacrete floor. A small man in whites appeared.

'He needs you!' Dido said.

The medic bent over the wounded warrior. He administered the injection, and in a few seconds the moans had reduced to the low whistle of breath in the tube.

'Why not put him out of his misery?' Dido said.

'The Emperor Protects,' the medic said. He came over and checked Dido's clipboard at the end of the bed.

'There's nothing there,' she said. 'You're just looking officious.'

He smiled and came round the bed to check her bedding. She had no control of her lower half, and sometimes she needed cleaning. He pulled the pad out from under her, put it into a bin and pulled a fresh one out, then lifted her lower half to slide it under her.

'My regiment are going into battle tonight,' she said.

He frowned. 'You shouldn't tell me things like that.'

Dido gave him a sideways glance. He didn't look like a spy.

He settled her back down again.

'My chest hurts,' she said.

He nodded as he finished arranging her bed sheets. He checked her records again. 'Give me a minute.'

The medic walked along the lines, checking on each patient, and then a few minutes later he returned with her pills. Two pink lozenges.

'Here,' he said, and tipped them into her hand. She motioned towards the plain presswood table at the side of the bed. 'Please,' she said.

He handed her the half cup of water. She took it and smiled. 'Thank you.'

There were two Cadian engineers waiting for Minka as she moved along the walkway. One of them was a slight, pretty trooper. She spoke in a low voice. 'This is as far as we go.' She gestured around the tower towards the gatehouse. 'You'll have to pull yourselves along from here. The wires are sturdy. When you get to the far tower the ladders appear still intact.'

Minka took this all in as her command squad formed up about her. The other squads paused behind. 'Harnesses on,' she said. Minka stepped into hers, buckled it about her waist and gave it a sharp tug. She checked her pistol, grenades, tube charges, knife.

Orugi clipped the plasma charge in. Yedrin's lascarbine was slung over his shoulder. He checked his pouch of fuses.

Minka paused briefly and looked about. Yedrin looked sick, Blanchez had a look of studied nonchalance.

The upper circuits of Tor Tartarus could not be more than five hundred yards away. The service wires were taut. They bowed slightly before them.

'Ready?' Minka said. She didn't wait for answers, but clipped the g-clamp onto the wire and swung herself out into the darkness.

THREE

Bendikt was only a few yards ahead of Prassan as the rest of the Cadian 101st marched the last mile along the assault pipes. Bendikt wore his ornate carapace armour and behind him came his command staff.

Behind Bendikt came the saint's grav-bier, with Gerent Bianca in her golden armour, and Mere in kasrkin armour. Then the banner bearers: Flynt carried the banner of the Imperium of Mankind, the golden aquila on a field of black. On the right was Aaronn with the banner of Cadia, and in the middle was Diken, who carried the banner of the 101st, with its icon of Ursarkar E Creed fixed to the banner pole just under the golden aquila.

The golden light of the bier cast a warm glow over them all as the arched tunnels rang out with the crisp precision of their footfall. Prassan felt that not even the Mordians could be so smart. For the moment this was all there was. He inhaled it. The comradeship. The fraternal sense of being part of a body of the finest troopers in the Imperium of Man. The honour of being a Cadian Shock Trooper.

Prassan thought of the last months of Cadia and he felt a wave of emotion build within him. Tears formed in his eyes but he refused to let them fall.

They reached a large subterranean chamber, one of the great marshalling yards. While this had once been filled with penal legionnaires, now the chamber was host to an honour guard of Rakallions.

At their fore stood Klovis Plona-Richstar, still wearing a feather-plumed brass helmet, though his double-breasted kossack jacket was now largely hidden by a breastplate of polished black steel.

Bendikt strode forward to greet him, and as he did so, the bier carrying Saint Ignatzio was brought forward.

'I transfer Saint Ignatzio into your care,' Bendikt said. 'May he inspire your troops to slay in the name of the God-Emperor.'

He also said farewell to Gerent Bianca. As most senior Richstar, she was going to fight alongside the Rakallions and Saint Ignatzio.

'I am honoured to fight with you this day,' General Klovis Plona-Richstar said to Gerent Bianca. 'Your ancestor's bier is safe with the Rakallion Grenadiers, I assure you.'

'Thank you,' Gerent Bianca said.

She had missed their level of ritual and formality during her time with the Cadians. In the field they were fine warriors, she was sure, but they lacked the social finesse of the nobility of the Gallows Cluster.

The Rakallions snapped to attention as the Cadians marched past, then they took a different tunnel, with the golden bier of the saint leading them to battle.

* * *

A mile of emptiness gaped beneath Minka. In the black she could see clearly the trenches and the fires, and the firing parapets below her, and a fortified rock wall before.

Sliding down the wire was easy, but halfway across the gradient of the wire turned upwards, so she had to monkey-bar along, wrapping her arms about the chain link and then swinging herself forward for the next. Arm over arm, she pulled herself up the incline. After a hundred yards her shoulder muscles screamed, her biceps burnt, her breathing was laboured, and sweat dripped through her eyebrows into her eyes. She risked a look forward. She was barely a quarter of the way there.

She could feel Orugi behind her. She had to go faster. She drove her muscles beyond pain until a stream of sweat ran down her neck. She would never have made it with a fully equipped pack. But now she cursed each ounce of equipment she carried.

She was three-quarters of the way across when her hand slipped. She clung on with the other arm and hung there for a moment, pulling in great lungfuls of air, and then started again, concentrating on each single movement so that there was no chance she could slip again.

The lights of the gatehouse grew gradually closer.

Minka kept pumping until she could smell the dry, dusty scent of earth just below her, could feel the gusts coming up off the rockface. Between her boots, fifty feet below her was the octagonal roof of a pillbox, and another twenty feet to her left.

Then, very suddenly, the rockcrete footings of the bridge support pillars loomed into view. Minka paused, hanging upside-down, senses straining in the darkness and silence for any sign that she had been discovered.

Nothing. Slowly and gently she unhitched herself from the wire and dropped to the steep rock face. Her arms were almost too tired to tap out the *all clear* in Cadian battle-glot.

She kept her fingers on the wire and felt the tapped response come back.

Coming.

Minka started to get her bearings. It always took a moment to turn a map in your head into real life, but the gatehouse made it fairly straightforward as an anchor point.

The gatehouse stretched away to either side. Before the war it had been a low, blocky rockcrete construction. Fifty feet of rockcrete roadway stuck out of the broad entrance like a black tongue. The entrance had now been sandbagged up and covered with camo nets.

Lights were visible through the old openings. Minka could hear the traitors at their prayers.

Her eyes were now well accustomed to the darkness. She started picking out the courses of batteries as Orugi dropped quietly to the ground. Blanchez and Yedrin came next.

They used hand signals as her squads followed. In the darkness about her Minka could hear the soft scrape of knives being drawn from their sheaths, the almost imperceptible click of safety catches being flicked off.

Barnabas, Dreno and Elhrot's squads were all in place when Minka led her command squad into position, and as she did so, more and more Cadians were dropping onto Traitor Rock.

Bendikt led his troops to the end of the assault pipe where lifts brought them up into the bowels of *Hatred of Iron*. Company by company, they marched down the assault ramp to the very edge of the void shield. He said a prayer as the Cadians massed behind him.

From the restless air, it was clear that the assault was imminent. Prassan looked about. He had never thought he would join General Bendikt in battle, but here he was, in full combat uniform, standing at the back of Bendikt's command squad. About him were the finest troops of the 101st, Ostanko and First Company on one side, Captain Irinya and Second Company on the other.

The troopers of both companies were turned out in the full carapace of kasrkin. Each trooper was armed with hot-shot lasguns, each platoon equipped with a deadly array of plasma, flamers and grenade launchers.

Surely nothing could stand in their way, Prassan thought. Until he looked up at the ruins of Tor Tartarus. And up there, at the top of the cliffs, the batteries of the fortress were as yet untouched. From high above, shots started to hammer against the protective bubble. Prassan had never stood like this, watching shells and las-strikes rendered harmless by a void shield. It was exhilarating as the blue light flared at each impact.

But he had a horrible premonition that this bombardment meant Minka's mission had failed.

He made the sign of the aquila as he prepared for his own death and looked to Bendikt to give the signal to charge.

The traitor batteries started to fire. All about them were flashes of smoke and flame, and the spreading stink of fyceline smoke.

Minka checked her chronometer. There were just minutes before the ground assault was due to start and it seemed that half of Seventh Company were still strung out along the wire like canine teeth on a necklace.

Minka clutched her knife in an underhand grip. 'We can't wait!' she hissed to Orugi.

He had his plasma gun ready. He nodded.

She signalled to her sergeants. *Move in.* They moved to their own objectives.

Minka shuffled across the rockface to the side of the pillbox before her. Light spilled from the embrasure. The rockcrete walls were nearly three-feet thick, but she could hear the talk of the gun crew inside. The squat, stubby bombard barrel filled the embrasure. There was no cover on the barrel. The dull factorum steel gleamed in the wan light.

She signalled Orugi and Blanchez to go around the other side. This pillbox was template construction and she knew the inside as if she could see it. There would be a sunken gun chamber, grenade pit to both sides of the bombard platform, and raised dais at the rear, with guard chamber and magazine.

She crawled along the dirt to the rear entrance. The gunnery crew had left the door open for ventilation. A screen net hung across the door to keep the flies out.

She pushed the screen aside and stepped in.

The front chamber was empty and unlit. A padded cloth hung between them and the firing chamber. Yedrin slipped soundlessly inside behind her, but she waved him back in case the hiss of his flamer might alert anyone. Orugi was ready. Blanchez had already clicked her bayonet into place.

They could hear the grunt of the artillery crew as they winched a bombard shell into place and struggled to slam the round home.

Minka was as taut as a garrotting wire as she crept to the padded cloth screen. There was a little gap between the curtain and the wall. It was all she needed. There were five of them. She held up her fingers, and counted down from five, and then lifted her bolt pistol.

She caught Blanchez's eye as if to say, watch, this is going to be messy.

The firefight was short, furious and completely one-sided.

The inside of the firing chamber was strewn with what looked like scraps of clothing. Minka knew it was shreds of flesh. The remains of the Guardsmen hit by bolt shots had been thrown backwards against the wall.

A heavy-set man, his body a ruin below the waist, was crawling for his gun. Blanchez shot him in the face. The las-bolt ricocheted off the rockcrete floor, coming back out of his skull with a hiss of steam, lit from within with the dull red light of a nearly spent round.

Another Guardsman – a middle-aged woman – was crawling towards the alarm rope. The lower half of her body looked intact, but she left a bright red smear on the ground. Minka pinned her down with a boot in the small of her back and fired, execution style, into the back of her head.

The bolt round decapitated the woman. From the severed stump of her neck, pints of blood flowed out in a great flood.

The power sabre slashed the alarm cord. Yedrin was already hammering spikes into the bombard's firing mechanism.

Minka had memorised the plans, but she pulled them out for quick confirmation, mentally checking off her list of targets.

'This way,' she said, and led them down to the right, towards an autocannon Chimera turret mounted on an angled rockcrete base, fifty feet below.

A flight of sandbagged stairs plunged down towards it. She took the stairs three at a time, skidding down the cliff face. She didn't need to break in. Some fool had left a ventilation grate open. She dropped a pair of grenades inside and stood back to wait for them to go off. The whole pillbox shook with the sudden blast, and then white smoke poured out from its openings.

Minka led her squad along a trench. Halfway along was an observation platform and another pillbox. She ran towards it with Yedrin at her shoulder.

There was a young man in the pillbox doorway. He was maybe twenty, a skinny lad, dressed in heavy padded coat and soft wool cap. He shouted out. His voice was panicked.

It seemed that in the darkness he had heard running feet and had assumed that it was his own comrades running to his aid. As Minka approached he said, 'There are intruders!'

His face fell as he saw who ran into the light. 'Yes, there are,' she said.

Her bolt pistol bucked twice. Both shots hit.

His chest exploded. The force pulled his ribs apart like wrenching open the fingers of a pair of cupped hands. The ruins of his body fell sideways and left a bloody smear down the wall.

She tossed a frag grenade through the doorway. Someone staggered out, blind and bleeding. Blanchez dropped him with a headshot.

Minka slid down another flight of stone steps. There was a latrine to the right. The stale stink of urine was strong, despite the sea air.

There was another gun emplacement further down the terraces circuit. She had barely a moment's warning before someone threw themselves at her. She saw the flash of a knife and caught his hand in hers.

It was a Swabian Fusilier. He must have been out to relieve himself and now he was on her back, trying to drive eight inches of cold blue steel into her kidneys. She flung him off and he scrambled up.

'Let me,' Orugi said, but Minka held him back. She wanted to do this for Dido.

The Swabian held the knife low, ready to swing into an overhand or underhand stab. Minka feinted once and then twice. He came forward with an uppercut to her guts. She stepped to his outside, knocked his forearm away from her, pinned it against her side and raked his face with the other hand. Her fingers were like claws as they found his eyelids and eyeballs and he dropped his knife in an effort to get them off his face. She was already moving, one leg wrapped about his, and a shove with all her strength flung him out over the parapet and down the rockface.

She watched him hit the cliff once, twice, three times. He did not shout as he fell, but he grunted with each impact, a low, painful, bone-crunching sound. After the last one he bounced out into the air, arms and legs spinning, and disappeared from view.

'Well done, lieutenant,' Blanchez said. She had a cocky manner about her, as if to say that she could do better.

'Thank you,' Minka said. 'Next one is yours.'

All across the top of Tor Tartarus, Seventh Company were sprinting into the battle. Some had scrambled down the support tower. Others had rappelled in, and even as Minka tore a bloody swathe through the enemy, reserve units were still hauling themselves across the wire and forcing toe-holds wider and deeper.

This was what it meant to be a Cadian. They were shock troops, elite warriors trained to drive deep with sudden raids of extreme violence and commitment.

Sparker led three squads straight into the gatehouse. They came in over the sandbag walls and found that the building was being used as a barracks for off-duty artillery crews. There were hundreds of them. Swabian Fusiliers, by the looks of it.

Most of them were asleep, shattered after a long night of artillery duels. Each soldier had a little pile of belongings, their helmets laid by their bed with what was left of their rations inside. The conditions were dirty, dank and squalid. They slept where they had fallen the night before, on heaps of old artillery sacking.

Frag grenades landed among them before they knew what was happening. The explosions were deafening. Many died in their dreams. The rest woke terrified and confused. There were shouts as a few grabbed for improvised weapons, but they were met with a searing hose of liquid promethium. Fifty died within seconds. Their bedding caught fire and reels of thick, oily smoke ripped out along the low rockcrete ceiling and then vented upwards.

Lieutenant Petr found a squad of about twenty traitors on guard duty who had stopped into an old hab-block for a warm brew. They were sitting round a cast-iron stove, watching a kettle slowly boil, chins resting on hands, leaning against the walls, oblivious, it seemed, to the massacre beginning around them.

Their lasguns were stacked by the doorway. Lieutenant Petr kicked the pile over as he stormed inside. There was a furious stand-off as the air hissed with stitched lasgun rounds. Grenades were thrown and kicked away. It was close quarters fighting, a desperate dash forward. Petr's chainsword roared as he plunged it into the chest of a stumbling warrior.

'That's it!' Minka pointed as they came around the ridge.

There was a large bastion fifty feet to their left, built into the mountainside. There were three levels to it, and an open parapet on top, reinforced with sandbags.

Coming from the embrasures they could see the puffs of fyceline smoke as big guns fired from within.

'We've got to get inside,' she said.

The parapet had been blown away by a shell blast, but the traitors had tied a knotted guide rope across. Minka held it one-handed as she hurried over. Rocks skittered away down the cliff face. The others followed. Someone shot at them as they crossed. Minka saw the flash of red in the corner of her eye.

Blanchez pumped off three quick shots in response and forced the shooter back into hiding. They scrambled forward. 'You all right?' Orugi said once they'd reached the shadow of the bastion.

'Fine,' she said.

He checked. The shot had skimmed the side of her helmet.

There was no time for any more chatter. The bastion had a thick, heavy door, reinforced with steel bands. It was locked.

She signalled Orugi forward. 'Stand back!' he said, as he checked the settings on the fusion core, then hefted the weapon up. 'You never can tell what mood a plasma gun is in,' he said and winked at Minka. She'd heard the same joke many times.

'Just fire,' she said.

He did. Two shots in rapid succession. Once the glare had subsided there was a hole where the locking mechanism had been, surrounded by heat-discoloured steel. Drops of metal had fallen to the ground.

Orugi kicked the door open and led them inside. There were war cries from within. Someone shot at him and Orugi fell. Yedrin stepped over his body, flames already jetting out from his gun. He hosed back and forth for nearly ten seconds.

Minka pulled him back. 'Save some!' she said. It took twenty seconds for the flames to die down enough for her to get inside.

Orugi had taken a las-bolt to his thigh. It was only a glancing shot but it had scored a nasty groove a hand's width across. 'Get that wrapped up,' she said and tossed him some stimms.

He bit the cap off, spat it out and plunged the needle into the middle of the wound, then pressed the syringe with his thumb.

There were three or four seconds before he said, 'Throne, that hurts!' He pulled the syringe out and fumbled with his medi-pack. 'Serves me right for making bad jokes,' he said. He wrapped a steri-cloth about the wound and bound it tight, knotted the end and stood.

'Good?' Yedrin said.

Orugi winced. 'Better,' he said.

Yedrin's flamer cleared the other floors as a wall klaxon started ringing and alarm lumens began flashing red. 'Took their time,' Blanchez said. Minka puffed out her cheeks. Stencilled numbers declared this to be Level 73.

'That means the main armoury is ten floors below,' she said. She looked at the bombard that filled the chamber. Blanchez had already immobilised it.

'There should be an armour lift,' Minka said.

Orugi touched Minka's arm and pointed. Behind her was a low metal doorway, solid iron hung on iron hinges, thick with oil. Minka dragged it open. Sure enough, there was an ammunition lift, and beside it a staircase winding down.

'Looks like we've found the magazine,' she said.

Even Blanchez started laughing as they plunged down the stairs.

FOUR

General Isaia Bendikt had spent many sleepless nights in the run up to this attack. But now that he stood at the fore of his army, fear and doubt fell away from him.

On Tor Kharybdis he had outplayed Holzhauer, but it had been a knockdown rather than a knockout. He'd bloodied his nose, twice. This had to be more than that. Today, he would deliver the coup de grace.

On his right were the neat ranks of the Mordians, to the left were the massed ranks of the Rakallions, with Gerent Bianca leading them, her golden armour bright against the mass of dark greatcoats. Behind him were the masses of the 101st, willing him on. It was as if he were a crucible into which they had poured all their courage, vengeance, implacable will.

Bendikt closed his eyes and said a final prayer before drawing the sword of Saint Ignatzio.

The blade caught the light of the rising sun and for a moment it shone golden. The light flared out until he thumbed the power stud and blue light crackled along its edge.

Bendikt stepped through the void shield, yelling his war cry, and the massed ranks of the 101st answered it as one as they followed him into the face of the enemy.

Cadia stands!

The massed bombardment that had kept them back for so long, and on which the traitors relied, never materialised. Bendikt marched forward almost unhindered, sweeping up into the trenches and the lower circuits of the fortress.

As he did, Seventh Company's attacks in the upper circuits knocked the traitor artillery crews reeling. Initial reactions were all the same. Alarm. Dread. Confusion. It was what happened after the first stab of panic that defined the course of any combat.

Poor troops never recovered. Panic swept them up like leaves before a gale and blew them away. Average troops fell back a safe distance, before going to ground to work out what the hell was happening. Good troops fought for every inch. The best, like the Cadians, counter-attacked immediately.

The Swabian Fusiliers were solid guards. They tried to rally a number of times, but the Cadians were running rampant. They plunged into the upper defences, killing, spiking, setting off ammo dumps, overloading void shield generators, setting plasma reactors to overheat. Demo charges were exploding all about them. Towers collapsed and ammo dumps set off chain reactions that went deep into the fortress.

Bendikt's charge carried the Cadians right through the enemy trenches. The Cadians crashed like a wave against the ruins of Tor Tartarus and the Elnaur Chasseurs roared hatred and defiance as they charged. For a moment the two armies struggled one against the other, locked in a vicious hand to hand battle.

The Elnaurs were dressed in their black carapace and visored helmets. They were a veteran force, honed like steel on the tough world of the Cadian Gate. But they were no match for the Cadians. The elites of First and Second companies shrugged off las-bolts, while the Elnaurs' armour was no protection against their hot-shot weapons.

Bendikt was always at the fore of the Cadian charge, his banners marking him out to friend and foe alike. The enemy threw themselves against him, desperate to gain fame or honour by killing the Cadian general. But Bendikt was a deadly warrior, with one augmetic hand that could punch through steel and rip out spines, and Ignatzio Richstar's sword swinging in the other. Nothing could withstand that blade. It carved through bone, flesh and steel as he cut a path deep into the enemy.

Mere was right beside him, power sword in hand, protecting Bendikt's back. And Colonel Baytov was beside him, power fist crackling with the blood that dripped from it.

They drove forward up the slopes, leaving a train of dead behind them. And all the time he called out the name of his enemy.

'Where is Holzhauer?' he demanded. 'Where is the undefeated general?'

Dido heard the thunder of battle and pushed herself up. She gritted her teeth as her body twisted, wracked by agony. The first time she fell back, and she had to go through it all again.

Sweat started to bead on her forehead and the small of her back. At last she managed to slip her hand inside the pillowcase.

She had to push with the opposite elbow as her fingers scrabbled into the corner where the pills had gathered. She pulled as many out as she could, and held them in her mouth as she reached in for more.

At last she fell back onto the bed. A white flare shell went off over the battlefield. The slowly falling light patterned the wall as it slanted through the shutters. The flickering white light moved up the wall as the flare shell slowly fell back to the ground. Another went off, and another. There was a low subsonic boom.

Dido reached for the water. She took a swill and swallowed as many pills as she could manage. She gagged for a moment, finished the water, swallowing the last of them back.

Dido did not go for the fawning crap that the priests told them about the God-Emperor. Her prayer was a quick, no-nonsense affair. No pleading. No begging. Nothing abject.

A simple request from one warrior to another.

As Bendikt plunged forward in the middle, to his left Gerent Bianca strode in lockstep with General Plona-Richstar at the head of his warriors. The presence of the saint's bier lifted them all to a state of almost ecstatic frenzy.

They had been barely able to wait for Bendikt to signal the charge, and as soon as he did, they rushed out like hunting dogs that had been held in kennels for too long. The Rakallion Chasseurs outpaced the Cadians, and were the first to scramble up against the trenches of their enemy.

Plona-Richstar and Gerent Bianca were ever at the fore, the general in his plumed helmet and Bianca in her suit of golden armour. 'For Ignatzio!' she shouted, leading the Rakallions through the trenches held by the Ongoth Jackals.

The enemy were no match for the Rakallion troops and the aura of Ignatzio Richstar.

Again and again, men and women claimed to have seen miracles performed by the will of the saint. Shots that were deflected. Blows that would have killed lesser men being shrugged off by

General Plona-Richstar, and it was said that the Rakallion general could not miss.

Every shot hit a traitor, and every hit killed.

On the other side of the Cadians were von Horne's Mordians. They marched, ten thousand guards in perfect step with one another, squares of red and white, defiant of danger.

The Mordians did not falter, even when their squares came under fire from heavy weapons in the rubble to their right and left.

The trenches opposite the Mordians were held by the bulk of Conoe's Swabian Fusiliers. They were a smart force determined to sell their lives as dearly as possible. They put up a furious salvo of las-bolts. But as one Mordian fell, another took their place, and all this time the regiment kept in step, the *thud* of each footfall sounding out like the beat of a bass drum.

It was chilling to see the Mordians come on without pause, despite the Swabians' best efforts. It was like watching a bull charge, knowing there was nothing that could be done to stop it.

When they were fifty feet off the Mordians stopped as one, fitted their bayonets and then charged.

A wall of steel swarming as one towards them. Many Swabians lost their nerve and threw down their weapons. Those around Conoe held firm.

Von Horne came straight for them. Like the Cadians, his was an orphaned regiment and tradition, and he carried that loss like a rod of steel through his will. In his hand was a bolt pistol that bucked over and over, each shot striking a traitor down.

He saw Conoe and called out his name.

As he strode up the rubble parapet, a traitor priest, dressed in a long robe embroidered with an embossed golden skull, and a breastplate and shoulder guards of battered carapace, stepped between von Horne and his prey.

'Step aside,' the Mordian ordered.

'You do not order me!' the priest answered. 'I am Father Bellona, the Bringer of the Word!'

'You are a traitor,' von Horne hissed.

Father Bellona thumbed the power stud of his eviscerator and shouted, 'For the Emperor!' as he charged.

Von Horne did not give an inch. His own chainsword was a plain field model, but while it lacked finesse, it was heavy, vicious and brutally effective.

The two weapons struck with a spray of sparks. They juddered against each other as both men put their own weight behind the blow. The Mordian met the eyes of the other man and saw fierce defiance there. A weighty conviction that he was in the right.

'The Emperor has abandoned you all! Your leaders have betrayed you!' the heretic priest cried. 'You will all die in darkness, away from the love of the Emperor! You and all your kind! Where is Mordia now?'

The words enflamed von Horne. He thrust the priest back but the wild man came again, blades sparking off each other.

'You are doomed!' Bellona roared with every great swing of his eviscerator. 'You have betrayed the Emperor! There is no hope. You have all been led astray.'

Von Horne had kept his tongue, and now he was on the attack and the priest was parrying desperately. The Mordian was by far the better swordsman. He strode forward, shouting, 'For Mordia! For the Emperor!'

The priest stumbled on the body of a dead Mordian. In a moment von Horne was upon him.

'For Mordia!' he spat as he plunged his chainblade into Father Bellona's belly. The priest twisted like a fish caught upon a barb.

Von Horne relished his pain before he thumbed the power

stud and the churning teeth of his chainsword opened the priest up from navel to neck.

Fighting echoed along every corridor as Minka led her squad down the long narrow staircase past level after level. 'Unless it changed, the munitions store is on level fifty-two,' she said.

At level fifty-three there was an access gate that had been forced open. It should have been locked from the inside, but someone had been careless, and carelessness was costing the traitors lives.

Minka pushed through. The tunnel smelt of damp. The arched ceiling was lined with sheets of corrugated iron and held in place with iron arches all bolted to one another, forming regular struts across the floor. The corridor went straight into the mountainside. Every fifty yards there was another flight of steep stairs. At the end they came to a ventilation door, and the first dead bodies. Three of the locals were lying in pools of their own blood.

Minka avoided the blood.

She pressed herself against the wall and came out into a wide chamber with a series of armoured doorways along the inner side. They had stencilled numbers on the front. The closest one was labelled '57'.

Minka's first experience of battle had been the fight for her home fortress of Kasr Myrak. City fights were deadly things. They strained the nerves and they killed the weak at a relentless rate, but for Minka, fighting in cramped conditions was in some ways just like coming home.

The magazine was located on the next floor down.

A team of labourers had been working to bring out bombard shells and they barely knew what happened as Minka and Blanchez strode in and gunned them down.

From the lift chamber, a series of arched chambers led away, one after another, each with their own heavy blast doors. The nearest door was open and an artillery trolley stood by the lift, already loaded with bombard shells. They were fearsome things, each weighing twice as much as a man.

Blanchez grabbed a ten-pound shell and quickly wrapped the detonator wires around it.

'I've got the mother of all bombs here,' she hissed as she spooled out the detonator wires, 'but I need five minutes.'

'Get the other blast doors open!' Minka shouted as she stood at the mouth of the tunnel. She could hear footsteps and braced herself as a response team of Swabians appeared at the end of the corridor.

She fired off a salvo of shots down its length. The bark of the bolt pistol drove the enemy back. She felt a few of the Swabian shots hiss past her cheek. Too close, she decided and tossed another frag grenade down the corridor, bouncing it from one wall to another.

After a few minutes she called out, 'They're coming again.'

Blanchez had a clasp in her mouth as she screwed the last wire into place.

'Nearly done,' she mumbled.

There had to be twenty of them. A firefight erupted. Las-bolts flashed up the access tunnel towards them. One hit a lumen above Yedrin's head. The glass exploded with a shower of sparks and he ducked back, tossing a frag grenade down the corridor just to give himself some time.

There was a sudden flash of yellow light. Minka cursed. She'd been hit by a spent round. It had rapped her knuckles and grazed her skin. 'Just a scratch,' she muttered and pumped another grenade down the corridor.

Blanchez was done. She set the timer as they scrambled away.

'How long?'

'Two minutes,' Blanchez said.

'Throne! This place is going to take half the cliff with it!' Minka said. 'Fall back!'

Yedrin and Orugi were already running to the stairs, but they ducked back into the room instantly.

'Swabians!' they said.

Minka looked about. The detonator was ticking. She had two choices. Up or down. 'Up!' she said and tossed two short-fuse frag grenades up the staircase. The blasts came moments apart. As she started up the stairs someone put their lasrifle round the corner and fired blind.

In response Minka hammered the shots out. Her magazine clicked empty and she slammed in a replacement. A few seconds later one of the enemy put his head around the corner and she nailed him.

She raced up the stairs, wild with adrenaline. 'Come on!' she shouted.

Another swung about, keeping low against the floor. She fired twice and hit him the second time.

'They're behind us!' Orugi cursed as he limped behind her up the narrow stairwell.

Minka flipped the timer on her grenades. The first was short. The next two were longer. She just had to keep their heads down. Had to distract the hell out of them. No one was going to be searching for detonators when grenades were blowing up about them.

FIVE

For months the traitors had relied upon the batteries in the upper circuits of Tor Tartarus to bolster their own defences. But this morning the upper batteries were silent, and in their confusion, panic spread through the traitor lines.

That moment of indecision gave the Cadians all the opening they needed.

Their charge was unstoppable. Within the hour all three battalions of Mordians, Cadians and Rakallions had broken into the lower levels of Tor Tartarus.

Explosions ripped through the upper stories. Whole sections of the fort collapsed and slid down the cliff-face, obliterating the ruins and wiping away all the cave mouths, tunnels and sandbagged gun nests.

The Cadians beneath renewed their assault. Bendikt led the charge up the freshly created rubble field. The traitor survivors were too scattered and stunned to offer anything more than a token resistance.

There was almost no one left to fight them. Within half an hour they had gained more ground than other regiments had taken with weeks of struggle and thousands of lives. Instead of digging in, they kept pushing forward.

For years the war's advances had been measured in mere feet and inches and now the sudden movement threw them into confusion. The traitors pulled back in terror. Imperial troops swarmed forward, seizing the abandoned trenches and turning the guns on the fleeing enemy.

The defeat looked complete. It was at this moment of maximum danger that Holzhauer threw his elite Elnaur Chasseurs into the battle.

Bendikt had just raised the banner of Cadia upon the lower circuits of Tor Tartarus when a wedge of Elnaur Chasseurs appeared in their black carapace and visored helmets.

'Where is the traitor general?' Bendikt demanded, and for the first time there was an answer.

'I am Holzhauer!' a figure declared.

The two generals strode towards each other. Both were dressed in suits of fine armour and both carried ancestral blades of ancient manufacture.

They came to a stop twenty feet from one another on the inner circuit of the firing parapet. Holzhauer was the taller man. He handled his broadsword with a practised ease. The Elnaur Chasseurs were famous for their swordsmanship, which had never been Bendikt's forte.

'Let me fight him,' Mere said, but Bendikt would have none of it.

'No,' Bendikt said, 'he is mine.'

Bendikt strode forward. He did not like to fight in a helmet, and took his off and tossed it to the side.

Holzhauer took this as a mark of arrogance, but he could

not be outdone with displays of bravado. 'I have never been defeated,' he called out, as he unbuckled his chin-strap and pulled his helmet up and back, letting it drop behind him.

Holzhauer's cheeks were blue, his gaze severe; he had the look of a man Bendikt might have respected once.

'General Holzhauer, I name you traitor,' Bendikt declared.

'By whose authority do you judge me, you who have lived a lie, and serve the high lords who failed your world?' the general sneered.

'By the authority of Lord Militant Warmund, and the writ of the Imperium of Mankind, whose peace you have disrupted with wilful violence.'

Holzhauer spat. He had no time for this nonsense. 'There are none so blind as those who refuse to see. You follow a dead faith, and a dying Imperium. You cannot put out the light of truth.'

'No,' Bendikt said, 'but I can cut out the tongue of a lying traitor!'

Holzhauer leapt forward, his sword hissing as it cut through the air. Bendikt charged into the blow, knocking aside the traitor's blade with his own. Paragon proved the better blade. Holzhauer's own sheared off, and its crackling blue flame flared and died, as Bendikt caught him by the throat.

There was a strangled gasp as Holzhauer plunged the blunt hilt of his sword into Bendikt's side. It cut through armour and padding. Bendikt swayed as he stood there, his hand still around the other man's neck.

Holzhauer stabbed Bendikt again. The Cadian held on. Despite the lancing agony, he smiled.

'What humours you, Cadian?'

'Look!' Bendikt spat as he forced Holzhauer's face to look up and about him. From the upper circuits of Tor Tartarus, a Cadian banner flew. 'Your Chasseurs lie dead. Your heretic preachers have been cut down. My forces have broken your own. You, the undefeated general, have been routed.'

'Never!' Holzhauer hissed, but his words ended in a choked wheeze as Bendikt's augmetic fist started to crush his neck. The traitor's struggles became increasingly weak as Bendikt ground his windpipe between his fingers.

'I am Cadia,' Bendikt said at last, 'and even after death, Cadia has broken you.'

With that, and with a flick of his augmetic hand, Bendikt broke the traitor's neck and flung his carcass to the floor.

He turned to his warriors arrayed about him, tired but triumphant, wounded but standing. He raised his bloodied fist to the sky, and spoke the truth.

'We are Cadia.'

SIX

As soon as the fall of their commander was known, the will of the traitors was broken. Most surrendered, but some fell back in confusion towards the Cathedral of Saint Helena Richstar. The Cadians pursued them.

Seventh Company of the Cadian 101st were in the fore of these attacks and Minka was among the lead. The resistance was half-hearted and sporadic. By the evening of the attack, the enemy had largely been driven from this quadrant, the last desperate commanders reportedly holing up in the bastion of Margrat.

Minka paused as her platoon regrouped and took shelter beneath one of the buttresses that lined the cathedral. Baine had found a bottle of grog somewhere, and now they were passing it along and taking long swigs from it, and laughing.

Minka was exhausted. She turned and looked about the scene of the battle. Despite the smoke and ruin there was a strange calm. As the last hour of sunlight cast long shadows, Minka found herself marching around to the cathedral front.

Void shields had protected it from the worst of the bombardments, but its east façade was scarred with impact craters. The stained-glass windows were shattered and half the niches on the façade were empty. The statues of saints that did not suit the Tendency had been pulled down and smashed.

However, it was not the ruins or the destruction that held Minka's attention. She was looking into the vast parade square before the cathedral where a forest had grown.

A forest of creaking gibbets.

There had to be ten thousand of them. She started forward. The stink of death caught in the back of her throat.

For a moment Minka was back in her home of Kasr Myrak.

She strode up to the nearest. The post had been driven into the stone square. Inside the metal hoops, the imprisoned corpse was brown with age.

The flesh had been picked by carrion, bleached by the elements. The innards had rotted away. It was now a desiccated skeleton, held together by skin and tendon, the lips pulled back, exposing a toothy grimace.

There was a stencilled sign attached to the gibbet. She wiped it clean of ash, and read the name and the regiment. *Trooper Maze. Ongoth Jackals.*

Unbeliever, the sign read.

Minka moved along to the next. Another Jackal. Then a Swabian Fusilier. Even a Chasseur. *Unbeliever*, the sign read again. And the next.

Minka did not need to see any more. She turned her back and walked towards the cathedral steps. Files of prisoners were already being led away through the gloom.

Minka knew their future. They were all guilty. The loyal troopers all hung in these gibbets. The Commissariat would execute the instigators, and the rest would be inducted into penal legions and labour squads and they would spend the rest of their lives in the service of the Emperor. Their final act of worship would be their deaths.

Minka reached the broad steps and mounted them. The cathedral doors were of thick ironwood. The portals stood ajar. Minka pressed her hand to the door. It swung inwards.

The chamber yawned overhead. She stepped inside. The walls were covered with ornate murals showing the Emperor, Holy Terra, the conquest of the Gallows Cluster by Ignatzio Richstar.

The shrine to Cadian regiments had been defaced, the faces of the bas-relief troopers chiselled away. The plaques had been pulled down, the banners torn off and burnt.

But there was enough evidence there for her to read that seven regiments had been stationed here. Their presence was recorded in brass plaques, each one bearing the symbol of the Cadian Gate, and the number of the resident troops.

One read, 'the 717th, Huntsmen', another, 'the 180th, Stalking Tigers'. She moved along the line of plaques lying discarded on the floor. At the end the newest plaque read, 'the 94th, Brothers of Death', with the crossed lasgun and combat knife.

The number startled her.

It was the regiment of Colonel Rath Sturm, who had led the defence of Kasr Myrak. He had kept Minka alive, many times. She touched the knife that he had given her. It still hung at her waist. The same image was pressed into the knife. For a moment the battle for her home kasr came back to her. Her heart began to quicken, sweat gathered in the lines of her palms. Her hands were balled into fists.

She wiped away the dust of years and felt her panic ease. The 94th had raised a plaque to pray for a safe passage back to Cadia. She checked the date. This was their last stop before returning to Cadia to fight in the Black Crusade.

Minka pressed her hand against the symbol and said a brief and heartfelt prayer. She felt a deep sadness as well, thinking of Rath Sturm coming here, five years before, wondering what his return to Cadia might bring.

If he had dared to hope in that moment, his hopes had been cruelly served.

Minka sat down and took in a deep breath. She really ought to go to her platoon, but just at this moment she needed a few moments alone.

At last she pushed herself up and looked about. This place felt less alien now, she thought. This church had seen centuries of devotion from loyal troopers. It had been seized by a brief madness, but she knew that the blood would be cleaned away, the defaced shrines restored, the statues of Imperial saints returned to their niches, and it would serve again as a place of solace for troopers like her, who fought and died for the Imperium of Mankind.

She walked out into the darkling gloom. She found her platoon where she had left them, but now the grog had done its work and they were lying back with their helmets in their laps.

Baine held the bottle up. 'We saved you some,' he said.

Minka took it and poured out a libation for the loyal souls of Traitor Rock.

EPILOGUE

Seventh Company of the Cadian 101st, 'Hell's Last', stood to alert at the graveside. In the front rank was Minka. She could not see the mass grave through the tears that kept welling up. In the trench there were the bodies of hundreds of her former comrades, but there was one there whose presence stung her hardest.

It had been a brief but terrible campaign. But the Cadians had conquered. They had crushed the rebellion. This meant that, at last, they could move on.

But none of that mattered to Minka now. Nor did the lieu-tenant stripes that she wore on her arm, and the confidence she had found in handling her troops in combat.

A trumpet blew as Father Keremm stepped forward and made a short prayer.

Once, Cadians had buried their own under Cadian soil in the fields of tombs she had trained beside as a Whiteshield. That was no longer a choice available to them. Their dead comrades lay wreathed in black shawls embroidered with the aquila and the Cadian Gate.

When Keremm's prayers had come to an end the troopers of Seventh Company filed past, one by one, and threw in a handful of soil.

Minka waited until Chief Commissar Shand had paid his respects and moved off. She did not throw hers until she was standing over the place where Dido lay. The lieutenant's body was distinctive. It was short and broad and lean.

Minka closed her eyes. She didn't want to remember Dido as someone who had felt she had to make that choice. She thought of a different world, one where she'd realised what was happening and had been able to help her out of that path. One where, years from now, Dido was training the next generation of Whiteshields with the same even hand she'd shown Minka when still a sergeant, sitting in the back of a Chimera rolling into the Evercity on Potence.

Minka recalled that moment as if it were yesterday. After the debacle of Markgraaf Hive, Minka had been a wreck, and Dido had taken her in. She'd been calm, confident, assured. Prassan had been there, Minka remembered. He had been prattling on about the cathedral and Dido had told him to shut up and Prassan had said, 'Don't you read any of the pre-landing reports?'

'No,' Dido had told him. 'That's what you bastards are for.'

Minka said a prayer to the God-Emperor as she looked down into the neat square hole. She was not stupid. This was the fate that awaited all of them. Death in the service of the God-Emperor.

But not today, she thought as she dropped the handful of soil in. It landed silently on the shroud below. The stillness was chilling. It was death.

Minka paused for a moment and lifted her head, taking in a deep, deep breath.

Father Keremm was standing shaking hands with each of them as they passed. Shand paused as he spoke to the priest.

Minka took her moment to slip away from both of them.

Away to the left the foundations for a chantry chapel were already being laid. A watch would be left and prayers offered up for the Cadian dead.

Minka turned her back on it all and walked slowly away. Their camp was already being packed up. Breve had reported that *The Saint* had been loaded onto a grav-pallet and was awaiting stowage in their transport. 'I got her a new powerplant,' he assured her with evident glee. 'Out of the tank graveyard. She's running better than ever!'

Minka forced a smile. Breve loved every unguent-soaked bolt of that Chimera. 'I'm glad,' she said.

'Lieutenant Lesk,' a voice called out. She knew who it was before she turned.

Chief Commissar Shand paced towards her. He looked strangely uncomfortable as he coughed to clear his throat, and then stood with his arms behind his back.

She waited for him to speak.

'I investigated that matter,' he started.

She waited.

'It appears there is some truth to your accusation. Captain Midha has been taken in by his Commissariat. They want to know if you will testify.'

'That he abandoned his positions? Absolutely.'

Shand nodded. 'Good.'

'Does this mean any censure is removed from my record?'

Shand paused. 'Yes,' he said.

She smiled. 'Thank you.'

Shand bowed slightly and returned the way he had come.

Minka turned to look about. Smoke was still rising from the remains of Tor Kharybdis. The ash gave the setting sun a spectacularly ruddy hue. It was like a red teardrop slipping into the sea, hanging for a moment before it was gone.

A hush fell as a bell began to ring out. Of course, she thought, it was the Eve of Sanguinalia.

Through the stillness, the cathedral bells tolled. Across the camp-city, each regiment was marking the festival according to their planetary rituals. Some spent the night in ritual feasts and dances, others in prayer.

The Munitorum were already repairing the bridge link to Tor Tartarus. How long would it take, Minka wondered, for all the scars of this war to be healed?

'Hey,' a voice said. It was Prassan. He was in his smart dress uniform. Despite his time away from the front lines, he'd lost some of his boyishness.

'I'm sorry,' he said.

Minka pursed her lips and nodded. She had no words. Not yet. It was all too raw. Prassan produced a bottle from behind his back. It was Arcady Pride. 'Bendikt asked me to pass it on with his compliments. He wanted to say thank you.'

Minka took the bottle. 'Bendikt?'

He nodded.

She half laughed. 'Me?'

Prassan nodded. He gave her a look. 'A drink?'

'Yes,' Minka said. She was exhausted, but that was exactly what she needed.

An hour later Minka and Prassan were sitting on the veranda of Minka's cabin. Minka was half drunk already, and the alcohol helped the words to flow. The rest of her platoon had found groups of their own. But two figures stood apart, not quite sure how they fit in, or what exactly to do.

Minka called out to them.

'Over here!' She turned to Prassan. 'Move over.'

Blanchez sat first, then Yedrin.

'General Bendikt has sent this for you two,' Minka told them as she filled up their mugs, 'to welcome you into the Hundred-and-First.'

'General Bendikt?' they said.

She gave them a matter-of-fact nod. 'Of course. Sent Trooper Prassan especially.'

Prassan gave them a non-committal look, but he was in the dress uniform of the HQ personnel so to them it must have looked true. They raised their cups in a salute and drank, and soon their tongues were running free with light words and laughter.

They reminded Minka of what she had been like, a few years earlier. She paused and looked out as the day faded about her. The sky was yellow at the horizon, and deep blue above her head, and between them it was shaded with green and turquoise and pale blue.

It was a beautiful evening, she thought. One to remember.

Perhaps one day, she thought, they would stand at her grave-side, and think fondly of her.

It was beyond her, at this moment. She refilled their cups.

'Here,' she said. 'Have another drink.'

ABOUT THE AUTHOR

Justin D Hill is the author of the Warhammer 40,000 novels *Cadia Stands*, *Cadian Honour* and *Traitor Rock*. He has also written the Necromunda novel *Terminal Overkill*, the Space Marine Battles novel *Storm of Damocles*, as well as the short stories 'Last Step Backwards', 'Lost Hope', 'The Battle of Tyrok Fields' and many more. His novels have won a number of prizes, as well as being *Washington Post* and *Sunday Times* Books of the Year. He lives ten miles uphill from York, where he is indoctrinating his four children in the 40K lore.

YOUR
NEXT READ

STEEL TREAD
by Andy Clark

Under the fell light of the Great Rift, Hadeya Etsul must battle her demons
while her dysfunctional Leman Russ Demolisher crew struggle for survival
against the Ruinous Powers.

An extract from
Steel Tread
by Andy Clark

Hadeya Etsul gritted her teeth behind her rebreather mask as smoke and heat haze danced about her. Gunfire poured down on her tank from the walls of the ravine, bullets rattling against the hull like driven hail. Fear and panic fought to master her, but Etsul thrust them to the back of her mind. She had her duties. Death would have to wait.

'The Emperor protects,' she told herself, then bit back a yelp as *Oathkeeper* rang like a struck bell. The Leman Russ tilted with the force of impact before settling back on the steel coils of its suspension.

'Damage report.' Commander Masenwe's voice was calm, projected over the vox from his bucket seat above and behind Etsul's gunnery station as little more than a static-laced whisper through her headset.

'Keep your mind on what's before you.'

It had been a favourite saying of her mother's, one of many Etsul still heard as clearly as though the woman stood behind her. Normally that sensation of connection made her feel by turns comforted or forlorn. Here, now, it brought the creeping sensation that her mother's shade lurked close by. The idea was incongruous, a nonsense, yet it sank its teeth in and wouldn't let go. Etsul felt the icy touch of imagined breath upon her nape and pictured her mother waiting to welcome her through the veil.

The hair rose on Etsul's neck and her skin prickled. She shook her head and spat a curse into the plastek muzzle of her rebreather.

'Throne alive, pull yourself together,' she breathed.

'Vesko, damage report?' Commander Masenwe repeated. This time his words came to Etsul more clearly. She shot a glance through smoke and firelight, to where Yvgan Vesko occupied the driver's station. Like her, the big man sat on a fold-out seat of plasteel and flakfoam. Sweat slicked his bald pate. Drops had gathered in his eyebrows and Etsul watched them clinging to hair, defying gravity.

'Hit to right flank armour, directed explosive, but she's holding, sir,' said Vesko. She saw his jaw move behind his rebreather as his mouth formed the words, but with the tank's power plant roaring and enemy fire hammering the hull, she heard them only through the vox headset clamped over her ears.

'*Oathkeeper* wouldn't let us down,' Masenwe replied. 'Maintain combat speed and stay close on Commander Lethwan's tail. Only two hundred yards to the end of the canyon, then we'll make the Emperor proud!'

Masenwe's calm did not reassure Etsul. Heat washed over her as though she stood too near an open furnace door. Smoke coiled about her, alarmingly thick and dark. She could taste it, overpowering her mask, worming in. Etsul's chest hitched, and she stifled a coughing fit.

Their loader, Osk, was supposed to be extinguishing the fire in the bowels of the tank, but he hadn't spoken for what felt like hours.

Etsul wanted to look back and check on him.

Fear of what might meet her eyes held her rigid at her station.

Today is the day we die.

The thought startled Etsul. It felt alien, an intrusion. She screwed her eyes tight shut and felt sweat trickle over the scrunched-up lids. She grubbed it away with the back of one fist then opened them again on firelight and smoke. The tank shuddered as it bulled along the canyon's rubble-strewn floor. Etsul had to look back, to see what had become of Osk, to check whether the fire was about to ignite her tank suit or touch off their shell magazine.

She didn't.

Couldn't.

'Etsul, target one-hundred-twenty yards ahead, fifty degrees right, elevation twenty degrees, confirm?'

Masenwe's voice broke her paralysis. Etsul applied herself to her instruments, checking *Oathkeeper*'s glowing auspex screen then pressing her eyes to the rubberised viewing scope. The tank jolted, mashing her face hard against the hot metal and plastek. She hissed with pain. Eyes watering, she tried to focus on the juddering blur before her. She caught snatches of dark ferrocrete rushing past to either side, canyon walls studded with the dark hollows of windows like eyes. Watercolour smudges of green showed where Croatoas' verdant undergrowth was reclaiming the ruins. Above the ravine was a strip of open sky turned bruise purple and umber by twilight. All around were the enemy, too many to count, too swift to focus on. Etsul made out humanoid silhouettes. Their outlines were distorted. Spurs and deformations rendered them nightmarish. Her one fixed point was Commander Lethwan's tank, *Restitution in Blood*, just ahead of them. Unlike *Oathkeeper*, *Restitution* had side sponsons. The terrain was so close they struck sparks from out-thrust chunks of rubble as the tank charged for the canyon's end.

'Gunnery Sergeant Etsul, do you have the target?' snapped Masenwe. She blinked, gasped, tried again. Still, she couldn't focus. The harder Etsul tried, the more sluggish her thoughts became.

'I… Commander, I don't…'

Restitution in Blood transformed from a speeding tank to an expanding fireball.

Vesko yelled through the vox and tried to rein *Oathkeeper* in. Leman Russ battle tanks might not be the fastest vehicles, but they could stop quickly and were almost balletic when manoeuvring. Yet in his eagerness to escape the trap, Vesko had left too narrow a gap, and the collision came regardless.

Etsul's head hit metal.

She sprawled between her seat and Vesko's, fire-heat raking her flesh.

Then came a violent cacophony. Rapid metallic clangs, the wasp-whine of ricochets, a sound like tenderisers thudding against meat in her father's abattoir back on Tsegoh. Something hot and wet splashed her face.

Etsul felt boneless, weak as a fever victim. She tried to stand. She pressed her palms to the hot metal of the deck and sought to push herself upright but could not. Etsul slumped and turned to see Osk's limp form sprawled amidst the flames filling *Oathkeeper*'s belly. Fire danced gleefully over his corpse.

Etsul dragged her eyes away. Beside her, Vesko leant against a stowage box. His gaze was unfocused. Blood drizzled from a cut on his scalp.

Etsul forced her head up, feeling as though she were deep underwater. And truly, she realised, her face was wet, but the liquid felt too warm to be the ocean. Commander Masenwe was slumped in his chair, limbs dangling like a doll's, blood running in rivulets down his arms and drizzling onto Etsul from his crooked fingers. The turret was a ragged mess of bullet holes. So was her commander.

A detached part of Etsul's mind noted that it would have taken an autocannon, or something even heavier, to inflict that sort of damage on a Leman Russ. She pictured hordes of mutants closing in around *Oathkeeper*, preparing to peel the machine open and drag her and Vesko out like morsels of meat scooped from a ruptured shellfish.

'We have to get out of here,' she croaked. Realising her mistake, she activated her vox-mic. 'Vesko, we have to get out of here! Can you drive?'

Etsul shook him by the shoulder until he looked up. She felt a spark of relief at the recognition in his eyes.

'Vesko, we need to go! Now!'

He nodded with renewed purpose, bending over his station while Etsul tried to calm her breath and turned to her own. As gunnery sergeant, she was the Leman Russ' second-in-command. Masenwe's burden now lay upon her shoulders. He had left her in charge of a burning tank, trapped prow-deep in wreckage and surrounded by foes.

'Worry what is, let the rest go,' Etsul told herself.

Another of her mother's sayings. They just had to clear the ravine before the fire consumed them. If they could manage that then maybe they could bail out and escape the enemy.

Somehow.

Etsul grabbed her controls, only to snatch her hands back as searing heat tore up her arms. She looked at her palms. They were scorched raw. It didn't seem possible that the fire could have heated the metal of the tank's interior to such a degree without consuming her and Vesko both.

Today is the day we die.

This time it was a whisper in her ear, the breath of a gheist.

Etsul turned to face Vesko and saw he was shouting. His eyes bulged with fear.

She tried to issue her orders, but it was as though her rebreather had melted to her flesh. She couldn't speak through its cloying mass. Blood pattered down, a carmine baptism of her short-lived command. Flames licked about Etsul, dancing over her clothes, her skin. The enemy were right outside the tank. She saw them in her mind's eye, pressed against the white-hot plasteel of the hull, flesh sizzling, fat spitting like meat on a griddle as they heaved inwards from every side.

Oathkeeper gave a terrible groan, a submersible gone too deep. Etsul cast about for escape. She saw nothing but flames and smoke. She imagined the venerable tank's machine-spirit straining to resist the mass of bubbling flesh squeezing ever tighter.

'I know you'll make us proud...' came her mother's voice from deep within the inferno.

Oathkeeper's hull gave way.

Hadeya Etsul screamed.